THE MAN WITH THE GOLDEN SWORD

by John B. Leith (1920 – 1998)

via Robyn C. Andrews, owner

Cover Design by Thomas M. Ware

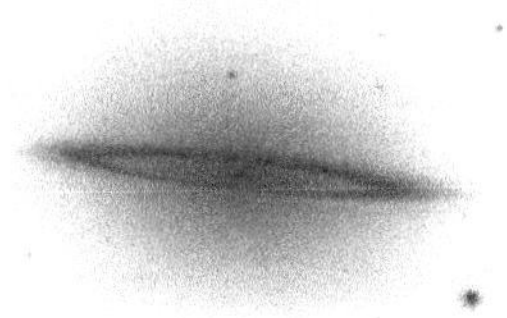

Library of Congress Control Number: 2014919665
CreateSpace Independent Publishing Platform, North Charleston, SC

TIMESTREAM PICTURES & BOOKS
4412 Wild Horse Court
Ooltewah, Tennessee 37363 USA

ISBN 9781503044326

THE MAN WITH THE GOLDEN SWORD

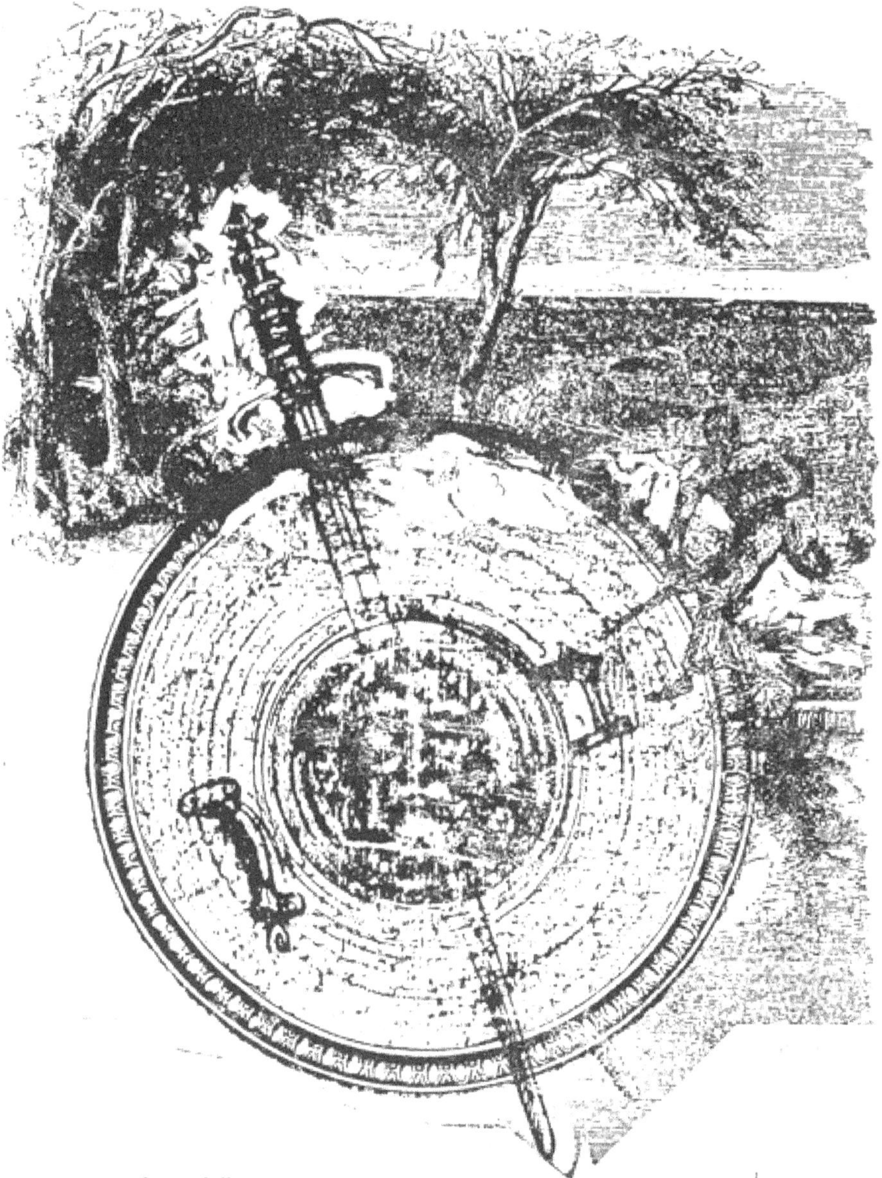

Original illustration

THE MAN WITH THE GOLDEN SWORD

TABLE OF CONTENTS

THE MAN WITH THE GOLDEN SWORD

This book is not organized in a conventional manner but rather is presented in the original style of the author. John B. Leigh (1920-1998)

PREFACE

This documentary-drama of a World War II hero concerns a brief span in his life as an agent in the overseas branch of the (OSS) Office of Strategic Service, United States Army. The narrative contains excerpts carefully chosen from the officer's diaries, as well as battle actions reported in official records and conversations with key military personnel.

Although the missions described did not begin till mid-1943, an unrelated happening six years earlier (1937) makes many of the book's episodes read stranger than fiction. So much so that believability may be questioned.

In 1937 the biographical hero of this documented story was a nineteen-year-old law student named Halford Williams living contentedly in St. Petersburg, Florida, U.S.A. when he felt a strong calling to discover the deeper reason for his existence. With this urge, he was suddenly drawn to Lhasa, Tibet. There, in the great monastery he was determined to search for the truth of why he was born and what was to be his ultimate destiny in the materialistic world in which he found himself.

Young Williams met the top lama of the monastery, an ancient Buddhist named Ho-An-Ti, the Enchanted One, who would become his teacher and watch over his development for the next eight months. On first meeting the young American, The Enchanted one's first words were: "We have been waiting for you. Your arrival was foretold."

For three of the following eight months, the searcher from a modern civilization would be confined in a small, walled-up cave, high up on a perilous mountainside. He would possess no light, no fire, and would sustain himself with a meager bottle of water and a scanty bowl of rice each day. For warmth, he survived the cold nights with only the set of clothes he was given.

In that Spartan abode, young Williams was expected to find answers to the riddle of his existence. Without material diversions, he would have to depend entirely on the strength of his spirit. To grow spiritually, he would learn discipline of the mind and body and eventually try to attune himself with the presence of the Almighty God. And if all went well, he would achieve nirvana, and in this harmony, his hitherto subjugated spirit would be freed and take him anywhere in the world. In the first few hours in the darkness of that lonely cave, he wished he were not earth-bound and that he could fly home to see again his mother and father.

But Halford Williams did survive his search for the truth -- at least bodily. He emerged from the proving cell and passed the strict monastic tests.

When the emaciated, bearded, scholarly-looking youth finally took his leave from the ancient monk, the parting words would be riveted in Williams's brain. "Your destiny was foretold before you were born. But, the outcome will not be made known until the sunset of your life."

As the awakened boy and the old teacher made their way to the point of departure, the latter stopped the somber convert, and placing his hands on his shoulders, uttered a revelation:

"Take heed, my son, and regard this statement as a testament! You were not accidentally placed in that spiritual refuge where you pursued your search for truth.

"Long ago, another chose that same retreat to commune with God. But he already knew the future path he must tread. That One was predestined to be the focal point of a sinful world. He was to become the Messiah -- the Christ."

William reflected in fright and despair. The Christ was in the same cave? He had been later rejected, hunted and crucified. Halford Williams was reluctant to think of his own future.

On returning to civilization, the pilgrim would abandon his philosophical dreams and put behind him the experience of self-denial in far away Tibet. Under the clouds of a coming war, his idealism would be placed in escrow. Hence, in 1943, Williams would be found engulfed in a bitter world conflict of which the Buddhist Lama had not forewarned him.

This biography of that unsung hero of World War II concerns only two years of his life as Halford Williams, Lieutenant Colonel, United States Army, Europe.

PROLOGUE

Hitler offered $300,000 in gold for the body of Colonel Halford Williams, dead or alive, a United States Army Officer of World War II. By war's end this bold, young adventurer had penetrated enemy lines sixty-two recorded times. The Nazi's could not catch or kill him in his rescue of countless prisoners from concentration camps.

General George S. Patton, U.S. Third Army, credited Colonel Halford Williams with turning the tide against Germany in the Battle of the Bulge. He called him the greatest hero of the war and stated that his actions behind the German lines shortened its outcome by several weeks. On another occasion, the valor of Colonel Halford Williams decisively tilted the outcome of "D-Day" in favor of the allies.

The missions attributed to Williams have not been chronicled before, but they were so important to the allied cause that he was awarded the highest international military honors from more nations than any other person in world history.

This book begins with one nation's attempt to find Colonel Halford Williams and publicly acclaim his unsung valor. Through a dozen missions deep inside Hitler's domain, the odysseys of Colonel Williams are traced. The narrative also attempts to unravel why he may have become invincible during his sixty-two missions. And why a high-ranking Nazi officer, discussing Williams, parodied the words of a great novelist: "Is he from Heaven or is he from Hell, this damned illusive Pimpernel!"

Subsequently, what happened to this OSS agent is verified concerning his last terrible ordeal inside the jaws of a notorious Nazi prison of death, less than a month before World War II ended--and only a few weeks before his twenty-sixth birthday.

MEDALS OF HONOR
PRESENTED TO
COLONEL HALFORD WILLIAMS
FOREIGN HONORS

Victoria Cross *Great Britain*

Order of King Haakon *Norway*

Croix de Guerre *France*

Order of The Elephant *Denmark*

Order of Lenin *Soviet Union*

Order of Knighthood *Great Britain*

UNITED STATES OF AMERICA

Distinguished Service Order

Congressional Medal of Honor (Posthumously)

ILLUSTRATIONS

* Illustration not available in this publication

Chapter 1

THE SEARCH FOR OSS AGENT DOUBLE XO-6

On a warm June morning in 1981, the Ambassador of Norway was granted special entry into the sacrosanct Central Intelligence Agency in the woods of Arlington, Virginia. Armed with a letter from the U.S. President James Carter, the Ambassador was searching for a single missing person--a nameless American soldier who had invaded Norway in February of 1944. With a team of only five men they had landed in the coastal town of Vaas and beat the occupying Nazis in recovering one hundred million dollars in gold bars from a hidden hoard on the side of a mountain. They had killed fourteen German soldiers and engineered a daring escape while alerting Nazi garrisons along the entire coastal area.

The gold, belonging personally to King Haakon, enabled the Norwegian government in exile to continue the war to reclaim their land.

In the years since World War II, an average of forty attempts have been made annually by journalists to locate the same legendary U.S. officer for even greater deeds of daring made in other Nazi occupied countries during the second World War.

Notwithstanding the relentless media search to find the mysterious soldier, all inquiries made at the CIA, FBI, National Defense, and

National Archives have met with blank denials of his existence.

But on that June day in 1981, the Norwegian Ambassador was prepared to persuade his listeners. He had come armed not only with complete details of the particular raid hut he jarred research historian Daniel Bent with his description of the officer's weaponry. He told of a Colonel leading a killer team while brandishing only a medieval sword—holding the sword at statuesque salute for three hundred teenage boys who participated in the gold recovery. The youths had been recruited to ski down a mountainside in falling snow, each ending his heroic feat by dropping a bar of pure gold at the young American Colonel's feet. But the raid to capture a quarter of Norway's hidden gold reserve was not the most memorable aspect of the mission according to the recollection of each boy in later years. What they remembered most vividly was that the American Colonel in charge of the mission carried a sword for defense.

The youths grew to manhood and were inducted as members of the Order of King Haakon for their teenage heroism. Each year they had sought in vain to locate the lost American hero who had silently received the treasure of gold and fled out to sea, never to be seen again.

That, in brief, was the story the Norwegian had delivered to the CIA historian thirty-five years after the incident took place. Of the hundreds of previous attempts to uncover the identity of the man with the golden sword, the Norwegian Ambassador came closest to establishing the true facts that such a person was real.

The CIA spokesman, under pressure from the President of the U.S., admitted for the first time that indeed such a man had lived. Furthermore, the American who spoke no language but English had led sixty-two raids behind the enemy lines into several European countries and escaped unscathed from his pursuers by commandeering boats, tanks, trains, rafts, cars, and even airplanes.

In addition, he had infiltrated the German Reichstag and observed the Fuhrer, was landed in Tokyo, in Burma, in the jungles of Brazil and the deserts of Africa. Each time he accomplished his mission without personally firing a shot; he was a pacifist. The Norwegian diplomat was asked why his nation wanted to find the American officer who was finally identified as an OSS Agent Double XO-6, code name Colonel Halford Williams. The Ambassador explained that the surviving boys of the illustrious raid, now men in their fifties, were about to hold their 1982 annual reunion and desired to honor the illusive unknown soldier whom they had toasted in absentia for years simply as "the man with the golden sword."

As the interview ended and the stranger asked for the name and address of the legendary hero, he was informed that further information was forbidden. The Ambassador had stared in disbelief at Bent, the historian. With apparent exasperation, he demanded what harm could come from the release of the man's identity.

The hero was dead.

The file showed the name was Halford Williams. It also disclosed his death as September 17, 1946. Later, he had been posthumously awarded the U.S. Congressional Medal of Honor which, among other international awards for bravery, made this unknown, twenty-six-year old American the greatest hero in the nation's history, and perhaps in the entire world.

But the ribbons and medals could not indicate the elements of sympathetic human interest, which evolved during the incredible missions to rescue nameless people in Nazi jails and concentration camps. Nor could the awards begin to express Nazi anger. Adolph Hitler went into a rage whenever a successful Williams mission was mentioned. Heimrick Himler was constantly frustrated because his Gestapo could not apprehend the offensive enemy predator, and General von Rundstedt secretly admired and praised the one whom he called "the American Fox", responsible for making fools of the Nazis. But George S. Patton, the great American general, made the most appropriate remark and committed same to writing, that Williams' actions on only one of his sixty-two missions, probably shortened World War II by several weeks.

As the Ambassador left the CIA he told his confidant that even without Colonel Williams being present, the 1982 reunion would still be held. At the head table would be a vacant chair. Lying on the chair would be a replica of their hero's golden sword and inscribed on it would be the names of each boy who had participated in the 1944 raid.

Did OSS double agent X0-6, Colonel Halford Williams, really die in 1946? Could a human being so invisible in war, depart this life in peace-time surroundings at the tender age of 27, only one year after hostilities? And where were those knowing the mystery that were bold enough to divulge the truth? These were the leading questions the author addressed following the Norwegian's visit to the windowless spy palace in Arlington, Virginia.

In the beginning the search was fruitless. However, initial attempts to unravel the loose ends showed one consistency. Nowhere could there be tracked the physical remains of Williams. They were not identified in the famed Arlington National Cemetery or his hometown. Nor in the remaining unoccupied crypt below the eternal flame in the hallowed garden of the CIA grounds. Nor could the remains be located in overseas military cemeteries. Nor was there ever a recorded memorial held for this hero.

Without a final resting place for his remains, the question therefore arose. Did such a being ever exist? And was there ever an intrepid agent named Halford Williams? Perhaps it all was a legend contrived by the CIA Information Services to satisfy insistent inquirers about the identity of several courageous agents.

In the storage vaults of the Smithsonian Institute the answer to one part of the riddle began to emerge. Secretly examined (without official permission) there was discovered, being kept for posterity, some strange items. These were officer's battle dress, World War II medals belonging to the same uniform, spectacles, and (out of context) a captured German officer's car 'borrowed' from the Nazis and driven through enemy lines. Later, the same car was freighted on an LST across the English Channel--destination London. There the car was presented on December 22, 1944 to Commander-in-Chief, General Dwight D. Eisenhower, as his Christmas toy. Last but not least there lay hidden from curious eyes in the Smithsonian a miraculous golden sword.

The former owner of all these items had been a nameless World War II American officer whose real identity had never been revealed. Therefore, apparently there once did live such a noble young man! But what happened to him that the public should be denied evidence that he ever enjoyed life or served his nation and the allies in general? Deep in the dead files of the CIA and the National Archives the revelations began to unfold.

Yes, an officer code named Halford Williams had survived intact sixty-one missions when he began his final assignment in 1945, deep behind enemy lines. It was only a few weeks before his twenty-sixth birthday and the end of the war in Europe.

With the account of his last mission, the reader accompanies Colonel Halford Williams deep inside enemy territory. As the story unfolds it becomes evident why he became the most feared soldier the Nazis sought to catch or kill in World War II.

ACKNOWLEDGEMENTS

Acknowledgements for permission to examine in writing documents relating to "The Man with the Golden Sword" are gratefully listed as follows:
The National Archives, Washington, D.C (old military records) - (modern military records)

Special Army Records, Arlington, VA (the Pentagon)
The Library of Congress, Washington, DC (Office of Strategic Service)

German National Archives, Bonn, West Germany (German records of WWII)

The French Archives, Paris, France (Battle of the Bulge)
Belgium Archives, Brussels, Belgium (Battle of the Bulge)

The British Archives, London, England (military records of WWII)

Admiralty Offices, London, England (submarine records)
The Vatican Archives, Rome, Italy (holy records)

Austrian State Archives, Vienna, Austria (Sword of Longinus. and spear and Hapsburg records)
St. James Monastery, Czechoslovakia (old Hapsburg genealogy book)

Archives of the Simka, Simpka, Spain (Catholic Church records)

Mont St. Michael, France (parish records on relics)

Chapter 2

PREAMBLE

In 1945, during the closing days of World War II, the Nazi menace had established a prison of ultimate torture behind the Polish border. Among the current inmates were foreign hostages, captured on the streets of London, Paris, and Moscow. Using these leading personalities as pawns in critical negotiations to end the war, the Nazis intend to achieve a favorable armistice. If they succeeded they would obtain complete amnesty for their remaining leaders,

Onto the grounds surrounding this extermination jail, Col. Halford Williams and his team of six commando rescuers had been dropped to foil Nazi intentions.

The date was early April, only a few weeks before his twenty-sixth birthday, and his last scheduled mission of the war.

Chapter 2

ALARM AT ALLIED HEADQUARTERS

Supreme Commander of the World War II Armies in Europe, General Dwight D. Eisenhower, somberly addressed the handful of senior officers assembled for an emergency meeting at Supreme Allied Headquarters, Trafalgar Square London, England.

Among those present were Lord General Sir William Claybourne, Chief Strategist, British Army; Field Marshal Bernard Montgomery, Commander of the British forces; General Charles De Gaulle of the Free French, and General William (Wild Bill) Donovan, head of the Office of Strategic Services (OSS), the United States of America.

The Supreme Commander began: "I've called this staff meeting to discuss our third attempt to infiltrate the infamous Nazi torture prison, which the Germans refer to as Prison 'X'." Location of this citadel is in Southwestern Poland. Colonel Halford Williams, an officer familiar to us all, led the six-man rescue team.

Since the night of the drop six days ago all contact has been lost.

The general exhaled a spiral of smoke and paused in his remarks. All waited in silence. Then he added, "The survival of those men is questionable. Intelligence consensus is that they've most likely perished. Reason: Col. Williams and his team could never be taken alive."

Speaking carefully, the Commander continued, "As you know, the team was sent to rescue only one person, a German scientist apprehended by the Gestapo and imprisoned in the subject jail. If he is still alive, he's being tortured right now to reveal specific information re: a particular weapon on which he refused further cooperation. The device is called an atomic bomb.

Col. Williams' mission was to free that scientist and bring him to London. Washington wants the man."

(Hitler had sentenced the scientist to death with execution scheduled the week of the mission's appearance. Such being the predicament, allied intelligence was determined the scientist should not be captured by the advancing Russians. In late January 1945, U.S. troops had overrun a Bavarian factory tunneled out of a mountain. The greatest surprise to the allied leaders and their combined scientific communities was unbelievable. The Germans had developed three finished atomic bombs, two of which were to be dropped on New York, thus hoping to prevent Germany's expected collapse. Destroying New York would swing the peace terms in Germany's favor. The U.S. Army of Occupation in February 1945 sent these three bombs to Los Alamos, New Mexico. However, U.S. scientists could not detonate the bombs without the missing German scientist who, only 60 days before, had refused Hitler's demand to get two of the atomic bombs ready to drop over the American city. So intricate was the bomb's detonating release within the larger bomb that the Germans themselves were unable to master it without explicit instructions from the scientist in question. Destruction of New York City was scheduled for the last week of February 1945. For his refusal, the ailing scientist had been sent to be tortured at this German prison with the ultimate fate for him, if he would not talk, to become food for the crocodiles. He had arrived only four days prior to the assault on the prison by Col. Williams' raiders and had not cooperated with his captors. It is not known how Allied Intelligence determined the whereabouts of this key scientist who alone devised the method of detonating the first atomic bombs, one of which was tested at Alamogordo New Mexico on July 16th. A second bomb was dropped over Hiroshima in August of that year as history has recorded.)

General Eisenhower was careful to The exact arguments for and against military intervention on Prison 'X' are not recorded.

As Commander-in-Chief of the allied armies in Europe sat down, he finished speaking almost as a lament, "The perplexing question remains in all our minds. What happened to our rescue mission? They were the key element who were supposed to supply the answers in this blundering affair."

General Bernard Montgomery traditionally chaired the meetings of the joint chiefs, but for reasons unknown, Montgomery had yielded the chair on this occasion. Lord General Sir William Claybourne therefore called for order as the group broke silence. An English colonel was pointing to a large, 10x14 foot, linen-backed map elevated on a side table. The map showed a section of Europe with roads in green and rails in yellow. The long pointer rested on a spot inside pre-war Poland off a main road about fifty miles from the pre-war German and Czechoslovakian borders.

"Here is where the mission was dropped. Location is roughly 300 miles by road from Vienna. They had a radio and were to have made contact on landing. We never heard from them. The pilot of the drop plane, Major Wilson, out of Vienna, reports the six-man team appeared to have parachuted safely at 0200 hours on the night in question, April 6. It was supposed to be Col. Williams' last mission. It was number sixty-two, all of which were night drops behind enemy lines."

The colonel turned to the Commander-in-Chief sitting at the head of the large table. "Shall I describe the building in question sir?" to which Eisenhower snapped, "Make it objective!"

"Subject prison is political in nature. Sources say it's an elimination structure. Those arriving are doomed to die. Nazi documents refer to the fortress as Prison 'X'. There are two aversions practiced there. These are mental and physical brutality committed against those incarcerated. Inmates are generally chained to the walls by their necks. End of the road for prisoners on the bottom wards is the crocodile moat where they are tossed alive into the putrid waters. The crocs are well fed..."

"Quit agonizing about the damn place, Colonel! Stick to the relevant information!"

The colonel apologized and began again. "The heavily guarded complex is located in a tight, impenetrable pocket of German resistance on the eastern front which Soviet troops chose to bypass in their rush towards Berlin less than a week ago.

General Montgomery broke into the dialogue. "I say Commander," he remonstrated, turning to Ike. "You mean that thousands of Russian troops couldn't penetrate the area, but you decided that Col. Williams and his six-man team could accomplish what a whole army of Russians decided was impossible?" Eisenhower, disliking the intrusive remark, glared at the Britisher but did not reply. He asked the English Colonel to continue.

"A road leads westward from the prison" the colonel said. "It's only a corridor at best. This thoroughfare at last report was still in German hands. Russians are closing in every hour, but German resistance has not yet been broken. Orders to hold-at-all-costs are coming from Marshall Herman Goring."

The colonel laid down his pointer. "In conclusion", he added: "Colonel Halford Williams and his men have disappeared within the walls of that hell-hole, but they never made it out."

General Claybourne called for General Donovan's report. Donovan began. "Heads of State in the U.S.A., the Soviet Union and Great Britain have ordered this meeting,for reasons of profound importance. Simply put, during the dying hours of the Third Reich, it is entirely probable (as General Eisenhower stated) that the Nazis may gain the top bargaining position in the forthcoming armistice--

although they lost the war.

The chairman asked Donovan to amplify the premise that the war's outcome depended on the rescue of the three Soviet captives about to be desecrated in Prison 'X', and why a superior military action was necessary on the part of the allies.

Donovan responded quickly. "I confess when I personally briefed Col. Williams seven days ago, we had not determined the full importance of the prison objective. Now we know.

For the last three months ominous reports from our agents have been arriving that the Gerries had drawn up the names of eight important but unknown allied leaders who were to be kidnapped, and smuggled out of what was regarded by us as safe havens. Once caught, the victims were to be taken by plane or sub to Hamburg for psychological shock.

There they would be intimidated with a terrifying threat: shown gruesome film footage of victims like themselves being torn apart and devoured by carnivores. The latest victims were informed that they too were destined to become live meat for the same crocodiles.

To escape such a death the hostages were required under duress to write letters to next-of-kin. They complied. The letters, hand-delivered by German agents, demanded complete amnesty for Herman Goring and ten other top Nazis before the coming armistice can be negotiated. Strangely enough, Hitler's name was not on the list.

Donovan continued as though presenting evidence in a courtroom. "We have received and confirmed the authenticity of certain ransom letters already. We believe half of the allies the Nazis were seeking has recently been snatched and taken to the so-called crocodile prison. Most startling are the names of other proposed abductees not apprehended. Two of these intended victims included British Prime Minister Churchill and U.S. President Roosevelt.

"We are aware that attempts to take Mr. Churchill have already been smashed, regardless of the cleverly devised plan to do so. Future documents still classified will also reveal that President Roosevelt was a primary target. Leader of that failed attempt was American Bund Leader Fritz Kuhn, now in custody.

"Arch Nazi fiend in charge of the 300-man espionage team is Otto Skorzeny. He reports to Marshal Herman Goring, mastermind of the plot."

(British and American war records reveal that attempts had been made to take Eisenhower at his Paris headquarters. Nearly all the Nazi force was caught beforehand. An attempt to kidnap De Gaule also was thwarted but Skorzeny escaped the net.)

Donovan continued: "To show the Nazi's desperation to pull off this plot I will pass around some pictorial evidence. It's a horrible picture made less than seventy-two hours ago, showing a young, frightened boy of fifteen years grabbed from the wealthy French branch of the Rothschild family living temporarily outside London. The day after the disappearance of their son, a messenger arrived at the Rothschild's English home, supposedly with news of their boy. The messenger was brought inside and insisted both parents be present before he gave out any information. After all were seated the so-called messenger broke the news that he was a German agent. Withdrawing from his jacket an enlarged photo. He passed it to the mother and father. The mother looked at the picture and burst out with a scream and later became hysterical. Shown on the photo was a ten or twelve foot crocodile with a person held in its terrible jaws between rows of visible teeth. On the entrapped body was a picture of their boy's recognizable head, which had actually be superimposed on an unknown victim.

For release of the young hostage from being eaten alive in a similar fate, Count Julian Rothschild was to use his influence in securing special peace terms that would permit leading Nazis who might be captured and convicted of war crimes in a forthcoming armistice, to be given safe passage to Brazil. Author of the demand was Reich Air Marshal, Herman Goring.

Julian Rothschild, a deeply religious man, had spent the remainder of the night that his boy was kidnapped in prayer' beseeching God not to allow his son to suffer such a horrible death. The next morning his wife had to be hospitalized. At eight a.m. Count Rothschild was ushered in to see General Charles De Gaule at Allied Headquarters, who then accompanied the distraught father to General Eisenhower. The top general could give him only one assurance: "That very night on which the messenger delivered the ghastly photo, there was a crack, secret team of rescuers expected to reach the same prison in which the Rothschild boy was being held. The team's single objective was to bring out one man, one man only, and get him back to distant allied lines at all costs." Eisenhower confided to the visitor that if there was a remote chance the team should stumble upon their son, then undoubtedly the team commander, known to have a soft spot in his heart for abused children, might pause to rescue him.

(March was the date chosen to complete the final round up of victims, but delays occurred which the Nazis had not anticipated. The list of intended abductees was impressive on paper and, had all been captured. There is little doubt the allied command would have vacillated from insisting on unconditional surrender of all German forces. Historical evidence shows the Nazi kidnap plot produced only the five persons mentioned. Concerning them, all allied leaders received mailed threats and accompanying photos appended to the ultimatum of surrender terms demanding amnesty for the Goring group. In the gruesome tug-of-war involving men's' lives, all allied leaders had agreed among themselves that if the hostages were killed, Goring and his henchmen would be shot immediately when caught, without waiting for the scheduled Nuremberg trials.)

After a brief discussion the allied leaders broke for mid-morning tea, a typical English tradition. Two orderly sergeants were admitted to the top-secret room. They served tea and cakes. English General Montgomery needled Eisenhower. "Oh I say General, tea is a gentleman's drink you know. How is it that tea is not your favorite beverage?" Eisenhower again ignored Montgomery while waiting for his brew to cool. All present recognized that Eisenhower's mind was deeply troubled concerning the apparent sacrifice of

Col. Halford Williams and his team. Some small talk ensued when comments of the assembly began to center on the private person of Col. Williams. Each, except Donovan, spoke as though Williams were already deceased.

Someone asked the English colonel about the state of betting on Col. Williams, a subject of common knowledge. As the colonel ruminated, attention of the senior officers began to center around him.

"As you know Sirs, we've only known Col. Williams for about eighteen months. At first no one thought he had enough staying power to last a fortnight. Indeed, he was a spit-and-polish officer when turned out for leave. But he didn't look the warrior type. Rather more of a scholar I would Judge. Looked as though he jolly well belonged in a library rather than in a skirmish. With his spectacles, his tall scrawny frame and his slow, deliberate walk, he appeared out of place as a solider.

On about his tenth trip into Yugoslavia, I think, he was forced to kill a man in self-defense. Would you believe it? He thrust the enemy through with that archaic sword he had taken on the mission. Afterwards he was quite tormented that betting began, weighted heavily that he was finished. They were even betting he wouldn't take off on another raid, let alone come back from one.

But he stuck in there, week after week. Gradually, his name became euphonic around headquarters, as most of you know. Instead of chaps joking about his boy-scout image, we began to regard him as possessing some kind of supernatural exemption from being killed. Although some of the missions nearly devastated him emotionally, he never seemed to be surprised that he came through okay,

Often, for instance, after missions he would turn up at headquarters like a cat dropped off across town. Instead of being haggard looking and frightened, he'd appear wearing that trademark of his, a silly grin. First thing he'd do was to apologize for being late on arrival as though expecting to be placed in room detention. Then the briefing officer would ask him how he managed to make it back through enemy territory and their front lines. Col. Williams would give the same maddening reply each time, "Quite decently thank you."

Actually it's common knowledge that the colonel escaped from the enemy using any means of transport he could steal, including German dress. He loved most of all to escape in a German officers' car. But he generally used what was available if there was no choice. He's barged through their lines on rafts, boats, tanks, and on one occasion, an airplane. He sure had more than just plain luck riding with him on those escapes. He once stole a passenger train and drove it right through miles of enemy battalions into allied occupied Vienna. The only escape method he hasn't used is horseback. He hates horses more than they hate him, he confides."

Someone exclaimed, "But what about the betting?" The colonel continued.

"By about the fifteenth mission, as I recall, bets were running one in four against his return. But, about the time of his fortieth raid behind enemy lines, all the believers of his invincibility dropped out except maybe two. All bettors agreed amongst themselves that odds were astronomical that Williams could continue his winning tenure. You have to realize why. The first hazard was the night-time parachute drop among the enemy and natural obstacles. If he survived the landing he generally had to fight his way into their strongholds, overcome, with his powerful team, an enemy guard or garrison, and rescue the victims if he could locate them in the concentration camp, or wherever. Finally, he would have to fight his way out and disappear from his pursuers, perhaps for days, along with his entire team and those rescued. Furthermore, to subsist, the marauders depended entirely on pillage of food and vehicles.

I would guess about 5000 pounds have passed hands here among the staff and those associates and planners connected with the team's field operations. One officer I know lost 300 quid. He invariably would let his five quid bet stand that Col. Williams would take a hit on his next mission. An English officer bet 100 quid that Williams would meet his waterloo on the current trip. But it's rumored there's one optimist here at Headquarters. He has bet consistently that the colonel would come back from each mission. On this final raid the same person has bet we all will see the hero again."

The English officer avoided glancing at Gen. Donovan. General Eisenhower gave Donovan a curious look and inquired. "Bill, do you know who bet Col. Williams would get safely home this time? It might be comforting to pessimists like myself."

(Wild Bill) Donovan replied, "You're looking at him Ike."

De Gaule, listening to the comments exploded. "Merci Mon Dieu! Such faith in an ordinary mortal I have never witnessed before."

Turning to Donovan with a praiseworthy look he said, "Mon ami! You should have become a man of the cloth."

All present including Donovan chuckled.

Lord Claybourne called for order and the meeting resumed. An orderly brought in an unidentified officer commanding the Vienna Reconnaissance Section of the Southern Army. The officer deposited several photos and spoke.

"Sirs These 5x7 photos, two of which are enlarged, show the aerial evidence of the mission led by agent double X0-6." The photos were passed around.

"Exhibit A shows a picture of the prison exterior on the morning following the presumed break-in. The black, irregular area shows a corner wall to have been well blown. The hole was not evident in the photo taken the previous day.

"Five other pics are aerial scans of the vicinity taken over a six-day period ending yesterday. They reveal absolutely no evidence of the escaping allied team led by the agent in question. Upon examination of the photos we saw no signs of the escaping commando team and no evidence of a hideout in the designated area, had they escaped from the prison. Nothing significant indicates they got out of the structure, but the enlarged photo clearly indicates they made it inside."

General Claybourne interrupted with an apology. "Tell us about the enlarged photo in more detail."

The visiting officer, still standing as required by the occasion, replied. "Sirs, that photo on close examination reveals the perimeter wire fence well cut, assuring that at least partial entry of the team was made through the outer defenses. The jail wall was certainly breached as already explained. However, there is no evidence from the photo as to how many managed to cross the crocodile moat, except to reaffirm that the jail wall was blown and presumed entry was made into the interior. Whether any of the team fell backwards into the crocodile moat cannot be ascertained."

The nervous officer shifted his weight, searching for words. "On the six successive days during which hundreds of other photos were shot at various elevations, our analysts, using third dimensional viewers, found no signs that the subject team ever got out of that prison interior. The day after the probable entry, much German activity was sighted and photographed in the area surrounding the main buildings, including what is thought to be an enemy Tiger tank blown up by some occurrence unknown to us. It is logical, in the picture of the grounds taken the day after the presumed entry attempt, that the enemy began searching for other saboteurs.

Sirs, in six days of dawn to darkness search, our rescue planes failed to find any vehicular evidence of the mission's survival anywhere along the roads or near the prison grounds.

From the pictures it is surmised that the commandos are either captives in that prison, or that they perished inside." The officer was questioned thoroughly and dismissed.

The mood of the meeting became downcast. Meanwhile, the last spokesman to appear before the emergency meeting was announced. The general, also from the Vienna U.S. Army gave his report as ordered by Allied Command sixty hours earlier. The sequence of military actions was briefly described: Initially a relief column had been dispatched the previous day. Its purpose was to intercept the overdue commando team, assuming there was a long-shot chance it had escaped the prison. The officer pointed out, on a different nap, the designated escape route the team was to have taken, the same routing on which the relief column would try to intercept them.

"Commander of the relief column is Lt. Col. Cromosky, a native New Yorker who had earned his commission in the field. A company of thirty-five battle-hardened troops was under his command. The lead vehicle was a half-track with a mounted anti-aircraft gun, followed by six well-armed jeeps. There were six trucks carrying rations, and equipment for road and bridge repairs. It was anticipated that blown bridges might add 200 miles to the dash through German controlled territory. Radio contact would be constantly monitored."

Now knowing where advance Soviet troops might be encountered, Russian military authorities in Vienna had been advised of the action.

The second phase called for five hundred troops from the Third Airborne Division, who were standing by. Their task was to storm the subject prison locale when the situation became clearer.

Third phase - Five thousand plus, paratroopers were already assembled in battle order to land and hold the prison area until Soviet troops broke through the German pocket.

However, the chiefs were reminded that the primary objective of the combined operation would be to find the missing allied team. If located, the search elements would protect the team from encircling German troops. Nevertheless, enemy capture of the allied team, with or without the prison captives was not discounted. After the usual questions were directed at the visiting general and he was dismissed, general Eisenhower stated for the record: "The world does not know the importance of this drama. Neither does Col. Williams or his top sergeant, Ian McCloskey, assuming they are still alive."

Fifteen minutes after departure of the Vienna-general a coded dispatch was delivered to Gen. Eisenhower. It read: 'Relief column to locate missing allied team, bogged down first day 35 road miles from Vienna headquarters.' The Joint chiefs concurred that the only action by which present orders could be countermanded would be the finding of Col. Williams' commando team.

As the staff offers dispersed, General Claybourne inquired privately of Gen. Donovan. He began in a subdued tone. "Did Col. Halford Williams carry that much-talked-about golden sword on the last mission? I say general, it's only a matter of simple curiosity, mind you."

As he asked the question, even in muted tones, three or four other staffers paused to hear Donovan's reply. "I asked him not to take it this time, because I considered it too cumbersome. I'm not quite certain how many times he's carried it on previous assignments. Sometimes he wore it unofficially, without anyone's knowledge.

Incidentally, he acquired it in Spain while on an earlier venture." Donovan smiled with apparent nostalgia.

"First time I saw that Toledo blade I teasingly told Williams he should carry it on his next mission. Damned if he didn't take me seriously. Since then he's taken it on four or five assignments that I'm aware of. There could be others, but I doubt it.

The sword must have some value to the wearer; otherwise, he would have discarded it long ago. The colonel is probably the greatest authority on swords you'll ever run into. He loves them. In earlier days, he drilled with them as though each one he used was a toy. By the way, he possesses a very ancient one of his own. It is said to have been used in the Crusader wars. Major John Schellenberger, Williams' first artillery officer, swears he has seen a certain sword glow in the hands of Williams."

"American baloney!" came a nearby reply, and all turned to see General Montgomery standing near.

"My reply Sir, to your baloney expletive", Donovan said while turning to Montgomery, "is that the sword has not brought Williams death on foreign soil as yet." Montgomery cut in.
"Let me tell you a truth general. It's not that ridiculous piece of hardware that saved Williams' life so often. It's my man Ian McCloskey, top sergeant and alter ego to your Williams. It's he who is the terror of the Nazis, not that archaic sword.

"Granted you're most likely right", spoke the head of the OSS. McCloskey's the brute power who protects Williams. I read all the reports carefully. However, the real power presiding over Williams is not McCloskey's weapon, be it gun or lariat. I would venture to say the power which genuinely protects him is not identifiable."

As the members filed out, Donovan turned to Gen. Claybourne. "I realize when you asked about the significance of Col. Williams' carrying the golden sword, you were not expecting a superficial reply. "I'm not sure my answer would satisfy you, so let me return the query by posing this paradox."

Is the sword in the hands of Williams some magical talisman to bolster his courage when he can't go on? Or does it actually possess some hidden power in itself?"

Lord Claybourne smiled and pondered the thought for a moment. "If your young officer survives this barbarism, surely higher powers already have marked him for a greater calling. Then, history will determine if the golden sword was a factor in his staying alive. Or, was it just one of the many props sustaining him toward a greater destiny?"elaborate on the expanding predicament, which focused on Nazi Prison "X" about which the meeting of the joint planning chiefs had been called.

The consensus given to the committee was that the allied team sent to rescue the German scientist must be considered lost, its goal of rescue unachieved. Another assault on a broad military scale would therefore be launched within thirty-six hours. Outlined for the Joint chiefs was a more pressing reason. In the last twenty-four hours, Nazi agents had whisked three of Russia's top leaders off Moscow streets. The names given were Gromyko, Beria and Molotov.

Summed up, the dilemma, requiring prompt military response, was this: One, to ascertain what had happened to the greatest commando team of World War II led by Col. Halford Williams; and two, an urgent request from Roosevelt and Stalin to find the missing Soviet kidnap victims.

The conclusion was alarming. The allies could not demand unconditional surrender from German peace representatives while the Russians were hostage to the Nazi torturers.

The meeting was opened for discussion.

Chapter 3

The Last Mission Begins

British Air Command simply called the outfit "Flight Group Number Nine". It comprised of three twin-engine, five-seater planes made in Britain resembling Third Reich silhouettes and markings.

The planes cruised at 300 + m.p.h., but the unusual characteristic of each plane was their ejection seats, a secret innovation developed during the war.

They flew over enemy territory with a full complement of rescue raiders, catapulted their passengers out in the dark of night, usually over German territory, and returned to England empty, accept for the pilot and co-pilot.

At 11:00 pm on April 6, 1945, Flight Group Nine's three planes took off at intervals from Floyd Croyden Airport north of London. Seven special passengers in full battle dress with weapons, ammunition and other espionage baggage hunkered down on their Martin-Baker aluminum ejection seats, each to be discharged by cartridges at intervals that were intended to carry them and their black silk chutes free of their planes. The ejection seats had not failed them to date, and Colonel Halford Williams thought of the sixty-one previous times he had been shot into the darkness over enemy territory the past two years. He wished he didn't have to go tonight. The war was winding down. Hew as conscious that so any circumstances had to come together just right, he had murmured before he got aboard. Otherwise his stream of luck, success, good fortune, fate, or whatever one cared to call it would end forever. One slip, he thought, or one adverse action of man or nature was all it would take for him never to breathe again the free air of his hometown or to see his English girlfriend, Pauline, daughter of an

English Earl.

The Colonel reached into a special pocket inside his insulated army jacket. He felt the twenty-two small envelopes from which he would intermittently follow instructions during the mission. He had received the unopened envelopes prior to leaving. The first one was 3" x 3" in luminous, non-toxic ink and handwritten by General Eisenhower on edible paper. It was to be read after ejection and landing in enemy territory. He knew he would eat this one rather than light a match to burn it.

Colonel Williams recalled General Montgomery's instructions the day before when he said, "You're the, third...I mean the second team to go on this mission."

Williams had caught the goof--so his was the third mission to the same objective he thought. The other two had failed.

The mission had to be his most important one of the war, Williams surmised. As usual, he hadn't even enquired the reason except as they explained, to rescue the most important man in the world.

General Eisenhower had said on departure as Williams saluted and said his usual sparse goodbye.

"Colonel Williams, this is the toughest mission in your career--also the most significant one of your life. The joint Chiefs of Staff who planned it say that the future oft he free world hangs on you."

Ike prematurely ended the farewell. "Colonel, fail this mission, and my advice is don't come back!"

Williams thought, "What a send off!"

By mid point on the English Channel, Flight Group Nine had risen to approximately 10,000 feet; where, above them lay a huge canopy of British bombers. The bomber squadrons had been alerted and, in fact, were part of the master plan to shepherd the three German-marked planes safely over the drop area.

The pilot of Colonel Williams' lead plane was waiting to hear only two words. Suddenly, over his radio, an English voice said, "Nestle in", and he climbed to 12,000 feet where eventually the three "Nazi" planes became an inconspicuous part of a British aerial armada headed east to bomb German positions on the Russian Front.

Williams knew only vaguely that the squadron routing was to be over France, Germany, and Poland. At 1:28 hours, the squadrons of bombers were over Poland. A green light flashed on Williams' plane and the three small unarmed craft left the protection of the fortified aerial armada. Williams was aware that when they had descended to drop level, they were over Southwest Poland in the province of Selesia. Above, the noise from the giant aerial armada was still deafening when the pilot of Colonel Williams' lead plane sighted a giant, luminous "X" staked out on the ground up ahead. The pilot knew the "X" marked the drop spot. He also knew he had only two minutes remaining to deploy above it and evacuate his mission and then the luminous "X" would disappear.

"Flight Captain to Colonel Williams and men. Prepare to eject," came over the intercom. The plane had slowed to 125 m.p.h.

Williams checked his chute, which he himself had packed. Then he disconnected his oxygen and his intercom to pilot. Colonel Williams counted 10, 9, 8,..0. Then a green band of light appeared on a cockpit dial and the pilot pressed a button.

Suddenly, three men from Williams' plane, sitting upright on ejection seats, were hurled above.

The three planes picked up speed and sped on. The noise of the bombers became a distant throb. Colonel Williams pulled his ripcord and freed his legs from the aluminum ejection seat. The ground marking "X" still glowed. The target would be lit only eight more minutes. He realized he was alone. The real mission had just begun. He could not see the other black silk chutes. He prayed that the landings would be safe, i.e. no trees, no water, no wires, no buildings. In spite of cold rain, he was glad the wind was less than 10 m.p.h. He adjusted for deviation and knew the unknown terrain was rushing up to meet him.

He landed in a huge tree.

Cutting himself loose, he dropped to the ground and began rounding up his six men from the three planes. All had dropped within half a mile. On landing, each had immediately buried his telltale ejection seat and black silk parachute.

The group was formed in a circle near the big tree in which the Colonel had landed. He counted roll. No injuries or sprains reported. Then he quietly called out the list of equipment and waited for answers on each piece. "Hack saws two, 40 feet of wire, 12 sets of jumpers, dynamite 48 sticks, plastic explosives 6 tubes, bolt cutters, portable stretcher, portable crawl bridge." The list went on. It included grenades and automatic weapons. Each looked at Williams. Finally, Sergeant McCloskey, checking the usual inventory in his own mind, came up and quietly said, "Sir, what happened to your golden sword?" Williams replied, didn't bring it tonight. I was ordered to leave it in London."

McCloskey let out a whispered oath. "I'll be go to hell. Our luck is broken," he speculated in a whisper and turned away.

Colonel Williams led the group in the direction of the fort.

They hid their three days of rations near the bend on a small creek that showed on their map. They expected to return and retrieve these after storming their objective. Each man had specific duties. They had left England only three hours before. It was now 200 a.m.

Colonel Williams took out envelope #2. He read the luminous scrawl. Then he ate it.

Heavy clouds moved slowly in the overcast sky as the allied group hurried three miles toward the objective, a square shaped prison now guarded by Germans but built some years earlier during the

Russian occupation of Poland. It was a political prison.

The mission reached the backside perimeter of the prison defenses in one hour, twenty-eight minutes--all well and all equipment intact.

Arriving at the 3000-volt electrified fences Colonel Williams knew he had reached the first obstacle. He took out his third envelope. It read: “You have arrived at the electrified fence. Sergeant McCloskey will jump electric current. Then cut wires and proceed through. Next obstacle will be a 10’ corridor of broken glass set in cement. Sergeant Stobel, prepare aluminum foot bridge.” The ex-Royal Canadian Mounted Policeman got his bridge sections ready to assemble.

Colonel Williams knew he could count on Stobel. He was good with a blackjack, a crack shot, adept with a knife, handcuffs, could pick locks, knew judo, and he could handle police dogs and prisoners equally well. General Montgomery had assigned the Canadian Sergeant Stobel to the team.

Stobel assembled the bridge and, thrusting it over the points of broken glass, he crawled over quickly with Colonel Williams following. The rest came on.

Beyond the glass deterrent the ground sloped on a twenty-five-degree angle and at the bottom of the slope was a continuous reef of barbed wire. McCloskey placed the jumpers on the wire in case it too was electrified. Then he cut through the innumerable strands and dragged out enough for a hole. Colonel Williams dropped to the ground and maneuvered his 130-pound frame to the other side. No one spoke.

Beyond was three hundred feet of open ground patrolled by guards. They sighted a small, one-man guardhouse where the patrolling soldiers met every twelve minutes. One German stood outside with his automatic weapon over his shoulder. Sergeant McCloskey would make the first kill. There was a gurgle from the soldier. His weapon fell to the ground as the Scottish Sergeant snared his neck from behind with the lariat. Seconds later, a second soldier came cautiously up to the small, one-man guardhouse. He bent over his comrade. Sergeant McCloskey dispatched him also.

Colonel Williams ordered those who could fit into the jackets and helmets to put them on. The Colonel was somewhat squeamish about taking off a dead man's clothing, so to satisfy his conscience he forbade anyone to remove German Jack boots.

The young officer assigned the two men who had donned the German helmets and coats to stand guard and hold their positions for an escape route after completion of the objective. They were to be relieved only by a birdcall that had been rehearsed long before.

The time was 4:00 a.m. The sky was still overcast--the night dark. They had about three and a half hours of protection from the moonless night.

Designers of the prison had counted on the outer defenses to make the prison impregnable. Hence, the group of seven men moving forward to the objective (now reduced to five) proceeded carefully over the remaining 150 feet of open ground.

Suddenly Colonel Williams brought his men to a halt. He was not prepared for this next obstacle. The envelope containing the instructions and subsequent warning of the obstacle had inadvertently been placed out of sequence among the packets.

The Colonel had almost stumbled over the ditch. He got down on his knees and peered over a depression which he noted was a cement and rock-lined moat, estimated to be about ten feet wide with undetermined depth. The water was unusually warm and from it rose a putrid smell. Vapor curled up into the cold air. Williams wiped his glasses and replaced them and sniffed the air again. A faint bellow came from the layer of warm water about eight feet below. He listened acutely and recalled his younger days on expeditions into the Florida Everglades. He turned his head around and whispered to Sergeant Stobel.

"There's a dozen or more crocodiles in that water, waiting for a meal. I faintly see their big snouts and I know their sounds."

What Williams didn't know, his superiors did. The prison was notorious because of the presence of the crocodiles. They were fed the victims from within the prison as the jailers saw fit.

Sergeant Stobel hurried back to the broken glass corridor and returned with the "bridge walk". Tying a rope around McCloskey, he crawled over the bridge with his knife in his mouth in case the support upset him into the cauldron below. With the sergeant safely across, ropes were tied on each man from both sides as they crawled on their bellies over the moat. The final barrier for the prison's defenses had been overcome. There was now no retreat.

The group was standing on a four-foot walk surrounding the prison. Colonel Williams' instructions told him that a second set of guards patrolled this walk. Cautiously, therefore, the team moved to the southeast corner of the windowless facade.

Sergeant McCloskey had his star drill (cold chisel) ready. He drove the point several inches into the wall about one foot above the concrete walk and inserted a dynamite stick. Then he attached a six-foot fuse. Lighting the fuse in his cupped hands, the group of six interlopers ducked around the corner to await the blast.

McCloskey was the best dynamiter the allies had trained. He had a natural eye and feel for the direction he wanted to blow a wall or other obstacle. A sound like a crack of thunder burst on their ears. The corner buckled and than came a muffled roar. Before the dust had cleared, McCloskey looked around the corner. A section of the prison's rear wall about 15 X 10 feet had peeled off and slid down in the moat. The shock attack upon the fortress and enclave had worked. This stronghold had become defenseless against a well-planed raid of seven trained men. McCloskey stepped through the opening followed closely by Col. Williams.

Colonel Williams had taken out the #6 envelope as the group waited for the burning of the dynamite fuse. He quickly scanned the 3" X 3" paper and memorized the instruction. "Inside the breached area of the jail, you will land in a guarded corridor on either side of which are five cells. The German National you will free is thought to be located in one of these cells. He may be ill and can't walk. The corridor is guarded at all times by three soldiers. Have weapons ready upon gaining entry!" Williams had put the rice paper and small envelope in his mouth, wet it with saliva, and began chewing. As he swallowed the directions he knew there had to have been an informer inside the walls.

As McCloskey and Williams stepped out of the dust inside the prison they saw they had entered on the backside of three barred, occupied cells, each fronted by a steel door that opened into a corridor. On the other side of the corridor were five more cells, all empty. Colonel Williams presumed they had entered at the exact location called for. Only one German guard appeared at the other end of the corridor. Apparently all the guards had fallen back from the blast. McCloskey leveled his automatic at the guard through the barred door who threw up his hands and blurted out in English, "Don't shoot! I speak English. I'm from Chicago. I was forced into the German army against my will in 1939 when visiting my mother in Germany."

Absolute surprise struck the small squad at the sound an English-speaking voice from within the Nazi torture prison.

"Shut up Fritz!" replied Colonel Williams after recovering. "I'll take your word for now till I find out if you're a traitor. Whether you live or die the next few minutes depends on what you can do for us! Do you understand, Fritz?" As he spoke the rest of his group stumbled in and the five allied soldiers filled three cells along with an assortment of prisoners.

Suddenly two more guards appeared. Seeing such a determined enemy they immediately raised their hands. Colonel Williams ordered Fritz to unlock the three occupied cells and let the six allied soldiers out into the corridor. The German hurried to obey, and the mission team burst out into the prison corridor.

As the team broke out, two more Germans appeared. There was a burst of automatic fire from one of the team and two Germans fell.

Colonel Williams spoke sharply to his men, "Listen! We're here for just one man. He's a sick scientist and we must free him at all costs. If necessary, we'll haul him across Europe to get to allied lines. We won't leave without him."

McCloskey looked over the prisoners. All were manacled by neck collars on three-foot-long chains. On one wall there were three men, apparent age about thirty. They conversed in Russian. He noticed none were speaking English. Next to them was a young emaciated boy, about 5'7, perhaps fifteen years old, who was chained by the neck to the cold wall. He dismissed him as being too young for the objective. In the center cell was a man, mid-forties, blue eyes, less than six feet tall, with a fair beard of several days. He was lying on a cot beside which was a slop pail used as his toilet. He was obviously ill and in pain from torture.

McCloskey told him in German that he was part of an allied British/American team sent to rescue him. "Who are you, Sir?" McCloskey asked into his ear. Slowly the prisoner looked up at the sergeant and uttered, almost inaudibly, his name and serial number. From then on he was silent.

Colonel Williams had memorized the man's name, and from a pocket in the jacket, rechecked the name and number against that written on the slip of paper. They were identical. They had found their man.

The prisoner looked forlornly at the British sergeant. McCloskey quietly surveyed the reaction of the prisoner, but it was apparent the man was too ill to comprehend, or else he had abandoned all hope.

Then McCloskey turned to Colonel Williams. "This is most probably your man, Sir."

Colonel Williams nodded affirmatively and called to Fritz. "Who is this prisoner?" Fritz replied in broken English, "He is a German big-wig from Bavaria they say. He hasn't spoken since his arrival. He's to be killed for crimes against the state. Others tried to rescue him before you. The first team became crocodile food only two days ago. They say in the Commandant's office that a second British rescue team never reached the prison area."

Colonel Williams ordered his men to place the scientist on a stretcher and delegated his men to get the feeble prisoner ready for a transport out of the prison.

The time was 4:13 a.m.

Williams called out to Fritz in an impatient tone. "Who are these other prisoners?"

"We got these three yesterday." Fritz pointed to the manacled, arrogant, hobbling prisoners chained by their necks to the wall. "I'm told they're top Commies," said the English-speaking German guard.

Colonel Williams approached the prisoners. They had a haughty look about them. "Anyone speak English?" Colonel Williams asked. One shorter, broad person with a small moustache and glasses who was fairer than the other two, said defiantly, "I do. You came to rescue us, no doubt?"

Ignoring his remark the American OSS colonel harked; "What is your name"

"Molotov of the Union of Soviet Socialist Republics. With me are Comrades Gromyko and Beria. Stalin will reward you highly after you free us." The Russian-speaking member of the allied team interrogated the Soviet prisoners.

Williams had an attitude that committed him to have compassion for the downtrodden and especially young people. All his life he often had been able to feel vicariously, another's pain, often the very limb or part of another's body experiencing the distress. But in the case of the three prisoners, who turned out to be Russian, a feeling of revulsion swelled up in Williams, particularly because of the vibrations felt from the one named Beria. Later McCloskey would land a haymaker on Beria's jaw for his arrogant demands.

"Well I'll be go to hell!" exclaimed McCloskey, standing beside his commanding officer. "Let those Commies hang here. We got our man, Colonel. We got what we came for mon."

Colonel Williams realized he could not go back to London and tell his superiors he perhaps had left Stalin's three top henchmen hanging by their neck collars in a German prison. "He noticed they were still wearing their street clothes in which they'd been captured. Better give those Russians the benefit of the doubt," he thought. He called over his torch man. "Cut these prisoners loose." The blue-flamed torch cut through the steel links close to the wall and Fritz dropped the hot end of the chains into a pail of water.

Williams ordered the three men to take the stretcher and prepare to exit the prison with the taciturn scientist. The time was 4:20 a.m.

The young twenty-six-year-old Colonel had cleared two cells, but alongside the Russians, manacled to the wall, the team was about to leave behind the young boy. Williams thought to himself, "Why is he here? What part could he possibly have played in this ghastly war?"

"Who is the boy?" he asked one of the Russians. "A Jew Kid" was the interpreted reply. "He's nobody."

Colonel Williams looked again at the gaunt boy. "He is somebody--he's a human being," he thought. Childhood terror was in the boy's features. He spoke to him in English. The boy did not reply. McCloskey spoke in German, then French. No answer. Sergeant Stobel, observing the interrogation, came forward. "Sir, the boy's in trauma; he hears but won't speak. That's terror in his fare. You're wasting time trying to parley with him."

Williams' concern for the boy was not holiness on his part, yet he certainly was a human instrument of divine righteousness. Thus, he was unable to betray his revulsion of an innocent boy condemned to a horrible death and his own need to prevent another human tragedy. Whatever would be the boy's destiny, Williams subconsciously determined that in future years the boy would discover it for himself, if he possibly could be saved.

"Cut this boy down!" Williams ordered the yank torch man, to which came the insolent reply, "Do it yourself, Jew lover! We got to save our own hides. The alarm's are going off all over this damned jail and you'd harness us with another dead weight--this Jew kid."

Williams moved directly in front of the dissident solider. "Jew or gentile kid--who cares? Somewhere this boy's mother and dad are crying their hearts out to God that their son be brought home alive."

"You understand this, you infidel." Williams hissed in anger to the man with the torch. "God will even try out cowards like you to answer the prayers of the righteous."

As Williams grabbed the torch and cut the steel chain holding the helpless boy by his neck to the wall, he warned the unruly torch man he could expect to be court-martialed for failing to obey his superior officer in the line duty.

McCloskey stared impassively at the angry colonel and tried to close the rebellious episode by proposing their final epitaph: "The condemned men heard a hearty sermon from their commanding officer before they were shot to hell by the Gerries." Then the top sergeant added hurriedly, "Colonel! We came to get only one man--a cripple at that, and now we have to haul out half the bloody jail inmates with us. Hoot mon, let's move our butts out of this stinking slaughterhouse."

Colonel Williams spoke up firmly for all to hear. "I intend we leave this death house like gentlemen. Fritz! Show us to the front entrance!"

Up spoke the disobedient torch man. "Now the colonel wants us to die like gentlemen--and at the front entrance too--where the German pack can enjoy cutting us to pieces."

The colonel had made a quick decision. Originally he decided to return through the blown back wall and familiar route in which they came in, and furthermore, it seemed the ideal way to team up with his two men guarding the back entrances. Suddenly; however, he reckoned he would lose too much valuable time trying to get the scientist on a stretcher and the dead-weight boy, as well as the obstinate haughty Russians, across the perilous crocodile moat and through the barbed wire and electrified fence.

Colonel Williams picked up the emaciated bundle of bones and terror lying on the floor and threw him over his shoulder as he called for Fritz to lead the way out through the front. Sergeant McCloskey held his machine gun in the back of the big German, and the mixed column actually quite unlike gentlemen in appearance, marched raggedly out, with weapons drawn, toward the main entrance of the notorious prison. Interspersed in the line of allied combatants were new yokes of added burden to slow them up--the Russians carrying the German scientist, the young Jewish boy flung over the commander's shoulder, and two German hostage guards, each handcuffed by Sergeant Stobel.

The rescue team knew nothing of the prisoner-boy's identity. If the captured Germans knew who he was they did not volunteer to tell. That he was Jewish, was the single statement acknowledged by the German guard, Fritz. In truth, the boy was Piere Rothschild, son of Count Julian Rothschild, the French scion of the Rothschild banking family. While in sanctuary in England with his family since the Nazi occupation of France, the boy had been kidnapped by German agents late in February 1945. Secreted to Liverpool and smuggled aboard a Nazi submarine off the coast, he had ultimately been landed in Hamburg and taken by train and truck to the crocodile prison of lost hope (or Prison "X" as it was referred to in German documents), having arrived only the day before.

(The year before Colonel Williams had dramatically raided the tower cell in another German concentration camp and delivered the sixteen-year-old son of Otto Von Schusnick, a leading Swiss/German banker, safely back to his happy parents.)

Following VE Day the Allied Intelligence teams who visited the Silesia prison site interrogated the German guards. They were horrified to learn that the other five cells on the same floor of Prison 'X' had been emptied the day before the Williams mission had blasted their way into the Jail. The unknown prisoners in those cells had been Jewish. They were undressed by the captors, taken out to the moat, and thrown in alive to the crocodiles. Many of those in the same prison met that fate. Allied bombers had strafed and bombed the crocodile-filled moat at an unspecified date after the Williams-led mission had left. The origin of the crocodiles is not known; but, prior to being placed in the torture prison, they had been kept in a basement of a Hungarian castle reputed to have belonged to Count Von Etherington, a top ranking Nazi officer who was a descendant of the illustrious Dracula. Count Von Etherington occupied the castle about the time of this episode.

Over in the prison courtyard, McCloskey kept his gun on Fritz who took the group to the main floor entrance in an enclosed area at the front of the jail. There sat the Commandant's small, five-passenger Volkswagen. With McCloskey's gun on Fritz, the German/American pushed a button and the drawbridge over the crocodile moat was lowered down.

"Pile in!" ordered Colonel Williams. The Americans got in with Fritz driving and Williams at his side, still holding the boy, and McCloskey behind Fritz with his weapon barrel on the guard's neck. The scientist was placed upright in the back seat with another team member supporting him. Those who couldn't get in, including the two handcuffed Gerries, ran beside. The road ran 400 feet up an incline on which the car left the jail with an assorted group of prisoners and raiders. They had killed four adversaries and lost no one so far, but at the top of the incline, the unexpected awaited them.

The German pulled the car to a halt and the passengers witnessed below and ahead a lumbering German Tiger tank inching forward. Its eighty-eight millimeter gun was pointed at the stopped car and alongside the tank Williams estimated about forty or fifty German soldiers trotting in full battle dress. The alarm that enemy raiders had breached the jail had reached the nearby garrison.

McCloskey was fourteen years older than Colonel Williams, but he was able to come up with a satirical, overstatement of the dilemma to his 0.C. "I'll be go to hell, mon. We have two possibilities: to get blown to bits up ahead in three minutes or retreat to the jail and get blown to hell ten minutes from now. Which do you prefer, Colonel?"

Colonel Williams threw out an order to McCloskey. "They don't know if we're friend or foe yet. Got any of the plastic explosives left?"

"Yes, one tube," was the reply. "Wrap it to the front of the bumper while we vacate the car and lock the steering in place."

The tank below slowed up as the incline steepened. In perhaps three minutes the big eighty-eight millimeter tank would nudge the raider's car.

Colonel Williams counted slowly. "25, 26...30...40" Forty-four seconds had gone by when McCloskey straightened up and ran back. The boy and the scientist were on the side of the narrow, rutted, dirt road as the six hostages and prisoners hunched down beside them. The car was in neutral, the steering column locked in position, and the front wheels were in the half-frozen, muddy rut. Colonel Williams' six-man team pushed the car and slowly it gained speed and timidly ground down the incline toward the giant monster of destruction.

As the allies and their prisoners hugged the side of the road they listened carefully.

It was less than thirty seconds. Then they saw it. The hollow below lit up in a yellow light, and almost immediately a great explosion deadened all other sounds as the car hit the tank. Then, a second explosion rose from what had evidently been an ammunition truck behind the tank. Metal shot into the air and fell randomly, but none of the Colonel's men were hit.

Even as the sky lit up and the ammo continued to explode, they saw a dirt path leading from their position and they moved off. The Russians and one of Williams' men carried the scientist on the canvas stretcher and the bony shoulder frame of Williams became burdened with another hundred-pound pile of skin and bones as he threw the boy and his chains over his shoulder again and moved off.

"With your permission, Colonel," whispered McCloskey, "let me take the lead. I know where we're going, mon." He gave a birdcall whistle and shortly the two other raiders came back through the fences and joined the group. They began to hear the cries of dying and injured men as they hurried downhill away from the confusion and struck into a small creek. Williams ordered them to take to the cold water. Walking ankle to knee-deep they hurried away from the destruction.

Before they struck the creek, Williams had released the two German guards still in handcuffs but retained the one they had nicknamed Fritz. One of the released guards had broken and ran back toward the Jail, but the other fell back and persisted in trailing the raiding team. When the team came out of the creek, 500 yards downstream, they heard noises from behind. Sergeant Stobel fell back and the group went on. There was a pistol crack and fifteen minutes later, Sergeant Stobel appeared with a German helmet,coat, and boots.

They had gone about 2-1/2 miles further from the jail and the raggedy group could hear the baying of dogs in the distance. The giant oak, underneath which they had stopped, obviously was their next rendezvous spot. Colonel Williams read another sheet of instructions that said in part: "Here is where you disappear from the Germans..." He laid the boy on the ground as Sergeant Stobel wrapped the cumbersome three-foot chain to the boy's arm. Then

McCloskey swung up into the huge, six-foot wide oak's trunk and climbed out on a long, horizontal limb that disappeared over a half acre of outlying rock covered with an impenetrable patch of briars and thorns.

Two men followed McCloskey upon hearing his low whistle. Then the stretcher with the sick scientist, followed by the boy, were painstakingly shoved and pulled out the limb without breaking any branches.

The Russians were made to follow, unaided, and Colonel Williams brought up the rear.

In the center of the mass of briars and thorns a rope was slung over the big limb enabling the group to be lowered down into a small, fifteen-foot clearing in the midst of which was a recently dug hole about ten feet in diameter and five feet deep. Instinctively, Williams knew the hideaway hole had been prepared by the earlier group of allied raiders who never got back to use it. All able-bodied men set out to deepen and widen the hole. An outcropping of a large rock to one side went underneath the briars and they tunneled into this to make a latrine. The group was packed into the small confined area and heat pouches were opened to help remove the wetness from the bottom and sides.

Williams wrapped a German greatcoat around the boy who still was mute. McCloskey covered the top with branches and pieces of canvas. Then he pulled the rope from the tree and slid into the man-made retreat. The rain had turned to heavy snow, and the abode of thirteen people--in reality all strangers to each other--became camouflaged from above. Sergeant McCloskey made the universal sound of caution, "Shh--Shh," to keep quiet. He cursed in his mind that his commander had not brought the Golden Sword! Without it, he believed they all could be jinxed.

A blanket of pure white snow covered the silent men, some of who had shed the crimson blood of perhaps 40 enemies. These Christians, atheists, and a young Jewish boy became subdued in a hideout of questionable survival.

Since the team had been dropped at 2:00 a.m., only four hours had elapsed. Colonel Williams tried to fight the slumber that overcame him. As he dozed off, he could hear new noises--the yelping of excited dogs and German voices under the old tree less than 100 feet away. He heard the rattle of a German mouser as the enemy sprayed the briar patch. Colonel Williams barely heard McCloskey whisper, "The Krauts have called for a half track. Looks like they intend to overrun our position."

Soon, reality faded into a dream as Colonel Williams slept, wedged among thirteen bodies. He did not hear the enemy half-track penetrate the rocky perimeter of their refuge.

Chapter 4

IN THE CAVE OF THE HOLY RELICS

Colonel Williams dozed fitfully in the snow-covered dugout in Silesia, Poland. It was to be his final mission. Because he had a congenitally weak heart and had exerted himself past the limit of endurance, his threshold of responses suddenly collapsed.

His prominent chin fell on his chest. His thought pattern became scattered despite his attempt to keep control. The smell of wet clothing and the rising odors from bodies permeated the already stale air. He remembered fearing that someone might break the sacred silence by a cough or scream. Inadvertently, he checked the temple pulse of the boy leaning against his side. He was still alive.

From beyond the hiding place the baying of dogs grew louder, then faded, and then came closer to the briar patch again. He hoped the thorns would discourage the dogs from sniffing them out of their secret lair.

Try as he would, he could not fight the fatigue. The physical and mental exhaustion had taken over his body, and now his mind also began to succumb in spite of his confinement in the stinking hole in a foreign land. The last thoughts he recalled concerned the five new personalities, especially the difficult Russians and the unpredictable Nazi guard. Every time Williams had observed him, he decided the man had lied about his identity. He resolved the man was not the simple guard he pretended but had commanded men. He was almost certain Fritz was a Nazi plant.

As the barking dogs were heard coming closer, the clear voices of the German searchers filtered into their hideout. Col. Williams barely reacted to the sound of a Hauser firing into the thicket. A bullet came through the covering above and buried itself in the dirt wall without hitting anyone. No man made a sound.

Williams would not yet discern whether it was autosuggestion or the old recurring dream that had seduced his mind as it had done often in the last year of his missions. Barely aware of those around him, he began to sink into a state of solitude. His subconscious emerged, and a purging of the present dispelled the sensory awareness of his surroundings.

Barely now, could, he hear faint baying of dogs and harsh voices. But as the sounds drifted into his hallucinatory state of mind he began to associate them with another time and place. He believed he was no longer in Silesia, Poland, hiding from a determined enemy. In a dream state he was running for his life somewhere on the coast of northern France on a cold November day almost two years earlier. The similarities were nearly identical. He was fleeing from vicious tracking dogs and Nazi pursuers.

Freed in mind, but not body from the present dangers, he imagined he was racing toward a towering church anchored beneath a tall gold cross on the steeple. They had followed the cross. Upon reaching the church they had bolted inside an unlocked door. There, standing beside an altar, was a young priest as if he were expecting their arrival.

“Vite,, Vite! Follow me,” the priest cautioned in a whisper. Then, carrying their wounded, the harassed team had rushed down into the basement of the old Catholic church and was rudely stuffed into a small crypt-like enclosure. They were barely settled with their wounded comrades when, from above there came the noise of rifle butts pounding the church door that was now locked. And from the air vent, or pipe, above their heads they could hear the baying of tracking dogs and the muffled voices of the enemy.

The sounds of the hunters faded, and they realized the smallness of their confinement. Sergeant McCloskey broke the silence beneath the church that day. "Mon!" he had said. "That bastard Hopkins was a traitor. I knew it when his chute landed first and the Gerries dinna fire on him. A hundred quid he's hunting us with them up there right now."

Later the priest returned with a doctor who pronounced the two wounded men dead, He gave last rites and left the corpses with them, and as the doctor departed the accompanying parish priest told them that the French underground forces would move them to a safer place when all was clear outside. He had left some bread and salami, water and candles.

Colonel Williams had lost two of his men to German firepower plus the traitor who stayed behind. Then, as he strained to hear outside noises, another American crawled in to share the limited space. He was a three-star general which uniform he wore beneath a priestly garb.

The young Colonel recognized that the Free French Forces of the Interior, often called simply The Underground, had saved them all from capture and death and that this church was a shuttle point for allies on the underground railway out of German occupied territory.

All the recollections sifted through Colonel Williams' mind in a split second as he sat in the scooped-out pit in the midst of a briar patch in Silesia, Poland, 300 miles from allied lines, only a few weeks before the total German surrender in World War II.

Rousing himself from the alpha state, again he heard the actual sounds of German trucks crisscrossing the surrounding terrain, and he knew the search was on in earnest to find the team which had delivered such mass destruction of property and life in Poland's Prison "X" and managed to escape intact.

But in his alpha state of mind, the Colonel kept calling for help to the "face in the shield" as his mind floated back to the cold crypt beneath a Catholic church in Brittany, France.

Another priest had come to the crypt, and after questioning, then agreed to help them escape. The next night, through a secret tunnel, the entire group came out on the Seine River beneath a bridge. A twenty-five foot channel fishing boat was tied up, and all boarded the boat and were taken below--all except the guiding priest who took off his hassock and hat, and assumed the appearance of a rough Brittany fisherman. Thus they left their refuge.

From below they could hear the captain challenged by a passing German patrol boat. Satisfied, the Germans allowed the escape boat to proceed. Then, an hour later, while in the channel, the escapees saw the rays of a searchlight flood the ship's deck and penetrate the hatchway. "Achtung!" said the German voice. The fishing captain gave his name as Pierre LeBlanc and also hollered an assigned number. The searchlight moved on, and the ship disappeared into the darkness.

Sometime later the craft touched a rocky outcropping and the allied escapees were beckoned on deck. They knew they were not in England. What each saw was a three-hundred-foot high, perpendicular cliff from above which the searchlight played on the water beyond the boat, and German voices could be heard. They were safe in the shadow of the cliff.

The priest/fisherman beckoned the men in the hull to come on deck and when they were assembled the Frenchman, in perfect English, asked Colonel Williams and his group to slip over the side of the boat into the water. The French priest went overboard silently, and one-by-one the five allied escapees followed him without question.

Colonel Williams' feet touched bottom at about six feet in depth. He held his breath and, following the priest, dove down and forward. Carrying out instructions, his hands touched an opening in the rock wall before him and he propelled himself behind the turbulence of the lead swimmer into a watery tunnel that sloped upwards. Suddenly he was standing waist deep in a basin, and he felt the cold air above him penetrate his uniform. He began to shiver as one-by-one the allied escapees surfaced. Williams followed the priest up a green, slime-covered slope that he knew had not been used for a long time.

They were in a damp, stone cavern with squared corners and the young American Commander sensed eerily that the place was ancient and perhaps, thousands of years ago, mankind had lived or met secretly here.

In one corner of the man-made cavern a bundle of wood had been placed over a stone grate. The fisherman/priest walked over and, retrieving a match from a small niche in the blackened wall, he lit the kindling wood on the grate and the fire sprang to life. In the corner, a hole sucked up the smoke and became a chimney. Following the lead of the French priest each man took off his clothes and boots, stood naked folding their wet garments towards the brisk fire. The French priest spoke, "I'm Father Brian, You must remain here forty-eight hours, and then we shall return and move you on to England." He added, "There are a few supplies, some food and candles in the other corner. Use them sparingly in case we are late in coming back." Then he disappeared into blackness through a small opening in the wall. The month was November. It was cold, and they could hear the sea gurgling through the tunnel.

After drying out by the fire, Colonel Williams asked the group to set their limited field rations and water flasks in the center of the crypt. A lighted candle placed in the small wall niche from which the fisherman/priest had removed the dry matches, obviously placed there in recent days. Blankets were absent and in spite of the faltering fire in the corner flue, each man quietly felt the clammy coldness that penetrated his bones.

No one had observed Sergeant McCloskey disappear into the crawl-hole through which the French fisherman/priest had also departed earlier into the adjoining caverns. Since McCloskey had quietly disappeared, Colonel Williams ordered the remainder of the men to stay intact. The room was estimated to be approximately 16 X 35 feet, permitting each man to claim his own section of the wall. Few words were spoken as each soldier collected his thoughts. The Colonel chose a corner of the room and the newly arrived American general stayed nearby and confided first to Williams and then to the entire group that he was an ordained Priest of the Jesuit Order and that as a Military Padre they would drop the title "General" and simply call him "Father John". The priest and Williams indicated by their expressions that they knew each other--more than casually. Beyond some unrecognized whispered words, no further mention was made of their earlier relationship. Such was the code of the OSS to which the soldier/priest apparently also belonged. Thus, the group had settled into the transitory stage of being prisoners in a dungeon, with confinement engendered by the raw, elementary nature of their primitive jail cell.

Within an hour after some consternation being shown by Colonel Williams, Sergeant McCloskey reappeared amidst a babble of questions. Without bothering to address himself to any questioner, he began:

"This place is a hole that leads to Hell and I couldn't find out where the Frenchy priest got out." he began in his Scottish brogue. Before McCloskey could resume his adventure tale into the Black Abyss, Father John interjected.

"I disagree, Sergeant. This place is most certainly not connected to Hell. Rather, I sense a divine presence all around us--but then I gather from the profane way you constantly refer to Jesus Christ, the Son of God, that you have no spiritual identity whatsoever."

There was silence in the dimly lit chamber as all eyes turned to McCloskey who was never known to back down from a challenge or dispute.

Walking over to the six-foot, two-inch priest with the big hands and rock hewn face, the five-foot-ten Presbyterian McCloskey looked up at the challenge to his brute authority and quickly noticed the a military garb, shoulder pips, and the Roman Catholic Chaplain insignia.

"Well, if it isn't a priest, and a mouthy one at that."

Sparse words were exchanged, and it was immediately evident

that the two men, one a cleric with high moral values and trained in religious dogma would be adversary during confinement to the tough, swearing, arrogant Sergeant who despised even the moral ethics of polite civility.

Colonel Williams ordered McCloskey to "back off" but intermittently McCloskey continued to slur the priest; and, in the flow of obscenity, finally called him a Pope lover and pagan traitor to true Christianity.

Father John had had enough of McCloskey. Forgetting differences in rank, the three-star Chaplain General unbuttoned his officer's coat and stepped back to the center of the wet floor from which McCloskey had thrown his verbal barbs at the cleric.

"We'll decide right now for God or Satan," began the priest as he raised his fists.

"And whose side do you represent, Holy Chaplain?" the Scottish Sergeant replied, and before he had finished the retort, Father John flung back the answer.

"You should know, son of Satan." Colonel Williams jumped into the center of the floor and stood between the two men as McCloskey was pulling back to deliver his first punch. He separated the two men and then asked McCloskey to explain his absence in the caverns, without using profanity, and tell what information he had picked up.

"Beyond the hole in the wall, I traced the French Priest's retreat about 100 feet along a narrow ledge hewn out of rock," McCloskey said while staring defiantly at Father John.

"I tell you, this place does lead to Hell. I dropped a coin over the side of the ledge and I barely heard it hit a hard surface, hundreds of feet below. I explored two small rooms but found only a log and a rough plank. I finally ran into a blank wall, but located no stairs or other openings out of the infernal place. This God-forsaken dungeon was chiseled out of the rock long, long ago. This much I'm sure, but who did it I cud-na-guess. Are we being watched?" asked McCloskey out loud. "Aye," was his reply to himself, "and not by the Gerries".

The men spent the next twenty-four hours with each trying to maintain his body warmth as the wood supply dwindled and the fire died. The temperature was constant,even into the night, but the thermal heat from the six bodies raised the forty-degree cold a few notches. Night came and the men removed their jackets and placed them between their derrieres and the cold damp floor. Colonel Williams propped his angular frame in his corner and the Chaplain took the adjoining corner over McCloskey's objections.

As time passed Colonel Williams was heard to mumble in his sleep, and Father John rose and went over to quiet him.

"What's the matter?" the cleric asked the OSS Colonel as he touched him gently on the shoulder. "There's a presence in this room which I can't identify," replied the Colonel. "Good or bad asked the priest. Good," said the younger man. "Do you feel it too?"

"Yes, it seems to come and go, but when I feel it, I'm overwhelmed." Father John whispered quietly.

"It's the same feeling I once experienced in a spot in Jerusalem, like being in the vicinity of a high alter used for Divine purposes."

"Are you psychic too?" asked the Colonel, to which the cleric replied, "On and off."

Colonel Williams' religion, like his father before him, was Christian Scientist: he told the priest and mentioned also that he had been aware of his paranormal ability to see apparitions and ghosts since he was a boy of six when he played in an old house in Bradford, Pennsylvania. He played with the ghost of a young girl whom he saw occasionally and with whom he carried on conversations, with no one else witnessing the apparition. His grandfather, discovering him talking to the unseen young girl beside the house one day, discovered his grandson's psychic ability and told the boy's mother that he had inherited a curse.

"There is definitely a presence in this room." responded Williams.

The men began stirring and evidently it was morning as their body clocks surmised. A candle was lit in the niche at one end of the room, and the few rations and water were doled out amid grumbling.

McCloskey scurried back into the aperture in the wall; and, in a moment, backed into the room again and stood up holding four or five bottles of wine.

"I forgot to tell ya about these pleasantries," he remarked with some glee.

Turning to Father John, the Sergeant asked, "Wi ya no hav a wee dockin dories?"

The Catholic priest; deferring to the unusual politeness and almost stunned by the conciliatory manner, replied, Why me?" "Because," said the Presbyterian soldier, "Ya nae did burn the precious candles in a mass when I was awa in the caverns."

The two laughed and turning their backs on the others, McCloskey, departing from his brogue, opened the first bottle and said, "Mon! Let's get plastered and give our senses a lift from this damn reality."

"I'll bet this stuff is five hundred years old," said Father John. "And who cares, Chaplain," retorted the Sergeant as he filled his empty water bottle with wine and passed it to the taller man.

Colonel Williams, a teetotaler, watched from his corner where he stood cracking his thumb and fingers. "It's a thin line between love and hate," he mused as he observed the two different inmates.

Father John, the Priest, and Sergeant McCloskey the hardened soldier, had indeed found something in common. First the two were the oldest of the group, the priest being forty-seven and McCloskey about forty-four years old. They soon discovered they were both of Scottish descent, Father John being American born. When the priest spun a few sentences in Gaelic, the native Scottish soldier replied mirthfully in like tongue. They both had risen through the ranks the hard way--notwithstanding, Father John was an officer graduate of West Point in 1916, which he had attended according to his father's wishes, later rising to the rank of general in Flanders, France, in World War I.

In the dungeon in which they hid beneath the French Monastery, a day and a half had elapsed since they first swam in through the water tunnel. Big Father John had been fidgeting and finally rose and walked over to the opposite end of the room. He was heard to speak in Latin and then was seen facing the niched wall and fireplace flue from where earlier the younger fisherman/priest had removed the matches and struck a light.

Father John studied the wall in the dim light. He ran his hands over the bare rock wall as though he were searching for a crevice and repeated the action several times. Then, taking the solitary lit candle he passed it in front of the area and observed the small, blackened shadows, finally tapping the wall with the end of his knife handle. Placing the candle back in the niche, he stepped back to a spot that he had carefully examined, then turned around and called over to Sergeant McCloskey. Can you give me a hand Sergeant?" he asked calmly.

The Sergeant moved to the priest's side and they exchanged confidences. The two placed their hands on the wall one set above the other. "Push," said the priest.

Slowly a section of the stone wall yielded and opened slightly revealing another blank void through a narrow aperture.

"My God, forgive us for what we've done," said the priest. "I'll be go to hell! Another bloody room." exclaimed McCloskey. The men gathered around the narrow entrance. The lone candle in the niche flickered out, and as the men adjusted their sights they believed they saw what appeared to be another room similar to the existing area, except the floor was higher.

The Chaplain lit a fresh candle and entered cautiously, followed by McCloskey. They parted to he left and right, each feeling the walls as they shuffled their feet slowly along a fairly smooth and much drier floor than the one in the first room that led to the sea. Arriving at the farther end of the room, they estimated it to be about twenty feet long and twelve feet wide. The remainder of the team peered through the opening as the two lead men independently studied a dim light in an aperture of the well. They came towards each other still touching the wall. As their feet shuffled along the floor, Colonel William met them after slowly crawling across the center of the newly discovered crypt.

Sergeant McCloskey felt it first. His hands touched the rock ledge projecting about a foot and a half from the wall with an interior depth of perhaps fifteen inches within. The total surface was more or less six feet long by three feet deep. The interior was maybe 20 inches high.

The Sergeant reached his arm in over the opening. His fingers touched a metal object. Quickly he pulled back his hand.

"Holy Hell!" he exclaimed. "The damn thing bit me!"

As the priest and Sergeant met, the cleric spoke silently, "I'm in its presence." He crossed himself and before the slowly gathering ensemble there rose a momentary glow that illuminated the interior of the aperture and flooded out into the entire room.

"Stand off!" admonished Father John. "We're in the presence of something supernatural."

"Bullshit!" replied McCloskey. "This stuff is just a pile of ancient junk." Reaching cautiously in again after the illumination subsided, he withdrew an old, silver-colored, metal goblet about eight inches high with handles on both sides. It was cone shaped with a lip-top edge.

"Look!" he replied. "A genie. Let's make a wish that we get out of this damnable hole before we all starve. McCloskey hurried out to the other room for his last bottle of wine that he had been guarding like the dog in the manger. He returned and picked up the ancient goblet, wiped the inside with his fingers, and finding no insects or sediments he poured a small portion of the wine from the last bottle he had freshly opened. Then he offered the drink to the priest.

"After you Sergeant," said Father John, and McCloskey took the cup and, raising it for all to see, offered a toast: "To the mighty sons of Scotland without whom the English would have already lost the war."

Then, raising the ancient silverish vessel to his lips with one hand he swallowed the wine. As the sergeant tilted back his head, his whole body arched out of control as though a sudden impact had given his spine a reverse curvature. Then his back flexed in a whiplash to a forward position, and unable to keep his balance, McCloskey spilled onto the hard floor, landing on his hands and knees.

The Sergeant exploded an oath: "May God help me! Who kicked me in the rear? This stuff hits you like a mule. It's more potent than the best scotch Whiskey I ever tasted."

Then, still leaning on his left hand, he touched his lips with the fingers of his right hand.

Profaning the name of Christ, he swore again, "My lips are burned where that cup touched them."

Then he rubbed his fingers together and exclaimed in abject wonder mixed with terror, "My fingers--they're burned too." The ancient cup he had dropped to the floor and as he rose he said, "I'm scared of nae mon, if I can see him, but what I canna see, scares me."

Father John reached down and picked up the battle scarred and tarnished mug. It was dented but not broken. Holding the cup aloft, the priest looked at McCloskey with a withering glance and said,

"God abhors profanity, especially the taking of his name in vain." McCloskey walked back to the other room and did not speak.

"Who else would like a drink from the cup?" asked the priest. No one replied.

Then, pouring the wine into the vessel, he slowly raised it aloft and gave a prayer: "Thank you, Oh Lord, for saving us undeserving souls from the enemy! And thank youfor leading us into this sanctuary. Surely our cup runneth over!"

He drank the wine and then walked over to the first room and, pressing the lips of the cup to a crevice in the wall, he drew an ounce or two of water and returned to teetotaler Williams, with the drink. The young Colonel thanked him and sipped the water, and then he placed the Chalice back on the shelf. "That feels good--real good I might say," said Williams. "Funny thing! The feeling lasts."

Father John and Colonel Williams returned to first room to confide, the room where McCloskey had already retreated.

Williams and the priest heard his top sergeant speaking to himself and finishing with the words, "For Christ's sake."

The priest, in solemn tone directly charged McCloskey with profaning the name of the Lord. McCloskey replied as though in deeper thought or trance, "It was not profanity priest, it was a prayer about something I've never felt before in my life. Something invaded my mind and purged it. I don't feel like swearing na more. What do you make of it, mon?" "I don't yet know," said the cleric. "You're supposed to know, priest. If you don't, who does?" Father John responded simply, "Great is the mystery of Godliness."

None noticed McCloskey's reticence to go near the objects as another lit candle was brought to the shelf and the men examined the ancient artifacts.

It was immediately apparent the items were not junk.

Colonel Williams, after standing aloof from the group, approached the shelf again as each item was passed around. Three of the group showed little or no curiosity. All concluded that the "stuff" was worthless for their immediate needs or survival.

Among the objects that were examined were the following:

A gold, Maltese-like cross with arched ends and the picture of a man's head engraved on the center; a four-inch-diameter glass object with sculptured edges which looked much like a modern ashtray, the base or globe on which it rested had been broken off; a metal headband pierced with many small holes placed at random; a silver coin the size of an American half-dollar which had been shaped to fit in the palm of a hand, drilled with a small hole for a chain to be worn around the neck. It had ancient writing on its face; a Jeweled dagger; a metallic bowl in which there lay three headless spikes about eight inches long; a still larger bowl with a few harder crumbs or cruets resting on the bottom.

Also, with the artifacts was a piece of perfectly preserved wood, jagged on one end and squared on the other. It was about forty inches long by ten inches wide and about six inches thick. In the wood was a large nail or spike hole. Several of the items were encased in what looked like sandalwood boxes and some had indecipherable inscriptions.

Colonel Williams felt the spikes in the first bowl and immediately he experienced a throbbing pain in the wrist. The two-to-three-inch band of metal then aroused his curiosity. He thought it part of some ensemble but could not equate its purpose. Toying with it, he finally placed it around his 7 1/4-inch head to measure its circumference and found it too large for a headband. Then, as the band touched part of his forehead, small piercing sensations of pain stimuli reached him where the object touched. Drops of what felt like sweat and blood came off on his fingers. Finally he thrust the ornament or band back on the shelf. He was angry with himself for having bothered to examine it so closely.

Without showing his anguish to the others, he perked up and handled the heavy piece of wood. He immediately felt as though his head was bursting and his heart began to fibrillate. Still holding the wooden piece with both hands, he inquired if anyone nearby was ill, because he vicariously could feel another's pain--a problem or curse he had experienced many times in his life whenever a friend or relative nearby was ill. No one acknowledged any acute illness.

Williams put back the wooden timber and the pain departed. Then, feeling in the base of the last bowl, his finger touched the hardened crumbs of some unknown substance and, before he was aware how it started, he was engulfed in depression. Suddenly he felt as though his spirit had been overcome by woe. The young officer wanted to double up with pain in his chest and head, but he withdrew his fingers from the bowl containing the hardened crumbs and returned to his corner in the outside, colder room. Placing his jacket beneath him, he sat down on the floor. He wanted to cry.

Father John, recognizing Williams' anxiety, followed him.

"What's the trouble, Colonel?" solicited the priest. "Everything," gasped the younger man. "I feel like I'm dying. Everybody's deserted me." to which the priest replied. "That's odd what you say. For some peculiar reason it reminds me of another time long ago at a place called Golgotha. Someone cried similar words."

The OSS leader of Christian Scientist persuasion from birth simply responded, "but what's that got to do with me? Too bad they crucified Christ. He was good man." "He was God," corrected the theologian.

Then, without prior conscious thought, Father John found himself saying out loud, "Surely He has borne our griefs and carried our sorrows yet we did esteem him not…."Father John no sooner had pronounced the Isaiah Scripture than he realized unbearable pain had overtaken Williams' body, and he found himself hurrying back to the shelf of objects. Grabbing the chalice, he rushed to the trickle of water coming off the wall, collected a minute quantity and brought the object and contents to Colonel Williams.

Drink," he commanded. The young man obliged and took the cup and obediently swallowed its contents.

As the priest looked intently at Williams' whitened face and mask of pain, he saw the facial lines relax and the face regain some color.

Then, turning to Colonel Williams, Father John asked what happened when he drank from the chalice.

"The depression left him, but strangely enough, as I held the cup to my lips, I saw Christ."

"How do you know he was the one you saw?" asked the Jesuit priest in wonderment. "I just know that I know," was the sole response of Williams.

"Those relics truly must he holy," said the priest. "Let us handle them only if needed, and he put them back in their hiding place where they must have been for hundreds and hundreds of years.

We mustn't tell anyone about these experiences with the relics or they'll think we're insane.

Time will reveal to us what happened here this last hour," said the cleric. "Time will tell," he repeated.

"Destiny certainly delivered us here. God knows none of us may ever be the same again."

The Colonel managed a smile and said, "You know, I felt like I was crucified a few minutes ago," at which remark the Catholic priest crossed himself and said, "Father God! Forgive him for the blasphemy!"

The group of escapees had eluded the German search parties for over two days since their fateful drop into enemy ambush. If the reckoning of Colonel Williams and his men was correct, they were most likely "smack solid" beneath a monastery or church converted to an enemy encampment monitoring shipping on the English

Channel. The meager supplies had been exhausted in the first 24 hours with the exception of water which was available from the trickles of seepage off the wall.

The original outside room connected by tunnel to the sea had been their main abode for sleeping, eating and toilet. The inner alter room discovered by Father John had been placed off bounds other than for the occasional curiosity in which they all soon lost interest.

Father John's meditation on the find was centered in the origin of the contents, but he also considered he was probably the only one who wondered about the metaphysical and supernatural aspects of the objects?

Colonel Williams, less knowledgeable about early Christian artifacts, had not become fully aware of their significance. In such a general attitude of unconcern, the priest elected not to speculate orally on the divine aspects of the objects or their origin, mainly because he recognized he was his own best counsel. He reflected that their discomfort was harsh enough without endangering theological discussion and so he excused the others for their indifference. The main concern for all was their close proximity, their basic existence and the shortage of food, as well as the dominating factor of escape that they never ceased to discuss. Colonel Williams forbade anyone to venture into the sea via the water tunnel, even to reconnoiter. "We're in the hands of the French underground and the Catholic church," he rightly surmised. "And they know what they're doing and have a proper timetable with our survival uppermost in their minds." He told them he was sure"London" already knew of their predicament and nobody on the allied side would panic if his voluntary prisoners remained calm.

One of the men smelled food sometime early in the evening. All likewise agreed. Then a faint rising of steam was seen in the small aperture where Sergeant McCloskey had disappeared to investigate the caverns. McCloskey got down on his knees and was seen to haul out a large steam pot and several spoons.

They quickly gathered around and found a note on the handle.

Then, peering and sniffing inside, they found a cauldron of vegetables and salt pork--enough for them all. Williams opened the note as his men began to spoon-feed themselves, each one with one eye on the provisions and the other eye on his neighbor's gluttony.

The note said simply, "Set watches for midnight! Swim out quietly and surface, signed, Father Brian." The predicament was that no one had a watch.

It was shortly after eating when Colonel Williams said, "Let's try and get some sleep!" Going to his corner and sitting on his jacket, he found the November weather of the coast of Brittany had become colder and the rock wall reflected the temperature drop as he leaned against it. He endeavored to bend forward and prop his head in his hands, but sleep would not come. Random disconnected images went through his mind as he tried to resolve the exact whereabouts of their hideout and the failure of his mission. He surmised, even accounting for the traitor, Hopkins, that his own leadership efforts had not been spectacular in spite of the fact he had kept cool and shepherded his men carefully, making sure of rehearsed teamwork to survive. But it was really the French Underground that had saved them. Still, why had he been brought into this mysterious labyrinth in St. Malo that was perhaps a retreat of the pre-Christian era and most likely last used during the Middle Ages. But, as he rationalized, he realized there was no pat answer--everything was plain conjecture on his part.

Without knowing why, he got up and walked over to the opening to the other room. He peeked through the stone door still ajar and looked at the end of the room where the objects lay on the shelf. Adjusting his eyes in the dark, he saw a faint glow from the shelf and he walked slowly towards the diminutive source of light. At the shelf, he stood quietly and then thought of the shield. He hadn't handled it before. It was a round shield, perhaps of Roman origin, he thought. In size it was about three feet in diameter, and as he felt it he marveled that the leather buckler on the shield, used to support the forearm of the spear-thrower, was still intact. The straps should have rotted hundreds of years ago if the shield itself were old, he thought.

He went to replace the shield on the shelf but considered the ridiculous idea that the shield belonged to him by inheritance and that he should hang on to it. Not knowing why, he began carrying the ancient armor back to his corner and mused at the sight of himself carrying an ancient shield, lost in a cavern beneath the sea, the victim of circumstances in a modern war totally beyond his control.

He managed a smile and reluctantly sat down again in his corner. His bones ached, but the dungeon no longer encapsulated his mind.

The cold seemed to vanish and his bones and flesh did not complain. Unexpectedly his mind drifted, and he was lost in time. Time, he thought of as though he were a bird in flight falling and soaring through space. His body became warm as he inserted his left hand and forearm through the leather buckler and brought the old shield down over his chest and abdomen. His head fell forward and his chin rested on the edge of the shield. He was a bird...a dove...and the space into which he soared became light. A light so bright like he had never been bathed in before, but so pure it hurt not his eyes. And so he slept and dreamed.

How long he was in oblivion he did not have the faintest idea. There were none of the usual body adjustments required for circulatory aid. His physical being and very existence had ceased to be a problem as his soul soared out and beyond, and his body reflexes did not complain.

Since settling down with the shield, the cavern occupants had suddenly quieted down also, albeit in various positions of unexplainable discomfort. Colonel Williams was not aware how long he had meditated into flights of fancy in time and space, except that in his subconscious state he gradually was attuned to an overpowering quiet around him.

Picking up a candle that he kept at his side for emergency, he struck a match, lit the wick and held the shield out from his torso perpendicular to his knees. The flickering light showed everyone apparently asleep. Then he held the light in between him and the shield and his attention was caught by a man's face shining from a mirrored portion in the center of the shield. The image swelled in size and Colonel Williams became hypnotized by what he saw before his eyes and the messages that flooded into his mind. Time stood still.

Looking up, Williams' eyesight adjusted itself and he saw the shadowy hulk of Father John standing at his feet behind the shield and staring down at the sitter's face.

"Colonel, do you hear me? What's up?" he whispered as he bent over to continue speaking. "You look like you've seen a ghost."

The Colonel looked up in a daze, his eyes blinking and said simply, "I have seen a ghost--a holy one. At least it was a vision or apparition right here in the face of this old shield."

"What did it look like?" asked the incredulous priest. "It wasn't an it--it was a he. He was: a bit older than I; bearded face, moustache, and long brown hair to the shoulders, white teeth and blue eyes. His countenance was grave."

Ignoring the description, Father John interrupted. "Are you sure you're okay? Is this confinement getting to you?"

"I'm quite all right, thank you."

"Good," replied the priest. "Glad to hear you acknowledge that. In that case what else can you tell me about the bearded man in the shield? I've seen an angel but not a bearded man."

Williams broke in. "The vision or reflection said it wasn't a person."

I certainly can believe that," replied the inquiring priest. "If it wasn't a vision then what did it call itself?"

Williams spoke slowly and soberly, "The being identified itself--or rather himself--in these exact words: I am Jesus Christ, the true son of the living God."

Conversation stopped as the priest pondered the last assertion, then whispered in Williams' ear. "You're telling me that vision--or whatever--called you all the way down into this cavern of total darkness simply to announce that he was the Christ? And he had to use an old Roman shield to get his message through to you? And why you?"

"He appeared because I called him--to help us all."

Recalling his own miracle in Flanders, twenty-seven years earlier, Father John acknowledged the distinct possibility of a divine miracle. "I certainly confirm and my church would also acknowledge the possibility that a miracle could easily happen, Colonel. But somewhat unlikely in the manner you describe, in spite of our awareness that there is something sacred in these rooms."

Colonel Williams replied. "He, the Christ, came to answer my prayers for getting back to England in one piece."

"What purpose did the vision--or should I say the Christ have in coming in person?" the priest asked with a slight hint of rebuke, to which Williams confessed, "He called me a doubter and accused me of self-righteous ego, but then categorically stated that I'd become a believer by the time I reached England--which I must question. He also prophesied about the future."

"And what part will you or I play in those eventful years after this unnecessary war is over?" asked the priest. "I'll tell you when and if I become a believer." smiled the Colonel.

"That's a lot of information you received for the last couple of minutes I watched you staring into the shield, young man."

Williams replied, "You didn't see the face or hear the voice so you can't believe."

Ignoring the remark, Father John asked for the shield, intending to replace it. As he picked it up from Williams, he casually remarked, "Oh, by the way, did the face say why he required an old shield to give himself third dimensional substance?"

Colonel Williams replied with quiet authority, "The shield once belonged to a Roman centurion by the name of Casius Gaius Longinus whose shield was placed over Christ's face and torso while the body lay temporarily on the ground beneath the cross of Calvary."

Father John replied almost inaudibly, "I'm familiar with that expunged portion of the gospels." He then replaced the shield. When the priest returned, he was ashen white.

Father John turned to the colonel and said almost as a warning, "I advise you, Colonel, and I shall do likewise, to omit this vision and its revelation from our reports when we get back to headquarters. If we try to explain, they'll put us both in a nut house or send us back home with medical discharges.

Why?" spoke up Williams.

The priest replied. "Mainly because you nor I have witnesses. And let me ask you one last question, as a priest of course: How does the one who called himself Christ intend to make believers out of skeptics before we reach England again--if we do?"

"He didn't say," said Williams.

In the tunnel below they could hear the gurgle of the sea as the tide rose and all the men stirred simultaneously from sleep, as though by built-in command, and got ready to move into the depths.

It was midnight on the third day of the mission that failed. They had been in the tomb seventy-two hours, Colonel Williams reckoned as he and his men, one-by-one, sank into the chilling waters and disappeared from the hiding place.

The commandos were fully clothed and sopping wet as the French crew pulled each one aboard and hurried them below decks into the low ceiling hold. The place reeked of fish as the men were told to lie on the planks and be covered with a canvas permeated with fish oil. The sea was rough. As the boat left shore, the waves rose fifteen feet or more.

Colonel Williams lay inert on the plank floor hoping he could breathe in spite of the nauseating odor of fish oil. He had felt the abundance of fish dumped over him and figured the French had caught a big catch, ostensibly to deliver same to a French port, but instead had picked up the English speaking captives and headed out to sea again. Once on board within the hold, the French had come back below and shifted the big fish haul to cover the entire canvas and captives in case of German boarding.

Colonel Williams reached down and felt his jacket. Then he felt the front of his pants and thighs. Only a few moments before he was wringing wet. He checked again. Now his clothes were dry, even the sloshing water had vanished from his boots. He knew his feet also were perfectly dry.

Most amazing, he had felt the fish loaded on top of his body and rightly expected that his movements would be almost impossible with the added burden of shifting weight. He noted as he moved his arm that surprisingly enough, his hand struck no obstruction above. There was no evident weight of fish on his chest, either, yet he had felt the burden when they first were shoveled on top.

Exploring with his right arm, he discovered a space existed next to him as though the canvas had been thrust upwards enough to enclose another person. Ridiculous, he thought. Turning his head he whispered, "Is that you, Father John?" A reply came back, "Yes, I'm still here but there is a space between us that wasn't there a while back."

Then he heard the priest exclaim, "I'm not cold nor wet; my nausea has left me; clothes are dry Williams, and so is my entire body, head to foot." They could hear the creaking of the ship's timbers and the wail of the wind above and outside and they knew instinctively they were well out into the English Channel.

It was then that it happened. A calm descended in the hold and the allied soldiers lay composed on the planks without any effects of suffocation while above them hundreds of pounds of fresh fish lay dead weight.

Up above the French boat, Captain Andre Lefebvre looked wildly around from his wheelhouse. The sky was dark with intermittent moon and stars. The waves were fifteen feet in height. He looked ahead one moment and saw a mountainous wave of at least twenty feet flowing toward his small craft. In a few seconds he knew he would be in a deep trough and a sheet of dark water would sweep over his decks. He yelled to his men in the fierce wind and hung on to the wheel and braced himself in the small wheelhouse space.

Captain Lefebvre stared in astonishment, glued rigidly to the wheel. The precipitous wave bore down and less than fifteen feet from the frail boat the water parted as if a giant hand had divided its mass into two parts. He looked back and saw the big wave continued on, joining itself behind the boat. Then, amid a crescendo of Hail Marys and Mon Dieus, the Captain looked around and saw the phenomenon. The boat was sailing on its own ocean, a calm, sea of perhaps thirty by sixty feet, fenced in by wild whitecaps and waves that should have invaded the oasis of calm water and half swallowed the boat and men.

Clenching the wheel, Captain Lefebvre eventually called to the first mate. He gave him the wheel and walked around the rails and looked down at the channel waters. Unbelievably, he made one distinct observation: their diesel motor was chugging along in the center of a mirrored sea where the waves and the wind had been stilled. He looked up and wondered if he were in the eye of some maelstrom, but the cumulus clouds hurried across the sky without apparent menace. His clothes were not billowing from the wind and the small marine pennant and fleur de lis flag hung almost limp from the mast.

"Mon Dieu," he said again in prayer and crossed himself at the stern of the boat. "Why this miracle of nature? As soon as we dock at Portsmouth with the catch and the Englishmen, I must get to the nearest Catholic church. Certainly, I must be crazy," he thought, "but if I am loco, my whole crew is loco too." Then he thought, "These Englishmen or Americans are no Jonah's, that's for sure! He crossed himself again.

Captain Williams knew they were in harbor when he heard the foghorn bellow and get a reply. A jarring of timbers occurred and it was evident they were tying up at the wharf. Suddenly, the hollow space the size of a man was gone, which he had felt between him and Father John during the entire trip. The weight of the huge fish catch was heavy on his chest and belly, pinning one arm across his face and the other at his side.

He faintly heard men descend into the hold and the canvas and fish were peeled back off Williams and his men.

A voice in English yelled, "Blimy! This chap in the Gerry uniform is done in. Let's get him to the shore medics first!"

Colonel Williams revived later to hear a voice in English ask, "Who is this stinking chap in the bloody Gerry uniform" The American soldier replied feebly, "Get me to a phone, mate."

As Williams finally walked unaided from the dockside shed in a makeshift English soldier outfit, it was still dark. French Captain Lefebvre rushed by to his boat. He did not recognize Williams as he hurried on board. The Colonel heard him say to an English provost at the gangplank, "In all my life at sea, I never crossed the channel so fast. I swear by God, I have never heard of such a strange thing. I've been to church and offered mass in thanks to the Holy Virgin for calming the wind and the waves when we crossed the wild channel," he said exaltedly in broken English to the provost, who looked up, rolled his eyes and smiled politely.

Colonel Williams climbed into a waiting lorry beside his new companion, Father John, and broke silence by inquiring, "Padre! How would a cleric like you describe the dangerous crossing from France?

The priest replied with some contemplation. "The face in the shield held the English Channel in the palm of his hand for our sakes."

Williams whispered reverently to himself. It had to be a miracle. He said I would believe before I reached England. But why me?"

He thought of the face in the shield and the promise made to him by Christ, that he would be with him when needed again and again.

The lorry driver got behind the wheel and they were on their way to Portsmouth railway station and Allied Headquarters in London--and possibly a new role in life.

Chapter 5

The Blood Ran Red

The unobtrusive pigboat pulled out of Yarmouth Harbor, England just after dark in November 1943, riding low in the water like an otter. She was headed on a kill or be-killed run.

Billowy wisps of thickening fog blanketed the entire ocean above the 55th latitude where the armor-plated boat would take he bearings from a radio signal beamed out of Newcastle. The boat would then head across the North Sea, destination: an island off Denmark's west coast named Romo. There, a garrison of Germans was about to kill the elite of Denmark's manhood.

The craft had been built in prewar Denmark and was approximately fifty feet in length with a 12 to 14-foot beam. Her hull drew a bare four-foot draft plus another two feet above sea level. This left in the watertight interior less than five feet of pigmy room. Yet on this trip she was designed to carry a cargo of humans instead of pigs. Topside of course, she was deckless, in that no one could walk the steel covering while at sea because it had a five-degree down-pitch each side of the center beam. Two diesel-run brass screws gave the low, sleek, black boat in excess of thirty-knot speed as she ran almost silent and invisible in the clinging, fog-bound sea. A German PT boat could easily overtake her, but her raft-like superstructure would make her a difficult target.

At each end of the big boat a fifty-calibre machine gun on a hydraulic elevator platform (resembling a small pill box) could suddenly be raised in the face of an unexpected attack. At mid-ship, the barrel of a Bofors anti-aircraft gun laid tucked in a groove, unrecognizable in its modified unmanned position. To an observer the craft was a sister to an unobtrusive garbage scow, rather than a sleek naval craft fitted with top armaments and hiding under her topside a foreboding secret.

The crew of six was entirely Dutch, including the commander. They had been carefully chosen from Royal Dutch Navy volunteers for the suicidal journey, and operated under the jurisdiction of the exiled Dutch government in Britain. Captain Stohl ran the craft and for this particular trip he was assisted by thirty-year-old Brigadier General R.V. Hansen, on loan from the Royal Danish Guards in exile. Besides aiding Captain Stohl in navigation, the main role of General Hansen was to come later as an experienced soldier during the planned raid. The night in question, Captain Stohl piloted his pigboat from a radio beam and retractable periscope in the front and stern of the boat, the latter from which the nerve center emanated. The crew kept the diesel engines in top shape while operating in wartime waters and also manned the sonar, radar, and radio equipment as well as armament. The boat was indeed a tight ship, man-wise and watertight too, with the topside often awash.

Special passengers aboard the pigboat that night were; Col. Halford Williams and his reorganized team of six, augmented by Gen. Hansen to aid him in his expected landing operation. It was Williams' first mission following the ambush and the three days spent in the rock tomb in France where he came upon the Christ relics. Old familiar Sergeant McCloskey was second in command of the Williams mission.

The new group had prepared for the raid for only four days, working out landing and siege coordination with McCloskey and Gen. Hansen, when unexpectedly, the night before, Major Davis of Allied Intelligence had come to Col. Williams with orders to report to the Allied Command for a change in date of departure. Revealed by the briefing were these essentials: "An estimated 240 key Danish nationals were imprisoned on the island of Romo, Denmark. Among those imprisoned were all the members of Parliament and certain intellectuals and resisters who had been rounded up after the Nazis had marched into Denmark. These prisoners were to be executed, without exception, the next morning. The German prison garrison was estimated to be approximately 250 officers and men." Allied intelligence chiefs were sending the Williams mission of six specially-trained troops to attempt the rescue with the additional help of the eager Dutch crew and the Dane who knew both the interior of the prison complex built during the Napoleonic wars, and the island itself.

Before departure, the briefing officer had frowned upon seeing Williams' startled expression when the size of the defending force was revealed, but the officer's frown later turned to puzzlement when he witnessed Col. Williams' buckle on his Sam Brown belt and attach to it a golden sword in its scabbard, the first mission on which Williams was to take his sword.

"May I ask Sir, why the relic you've tied to your waist?" the briefing officer said jokingly.

"It, the relic as you call it, is exactly what it appears to be--simply an officer's dress sword which I recently acquired for reasons of my own," replied Williams.

The major retorted in jest. "May I inquire Sir, are we still fighting the civil war?" Then he added seriously, "Sorry Sir, good luck and good killing," and turned briskly and left. He probably could feel Col. Williams' glare piercing his back.

Now, aboard the pigboat Williams lay in an improvised bunk with little headroom, sprawled over a straw pelisse. Beside his quarters sat a 50-calibre machine gun and its Dutch gunner. When the pigboat hit land, this Dutchman would be responsible for opening the upper hatch and extending forward the motor driven gangplank on which the assault team would storm ashore. Williams' men lay in nearby bunks trying to rest. All were agitated because of the new British-made, short-barreled, 100-round automatics that Gen. Montgomery had insisted they use for this mission, in spite of the team's unfamiliarity with them. The ammo was tension-held in a throwaway canister. Soon, even this gripe subsided as the men worked their weapons.

At the halfway point in the eight-hour journey, the waters were still comparatively calm with long swells as the Captain sent word that they expected to reach their objective at least a half hour or more before daylight. Williams did not bother to rouse his crew and pass the word. They needed the rest, or half-sleep.

Yet Williams remained uneasy and sleepless. He disliked the confinement. He couldn't stand upright and pace the wooden plank floor, there were no chairs, and he couldn't get accustomed to the hum of the diesels and the vibrations from the twin propellers.

He wondered what his girlfriend, Pauline, would do tonight when he didn't show up at the rendezvous. And McCloskey, his tough squad leader, had been invited to a family gathering the next day and he would not show either. Williams pondered that he hadn't heard McCloskey swear since coming back from Brittany. Would he still be able to kill or defend himself against an enemy, he wondered. He was aware that his sergeant had been to a Presbyterian minister to seek counsel as to why his anger and swearing had ceased, generally taken in the name of his favorite deity, God or Christ. His family had told how the malice left him and how Christ took over, although his minister preferred to wait and see about the latter spiritual change.

Back in London after the Brittany mission, father John had only been able to spend a half hour with his friend Williams, and then without explanation he had slipped away without further ado concerning their experiences with the relics. In his meandering thought pattern, Williams wished McCloskey had not inquired from the briefing officer about the enemy garrison count guarding the island prison. The allied team would be outnumbered by 250 enemy to his six and the Dutch crew. To Williams, the outcome was hopeless.

Yet he must consider the odds. Therefore, one thing he kept pondering, "No use to storm the objective, the tactic used in training. With that many defenders, his team wouldn't have a snowball's chance of survival in a fiery furnace, even with fire support from the pigboat's machine guns." He recalled that another paramount requirement was that once inside the prison, they should avoid automatic fire in order to save the lives of the Danish prisoners. Williams concluded he was on a no-win course if he followed planned procedure.

He knew instinctively he would abandon the plan. Instead, he would lure the German garrison out in the open at all costs. Thus, Williams kept rehearsing in his mind the apparently unsolvable problem: "Save the lives of the Danes but don't storm the prison complex. And lastly, remember the entrenched enemy was over thirty-to-one in manpower. Williams' misgivings increased by the moment. Without a sure plan to succeed or even survive, he had only one potential element in his favor--surprise.

Besides his sword, the colonel carried only a German luger that had been altered by the ordinance gunsmith into a .32. A new sleeve had been inserted into the .45 barrel and the Nazi swastika had been honed off with a U.S.A. insignia superimposed. Now the gun did not kick. Williams had told the gunsmith to ignore its killing potential in the original design. He had asked simply to be provided with a smaller bore, accurate at close range for his own protection.

He continued to ask himself the question, how could this mission succeed in the face of such odds? He reached into his jacket, took out his glasses and wiped the lenses. Of one thing he was convinced. He would have to die fighting. There could be no allied survivors. He thought himself as crazy as Custer if he actually carried out the attack on the superior German battalion.

Nevertheless, he reasoned, once ashore he would seek an ideal defensive position although he was not sure that such a place existed on the bare rocky surface on which he mused it would require a jackhammer to dig a fox hole. He would be careful to mask his pessimism from his men, he assured himself.

The Dutch machine gunner came over and asked Williams if he wanted to discuss anything with the Danish landing officer. Williams had replied--not till just prior to beaching. Then Williams asked the Dutchman his name.

"Juss call me Huiscamp. Charlie Huiscamp. That is not my real name," to which Williams replied, "tell me Charlie why you Dutchmen are so dedicated as to take on this mission into the jaws of an outnumbering German force," and the young Netherlander answered: "Val colonel, I don't vish to say something abouz myself, except that my grootmudder was Jewish, and I have a family still living in Holland broken up by the occupying Germans. But zis I tell you, about zee Captain of zis boat. He already did see his fazzer and mudder and vife and kids killed before his eyes. So you can be sure he vill give you all zee firepower you need and which you haven't got with your scrawny outfit. Don't voory colonel! I juss vish ve all vere landing on shore vith you so that ve could get many Nazi swine vith our knives to settle our own scores."

Col. Williams answered: "Very interesting Charlie, but this is not a mission of vengeance to settle scores—remember that!"

"Maybe you are afraid to kill Germans?" replied the Dutchman."

"I don't want to kill anyone," was the brief answer.

A cold air mass had settled over the North Sea and the fog increased in density. The captain now zeroed in on a radio signal beamed from Copenhagen, and with his Danish copilot he made allowance and corrected course. On one occasion the captain's communications operator picked up from the water what sounded like another engine noise that he judged to be either a German PT boat or a surfaced sub, probably out of Hamburg. All engines thereafter were stopped. They waited twenty minutes before slowly resuming speed and course.

It was 4:30 am when the captain had announced a noise blackout including conversation. The next announcement said daylight was to arrive at 6:55 a.m. and they expected to land only thirty minutes prior because of the delay caused by the unknown vessel entering their vicinity earlier. Up ahead the front periscope picked up several pinpoints of light as the fog shifted momentarily. General

Hansen, the Dane, knew they were on target. Ahead, about a mile and to the right of the lights there would be a sandy beach. The captain must miss this section and nudge shore north of the beach in deeper water from which the land rose abruptly to five or more feet, enough to lend visual protection from German eyes when dawn broke. The captain cut his speed and one motor entirely and probed slowly the darkness and shallow waters ahead. Daylight was appearing almost imperceptibly over the horizon in front of them, when the pigboat and its occupants reached destination and secured moorings.

Col. Williams alerted his men and waited. They had felt a slight jar and knew they had touched the rock outcropping. Then, at his side there appeared Gen. Hansen. The Dane laid out a blueprint of the prison and adjoining property, and he and Williams scanned the map.

"This prison has had many uses, among them a naval training school with which I am familiar", said the Dane in low tones. "I believe the Germans have not noticed our arrival but once they discover us they will either attack in mass from the large, front doors and side exits or they will counter from several windows in the front of the complex and perhaps the roof. They may also have positions back on the higher slope.

There is one advantage in defending our positions. They must attack from only about a 95 degree frontal arc so that we should be able to direct fire power at them at all times keeping in mind we can't afford to lose any men. On the spot where I've marked the map as you notice, they will likely begin the executions, sharp at dawn, That is, if they don't detect our presence first. That huge flat area in front of the building is the parade square, he said pointing again to the map, I expect the German execution squad will fire from there in our direction, that is out to sea. Are you fully prepared, Colonel?"

"Well I guess we are as ready now as we'll ever be," responded the American. "I thank you for the last minute briefing, General but there are a few points we should take a second look at on the map if you don't mind. I notice you have marked the map up from the shoreline topographically in feet. I see that about thirty feet from high water mark there is another sudden rise in the elevation of five or six feat. The question is, do you think my men could take full cover at this point?" Williams inquired.

The Dane replied, "Yes, temporarily at least, but you must keep up continuous fire power to check German advance from overrunning your position--or rather our position, because I shall be with you."

Just then the machine gunner picked up the phone and called quietly in his Dutch accent to the assembled men. "Captain Stohl says the fog is clearing and he recognizes the outlines of the prison through periscope. About half way from here to the prison entrance he can barely make out the outlines of twelve posts."

McCloskey, turning to the Danish advisor, spoke up. "That means the execution posts are in place mon. It looks like the massacre will begin on time. We'd best get into position before the firing squad is in place."

Col. Williams turned to his crouched men and said "Form up!" He then buckled on his sword with painstaking deliberation and everyone stared at him in disbelief as silence reigned among all. Williams' hands perspired and he could hardly keep from shaking. Like the others, he was frightened as he prayed for guidance.

"Prepare to land" came the barely audible order from the boat captain's hidden microphone.

Noiselessly the forward section of the pigboat parted above their heads and seven hunched bodies straightened up. Daylight and its all-seeing eyes would soon light up the area. A three-foot metal gangplank powered by an electric motor folded forward and attached itself to the rock using rubber footings. The Dutch gunner ran up the plank and added a further extension of about ten feet to assure the men agile tracking on the slippery rock.

The OSS colonel climbed onto the gangplank with its pocked

surface and started ashore leading bent-over men with shouldered weapons and belts strung with grenades. The colonel glanced back and saw the gangplank being withdrawn into the pigboat and he knew there could be no retreat.

Reaching the first elevation as the map showed, they found the natural abrupt rise in the rock, offering limited protection. The team separated, and McCloskey and two of the men spread out to the right and located a similar defile about seventy-five feet away. Now the two teams could direct crossfire on the front entrance to the jail from where the main exodus of opposing troops would erupt. The Colonel raised a small folding periscope and observed the terrain of the parade ground. No movement was taking place as he saw lighted windows show up in the complex and he knew instinctively the inhabitants of the prison were rising. As he watched intently, the front doors of the jail were flung open and two German soldiers marched out a blindfolded man with hands tied behind. Immediately the grim scenario was repeated and in less than five "minutes twelve Danes had been tied to the posts and guards returned to the jail except two standing at each end with rifles drawn on the tied prisoners.

Momentarily, with typical German precision, an officer marched out twenty-four soldiers who were brought to a halt about 250 feet from the jail and about 60 feet from the posts. An order was barked out, and the platoon was broken into two squads with the front twelve taking a kneeling position and the rear squad standing at attention.

Still using the periscope, Williams watched as the two soldiers guarding the flanks of the prisoners took new positions beside the firing party, and the American colonel listened as the German officer gave his next orders. Williams did not understand German, but his observations told him explicitly what would transpire within 60 seconds. He waited for the German commands to shoulder arms! Aim! Fire!" Williams, in a side-glance, saw McCloskey give a low, preliminary hand signal that meant less than a ten-second interval remained after the command to shoulder arms had been given. Then Williams watched closely and saw the unfolding finale of the tragedy about to take place before his eyes. He heard a Dane at one of the posts shout a patriot call. The German execution squad held fast. Each German was about to place one bullet in the chamber of his rifle. When all completed the precise motions, the first twelve political prisoners considered a threat to the occupying masters would slump down in their rope harness that held them fast for death.

The colonel continued to watch. His men were waiting his next order as the enemy guards brought their rifles to their shoulders. Williams heard the order in German to load, then he saw McCloskey's final hand signal as each German reached to his belt for a single cartridge and place same in his weapon chamber. Williams knew the time to act was now or never.

Before the enemy guns could be loaded, the OSS colonel gave the signal and his team exposed themselves to the startled execution squad as five short-barreled machine guns began mowing down the almost defenseless Germans. The moment of destruction was swift. In the place of an aggressive, disciplined team of executioners there lay an unrecognizable heap of men blotted out from further life. The allied guns were hot and the raiders stood fast and held aim on target.

As previously understood, Col. Williams ordered the Danish general to make haste up the incline to the posts. Doing such, and articulating in Danish, Gen. Hansen boldly yanked the blindfolds from each of the condemned men, cut their ropes and quietly assuring each he was still alive, he urged them to take off toward their rescuers at the water's edge and not look back. One by one they did just that.

Stumbling as they ran, the prisoners hurried toward the allied group. Williams wished they would move faster. Then he looked back to where the pigboat lay and behold, he noticed for the first time it was docked parallel to the shore instead of prow first as when they landed. Half the upper roof along its whole length had been hinged outward to provide its own boarding wharf and at each end, the machine guns had been elevated, manned and pointed toward the jail, over and above the heads of the rescue team. In the middle of the pigboat, stocky Capt. Stohl was waving the escapees aboard. They were ordered to lie down and be calm.

Williams thought, "Twenty-six Germans dead, twelve Danes saved, two hundred and twenty five more enemies still inside the jail." A cry interrupted his thoughts as an anguished moan came from among the fallen enemy. Out from the front doors of the complex rushed an officer and a short burst of gunfire from one of Williams' men dropped him, but he dragged himself back inside the jail. The alarm had been sounded.

Above the one-sided battle the sky was heavy with haze but ground visibility was now clear. The initial firing on the square had apparently been mistaken by those inside as coming from the execution squad, but when the wounded officer crawled back inside the jail, the ugly truth was made evident: The German commander reacted quickly and efficiently. He assembled an attacking force of armed infantry troops and on command a stream of men rushed out the opened doors toward an enemy that had momentarily ducked out of sight.

What the Germans first observed were two machine guns pointed at them from an elevation at the waters edge. The commanding officer ordered his men forward on the double towards the machine guns, firing at will, while two-man teams began setting up their own machine gun emplacements on each advancing flank.

The distance from the jail was about 500 feet, slightly downhill: The advanced Germans had covered 150 feet and were being crowded by a continuous stream of reinforcements from the jail entrance. The allies held their fire. The garrison troops fanned out and began searching for response in their field of fire. Puzzled by apparent allied inertia, the enemy slowed down. Neither the German officer commanding the first wave nor Col. Williams had yet given the order to commence firing, such was the discipline of the allied team and its enemy. As they came close to confrontation it was obvious that neither could ever retreat. Either the rescue team or the enemy garrison must die in place.

Imbedded deep in the innermost layers of Col. Williams' mind was the need for self-preservation. But the need for survival was less pronounced than his training and character to lead his men now waiting to receive from him a symbol or recognizable motion to stand firm in front of an enemy, before that enemy ran over them and killed at close quarters. His men saw their officer leave his group and run in a crouched manner to a point midway between the two pockets of rescuers.

Suddenly the advancing Germans were aware of a lone military target rising before them on the stark surface of bleached rock. He stood erect, over six feet in height, perhaps 350 feet from the first enemy troops. All eyes stared and all bodies hesitated. Was the peculiar being a challenge or a confrontation? Was he friend or foe?

What all saw was a rigid man with a golden sword take position and present his sword at parade rest. The troops watched in amazement as the man swung the sword up and held it perpendicular before his face in salute. The enemy knew instinctively the incongruous person was out of place in time, and in the art of war, yet he was a perfect bull's-eye. But to an officer familiar with military sword drill, he would know a sword held in salute was in honor of a superior officer or an arrayed formation of troops or a flag. Thus, before the advancing Germans stood a neutral anachronism welded into the cold, rocky landscape.

Still, the air was silent of gunfire. Col. Williams shook and then stood firm as he offered himself a substitute for his men. Methodically, he had brought his sword from parade rest to salute. All watched. As the awe-struck Germans advanced, he prayed for support to the One--to the face in the shield--to the Christ he had met a fortnight earlier in Brittany.

As Williams-the-man called silently for help, he cried that he could not kill. As if in answer, there appeared before him and between him and the advancing Germans a familiar face. It was the same countenance he had seen before. He watched the eyes move in recognition of him and the mouth formed words, "Do not be afraid! I stand before you."

The young American colonel stood his ground as one hypnotized.

His men took the sword being held in salute as the order to attack. From behind, his team recovered from mild shock and opened fire on the enemy from two positions. Then the big pigboat machine guns chattered and the engagement was on.

Now the enemy had a target, and practically all their forward troops advanced firing at the helpless man holding a golden sword. They symbolically recognized him as the leader of an adversarial force. As they moved on in sprawling knots across a 160-foot front they saw other less visible forms firing machine guns from well-protected positions at the shore.

Without realizing why or when, the guns before Col. Williams were silent and he knew the German contingent had been annihilated in a withering crossfire. He held position and returned his golden sword to parade rest, as those of the fallen enemy who tried to rise were gunned down.

The OSS colonel was unaware, but one of the Dutchmen had brought an armful of newly loaded, fresh machine guns to the two teams during the lull in fighting. The man simply dropped them at the feet of each team and then raced back to the boat. On the pig boat the gunners of the 50 caliber weapons reloaded and waited.

There was a pause in the battle that seemed to have lasted a lifetime. Before them the situation was as critical as when they landed. To Col. Williams, scouring the hill of dead men he cringed at the offense his men had committed against the highest morality, and he decided that he was part of an instrument of evil--not that he was motivated by evil, but that war was evil. He did not see the dead men before him as Germans but as men--even brothers. He did not try to rationalize the devotion of the enemy to kill him or the condemned Danes.

As Col. Williams stood with sword at parade rest, the remainder of the German garrison began pouring out of the jail from all exits. The square was filled with men rushing toward their fallen comrades. They fired at random as they ran and Col. Williams brought his sword to salute once more. His own men opened fire.

The solitary exposed figure felt the bullets nick the tip of his blade. He saw fragments of bullets fall before and around him in increasing volume that begin to pile up in an arc around the front of his position.

He was the pivotal point for enemy vengeance. They focused on him and came on from all directions as his men kept up a constant fire on the German melee. As Williams thanked God for protection he did not use the sword menacingly. A German sergeant broke through with fixed bayonet and overran the American officer's stand. The soldier came directly in front of the colonel, unstopped by the mission's hail of bullets in his direction. Williams stared at the man lunging at his middle. He could almost feel his belly torn by the blade as he stood firm and believed the soothing "Be not afraid!" voice of his divine patron.

Then he watched awe-struck as the bayonet meant for him struck an invisible shield, and he witnessed the sergeant bowl over, his bayoneted rifle sill gripped tightly. As the man fell forward against the sword's unseen barrier and onto the rocky surface, he remained bent in a running position with stiffened body and eyes staring blankly into space. He saw no enemy because his muscular system was atrophied.

Next there came at the allied officer a young soldier who fired point blank not fifteen feet away. Still running, he thrust forward his rifle and vainly attempted to bayonet the man with the golden sword, who himself stood as a living target and had not attempted to retaliate or kill. The young German fell grotesquely beside the sergeant by a cosmic force.

In the intervening two or three minutes, three more German troopers rushed the statuesque colonel and they sprawled helter skelter before the astonished eyes of Williams. They resembled a football pile-up frozen in final position staring blankly into space with fixed glares of hate and weapons held tightly for hand-to-hand killing.

The last one of the storming German soldiers overran the teams and rushed the boat where Captain Stohl waited. The battle-hardened seaman ducked the thrust and with his own long knife he countered and opened his opponent. He had smelled the blood of the enemy. As Stohl ran on to shore to finish off the straggling attackers, he heard Williams' voice. "I am in command on shore. Do not kill for vengeance!" All of the enemy had fallen.

Simultaneously the Dutchman glanced over to where Col. Williams stood at salute and saw him bring his sword to parade rest as his trance ended. Then he replaced the bloodless sword in its scabbard and yelled for all to hear, "Cease fire!"

The allied unit raided the jail and freed the remaining prisoners. They counted 226. The German garrison numbered 238 dead with five alive--but frozen.

Within an hour the Danish prisoners held for death on the same day, were herded into the pigboat's cramped quarters and made to sit in tight formation alone with five carefully guarded German hostages. The body muscles of the Germans were still stiffened as their bayonets and ammunition were removed from their rifles. They also lay minus their jackboots, yanked off to be worn by the team members or crew.

Within the jail many allies had taken a spoil and this had angered their commanding officer that denounced them by saying in furry that "people who rob dead people are no better than those who plunder graves." That remark had ended the spree of luger, boots, and miscellaneous thievery.

The team had crisscrossed the horde of slain men and those who lay dying. No medical aid could be given, of course, because orders called for swift evacuation. The soles of the raiders boots were soaked in blood and human carnage as they headed, on order, for the pigboat. Williams vomited before he reached the boat at the sight of such ignoble deaths, and the thought of so many worthwhile humans who had been sacrificed by a dictatorial system that killed all who dissented, or who might lead an uprising.

The pigboat, burdened by such a heavy load, moved ponderously into deep waters under cover of the heavy fog hanging offshore. Beneath its top covering was a cargo of free men, stunned by a salvation that none had thought possible. The problem now was to reach England and safety.

Col. Williams and Captain Stohl exchanged thoughts that perhaps the German radioman had gotten out a message. In fact, such a message had gone out in plain German during the fighting. The crisp wording simply said "garrison being attacked from sea by superior invasion force--many casualties suffered--send reinforcements--urgent." The sender identified the regiment and sent the SOS to battalion headquarters and waited. It was soon in the hands of divisional headquarters, and reinforcements were dispatched by ship. Additionally, all available German PT boats and light naval craft were dispatched to the area.

The fog still hung heavily over the boat and the surrounding waters. About twenty minutes out from shore with his frail cargo, Capt. Stohl sounded his muted foghorn and a reply came back. Captain Stohl heard the answer and knew the reply was foreign.

The passengers heard the machine guns and anti-aircraft gun platforms ascend. At the same time they felt the hammer strikes of a dozen shells ricochet off the low overhead and echo inside. Now above ship, the three Dutch gunners searched the fog and Col. Williams shifted in his bunk as he felt the engines stop and the boat turn hard right. On signal, the two machine guns began firing over open sights and spewed out crossfire of shells at an unseen enemy hidden by fog. The Bofor lowered its muzzle and fired horizontally across the fog-enclosed North Sea as Captain Stohl slowly turned the pigboat clockwise for a wider sweep. The pigboat passengers heard a muffled explosion, and suddenly all realized the enemy ship that had found them was silent. The guns were retired inside and the diesels went pocketa-pocketa again. Shortly thereafter, the enclosed Danes heard the foghorn again and braced themselves for further action. Suddenly half the roof on the starboard side was raised and folded out to form decking. Hurriedly the Danes were asked to divide and as half the men raised themselves onto the folding deck they saw an identical pigboat alongside. Freed Danes, numbering 120 men were transferred to the sister ship of the number one pigboat, and the decks were lowered quickly into place and became protective roofs again as Capt. Stohl exclaimed across to the other bow, "Beat you to England!"

Col. Williams called Sgt. McCloskey to his bunk and told him to look after the young Germans whose body reflexes were returning to normal. He was concerned with their ration of soup and protection from their former prisoners. Capt. Stohl had stowed provisions for the return voyage, and with the welcome ration allotment he continued to enforce silence. Passed along by word of mouth was the warning, "We're in enemy waters--don't talk." With the strict silence broken on several occasions the captain went amongst the refugees and in salty language proclaimed: "If you want to reach England alive, don't talk but pray damn hard the fog stays and the Gerries don't find us." He confided to Williams that German subs got many kills at night while riding surface. By staying up the enemy had greater mobility and might even fire flares on a suspected target and then outgun or torpedo the victim.

"But don't worry, Colonel," he confided, "we lie lower than a snake's belly, so that even German radar would have a hard time bouncing an echo off of us. But if they did cross my bow, I would be quick to ram them--what with our heavy cement-filled keel."

Lying on his bunk, Col. Williams began to unwind and return to the world of reality. His fear of sea disaster was somewhat assuaged by the optimism of Capt. Stohl. But Williams wondered what was real and what was imaginary in light of his re-acquaintance with what he believed was the divine. Shocked from the sights and sounds of killing more than ever, he despised his role in the massacre. Seeking an answer, he reflected on the unexpected presence of the Christ during the battle whose presence gave him vicarious strength to stand alone. As he pictured the face again (the same as he had seen in the shield) he felt a presence and heard the familiar voice break into his thoughts:

"God is neutral in this evil war. Against your will you have become a part of it. I hear your cry 'Why me!' and I feel your anguish. But, do not be afraid. I appear before you as I have done many times in the past, often unbeknownst to you. As long as you fear God and do not exalt yourself or hate your enemy unmercifully, I shall stand with you in the mortal destruction of man against man. Remember this: you cannot escape your destiny, as I could not forgo Calvary."

Williams felt great warmth inside his whole being that surged through his veins and bones. It cleared his mind and left him with a limited understanding about his role and surrendered him to peacefulness. He envisioned two supernatural powers presiding over the great and small affairs of men. It was apparent that a supreme God in his divine logic had allowed the lesser evil power, Satan, to control the planet Earth for a brief period. In contemplation, Williams tried to distinguish if this were the final conflict of the age, when he fell into a deep sleep.

Sgt. McCloskey was standing over the colonel's bunk. "Sir, you've been out like a log. We're home mon, back at Yarmouth. There's a Royal Danish band outside to welcome the freed men."

"Good," responded Williams almost inaudibly. "And what's for us?" to which came the reply, "A cup of hot English tea for you and a waiting jeep to take you to London."

The colonel pulled himself out of the bunk; smiled feebly and said, "English tea again. That is a hero's welcome? They always boil it till your spoon stands up and your innards turn to cast iron." McCloskey chuckled obediently as his officer said, "Take charge, sergeant," and Williams gathered his belongings and stepped ashore with his golden sword strapped to his Sam Brown belt.

Two days later an orderly woke Col. Halford Williams from sleep. "Sir, you are requested to report within an hour to General Headquarters and be prepared to attend a thanksgiving service."

Williams sat in the front pew of the St. Paul's Church of England wedged between three proud generals: Eisenhower, Montgomery, and Danish General Hansen. Williams heard the priest honor the

238 Danish parliamentarians and countrymen freed three days previously. The priest told how they had been saved from death by a miracle, and in this reference to a miracle the Anglican priest defined it as "the absolute love of God that transcended the laws of man to achieve divine purpose." Then he said "It is often God's method to perform a miracle by using a human accomplice, in this case one man who believed God, along with the help of his team of six." Sgt. McCloskey smiled from his seat in the second pew. The priest told the Danes they had been saved from death and to use their remaining years wisely for God's sake.

Then General Hansen rose and proclaimed, "Because of the unbelievable courage exemplified by Col. Halford Williams we Danes shall recommend to our sovereign that he be given Denmark's highest award, THE ORDER OF THE ELEPHANT."

An honor guard escorted Col. Williams to the door and his proud commanding general stood aside as scores of Danes waited to shake his hand.

The minister reached him first. He said: "Everyone is talking about your great faith, I surmise it enabled you to stand firm in front of murderous firepower that should have annihilated you a hundred times or more. Colonel, you are the greatest example of courage and faith I have encountered or studied including the book of martyrs. Williams thanked him and replied humbly, "Sir, I didn't possess the faith you mentioned. Rather, fear overcame me. In fact, I stood there helpless before withering firepower. Momentarily, I think I emptied my mind of myself. I was helpless."

The priest's theological learning was somewhat shaken but he recovered to say, "Oh, as a much older man I must chide you Colonel. Are you not over playing a mortal weakness out of modesty? Williams retorted, "No Padre. I repeat. It was naked fear that filled me, not courage..." to which the priest interrupted again..."but with enough courage to stand alone?"

Williams continued. "I got my strength from a divine being-- and that was the miracle you referred to in your fine sermon."

But the Anglican minister would not let Williams off with so human an answer. Searching for a heavenly clue he asked: "Then lacking courage which you freely admit, how did the divine intervene?" The young soldier countered.

"A divine being commanded me to stand fast as I held an exposed position to rally my men. Truthfully I was so frightened I froze. Suddenly the divine one proclaimed He would stand before me--and that he did. From then on I trusted my protector. It was during the ordeal that followed that I realized for the first time in my life that our creator cannot lie, and that every single word he states becomes truth absolute. Even as he spoke to me his words became reality. I stand before you reverend, as a living witness that God is true. I believe that that very revelation is my only claim to fame."

Then the priest again shook hands with Williams, and as the crowd pressed to do likewise, he finished with a parting query:

"Talking to you colonel has been like speaking to Daniel after his rescue in the lion's den. But tell me if you will... "Who said you wouldn't be killed? Was it God or Christ?" "Take your pick Father! Are they not one and the same?

The bells of St. Paul's cathedral were ringing.

CHAPTER 6

THE CHAIN GANG versus DEATH SQUAD

Col. Williams lay in the wet ditch near Mens, France agitated because of the aerial operational blunders involving his team since leaving their London headquarters via Algeria. The six-man group was now shivering against the side of a deserted road, while a cold October drizzle soaked through their uniforms. They wished they had brought ground sheets or greatcoats.

Williams' irritation grew. Lack of adequate weather information by London briefing officers had dampened team spirits. He recalled the final send-off: "Overcast--possible rain--perfect conditions for a night drop. That's your mission, Colonel," the officer blithely predicted and wound up the briefing with the words, "happy landing." Now as Col. Halford Williams shivered in the ditch on the side of a French hill Col. Halford Williams was most unhappy. So were his men.

None thought they had a smooth parachute drop that night. Williams' top sergeant, McCloskey, groused out loud "Those domm desk soldiers in London should be shot for tonight's foul-ups. Here we are damn it, stranded somewhere in Europe and we haven't even got wheels to get to our destination. And once we get there what's our job? It's to save some punk the world has never heard of."

McCloskey turned to his colonel and demanded: "Why did you enlist us for this lousy mission? Six good lives are on the line for an unknown foreigner. Give me a straight answer mon!"

There was a long pause and the disgruntled group waited for the reply. Finally the young commander said in self-defense. "I guess they chose us because we're expendable."

McCloskey, in a manner bordering on insubordination, got madder at the reply, "Whatdaya mean mon that we're expendable?"

"Well," volunteered Williams, searching for an answer to cool tempers, "I'm sure London's not losing any sleep over us once we free the hostage."

The sergeant, still angry interjected. "Is that what you mean by being expendable," and his commanding officer replied feebly, "I suppose so. Let's drop it!"

Wanting the last word, McCloskey insisted in summing up their dilemma, "As I see it, colonel, top brass makes a deal and we men are the fall guys. Believe me mon, this trip's a one-way ticket to disaster. The blokes in London draw lines on a French road map for us to follow and then they drop us off in the wrong sector. Then if we finally manage to get reoriented and get their dirty job done for them, we're expected to get back to England on our own. If you ask the bastardly intelligence guys how we're to escape if we get ambushed, they have a stock answer: The French marquis will contact you as the mission progresses."

Co. Williams ignored McCloskey's outburst. But now, totally unenthusiastic for the operation himself as he lay in the wet roadside ditch somewhere in the valley of the Rhone, Col. Williams contemplated the inadequate briefing instructions they had received. Worse still, he decided that if he weren't careful, he could have an insurrection on his hands. He reasoned that if his top sergeant decided to abandon the mission, all would follow. His men were fidgeting and grumbling as never before. And to top the aggravation, he admitted to himself he couldn't find, a strategic reason for their being here. Williams concluded: The hostage they're after cannot be worth the lives of six men.

The rain turned to sleet. A German truck ended the beef session. The vehicle came along partly obscured by sleet and was upon them before they were prepared. It slowed down on the incline and moved past their vision at a bend of the road. Col. Williams touched McCloskey. "Keep low till I signal. We need an officers' car for this Job." They waited and shivered over an hour. Someone gave a raspy cough. Tempers rose. Daylight was less than two hours away and with it, the mission would have to be aborted.

Col. Williams, trying to divert attention from their predicament, touched his ankle and said quietly, "I think I sprained by ankle when I landed on that stone fence."

"Too bad Colonel, I can't hand out any sympathy," said his sergeant. I have my own problem. My right foot landed in a fresh cow pie when I came down, but I'm not complaining."

Someone broke in. "We're getting the drift sergeant, Get downwind!"

Ignoring the jokester, McCloskey boasted, "Soon as I pick out my first kraut with the right size boot, I'm going to get a clean pair."

Upon landing, they had heard their drop-off planes disappear south toward Toulons and Williams figured the pilots were returning to North Africa. All of the two planeloads had landed intact except for minor bruises. Now they were reformed and ready to go--but without transportation. Fears and frustrations flourished in each commando's mind. Behind the infiltrators they heard a bull snorting in the pasture, and glancing back they could barely discern its massive shape moving near their position. In spite of the stone fence at their rear, the animal had made them all apprehensive. Its intimidating presence seamed a bad omen. Uncomfortably, they lay huddled at the bottom of an embankment about five feet high, unseen by occasional German and French traffic that passed.

Someone made a rude remark and Williams ordered, "quiet". The response broke the tension and produced a weak laugh when Marlis whispered, "Who? Us or the bull."

They all heard the new sound. It was what they had been waiting for--and it was like music to their ears. Williams spoke to McCloskey. "That's it--I know the sound--a German officers' car is coming slowly up hill. Get in its path and halt it without firing. Tell them our car has gone off the road."

The sergeant replied. "How about asking them if they could exchange one shitty boot for a new clean one?" Williams ignored his man but was pleased they were going into battle with composed minds. The German car, driving in low gear, came into view. It was about to take the curve when its driver noticed a sergeant in German uniform frantically waving a flashlight.

The car stopped and the driver peered out. McCloskey yelled as though in distress. "Our car slid off the bend. My general is pinned beneath it. We need manpower to save his life."

Responding at once, the driver pulled the car off onto the narrow shoulder of the curve and his officer and four non-commissioned men jumped out ready to come to the aid of the victims. Together they rushed over to the ditch. They stopped abruptly on the shoulder of the road, and to their surprise found themselves staring down into the cocked weapons of five enemy soldiers. Behind them Sgt. McCloskey's automatic kept them covered. As he eyed the boots of the driver, he yelled in Germen. "Hands up! Don't reach for your weapons or you're dead."

"Get them out of their uniform," Williams snapped at his sergeant, "including their caps!" The team was lucky. They had captured a German general. He was also a brave man. Immediately he demanded to know what regiment the team belonged to, and McCloskey shut him up with an oath and led the protestors down the incline accompanied by Marlis.

Shortly thereafter the allied team, poorly outfitted in German uniforms, climbed into the German officers' car with McCloskey driving. Someone remarked that the Germans looked like a decent lot of men and asked McCloskey how he had disposed of them to which the tough, older soldier replied. I don't wish to offend your finer qualities, but I hope that old bull enjoys his new company. All knew the answer was deliberately evasive. The Scottish sergeant was wearing a pair of German jackboots.

The Wehrmact officer who was captured turned out to be Brigadier General Carl Wickhorst, a professional soldier. He had been badly wounded on the Russian front, and according to German Archives in Bonne; he was sent home and subsequently placed in charge of prisons in Northern France with headquarters in Nancy.

The team was on a secondary French road a few miles from the town of Mens, southeastern France. According to their newly discovered orders removed form the general's pocket, they were on their way to a staff briefing in Mens. It so happened that Mens was also the team's objective--the political prison. In that prison was housed the Crown Prince of Morocco, whom the Germans had kidnapped and were holding for ransom--the ransom being German control of the King of Morocco and his territory, thus assuring the Nazis that the king would remain on their side in the North African fighting.

The German officers' car with its new occupants stopped twice to ask for directions to the subject prison. Before the first rays of a chilly autumn dawn began to stir the city, the saboteurs, led by a gold braided general, pulled up the to the front of the prison.

The team functioned like a well-tested machine. Twenty-two minutes had elapsed since they had overpowered the guards, broken into the prison and freed the Crown Prince. Behind them lay twelve possibly dead Nazi jailers and, added to their team, was a member of the French Underground who, by pre-arrangement with allied headquarters in London, had aided them in the rescue raid and who took over as driver of the escape car.

The young prince had shown arrogance continually while in the jail cell and in the escape car, when Col. Williams, intolerant of the young man's attitude, ordered him silenced by whatever means chosen by his friendly abductors. In the nearby town at a pub frequented by Germans, the boy was placed in the custody of a colonel in the former regular French Army prior to its surrender. After delivering the Moroccan, the allied team began their disappearance. "By mid day," confided Andre, the French driver, "we must be in safe hiding." They all knew the enemy would soon be searching all roads in the area looking for the trail of those who gunned down the jailors and escaped with a valuable prize. To generate optimism the French driver said to Col. Williams, "Don't worry Monsieur! All will be well. Soon we will have put many miles in between us and Mens."

In truth, Andre could not see the trouble that would engulf the restless passengers before high noon, the same day.

The car sped over back roads through the countryside of vineyards. The plan that had been confided to Col. Williams by the Frenchman was to have the soldiers holed up for three days in a chateau to which they were heading, and on the fourth day they would be taken to Marseille for pick-up at sea by a British submarine.

They would never make the rendezvous with the sub.

The drizzle turned colder as they climbed in elevation. Two hours on back roads, Soitzman, the machine gunner made a comment for all to hear. "Can't we speed this German car up and get onto a fast road?"

Williams turned angrily to Soitzman and replied. "You delivered a lethal dose of lead back there in the prison. You couldn't wait to kill those German jailers--half the kill was unnecessary. Now, you hold your hot temper during this escape and keep quiet, if you please." Before Soitzman could reply the bilingual French driver turned to Soitzman and asked, "Monsieur, you don't like the way I chauffeur for you? Maybe you would like to get behind the wheel, yes?'

"Ya," said a young marine private, "and deliver us right into the hands of the Gerries."

The French driver added for all to hear, "I know where I am going.

Don't worry. Every ten or twelve kilometers there is a French lookout posted that watches us and keeps their eyes on the whereabouts of German patrols.

Shortly, we will take another back road to bypass Lyons. In an hour, if all goes well, we shall arrive at St. Etienne and be close to the hideout. I think the German net will not reach so far for you." "Merci beau coup for your travelogue," replied Soitzman, with a tinge of ridicule as the driver left the narrow asphalt road and turned briefly onto a dirt path to avoid an unexpected German checkpoint. The light rain came through the side of the open touring car as the men turned up the collars on their German coats to keep their necks dry. The day had started bleak and cold; it warmed only slightly. The bare-limbed trees, the brown grass and the foreboding sky made the mood of the team sullen. Beside a haystack looming on a curve of the road, the driver stopped for a toilet break and some refreshment. From across the fields an oxen-drawn, two-wheel cart pulled up. The farmer spoke briefly to the car driver. Then from under some turnips the farmer withdrew a container and two earthenware cups. Hot tea was shared and two sandwiches were issued to each of the team. Col. Williams let the men drink first, then taking his mug of tea he thought of the gold braid on his coat indicating it was worn by a three star general only hours before. Calling his sergeant to one side out of earshot of the others, he asked McCloskey, "Did you kill those men when we pinched their car?

McCloskey replied with irritation. "Hell, yes! This isn't a gentleman's game played by cricket rules. It's killing--not being killed. Once we land among the enemy, no holds are barred. Bluntly colonel, we bleed them or they bleed us. But I prefer the lariat.

"No Colonel, we didn't lead these men into the field and say do you mind if we tape your mouths and tie your hands and feet so you won't blow our scheme to your bloody comrades. We executed them, damn it. I don't like it either but if you and the rest of us want to live to get home in one piece, we must kill the enemy before they kill us."

A torrent of words continued to cascade out of McCloskey, and Williams suspected he had somehow been able to spike his tea with cognac. McCloskey continued, "You were never in a life or death struggle colonel when you were younger I was. I learned how to survive in India among Gurka thieves and cutthroats before I was twelve. They killed first and never bothered to ask questions. You know as well as I do the price on our heads if we're caught here in occupied Vichy. Torture and more torture, we have enough knowledge about allied operations to give the heinies a field day, plus a nice plumb for nabbing us. Sure mon, Soitzman is gun happy. That's why I didn't try to stop him when he mowed down those Nazi jailers. But he has reasons. He hates all Germans for what they did to his relatives in Poland. The Nazis haven't a friend in all Europe. And to tell the truth mon, half of Germany is ashamed of the Gestapo brutes and SS bullies. All of the Germen objectors themselves have been done away with already or are dying in concentration camps. I know what excuse the Nazis give. They say 'I'm only carrying out orders.' They'll tell you that crap right up to the moment they shoot you between the eyes. I say they're all guilty at both the top and the bottom of the Nazi structure. I don't need a magistrate to tell me that, colonel"

McCloskey waved his arms, and raising his voice, fulminated against Williams.

"Sure mon, I'm here to help rescue the prince, but if I must kill to save our own lives, I'll kill. I admit you're a born leader Colonel; you draw men to you. God knows why. But none of us can tell why they chose a leader so different from the rest of us. We have to be a killer outfit at times. You have to go along with the idea, Colonel or one day find yourself without a backup. We can't rescue the innocent people we're sent to free without at times killing others. No peace lover can survive in this jungle of kill or be killed. The alternative is to be taken prisoner and die a cruel death."

McCloskey continued. "Understand me, Colonel? You don't--do you mon? Sir, say yes or no!"

Numbed by the barrage of words and an unexpected confrontation,

Williams replied. "Yes, I understand you McCloskey. You're the best soldier in the whole British army, but you also have the primal urge to kill, just like Soitzman. I'm glad you're on our side. But as for me, I just can't kill deliberately I would die a conscience-stricken man."

"OK Colonel. For the time being leave the killing to us. But you'll kill later. Before you're out of this dom unit, you'll kill or else be killed. One day there'll be many dead Nazis on your timid conscience."

They heard the driver call, Allons! Vite! Let us go from here.

The French driver, avoiding Lyons and German troops, had driven well over an hour when he pulled over and spoke to Col. Williams. "We will shortly pass through St.Etienne. All local road traffic must pass through the village because of the narrow, old Roman bridge that takes only one vehicle at a time. There is a bar near the bridge where you may run into some German vehicles. Pay no attention and don't get out of the car, I strongly advise you. Your German officer outfits should get you through without being challenged. So, I must say au revoir, Colonel." The Frenchman got out and Sergeant McCloskey took the wheel.

The six-man team straightened up like good German soldiers, adjusted their ill-fitting uniforms and set their caps on squarely. The time was 1045 a.m. The village was strangely deserted and there was no activity on the streets. A dog crossed the road and disappeared between two shuttered houses. The team wondered if the locals wore in the fields or had fled.

The narrow street was straight and led to the old stone bridge. In their line of unrestricted vision to the left they saw the bar that the French had mentioned. Parked on the street adjacent were three German personnel vehicles and three officer's cars. The team, therefore, surmised the building was full of soldiers and some officers, maybe twenty or thirty, likely grabbing an unauthorized break. McCloskey turned to Williams and reminded him that the town was crawling with Germans, perhaps a hundred or more, he reckoned. Because of the parked vehicles, the road into the village was accessible by only one lane and McCloskey slowed their German car to a ten- kilometer speed. Pulling wide of the parked vehicles, he looked up the road and beheld it was blocked tight with a convoy of fifteen or more parked trucks, about 700 feet total.

It was then they determined the make-up and contents of the convoy. The seventh vehicle, a side-stake open truck to which they came abreast, was a common carrier used by the Wehrmact to carry bulk freight. Ahead they identified twelve such vehicles, all stopped.

Col. Williams blinked at what he observed but the sight did not register right. He stared again at the first vehicles that caught his eye in passing, and then he swept his glance up the line at the remainder. Each was filled with a mixed collection of people. They were cramped tightly together, unable to move. Williams turned and looked back again to the first truck and touched McCloskey on the leg saying "make this thing crawl."

The young American colonel studied the people in truck number two and so on. They were dressed in assorted civilian clothing, some adequate, most not, so he ruled out jail inmates being transferred. The majority was hatless, possibly having lost them in the cold breeze on the way to St. Etienne. The officer studied the rectangular islands of tragic and forlorn faces and was struck primarily by the looks of terror on many. There was occasional anger and defiance--some were like zombies. He knew that these were people whose spirits had been demeaned and broken.

He again blinked his eyes. Unbelievingly he stared at the faces of the sixth and last truck containing unknown prisoners. Then reality dawned. He was witnessing, for the first time in his life, truckloads of human cargo. They were of both sexes, from twenty to seventy years old, relegated by totalitarian authority to a non-human status. Like animals they were being taken unwillingly to a stockyard for slaughter, it dawned on Col. Halford Williams. A lone soldier ran between two of the trucks and prodded a woman with his rifle barrel. McCloskey heard him say, "That will stop your screaming, you bitch."

A military provost stood up front in the roadway with his hand raised to stop the team's escape car. A civilian car had already been halted ahead of them and the driver had gotten out. The driver was gesturing as he turned his car around to retrace his path. McCloskey turned to his officer and requested instructions. Col. Williams (General Wickhorst according to the captured papers which McCloskey carried) swung his head slightly and said, "Keep cool sergeant and when he stops you, answer with authority. We'll back you."

The car with the English-speaking commandos and one German voice that, of the sergeant driver, came to a stop and a husky German provost marched over to McCloskey and peered inside scrutinizing the occupants.

Without speaking, McCloskey handed him the papers taken off the ambushed German officer group the night before. McCloskey spoke. "We are returning home from a staff meeting in Mens. I got lost detouring past Lyons and need help to get back on the road to our headquarters.

The German policeman glanced at the papers and was duly impressed. Whereupon he looked apologetically at the stern soldier seated in the car and said, "Sorry Sirs! The bridge ahead is on the only road through town. There's a truck stalled on its approaches. We will have it out of the way shortly I expect. May I apologize for any delay you may have, but there is a bar back there and if you wish, you might drop in for some refreshment. Only trouble is that about thirty-five others are in there at present trying to get a quick drink."

"Corporal!" said Sgt. McCloskey. "We thank you for the kind suggestion, but what is the convoy parked along this road. We don't recognize the vehicle markings."

The German replied. "We're not too common in these parts." Then he pointed to his shoulder and helmet patches. The team looked as one. For the first time, each of them saw the dreaded emblem of the "UNDESIRABLES--ELIMINATION SQUAD". The logo was a skull and crossbones.

Immediately the allied team understood the obvious. The people in the trucks were Jews. They were being rounded up and carted off to death.

The German smiled. "No, this isn't a regular army unit. We're making a sweep through these French towns picking up Jews for the gas chambers. We cleaned out most of the Jews from Toulons, Lyons and Marseilles, and this lightning raid in St. Etienne is to catch them where we haven't searched before. We have six full truckloads already and expect another six before nightfall. The provost laughed. "You Germans understand that we're destroying the scum of society"

McCloskey raised his hand and belched; "Heil Hitler!" The provost corporal returned the salute.

Mollified by the Nazi salute, the corporal continued, "Look ahead. There are six truckloads of them--about three hundred old and young men and women, as well as the odd kid too. We've even squashed in two or three blacks. Today we should net another couple of hundred in surprise raids. About fifty are packed into a truck--would you believe that?" he said, beaming at the officers for approval.

He continued. "Look at them! They're standing like posts in the rain! They can't even bend to piss--ha! But within seventy-two hours they'll all be fodder for the portable gas furnace up la Alsace Lorraine."

Col. Williams smiled with disguised appreciation on the recital of human brutality. The Nazi death Squad corporal stepped back and McCloskey said they would move their car up to the side street near the bridge. There they planned to wait until the stalled truck was moved, while hoping not to draw attention. McCloskey gave the Nazi salute once more to the German corporal and told him his General Wickhorst might want to pass the time of day chatting to some of the officers near the bridge, and show his appreciation for their work in getting rid of the Jewish problem for the fatherland. McCloskey thought it best not to translate his last remark to Williams.

As they pulled away, the German corporal shouted, "You may run into our Commanding Officer, Major Klaus Barbee. You'll be parking on the side street that leads to St.Etienne Catholic Orphanage. There should be some action near that spot which you may enjoy while waiting for the bridge to be cleared." McCloskey figured it was another three hundred feet or more to the intended parking area.

Someone in the back hissed. "Damn you Sergeant, you're setting us down in the midst of this butcher outfit. Let's turn back and wait it out on the outskirts of the village where we won't draw attention,"

McCloskey replied. "The colonel and I have decided to sit it out in the village. Were not retreating."

But Williams as a man was reflecting on something more serious. His thoughts kept turning on the plight of the trucks filled with forlorn Jews. He was sure of one thing. None of the destitute human cattle had a choice. An unknown person or persons in a totalitarian structure of hate had condemned them to die. Someone soon would take their clothes, shave their heads and bundle the hair for storage in warehouses--and after they were gassed, their teeth would be extracted if they contained gold. Williams kept repeating: No freedom of choice--no freedom of choice--no freedom to choose their destiny. They had been condemned to die because they were born Jews.

Col, Halford Williams knew he had been placed on trial in the highest court of divine judgment. He was appearing before the court as a free man about to be tested. He himself had freedom to choose and today we he was wrestling with the alternatives. He came to believe he had been purposely led into this evil drama by a higher power, and he could not resolve the dilemma without using his own God-given freedom of choice. His alternative choices were recognizable. They were good versus evil, bravery against cowardice, unselfishness opposed to selfishness. In the final analysis his choice would have to be the voluntary sacrifice of six men for whom he was accountable to try to save fifty times as many strangers who had no choice in living or dying.

He knew it was not a moral issue he had to resolve.

And it wasn't a matter of valor. It was an infallible, involuntary decision that required no philosophical or religious determination. It was the ultimate surrender of self, come what may.

They parked the car at the entrance to the side street that proved to be a dirt road down to the orphanage mentioned by the provost corporal. Up ahead, less than three hundred feet, was the bridge where a growing collection of soldiers was gathered. Practically the entire personnel of the whole convoy were there minus those in the wine bar. A large truck with a broken axle was stalled on the near entrance to the bridge and on the far side they could make out a large German vehicle trailer loaded with equipment, perhaps officer's baggage and possibly some loot from the forsaken Jews.

Col. Williams asked each to do a slow, 360-degree scan of their surroundings. They then came up with this composite picture of the alien land they had entered: Most of the enemy was congested near the bridge for some unaccountable reason. There were also a couple of German officers' cars on the near side of the bridge with what looked like another loot-filled baggage trailer. Behind the team were six empty, open trucks and behind these were the six other open trucks packed with apprehensive and broken-hearted Jews. Farthest away were the transport vehicles for soldiers and officers.

The team estimated the convoy was over 700 feet form the bridge to the front vehicle. A guard of only three men kept eyes on the trucks filled with Jews, meaning the drivers and driver mechanics were either in the bar or up at the bridge. Col. Williams concluded that the usual German orderliness was absent, otherwise the men would have been standing beside their vehicles and the soldiers, presumably those used to round up the Jews and protect the convoy, would be stationed at intervals on the road. They apparently had left their jobs to one provost and a roving guard or two. It was also evident, as the provost corporal had revealed, that the top officer in command was a Major Klaus Barbee directing activities near the bridge.

At the foot of the side street on which they were parked was the orphanage about 250 feet down the slope. All the team noticed the action around the orphanage and the shouting from within with occasional screams. From among the convoy of captive adults behind them they also heard much crying and sobs of hysteria, mostly female sobs.

After doing the combined eye-sweep, the team concluded it would be folly to mix with those at the bride and instead to stay put and keep their noses clean. However, discussion revealed that the weakest spot in the Nazi garrison's disarray of manpower lay next to the truckloads of Jewish victims whom they had just passed. They decided those guards could be easily knocked off if necessary. They reasoned that the whole convoy, and particularly the front end, was the most vulnerable at the present moment.

The theoretical military exercise on how to dislodge the enemy bolstered their egos and lifted their thoughts from the reality of the predicament. The panorama was clear. They were a small island of people engulfed in a sea of enemy. Such a conclusion left the military alignment static unless some incident of aggression was to occur by either of the adversaries. Therefore, the allied team must stay cool. These thoughts were churning in the head of Col. Williams. He decided they had perhaps an hour to kill, or as Sgt. McCloskey speculated, an hour in which to kill or be killed.

Their combined Intelligence appraisal took less than two minutes of observation and discussion when Col. Williams volunteered a question. "What's the weakest part of this convoy?" All agreed it was the front end beyond the bridge action. "Then," asked the commander, "where is our greatest opposition in the enemy outfit?" and all surmised it would be from the soldiers in the bar. They probably were carrying their weapons and hence would develop the quickest response and most effective firepower.

Turning around in the car for all to hear, Col. Williams said, "Do you guys think we can stampede these Nazi gangsters into doing something they hadn't planned?" At that point he turned to speak to McCloskey, but his words went unsaid.

They all heard the distinct yelling and screaming at the orphanage; guttural German hollering from adult men and screaming replies in French from adult women and children. In the sudden commotion in front of the orphanage, a loose knot of children appeared, boys and girls. Soldiers were herding them into a marching formation but the children kept breaking away. The team could see the rough tactics in which the young objectors were hurriedly grabbed or wrestled into position, only to break away again. Most stood silently. A girl, perhaps ten or eleven, fell down in a heap and began to sob. A young boy of lesser age ran to comfort her, perhaps a brother. A boy of about twelve stood to one side in shock, oblivious to the confusion around him. A brute of a soldier had pulled down his trousers and examined his private parts. Another soldier chased a girl, barely in her teens, back inside and came out somewhat later with a nun chasing him as he dragged the girl.

What was transpiring was only speculation on the part of the allied team; but whatever their thoughts about the helpless, abused Jewish children, Col. Williams reacted."What are they doing to these kids?" he exclaimed for all his team to hear.

McCloskey added, "What are they doing now? Those kids are being sexually molested or worse."

A soldier came out and shoved the dazed, stumbling boy whose pants were down back into line of three abreast and fifteen children long.

Williams asked the question again, "What's going on?" Gannon, the French member of the team spoke. "Those deviates, or whatever they are, are having fun with the kids and the nuns, whatever their preference. I figure they're having an orgy of unbridled abuse inside the orphanage." Gannon had the look of vilest hate and this look was transmitted to Williams and the rest of the allied crew.

Two men pulled an anvil from a truck parked near the bridge and an older, heavy-set sergeant--obviously a blacksmith--came over with a box that, when opened, proved to contain leg shackles. He stepped in front of a pile of iron or steel that, on second glance, the team members finally recognized, was a continuous length of chain covering a twenty foot area of the ground. The blacksmith set his anvil up beside the chain and waited.

McCloskey spoke. "Sir! Allow me to saunter over to that blacksmith and find out what's going on. I'll get the story firsthand. Before replying, Williams observed the raggedy file of urchins and early teenagers being marched up to the top of the street. The column would obviously stop beside them and near the blacksmith.

"You have five minutes, Sergeant," said Williams quickly. As McCloskey sauntered casually over to the blacksmith, Corporal Erbstien got out, raised the hood and tinkered with the motor. Soitzman went to the back and untied a Gerry-can of gasoline. Two of the team sat inside with their automatics ready beneath their coats and Col. Williams paced slowly up and down beside the car, waiting for McCloskey's return.

A fragmented part of the orphans' tragedy was told to Col. Williams upon the return of his sergeant. McCloskey explained that the Nazi blacksmith was stationed there on his own accord to shackle the forty or so Jewish orphans being brought before him. The homeless children had been wards of the convent since their parents had been rounded up and taken away by the Nazis earlier that year. The burly blacksmith's technical Job was to clamp leg shackles on each child or adolescent, but his animal instincts were much more refined as he looked over each victim. Once the shackle was placed on the victim, the open ends would be hammered onto the heavy nickel-steel chain with the same technique done on the next child, and so forth.

The evil looking smithy had laughed when he told McCloskey he enjoyed watching the faces of such kids particularly the young boys emerging into their teens. He boasted he liked to hear them beg for mercy as they were shoved before him and held while he riveted them into the chain of human bondage. Of course, after an interlude of a day or two at the most the children would be on their way to the gas chamber. McCloskey had noticed the blacksmith had singled out three of the early teenage boys, which he shackled together, apart from the rest. He had blatantly examined their bodies with his bare hands and greedily set them aside for his own deviate satisfaction that night. McCloskey, visibly moved with emotional anger, finished his evaluation of the terrible scene by estimating the children would all be shackled and loaded in one of the trucks within the hour.

McCloskey had remarked that the blacksmith enjoyed his work. He had, in fact, asked McCloskey to stay and watch, commenting he would attach most of the group by shackles to one piece of heavy chain, and keep selected ones for personal reasons.

Williams' first question was academic, "How much chain is there in the total length?" "Over 400 feet," replied the sergeant. "There is also an ammo locker full of grenades in the blacksmith's truck. The blacksmith boasts he can hit a running Jew with a grenade at sixty feet, so that none of the victims would likely escape." They are all sadists and sex deviates and some like the metal monger, with both evils combined," said McCloskey. He called them the dregs of German society, all of them serious offenders recruited from jails.

McCloskey added a final comment: "They are the goons the regular German services would never enlist. I've never felt so sick in my guts since I witnessed the innocent kids about to be sacrificed in death one way or another. I'd personally enjoy cutting up every one of those evil bastards," McCloskey swore.

According to records, the bear-like blacksmith was a homosexual whose preference was young boys. His name was Pierre Blanchett from the province of Saxony. His father was French and his mother

German, records show. The Gestapo had recruited him from the prison for insane where he had spent several years of a lifetime sentence. His crime was kidnapping, sadistic sexual pleasures, and murder of thirty-four young boys whose remains had been found buried beneath his shop and yard in the late 20's. For agreeing to serve as blacksmith manacler on the roving death squad, Blanchett was freed from incarceration and promised all the young boys he desired with no questions ever to be asked about their ultimate use or disposal thereafter. For cooperation, he was made a master sergeant with honorary discharge promised after hostilities, to live anywhere he chose within Nazi controlled territory--except the province of Saxony where he would no doubt be killed in revenge if he were to return.

As Sgt. McCloskey stifled his anger, Williams too was overcome with a fixation of adult humans sadistically killing young innocents. Pausing to consider the bestial pleasure being displayed against children right before their collective eyes, Col. Williams began to listen to his inner-self emerging strong and clear. He leaned against a fender, closed his eyes to obliterate the sights before him, and dropped his chin on his chest. His first reaction was gratitude--gratified that he was not one of the evil molesters.

He pictured himself simply as a bystander, but as he thought about his neutral role he wondered if he were indeed a non-interested observer. In a subliminal way he was acutely conscious of a divine mercy protecting him and his men during the last twelve hours. He reasoned he and his group might have been preserved to save these tragic children. As he thanked God with tears, a voice like an old-testament prophet welled up within him.

The evil indignation you are witnessing against the children will not pass. I give them over to you from destruction. Will you save them?"

All within earshot heard their commanding officer's spoken words that sounded meaningless. He cried, "I will!" and that was all. Those who heard stared at Williams as he tried to comprehend his outburst. As they watched their leader they saw him snap to attention and heard him say, "Here's the plan, Sergeant. Now listen carefully and we'll make something really happen around here... First we'll create a diversion and by so doing we'll free those kids before we leave town."

Everybody now realized they were not leaving St. Etienne in a hurry.

Surveying the astonished expressions of those around him Williams said, the die is cast. We stand and fight.

Soitzman exclaimed, "You're crazy! There must be 150 Gerries in this forsaken town. That leaves odds of twenty-five to one again at us."

McCloskey stopped in the middle of an oath, but he knew that expediency was the order of the moment as the children were being quickly riveted onto the chain.

None of the Germans so far had challenged the allied team as they moved about inconspicuously. After all, Williams wore the braid and insignia of a Brigadier General and the others were dressed in outer garments of non-commissioned officers and private soldiers of the German Army. The German diversion at the bridge was the incident that preoccupied enemy attention, either as workers or spectators, and this diversion enabled the team of allies to move unobtrusively about the perimeter of activities.

Saving orphans was not their bag that particular day, inasmuch as all roads into the area would soon be patrolled by Germans checking for the unknown assailants of the Mens jailers fleeing in a stolen German officers' car. Furthermore, the team knew they could not withstand direct questioning. But to ignore the unfolding tragedy of helpless old and young persons being rounded up for barbaric killing roasted the conscience of Col. Williams and his buddies. They themselves had often killed or been responsible for the death of German soldiers in self-defense for which they were later penitent. But on this occasion, thrust into the killing arena as unwilling spectators, each became an inflamed adversarial combatant with a role yet undetermined.

Col. Williams' logic to improvise showed his unusual discernment to sort out primary objectives and move in an orderly manner to complete them, even in the face of imminent danger. His reaction in a sea of potential trouble was generally intuitive, or in this case he may have been guided by an unseen power within him, because his strategy was so uncanny and the timing so perfect

The colonel told his team during a quick huddle that time was now of the essence. In another five minutes or so, the Gerries would be close to pushing their broken-down truck off the bridge approaches and then the convoy could cross. And when they departed, with them would go three hundred fifty or more people straight to their untimely deaths. Williams warned his men that at any minute the enemy also might come to their car and get inquisitive. "We can only fake it for a few minutes if they once start asking questions to a bunch of guys who can't speak German," Williams concluded. Immediate action to put the scheme into effect then preoccupied the team. "McCloskey!" he beckoned urgently. "Take fuse wire, matches and your knife. Walk openly to the officers' car at the front of the convoy, farthest from the bridge. Puncture the gas tank and do the same with the next car. Try and get three vehicles. If necessary, run a soaked fuse from one vehicle to another. Give yourself a couple minutes of lead-time to get back here before the cars go up in flames. And don't pick the daisies on the way back. "Soitzman! You're still itching for Nazi blood. You cover McCloskey in case the traffic policeman or any guards of the other two convoys questions McCloskey. After all, they are a closed group and recognize strangers. Each of you, walk down there arrogantly like a true Nazi soldiers minding his own business.

"Gotcha Colonel," said Soitzman as he followed McCloskey already on his way. McCloskey was a veritable arsenal and was the team's expert saboteur. He carried fuse wire, grenades, matches and miscellaneous paraphernalia for sabotage tied beneath his coat.

Corporal Erbstien put down the hood of the German car and stopped beside Williams. "I guess you plan to fire the end of the convoy and divert the Germans from the bridge and the bar That idea should work but what about the krauts near us in particular, the top slime--the blacksmith?"

His commander replied. "The fire will attract the blacksmith and the whole corps. If not, you and Gannon take care of those depraved reprobates rounding up the kids. Strike quickly, the way you were trained, take no chances because these creatures are not predictable. If McCloskey handles the fire right, the entire death squad will be needed up front and there'll be no witnesses to what we intend to do."

Corporal Erbstien cut in. "Need I remind you, I'm a German Jew. I understand German and I heard that blacksmith swine say what he's going to do to three of those adolescent boys tonight. They'll die horrible deaths after he's finished his pleasure.

Williams raised his voice, which he seldom did. "Hold it Corporal, You're a Jew all eight. If you want to stay one, don't try your Yiddish on that gang or you're sure to end up on one of their meat wagons. I know your relatives were killed by goons like these, but if you want to come out of this fracas alive, quit playing the avenger role for all murdered Jewry. Take that chip off your shoulder and keep cool till we've done our job."

"Okay! Okay!" responded Erbstien, "but grant me jut one favor. Give me the rotten blacksmith. Let him be mine alone!" Replied Williams simply, "Okay, he's yours. If you think you've been called to be his judge, and you get the chance to become his executioner also, let the decision of either mercy or killing be on your conscience,

Corporal Erbstien thanked Williams with a look of acknowledgment and continued. "I realize you won't be so foolish as to attack this enemy company head on. So what may I ask is the plan to get out of this rat hole?'" Erbstien became madder at Williams' attempt to mollify him as he heard the colonel confess. "I intend to invite these kids to follow us across the bridge to safety. It's that simple."

Erbstien retorted, "You're joking of course," and his leader responded that he was never more serious. He openly lamented that a more complex problem was how to eliminate the 150-man death squad in order to steal the kids from under their noses. Erbstien turned in disgust.

Williams ordered the corporal back for a direct confrontation. "I've got a much bigger job for you than wasting time thinking how to knock off one evil blacksmith. I'm placing you in charge of the safety of these kids. Keep them intact and be prepared to escort them to the safe side of the bridge when I give the order, Use Gannon too because he speaks French. Then Williams pointed to an officers' car with motor running, on the near side of the bridge.

Attached was a trailer filled with Jewish loot. "When the signal is given," said Williams, "you will start a fire in that baggage, big enough to be seen a mile down the road."

Colonel Williams glanced at his watch, anticipating McCloskey's return. Down the road from the front of the stalled convoy he saw his top sergeant walking briskly, followed by Soitzman.

Asking McCloskey upon arrival when they could expect the fire, the sergeant smiled and confided, "We took a wee bit of extra time subduing the road bobby and that jerk of a guard who prodded the poor lassie with his rifle barrel. We took the courtesy to place their carcasses at the site of the fire we started. Their comrades will think for some reason they started the fire and then killed each other in a fight. In this insane outfit it's not hard to imagine such a weird thing."

Before McCloskey could embellish his story, a black cloud went up at the front of the convoy from which they had just departed, followed by a terrific explosion.

"I like tires, don't you Soitzman?" smiled Sgt. McCloskey.

The enemy at the congested bridge approaches had just finished moving the disabled truck off the bridge. The commander of the death squad, seeing the smoke and fire,yelled at the top of his voice, "Everybody to the fire," and the command spread. Blanchett, the blacksmith, dropped his hammer and ran inside the orphanage, bringing out several henchmen whose presence was unknown to the allied team. They had been inside violating the nuns and other victims (See Appendix B). The entire platoon in charge of the orphan roundup took off in the direction of the fire, its flames and smoke now billowing high into the sky above the village. Blanchett grabbed his pail of water and ran toward the fire, while up the street the doors of the bar burst open and knots of soldiers joined the stampede.

Alone and unattended stood the group of frightened children, cowering beside the chains and the dreaded anvil.

Six truckloads of destitute human beings in open trucks tried to turn their heads toward the front of the column and the pall of smoke and fire. The lone guard of the adult Jewish prisoners obeyed the order for all able-bodied men to help put out the spreading fire that was mysteriously moving up the convoy. Around the engulfing fire there was pandemonium, sharpened by the occasional popping of live ammunition.

Out of sight because of the smoke and out of mind because of the fire, the convoy of over 400 adult Jews stood unguarded.

The diversionary fire had been well conceived but it was another matter to take charge and evacuate the helpless prisoners.

McCloskey had lit a good flame. He had piled clothing and a tire on the original material of mixed baggage. Then with raw petrol he ran a burn corridor to the front car and used a fuse to the baggage and gas tank. The technique gave the allied men just enough time to vacate the scene. When they first arrived back to their commanding officer, the first car went up in flames followed quickly by the next two vehicles in line. They were all burning before the enemy troops arrived.

As the smoke from the tires and clothing rose in the air, the death squad could no longer see the blind approach to the bridge, nor a car full of "disguised Germans in transit" that had not responded to the urgent order to put out the fires.

Racing over to the children, Erbstien and Cannon tried to calm them. Little did they realize that their German uniforms made them suspect as benefactors. Nevertheless Gannon assured them in French that they were about to be rescued and Erbstien confided that he too was Jewish and cared about their safety. They were instructed to follow Erbstien across the bridge where they would be placed in a German trailer for escape before the evil German Nazis returned. Hesitatingly, and with reluctance, the children followed after the links were split on the first shackled boys. One-by-one they all broke and trotted away. The bridge was about 200 feet in length, and in less than a minute the children were across on the safe side where there were no visible Nazi persecutors.

On Col. Williams' instructions, Sgt. McCloskey attached the end of the four hundred foot long chain onto their car and pulled it onto and over to the far side of the bridge. When the car stopped, about forty feet of length remained on the near side and the longer length on the far side where the orphans now huddled.

The forty-or-so feet of chain on the near side would be used to block entrance to the bridge by the overtaking Nazis. The longer length on the far side of the river would be hauled back by hand at once to form a huge cone in the center of the bridge,

Col. Williams assembled the team for quick instructions:

"Soitzman! You string the heavy chain across the near end of the bridge approach "

McCloskey! Take six sticks of dynamite and set them among those three or four-dozen German hand grenades you found. Plant the cake dead center on the bridge. While you're doing that Marlis and I will pull the chain from the far side back onto the bridge to form a giant cone or beehive around your bed of explosive."

"Erbstien!" Your first Job is to fire the officers' baggage trailer on the near side of this bridge. Pour gasoline on the truck next to it also. I'll signal you when to light the match and toss a grenade into the flames."

"Gannon! Double back and warn the people in the death trucks. Tell them when they see a car catch fire up here, and hear a grenade exploding, to jump out of the trucks and flee--away from the bridge. Warn them not to jump off the meat wagons till they see the last Nazi pass them on his way to this bridge. Tell the to pass the word among themselves in French."

Williams continued his brief instructions. "We're taking a big chance the Nazis won't gun down the adult Jews if they're caught escaping but at least they can't get at the kids.

I Judge the time slot to be no more than five or six minutes to get our work done. It seems impossible, but we have to do it or the Gerries will be back upon us in mass. Go to it!"

As it turned out six minutes was not enough to wind the enormous chain length into a cone around McCloskey's handiwork. It was the eighth minute before Williams saw Gannon begin his sprint back to the bridge after warning and instructing the adult Jewish people. He had taken extra time to remove the bolts from the tailgates of the trucks so the weak and feeble could be helped down by the able. Gannon had openly moved around the death trucks without slinking, and the Germans attending the fires apparently thought he was a guard left to watch the condemned prisoners. Now, as Gannon staggered back to the bridge, the last pall of smoke floated away from the convoy of parked vehicles several hundred feet away. The attending Nazis looked back toward the bridge to witness more trouble from an unknown source.

Upon Cannon again reaching the bridge, Williams gave Erbstien the signal to fire the nearest enemy vehicles. Soitzman had finished cordoning off the near side of the bridge with the chain. A cone of heavy chain now stood in the center of the bridge. It was over five feet high. Its base stretched across the full width of the bridge.

As Erbstien lobbed a grenade beneath the flaming car and truck, McCloskey straightened up on the bridge and began unwinding his fuse wire. He yelled for Williams to hear "cake is baked" and carefully headed off the bridge to the far side where the children were waiting beside the lone German baggage trailer.

The far away death squad contingent saw the new conflagration and heard the grenades near the bridge. Unable to identify the saboteurs in their midst who were burning their convoy at both ends, the Nazis began running back toward the new source of destruction.

As they ran down the hill the Nazis ignored the Jewish prisoners in the death trucks.

The first of the German Death Squad began closing in on the near side of the bridge. Far in the lead was Blanchett, the blacksmith. He had jumped the gun and left first to make sure his orphan wards were still at his disposal. As he reached his anvil and saw that his victims were gone, he spied a lone "German" waving frantically for him to continue to the bridge. Blanchett took the bait. In sixty seconds he came face to face with Corporal Erbstien

Col. Williams watched from a knoll across the bridge and noted the confrontation with his captured German binoculars. He was suddenly angry because Erbstien was jeopardizing the timing of the entire operation. Apparently the corporal was not content with the sight of fire and the sound of grenades to lure the Death Squad back to the scene. Still fuming at Erbstien's disobedience, Williams witnessed the young Jewish corporal stand boldly in the open as though inviting the Death Squad and their accomplices to the coming attraction--the cardinal point of destruction.

Williams saw the first of the enemy arrive. He was a burly, heavy set, somewhat ponderous man. Erbstien and the blacksmith met. To Williams it looked like an embrace. Then he observed the flailing of arms. In the next moment the newcomer was on the ground and scuffling. Horrified, Williams observed the one he knew raise a knife and rip open a man's tunic and pants, exposing his front. He saw a razor sharp knife slice across the man's groin and in the next movement it slit up his belly.

Williams knew Blanchett, the blacksmith, was dying a horrible death. He had not been hanged or quartered but an expert had drawn him. Williams saw Erbstien wipe his knife across the dying man's cheek, glance quickly at the onrushing Nazi hoard, then bolt toward the bridge. Seconds later Corporal Erbstien dove for cover into the defile beside Williams' observation point.

"I saw what you did," snorted Williams still grieved. "That action will haunt you till you die."

Still panting Erbstien gasped. "I only killed a beast. His time for Hell was long overdue."

Replied Williams in a low voice of reprimand, "Maybe, but you put a vengeance killing on your eternal tally."

"Keep preaching!" yelled the Jewish boy from New York. Then he placed his hand over his face and sobbed. Col. Williams laid his hand on the younger man's shoulder.

From their concealment behind the rock cropping, the allied team watched the enemy arrive at the bridge and examine the chains. There was a babble of voices. One soldier ventured to the center of the old Roman structure and felt the cone of chain, then retreated. Out of the confusion, order came when the Death Squad Major arrived.

One thing was most obvious to Commander Barbee of the Death Squad. Sabotage was spreading throughout the convoy. The chain strung across the bridge entrance and more of it obstructing the bridge roadbed proved to be deliberate harassment. McCloskey listened to the Nazi major call out to his men. "The murderers. They got away across the bridge and barricaded it behind them."

Surveying the annoying situation, the Nazi officer ordered a second empty truck to be driven up to the bridge. He gave orders to snap the chains stung across the bridge entrance, then winch off the pile in the center.

Simultaneously, as the officer gave the order, the watching adult Jews passed Cannon's instruction to flee throughout the six trucks. Cautiously at first they began evacuating the vehicles and fleeing in the opposite direction from the Nazis preoccupied at the bridge.

McCloskey heard the German O.C. exclaim, "They won't get far," as the truck moved slowly up to the strands of chain blocking pursuit of the saboteurs. Through his glasses, Williams saw the German O.C. stare quizzically at the carefully built cone of chain placed in the exact center of the bridge. Williams observed him study the moving truck about to snap the leading chain tied across the bridge approach. Suddenly, the Death Squad Commander turned and rushed to the rear of the gathering. Then he ran. Williams watched him disappear between two buildings.

The truck inched forward and the chains became taut as the driver put his vehicle into low gear and gently accelerated. He had an attentive audience. The entire Death Squad personnel of 137 viewed the action from within a theater of less than a hundred feet deep, each standing exposed to witness the spectacle prior to pushing on to nab the escapees.

Except for Erbstien, McCloskey had been the last of the allied team to cross the bridge now set for total destruction. He had unrolled the fuse wire and checked the end connections as his trained eyes backtracked the fuse to the chain cone. As the Germans raced toward the burning cars and bridge approach, McCloskey disappeared from view as he did a double barrel-role and landed beside his O.C.

The orphans and allied team were approximately one hundred feet from the bridge, gathered tightly on the side of the road as it sloped downwards through a deep defile in the terrain that offered maximum protection from blast or bullets.

"Here they come," McCloskey called as the truck began to grind toward the chain barrier.

The sergeant took a moment to ask Williams where he had learned the chain trick. He received a flat response. "At military school." Then Williams asked if all was set for the explosion to which Mc-Closkey replied gleefully. "Full house Colonel--standing room only. The chains are in place across the stage, and I'm waiting for the Gerries to burst them. Then the show begins."

All heard the snap of the, chains at the other end of the bridge. Mc-Closkey touched the two charged wires.

There is a remembered moment in the affairs of human creatures involved in total war that stands starkly out of ordinary perspective--when the laws of nature and creation are aborted as chaos takes over. Such was the next moment that transpired over the village of St. Etienne that morning on October 22, 1943. It would rightly have been recorded as the day World War II came with all its terror to the village. The world around exploded as Col. Williams and Sgt. McCloskey took one startled glance upward and saw briefly the blinding flash followed by a deepening roar. The freed children held their fingers in their ears as they lay on the hard ground beside the rocking German baggage cargo. Two of the youngsters were tossed about.

Williams took another cautious and frightened look upwards following the explosion and identified the sheered-off tops of trees sailing over the defile in which they lay. He identified a boot and leg, a knife, and an entire motor as well as other unidentifiable parts of metal and sheered human bodies and limbs. It seemed like an age had ended before the colonel dared raise his head sufficiently and look about. Two of the children were sobbing hysterically but none seemed to have been injured. Others were in mild stock.

In spite of the group's need to evacuate the area with utmost haste, he realized he would have to handle the children carefully. Their minds had been scorched by brutality and traumatized by a cataclysmic explosion.

Someone started the car and began throwing out the German baggage. After boarding the kids, the team attached the trailer and pulled back onto the road and away from the destruction. Three of the more frightened children were carried in the car, one on Williams' lap. They drove slowly as though all were in a trance.

At the edge of town, a man of the Free French Interior stepped out from behind a bush and took over the driving. His first words were: "Mon Dieu! What happened in St. Etienne? It must have been blown to pieces" Then he added, "Where did you get all the children?"

As they left town they passed a German vehicle, the top of which had been sliced off as if by a knife. A mile from the scene on the other side of the river, the blacksmith's anvil would be found.

Buildings on higher elevations in the village of St. Etienne were destroyed by the blast and there was total destruction in the immediate vicinity of the bridge, including all of the German transport. The two-story post office was leveled and all that remained standing was the flag pole, although the orphanage--located in a hollow--missed most of the concussion. For years afterwards the returned residents were removing pieces of chain from mortar, trees, chimneys and dwellings.

With the exception of the one escaping officer presumed to be the Battalion 0.C., the entire German Death Squad was no more. So terrible was the explosion that those death squad participants gathered at the doomed bridge were blown to pieces, decapitated, cut in half or riddled with chain or grenade fragments that made the bodies unrecognizable.

Within 24 hours word had gotten out to the German area command. Clean-up crews were sent to St. Etienne, as well as political police to find the perpetrators of the massacre of 137 Nazis. It is unfortunately true that the Germans suspected the Free French had engineered the demise. Nevertheless, lowboy trucks and cranes removed the vehicle remains. A large hole was dug with a bulldozer near the massacre site, and the human carnage and unrecognizable bodies were interred. No marker was placed above ground.

For years Jewish organizations in France, particularly the surviving orphans who grew to man and womanhood, looked for the tall, gangly American who, like the Pied Piper of Hamblin, was responsible for befriending the condemned children. But he was never heard of again. To this day they do not know who he is or from where he came. The same Jewish people of French nationality sought to erect a monument or cairn to their savior commemorating that terrible day when they were without hope. But German pressure exerted on the councils of St. Etienne from higher authorities, including the United Nations, prevented recognition of the marvelous feat of caring by the entire team of allied soldiers and particularly the man who devised the chain method of total destruction of evil men. In fairness to the German stand on the subject matter, it was only natural that they did not wish the perpetrators of the debacle to be immortalized by a public monument. They preferred, and still do, that that day be forgotten. The German archives file on that particular incident reads: "UNDESIRE-ABLES--ELIMINATION SQUAD, it is marked closed," and the actual German words appended say: "Good riddance to evil men."

It was, in fact, the one day perhaps in the history of World War II Jewish annihilation that the tables were turned against some of Hitler's death merchants, and they themselves became the sacrificial objects en masse. Besides the forty-three original orphans who escaped the gas chambers, for some unaccountable reason of fate, another one hundred children later found their way to the orphanage and then on to the final chateau staging area near town where they asked to be protected. All reached England through the humane efforts of the countess at the chateau and the untiring work of the French Underground who smuggled them out of the country in twos and threes in the weeks following the St. Etienne massacre by the chain gang. They were sent to English orphanages and foster homes, and after the war most returned to France and tried to emerge into adulthood in spite of their terrible childhood scars in which some of them witnessed their parents and other family members murdered before their eyes.

The adult Jews who fled had no immediate pursuers. They eventually filtered into the countryside where compassionate French peasants, aware of the massacre of the Nazis, hid them safely and later helped to expedite their passage to England and Switzerland for the war's duration.

The raiders had come unannounced into the town about 10:30 a.m. and departed at 12 noon without losing a man. No one in St. Etienne has ever been able to fathom the mystery of how an unknown presence came to their town that day, spent ninety minutes, freed the innocent humans from death, destroyed their would-be destroyers, and quietly disappeared.

Two of the bewildered young boys jumped out of the trailer on the way to the chateau rendezvous but later found their way to the hiding place. The car, and trailer were shoved off a cliff out in the country and the band of people walked the last mile on foot with the team carrying and helping the children. The Germans found the escape vehicle two days later and traced its origin and trail to and from the Mens prison. Finding no bodies, the Germans did not close the case and kept searching for missing links in the abduction of the orphans.

The anti-climax to the St. Etienne massacre was like a fairy tale. At the chateau door where it was designated they should hole-up a beautiful lady appeared. She had a regal bearing, beautiful blue eyes and perfectly shaped features. Her hair was blond but the description that all the team agreed on most was her melodious English voice. Not divulging her nationality, nevertheless, she did say she liked to meet Americans. She quickly kissed each of the team and asked them where they had found the children. They told her. Changing plans regarding the team's proposed underground hideout she put the children there instead, and placed the team, with their weapons ready, in a hidden room within the chateau tower. The German patrols who came searching for the group never located anyone and took the word of the countess that she was not harboring undesirables. She gave the orphans complete attention and the French Underground collected food from the nearby farmer to feed the children that they inherited for a short time.

The submarine waited off Marseilles for two days for the team to escape from France, but they abandoned the wait when the mission failed to show. Col. Williams and his men were taken from the chateau the following week and ended up in Bordeaux where they were divided into two groups and placed on fishing vessels to be returned to England. Of all their trips together, the one on which the team had begun with so much dissatisfaction turned out to be the most morally and spiritually satisfying of their military careers. For their performance they received basic army pay and no medals or honors--or recognition. Nor did they ever seek them.

Arriving pack at his London headquarters, Col. Williams was required to make the usual report. At first those who studied its contents found the subject matter confusing in that he spent so few words on the object of their mission--the rescue of the Crown Prince of Morocco.

Before obtaining a more complete report on the entire French operation, General Eisenhower took the young officer aside. His major interest was how Williams had used the chain to annihilate a company of 137 Germans. The younger man explained the tactic. "They taught us the technique at the Nashville OSS school back in the States," to which General Eisenhower remarked, "They showed how to do some wacky things in that place in order to survive, but I would have bet no one would ever believe the chain trick would work."

Less defined than the work of the allied mission under Williams, but nonetheless heroic, was the role played by the countess who mothered and provided shelter and affection for the orphans. Gen. Eisenhower asked Williams if he had recognized the countess who had harbored them at the critical time during their escape.

Col. Williams, of course, replied he didn't know because she refused to tell her name.

"Let me fill you in, but first I must swear you to secrecy," to which the younger man agreed. Then the top general told him. "Her name is Madylene Carrol, the sweetheart of movies in America and in

Greet Britain,"

Williams confessed he had seldom attended a movie and never heard of Madylene Carrol.

Four-star General Omar Bradley had been listening to the conversation. He rose and came over to offer congratulations to Williams. Bradley opened. "I read your file report on the St. Etienne massacre. Pardon me but I was a bit amused by your written statement that you and your five men accidentally, I repeat, accidentally drove your car into a set of circumstances in St. Etienne from which you could not honorably retreat. Pardon my view-point Colonel, but I can't help wondering if that set of circumstances was so accidental after all."

The general continues as Eisenhower also listened. "I realize, after the fact, that the thrust of that last drop was not primarily to rescue the Moroccan Prince at all. We know that now. Instead, could it be that your real task was to save from death those helpless people? Colonel, you were given a precise appointment that day and that very hour to stop the clock of death for 450 kids and adults by a power higher than all of us."

Williams replied with a subtle query and a hint of teasing. "Are you sure it was a divine appointment General?" Bradley broke in. "Look young man, you were the main character in the drama. You flew roughly 1000 miles in an airplane at night--you were ejected without injury, helped yourself to stolen German transport and took a side trip 100 miles or so out of your way because of an unexpected detour. You drove uninvited to a Nazi lynching party as it were, and quietly went about without interruption to work out a plan to kill the enemy with one piece of chain, which they even provided for you. And most unexplainable, how do you account for the stalled German truck blocking your escape across the bridge? That delay alone prevented you from leaving town before your appointed task was ready to begin?"

Bradley waxed eloquent, out of character for him. "Now if that whole episode was pure chance, I've lost my faith that divine intervention is possible in the affairs of men. What's your comment, Colonel?"

Williams slowly contrived a reply to Bradley's attempt to analyze the mission in spiritual terms. "Well General, your explanation seems quite all right to me. But I have one comment on your theory, and it's this! If the circumstances were so divine why do you suppose I was allowed to twist my ankle early in the mission?"

As Eisenhower chuckled at Williams' response, General Bradley suddenly realized his junior officer refrained from being serious in order to keep relaxed. So the general replied, "That accident was so you would have to rely on your head instead of your feet." All laughed.

But Bradley continued. "Stay a minute Colonel and drink this fresh cup of tea. I do have something serious to address to you."

He waited for Williams to stir two teaspoons of sugar into the strong brew and continued. "You were always squeamish about killing the enemy. We all know that. What altered your opinion at St. Etienne?"

Williams deliberately sipped his tea and constructed a reply. "In St. Etienne, the brutes I met were not Germans as I have come to know Germans. What I saw was a universal type of evil found in every world society--bar none. Except these were social degenerates released from confinement and approved by the state to satisfy their own lusts. Their assigned job was to plunder, rape, torture and kill for pleasure. That's why it didn't bother me to fashion a device to execute these sub-humans.

After the goons were blown to Hell, literally speaking, on the way out of town I laughed at their death, and that's that."

General Bradley remarked, "Perhaps your laughter was a release of emotions--maybe even hysteria"

"You could be right General, but they'll never again hunt Jews or anyone else for killing.

General Bradley looked at Ike and, turning to Williams, tried to sum up the moral of the episode. He spoke haltingly, with a ring of the philosophical.

"You know gentlemen, hunters know that death nurtures life in the wild. The captors you killed, Colonel, had to die to nurture life for those they captured. And you,Williams, were the instrument chosen to intervene in the timetable of who would die and who would live."

Williams answered with meekness. "I never quite thought of it that way, but I'm glad I made the right choice."

General Eisenhower expanded on Williams' sentiment by adding, "So are 450 others. God knows what good will come out of this tragedy of death which became a miracle of living."

Gen. Bradley ended the conversation. "But that outcome is in a future timetable, isn't it Colonel?"

Williams did not look up. (See appendix B, the Nun's Story)

THE SEQUEL TO THE CHAIN GANG MISSION

The sequel to the mission to save the orphans really began the night Col. Halford Williams left the chateau over which the Duchess, the late Madylene Carrol presided. She and Williams sat down by the river below the chateau talking about the western world, particularly America and Hollywood, like old friends. He had thanked her for taking in he Jewish children, and she had admonished him. She remonstrated there were no Jewish kids in her vocabulary, or French, or Chinese or black kids. Just children of the world she said. It was adults who put the descriptions on children for prejudice or whatever.

They said their goodbyes and Miss Carrol was warned by Col. Williams about the danger of trying to be the den mother of all the homeless children who were brought to her. She confessed she could not relinquish that calling on behalf of downtrodden humanity for it had become an abiding role that she must continue.

They parted and the beautiful actress told him she would be ever grateful to him for bringing the condemned children to her home and that she hoped to meet Williams again after the war.

Seven months later Col. Halford Williams was assigned another rescue mission to a Gestapo prison in France. His job was to rescue two unknown people and get them back to England intact. The prisoners were a man and a woman.

Taking with him Sgt. McCloskey and a partially new team, they were dropped by parachute at night and eventually breached the notorious prison, defiantly shooting their way into the basement area where the prisoners in question were located and being tortured to confess names of their collaborators. The team found the two people in primitive circumstances and the woman was so beaten she was unable to stand or walk. They placed her on a hand-hold stretcher of cotton and made their exit as violently as they had entered, blasting their way out with gunfire.

Halford Williams did not recognize the new ward that had been in the prison bowels for months of psychological and physical torture. The woman did not speak. Her eyes were puffed and closed. She was so emaciated and haggard looking in appearance that identity was impossible.

Williams would not know till later, but he had just saved from lingering death the brave and beautiful Madylene Carrol whom the French Marquis had finally located. They radioed London to affect a rescue if possible.

In addition to the American actress, the accompanying prisoner, located and also severely tortured, was Jeane Lefebvre, the captain of the fishing boat who had brought Williams and his team across the channel when there occurred the miracle that calmed the sea and stilled the wind.

The prisoners were driven to a pre-arranged rural area. After arriving, to Williams' surprise, a score of figures in black removed dozens of shrubs and bushes and stacks of hay to reveal a short runway. They were barely finished when a small British plane came in and was guided by lights to a landing. As the plane taxied to a stop, a dozen German soldiers emerged onto the clearing and the allied team confronted them with machine guns and grenades.

Williams and McCloskey lifted their unknown wards onto the craft as the pilot and an English nurse battened them down. The plane turned around and took off--without one member of the rescue team boarding the craft to escape. Before the plan was airborne, the figures in black began camouflaging the area again while the allied team, still intact, left the scene in the direction of the English Channel.

But before departing from the area, the team went boldly back into a nearby town and, with the help of a French Marquis, located the informer who had turned in Madylene Carrol to the Gestapo. Sgt, McCloskey executed him by lariat outside a cafe. Then they took their leave.

Chapter 7

THE SPY WHO WAS NOT, A SINGLE MISSION ASSURES VICTORY IN EUROPE

In the spring of 1943 Col. Halford Williams and his team was asked to participate in the most crucial spy episode of World War II. Upon success of the mission hung the outcome of the proposed June 6 allied landings in Europe. Col. Williams never was made aware that he was to carry out the cunning scheme for General Eisenhower and the allied intelligence apparatus.

General William Donovan, OSS Chief, drew up the counter espionage plan. General Charles Wilson, Deputy Head of the Office of Strategic Services, prepared the master deception. Gen. Wilson, a confident and friend of the younger man, Williams, had decided that even Williams must not be told of the operation.

Hence, following the usual ordeal of sleeping off a mission in May 1943, Williams was called before Gen. Eisenhower and in a frosty meeting was given some abrupt news. He was told, without reason, that he had been posted back to the Panama Canal Zone, to the 103rd Panama Infantry Division from which he earlier had been sent overseas. Williams took the posting disconsolately, principally because he surmised the abruptness of the orders indicated either he was a failure or considered by higher-ups to be breaking under pressure. As Gen. Eisenhower dismissed Williams, his only justifying rationale was that Gen. Donovan, operating from his New York office, had requested his presence in the Latin American hemisphere.

So, under these circumstances of departure from London, Williams started out to the Panama Canal Zone via Lisbon, Dakar, Rio de Janeiro, and Caracas. He had said a quick goodbye to his London sweetheart and in a state of numbness, sat sadly on the first leg of his air hop that would set him down in Lisbon for a brief stopover.

He arrived in Lisbon on the morning of May 28th with the feeling that he had been watched during the short flight. Upon arrival in Portugal he found his flight schedule gave him ten hours of free time. Dropping into a restaurant, he ordered a lunch of broiled fish, hard rolls and flan, his favorite egg-custard dish. He still felt he was being observed. After the meal he decided to visit the St. George Palace and then drop over to the Portuguese archives to browse.

It was almost 6 p.m. as he walked slowly down the street still pondering his unexpected posting and already lonesome for his English girlfriend. He saw the big black car pass slowly and pull over to the curb just ahead. As he approached the limo vicinity the doors opened and two men got out and confronted him.

Williams knew he was tops in unarmed combat and he considered dropping one of the men with a judo chop on the Adam's apple while getting into position to throw the second attacker over his shoulder to the pavement. Then he noticed Lisbon policeman standing a few feet away watching the developing situation and he therefore elected to stand guard and wait for the would-be adversaries to make the first move. One did.

"Colonel Williams, we are from the United States Embassy. We need to talk to you. Would you mind accompanying us to our offices?" While speaking, the stranger showed his I.D. card with picture and U.S.A. coat-of-arms imprint. At the same time he flashed a picture of Halford Williams before the young man's face. He continued.

"We've been tracking you since you landed. There's been a change in your plans to leave Lisbon."

Williams countered the unique introduction by asking the name of the ambassador and other related questions. Certain he was talking to bona fide American representatives,Col. Williams got into their chauffeur-driven auto with some trepidation. Before 6 p.m. struck he was sitting in the U.S. Embassy in Lisbon at a large oaken table with the U.S. military attaché' before him.

"I'm sorry Sir that we had to bring you in this way but you gave us the slip for a couple of hours at the museum and there is no time left for civilities." Williams then heard the astounding news that it was never intended he reach Panama because his next mission had already begun. To all intents everyone was to believe he was outward bound for his home unit but the orders were no longer in effect. By 10 p.m. that very night, Col. Halford Williams would be on his way to accomplishing his real mission--destination unknown.

Col. Williams listened and then asked for one consideration. The attaché must bring in the ambassador and have him confirm or he would phone allied headquarters in London. Realizing that if Williams got in touch with London the scheme would likely be cancelled, the attaché brought down the Ambassador.

"Yes Colonel," said the ambassador, "Coded messages indeed confirm you have an appointment of utmost secrecy this very day. Please, I urge you, do not decline. It would be listed on your record as failing to carry out an order from the Supreme Allied Commander General Eisenhower himself. You must decide on the wisdom of our using such secrecy in this operation for which there is obviously ample reason."

Col. Williams reluctantly accepted the explanation and on asking why they did not trust him enough in London to advise him confidentially, the ambassador replied, "It isn't you our people are worried about, I gather it is the enemy."

At 9 p.m. the attaché and Williams left Lisbon Harbor in a fast yacht and headed out to sea. Seven miles out a faint light blinked before them and suddenly there loomed above the surface of the

Atlantic Ocean the shadowy hulk of a submarine conning tower. It had no visible markings anywhere and no numbers painted on the tower.

Williams heard himself remonstrating that he would not board any submarine in any waters at any time in his lifetime because he had claustrophobia. He heard the abrupt warning from the attaché, "You will either board now Sir, or ruin your military career forever, perhaps by dishonorable discharge." Williams saw the sub commander standing forward of the bridge and heard him call to make haste; he must immediately submerge with or without the unwilling contact.

Finally Williams reluctantly allowed himself to be pulled aboard, and before he could react he was on the bridge and in the conning tower climbing awkwardly down the near vertical ladder. He heard the words, "Clear the bridge!" and listened to popping noises as the ballast tanks went open and four lookouts slithered down the ladder from their upper platforms hugging binoculars as they landed. Soon Williams, being escorted away, felt a slight pressure on his ears and remembered saying to him self, "I hope they closed the hatch." He was certain the bow of the ship was tilting downward. It seemed to him the commander, superintending the diving operation from the control room, took the ship down quickly, but later he found it was a fairly gentle dive. "The ship kept perfect trim." He heard an officer say, "twenty fathoms, and Williams was aware of his apprehension and fear of the unknown world of the sea. He knew he was riding silently under the sea in nothing but a fragile watertight boiler, headed into deeper water. He was sure the overhead lights dimmed slightly as they picked up unwarranted speed.

Thus unaware of its real significance, Williams began the most important single mission of World War II.

A yeoman took him to his quarters and Col. Williams lay on the bunk attuning his mildly shocked mind and body to overcome his abiding fear of a submarine. After tea and toast was brought to him the sub commander came over and said hello, apologizing for the abrupt reception above.

"Plenty German subs off Lisbon," he volunteered. We could not afford to be observed by one of them with you coming aboard."

The commander then dispensed with courtesies. "We won't be asking for names on this trip in case you get curious, and we don't like questions. We have a two-day run, submerged whenever possible. If the sea is calm we'll occasionally use the snorkel but there'll be no docking and little if any surfacing."

Williams noted the commander had an English voice and the one who brought him tea and toast probably was a Londoner. He saw most signs were painted out but noted the British Crown insignia stamped in various places. So, he was on a British sub which he surmised may have been American-built because it was spanking new.

"Commander! Where are my orders for this mystery cruise under the endless ocean," Williams asked furtively and the lieutenant commander replied. "I have them Colonel. I'll hand them over as instructed when we reach destination, only then. Until that time, make yourself at home. But before you retire, follow me please. I have somebody I want you to meet." The two went down single file to the crew's quarters, past switches and controls and silent men. To Williams it seemed he was under house arrest.

Ahead he distinguished a group of men strung out in the aisle chatting away, oblivious to the commander's quiet arrival, The one doing the talking was broad shouldered and of stocky physique. The man suddenly wheeled around with speed of a wrestler and faced the commander. Williams peered around the English officer and got his first startled glimpse of the men blocking the passageway. He already knew the voice. It was Sergeant McCloskey. Wildly, the two shook hands. Two others crowded up to do the same. The lieutenant commander almost smiled as he stood back and watched the group slap the colonel on the back and exclaim a dozen army clichés of gross familiarization. The commander was observing a family reunion that did not follow procedure running fast and sure. They also knew they were on a ship laid down by the King's Rules and Regulations. He left them alone.

McCloskey finally said, "I have your instructions for the mission Sir," and he went over to his bunk to get them with Williams following. Then McCloskey whispered, "This is a routine job from what I learned at HQ, but since I got on this stinking boot, I've observed and heard enough to know we're not starting the hunt immediately. There's another matter to attend to first."

"How so and why?" countered Williams, and McCloskey whispered. "It's something to do with a damn package--yes, a package Sir--which that granite-faced commander may show you when you're finally settled."

"What's in the package and what do we do with it McCloskey?" asked Williams, normally so taciturn that he didn't exhibit interest.

"Nobody knows, except the Commander and the Approach Officer. Those two are forever checking the condition of the package in a guarded area out of bounds to us. As I read that clam-mouthed Commander he wouldn't tell his old lady her dress was afire."

So, the submarine moved through the depths, and the mission team languished in the hot interior. They knew the second day that they had passed through the Straight of Gibraltar and were in the warmer waters of the Mediterranean avoiding enemy action or being seen by an enemy, from either surface or undersea. All were closely confined to their quarters; hence their bunks became their abodes.

The sub had been on destination course over forty-eight hours and had altered direction and changed depths periodically. Someone in the team said she could make over twelve knots under water but not for too long because her battery could give juice for only about sixty minutes at a high rate of electrical discharge. But on the other hand, the commander didn't rely entirely on the snorkel breather either. On one occasion the allied team awoke and felt the warmth dissipating quickly and fresh air flooding in. Gradually there seemed to be a slight sway induced by a lazy running sea. They could hear the drone of engines as the sub cruised along on the surface with full watch above and recharging of her batteries below.

Suddenly Williams was startled at the muffled sound of distant gunfire, but he specifically noted the Commander called for no particular evasive action, nor did he order battle stations. The sub continued on the surface, apparently away from the gunfire, as the Commander ordered a true north bearing and a reduced two-thirds speed. The Commander seemed pleased that the sea was running smoother, and after observations he took the ship back under. The team had fallen fitfully asleep again, and Col. Williams dozed off only to be awakened by the same yeoman.

"It's 10 p.m. Sir, Greenwich time. We're off southern Spain. I have tea, toast and sausages for you. The Commander asks you to dress and be ready for orders within an hour." Then the yeoman left as Col. Williams swung his feet onto the deck.

He felt the sub incline upward and as the forward ballast tanks began to empty he knew the periscope would soon be on the way up. The ship was stabilized as the scope broke surface. The Commander spun it around quickly four times, then spun it in a narrowing arc, lingered on one sector and returned the scope to its well. Obviously he had seen the object of his search. The allied team heard the bong through the ship as general alarm sounded briefly and went silent. The sub began surfacing and the engines stopped, The Commander and the Control Officer went up the ladder through the conning tower, the hatch, and finally onto the bridge. Before ascending, the Commander ordered the package delivered topside and four men were involved in hoisting something to the surface. Then the Commander returned downside and got Col, Williams. Together they picked up Sgt. McCloskey standing ready. Each man had been assigned black naval clothes, black cap and black deck shoes.

Williams and McCloskey held onto the deck chain and saw the calm sea lolling over parts of the submarine. Held fast by two sailors was a black raft with four oars, and along the middle of the raft bottom was an irregular object roughly about six feet in length and two feet wide that went from end to end. In the distance Williams could see lights on shore and at one short interval in his gaze he saw distinctly a blinker light from the land.

The Commander spoke to Williams. "Meet the third member of your crew. He is a well-trained, powerful, long-distance swimmer. You three are to row this craft to within a mile of shore and drop the package that we have placed on board. The blinker light on shore will be your guide. As you get closer to shore, the frogman will go overboard and help guide the raft--same on the return trip. Have you got your knife Colonel?" The reply was affirmative.

The Commander continued, "I advise you to slit open the package sometime past the three-quarter-way mark. Under no circumstances are you to lose the plastic wrapping, and you must account for it as the first item of priority on your return to ship." The Commander added, "We are about three miles from shore and we will endeavor to hold this bearing till you return. The lights you see are from the Spanish town of Palamos. I repeat: Instructions are that you go no closer than one mile to the beach before dropping the package. Got that distance Colonel?" A glum "Yes, I understand English," was the retort.

The Englishman went on carefully and quietly. "The beach is patrolled regularly by a Spanish/German team. You are not to discuss the contents of the package before or after you return to the ship. God speed Colonel." The three men got in the raft and they shoved off. After an hour of strenuous rowing Williams and McCloskey wished they had been provided with a full meal. Behind them, the outline of their submarine soon disappeared and in front of the raft the lights on the distant shore grew more distinguishable. There was no talking except where necessary, and each man rowed quietly in combined unison, dipping his paddle in the black depths.

The frogman whispered that there was about a mile left to row. Then he mentioned with some alarm in his whisper that they had begun to drift away from the particular shore light. Williams had to make his first major decision of the trip--that is to disobey the order to go no farther than the last mile toward shore. There was obviously no way they could make the drop of the package as required by orders. It was apparent to Williams that unless they got inside the lateral shore current the package would never be found.

The frogman whispered again. "The current is shoving us westward off target," and each agreed, in spite of their increased rowing. Then, slipping off the raft, the unknown man took the raft's rope and with powerful, silent strokes he swam shoreward while McCloskey and Williams put their remaining strength into longer and deeper strokes to take them through the surface current and eastward to the general point of delivery.

Hanging low over the area there still was the blackness and a subtle mist clinging to the water. At one point while in the current a gentle swell from seaward caught up the raft and passed under it. "Something huge and fairly close to shore made that swell," whispered the frogman. Then the man finally gestured that they were out of the current, and pulling his face over the balloon side of the raft he asked for instructions. "Continue swimming toward that signal light behind town," Williams indicated. The surface of the sea was calm, still encased under a canopy of blackness secure from observation. "Suddenly the frogman whispered, "I've touched bottom, we're sitting ducks." Ahead of them lay the target area and the beach was only 150 feet away. They had gone too far.

Williams quickly took his knife and slit the package from top to bottom. From inside there came a sweet, rather nauseating odor. Reaching his hand inside at the top end, his fingers began to explore the contents for a grip. Imperceptibly he felt the outlines of a person's nose, closed eyelids end cold lips. Then he touched hair--human hair--and Williams knew he had drawn his hand across the face of a man who was dead. Williams reflex was to yank back his hand as McCloskey knelt beside and stared into the opening.

"Give me a hand!" Williams whispered. "Hurry!" Together they lifted the head out of the bag as Williams pulled the plastic away to one side. Task completed, the two cronies stared at the body of a British Major with two bullet holes in his tunic. On his wrist was strapped a leather briefcase and his inside pocket contained a plastic envelope. He wore boots. The major was fully dressed, except for his cap. Carefully, the frogman pulled and tugged the body into the water beside him, turned it face downward, and quickly the team of three propelled themselves seaward. Approaching so close to shore Williams had taken a chance that they had been detected and observed, but nevertheless, they departed the scene believing they had not been sighted.

As they got out of earshot from shore, Col. Williams raised his hand in salute and whispered, "Goodbye Major! Rest in peace." McCloskey croaked, "What was that for?" to which Williams replied, "A burial prayer. I said it on impulse out of respect for whoever the poor guy was,"

The raft was 160 pounds lighter, and with the help of the frogman they got through the offshore current diagonally and headed out to see, correcting course. An hour later they sighted another raft unexpectedly.

Before they could take action the two rafts almost touched and in the other raft they saw hazily three men, one with field glasses. The man let the field glasses dangle on his chest and pulled alongside Williams' raft. He immediately identified himself as General Charles Wilson, the OSS Deputy Chief in charge of preparing the body and providing the secret information left purposely in the briefcase and the envelope. Gen. Wilson did not disclose to the team the reason why the body was to have been dumped near shore. But he challenged, Williams as to why he had jeopardized the entire operation by almost landing in Spain. He accepted the reasons from the Colonel, but curtly advised him that the frogman should have towed the body through the current and left it to drift onto the beach without having exposed the silhouette of a raft and its occupants to a likely beach patrol.

As they spoke, the raft people saw debris floating in the water from the hulk of a strange submarine towering nearby. They knew then why they had felt the swell sweep under their raft earlier and guessed correctly that the floating life jacket and pieces of marked and splintered wood were part of a scheme of unknown intrigue. Whatever it was, Williams thought, it had been cleverly executed in London and completed with the dropping of the Major's body off the coast of Spain. Williams recalled the gunfire at sea when the sub had surfaced earlier in the night and he also surmised that a decoy ship had been sunk for a purpose connected with the body incident. He believed that the gunfire action at sea heard earlier had destroyed the decoy ship and correctly surmised the action was intended to be heard by the beach patrol on Palamos.

The "package" team rowed to their submarine nearby, pulled up to the wooden decking, and embarked.

The first words of the skipper were, "Where's the wrapping?" McCloskey could take no more intrigue. As he got off the raft he growled. "We left the bloody wrapping on the body and tied it with a red ribbon." As he spoke he threw the gooey and blood covered sheath to the Commander and scurried haltingly onto the surface of the deck.

The Commander glowered at McCloskey and ordered all hands below. The sailors helped Williams and his sergeant to board and the skipper gave orders to dive. The unmarked submarine slipped under the Mediterranean southeastward from the shore. They intended to create a reaction at the first light of morning.

Williams had left London on the 26th of May 1944. It was now early on the morning of May 30th. D-Day in Europe was only six days away. Forty-six German divisions stood posed for any allied attempt to land on the continent and reclaim Europe from the Nazis. Only one man could reduce the number of German divisions facing the English Channel, waiting to cut down any allied advance. That hope lay with a dead man.

On the person of the dead major he carried the military ruse that caused the Germans to abandon their commanding defensive positions on the Normandy beaches of the English Channel and rush to southern France to interrupt the "real invasion" from North Africa.

"The spy who was not" washed gently up on to the beach at Palamos. The deceased soldier waited for the enemy patrol to find him. They did.

Major Paul V. McPherson, a Scot with His Majesty's Royal Marines was a Special Duty Officer who had been wounded on a pre D-Day exploratory raid on the beach of Normandy. His unit had gotten him safely off the beach, but he died before reaching the English side of the channel.

Allied Intelligence, with approval of Major McPherson's family would provide the decoy washed ashore in Palamos Spain from a "sunken" allied ship on the night of May 30th. The remains had been kept frozen on ice since its preparation for the mission. The body was gradually thawed aboard the submarine on which Col. Williams and his team sailed incognito to the Palamos destination. The carefully prepared plans of a massive sea-borne invasion into southern France was to be the misleading information which would fall inadvertently into the hands of German agents in Spain who would conclude Major McPherson had been a victim of an unplanned accident of a British ship bound for Naples from Gibraltar.

According to the papers found on Major McPherson's body, they incorporated complete plans for an invasion of Southern France. Agreement for the operation had been originally made in Teheran in 1943 under code name "Anvil". It was considered possible by British Intelligence that German agents had long anticipated that such an invasion might some day take place, knowledge of the "Anvil" plan possibly having been ascertained by clever German agents. So finding detailed plans on an allied courier no doubt gave assurance to the German high command that the allied operation named "Anvil" was about to become a reality.

However, the dilemma for the Germans was that they had only one week to assess whether Anvil was authentic and if so, to take action.

As anticipated, the body of Major McPherson was discovered at first light on the morning of May 30th 1944. Two German soldiers accompanied by Spaniards were patrolling the beach when they came upon a body half in the water. Placing the corpse in their car they drove to police headquarters in Palamos and laid out the remains in the back room. There, two German officers who were Gestapo, made a thorough search of the clothing and other paraphernalia. Quickly discovering the packet of secret papers in a watertight plastic bag, they excitedly telegraphed a coded message to Berlin.

The same day a high-ranking officer of the Third Reich arrived by special plane and departed immediately for a return trip to the German capital with the "Anvil" docket.

Meanwhile, Palamos military authorities informed the British Embassy of the body because identification showed he was a Major in the British Marines. The British ambassador arrived on the scene after departure of the Germans who had stripped the body, and he vehemently protested that he had not been sent for sooner.

The deceased who apparently had drowned at sea was taken to a funeral home. The next morning at 8 a.m. graveside services were held by the Spanish authorities. With honor befitting his rank, the remains were lowered into the grave as a squad of six Spanish soldiers fired three rounds over the casket. Then taps were blown. A twenty-four-hour guard was placed on the site. Later, a simple cross with the name of the deceased, as shown in his identification, was placed over the grave.

Thirty-six hours after Major McPherson's body fell into Nazi hands, Berlin experts would examine the allied plans to invade the continent of Europe on June 6th, using the back door of Southern France.

The truth of the matter was that "Anvil" had long been proposed by British Prime Minister Churchill, General Montgomery, and their European allies. But the Americans, especially Roosevelt and Gen. Eisenhower, rejected the breaching of the continent through Marseilles, etc., and traveling over 500 miles of roads through the Rhone Valley and on to Paris and Germany.

The unmarked British submarine carrying Col. Williams' team lay off Marseilles past midnight on June 2nd. A blinker light signaled from shore. The allied team of six embarked in the raft and quietly paddled towards their next mission. It would be a combined operation with the French Underground.

Col. Williams' notes provide a spectrum of activities: May 30: Came ashore vicinity Marseilles. Taken to safe house. Slept all day. Departed after dark in two French cars. June 1: First drivers relieved by locals familiar with roads, bridges and checkpoints. Slept, bathed and ate at next stop. French woman washed and dried clothes while we slept. All feel refreshed. After bath, McCloskey boasted he felt so good he could "lick the world". Didn't understand the saying. McCloskey said, "Colonials were so dumb they'd forgotten their mother tongue." All laughed at the 19th century view of history. McCloskey interpreted the remark by saying, "Gerries, get out of our way--here we come." Truth is we might soon be getting out of the Gerries way. Tough, sharp, trained German soldiers are being seen who are quite our equals. Mustn't run afoul of these guys.

McCloskey (on behalf of men) asked where we were headed. Told him London, via Lyons, Nice, Metz, Paris, and Calsis. Team complained, food fair but beverage service poor and particularly short on cognac and wine. Late in day French guide handed Williams a note that said: "Thanks for delivering package. Well received. Make haste to destination. Repeat: Hurry!" There was no signature other than code number 61ICX. McCloskey commented, "London seems to know where we are every night." Arrived vicinity Lyons. June 2: Poor progress. French drivers insist on staying off main roads. Occasional German military cars being sighted going south at high speeds.

June 3: New French driver LeBlanc. They all call themselves LeBlanc. LeBlanc was handed note which translated said: "German infantry, armor and artillery units pulling out from Normandy, Brittany, etc., headed south into Rhone Valley. Take extra precautions in travel and bivouacs." Tempers frayed riding in small French cars. Hot with German coats and helmets worn over our allied uniforms. The team is beefing because they haven't been made privy to destination or mission. McCloskey, as their spokesman, cornered me and demanded a satisfactory explanation. I walked away pondering a reply which irritated McCloskey who taunted, "You throw out your feet, thrust your chin and clasp your hands behind. Does being in France make you think you're Napoleon?" All eyes were on the confrontation. Omitting McCloskey's profane description of me I finally stopped and said quietly, "Thanks for the backhanded compliment. I like Napoleon, especially today. He planted all those trees along the French roads we've been traveling. If you guys had been soldiers in the 1800's you'd be marching under the shade of those trees. But you're lucky. You were born in this century so you could travel these pretty French back roads in fine automobiles." Little speech didn't go over well. Everybody gasped waiting for the punch line. There was none. Silence continued as the bilingual French driver apprised the passengers. Finally McCloskey blurted out, "OK. General Napoleon--where the H are we headed for?" They wouldn't believe me when I turned around and ended the conversation by saying, "I don't really know except to say it's near the town of Metz in Alsace Lorraine. Am having trouble with one of the men who's become an alky, always taking a nip from hidden bottle. Good man but will drop him next trip. He's burned out already.

June 4. Forty kilometers from Nancy--Main roads crowded with German traffic. Country is crawling with Gerry divisions. Forced off road unexpectedly by regiment of Nazi motorbikes with attached sidecars and machine gunners. Mean looking lot.

1.30 p.m.: Delayed two hours at rail crossing. Long freight train with German tanks chained onto flat cars passing by. All civilian vehicle priorities cancelled to allow German troop movements. Falling behind in our itinerary. French driver tries secondary road. Too clogged with German truck and personnel traffic heading south. Stopped by German provost at bridge. Won't permit our crossing in spite of our German uniforms. Got out and marched on foot. Took salute from provost. Finally located another car. Crawled along northward towards Nancy.

June 5: Noted radio silence re German troop movements. All vehicle markings painted out or covered over. Roads filled night and day. See German infantry in backs of trucks, but none on road. Have passed many self-propelled heavy artillery units the last 72 hours and other artillery hauled by half-tracks and trucks. French drivers have conference. Decide to re-route as far east as possible, as all available western and Rhone Valley roads are bogged down with German troop traffic. The whole team is perplexed, including me. Unaware why division after division of German troops is heading south. Except for the smelly sweat, that's all we talk about.

Finally one of the men gasps, "I've got it. The allies have started the big invasion from southern France. We just beat them ashore." Everyone agreed and yelled Hooray. French driver disgusted with us. We sobered up emotionally when someone asked me why we were running from the action, and I had no comment--simply because I didn't know.

On the morning of June 3 the leading German Generals were gathered in Berlin. Hitler chaired the continuing meeting attended by Rommel, Spiedel, Von Runstedt and other leading generals from the western front. The elite German armies waited for the expected allied landing that had not yet materialized. Now, as the military leaders met in Berlin at Hitler's call they had left their commands that were under a cloud of deteriorating weather forecasts. The consensus was that the enemy invasion fleet, that lay camouflaged in the harbors of southern England and the surrounding countryside waiting to invade the continent, would not move in the next week or ten days. The channel would be too rough. On the other hand it was ideal invasion weather in south France.

At that Berlin meeting of June 3, the ominous words had already fallen on the ears of the top generals like a hammer on an anvil. "We have picked up completed plans found on a drowned British courier at Palamos, Spain, for an enemy invasion of 16 divisions to be landed in three assault groups; on the French Riviera, Marseilles, and Toulon. The enemy date to land is June 6, three days away,"

Wiser counsel among the German general's prevailed, and they asked for further evidence. They got it. German reconnaissance observations in the Mediterranean had been filtering in for days. Number one item: British General Montgomery, who had routed Rommel in North Africa, had been seen by German agents moving hurriedly near an English Port.

His presence coincided with heavier troop activity.

From Naples in Italy there was evidence of troop concentration and verification of shipping being assembled for an allied sea evacuation to points unknown. Also noted from Italy was observation of LST landing craft gathering at various points.

Gibraltar was in a state of hyperactivity on the docks.

At sea German submarines were reporting a virtual covering of the Mediterranean surface by newly concentrated enemy shipping. Observed were large elements of British naval forces and the entire U.S. 7th fleet. Most alarming, it was apparent the 7th fleet was being assembled for one purpose--to guide and protect an invasion force seen embarking on every type of craft that could move over water. Camouflage netting in various North African ports was being used to cover smaller vessels, but German aerial photos had picked out at least 150 LSTs moving to assembly points for towing seaward. Photographed on these advance landing craft were enemy soldiers covering the decks.

The generals asked Intelligence for further corroborating information as to the possible destination of the naval activity. It was estimated it would take these flotillas forty-eight hours of leisurely travel to cross the Mediterranean and be abreast of French ports for assault.

While this enemy strategy was being discussed, alarming aerial and submarine reports came flooding in to the Berlin headquarters. They said in part: "Enemy traffic protected by the entire U.S. 7th fleet including battleship, two flat-tops, and many destroyers are moving out of North African ports. Photos show naval ships covered with soldiers and long lines of invasion barges being towed out to sea." Weather was reported favorable and the sea relatively smooth for a crossing into France.

The leading generals were still unconvinced. These military men, like Von Runstedt, wanted to wait further and assess more closely the character of the invasion fleet particularly the LSTs, and they also asked that they be furnished the latest photographs on the number of LSTs and enemy troops assembled on the decks of the invasion fleet. There remained a day for good photography.

Adolf Hitler made the final decision based on the preliminary evidence. He overruled his generals and demanded immediate response to the new invasion threat. Consequently Hitler made his second blunder of the war for Germany. The first was at Stalingrad and the second would be southern France. The meeting adjourned, swayed by a grand deception.

On June 3, 1944 forty-six German divisions stationed at the English Channel waiting for an invasion from southern England faced a new threat. Their Panzer units, their proven Blitzkrieg units, their toughest and best-trained troops they could muster might have to be suddenly moved and regrouped on another front hundreds of miles away. When the Berlin-staff meeting was over Adolf Hitler decided that the main allied invasion onto the continent of Europe would be launched first through southern France and up the Rhone Valley. No one was allowed to dissent.

Twenty-seven of the best German troop divisions dug in along the English Channel defensive positions (two-thirds of the total defense forces) would be ordered detached and sent south. All personnel were recalled. Advance petrol units and supply depots moved out first and the fighting units followed on their heels as all headed toward Marseilles, the Riviera, and Toulon. All French trains were commandeered for German heavy equipment and troops. All available French autos and busses were confiscated for German service. On June 4th the bulk of the hardened, trained soldiers, the best of the Wehrmact began pulling stakes and heading south to stop the invasion at their back door--the secret plans of which Col. Halford Williams had deposited 150 feet from the Palamos beach in the dead body of Major Paul V. McPherson.

Nineteen German divisions, mainly green troops, were left to halt any unlikely enemy thrust to be launched from English ports 26 to 30 miles away against the beaches of Normandy. The one unchangeable but severe element left in the German defense of northwestern France would be the big stationary gun emplacements, the beach-mines, and the tank landing obstacles put in place by Rommel after the 1942 Dieppe landings.

General Von Runstedt was chosen to prevent the imminent invasion in the south and he flew to Marseilles and set up his headquarters. When his heavy artillery guns and self-propelled vehicles arrived on a non-stop rail and road dash, he would be ready--in time he hoped--to blow the first enemy landing craft out of the water.

General Von Runstedt had less than 48 hours to get his first gun in place along the areas of anticipated enemy infiltration. He had orders to stop an enemy beachhead at any cost. Sleepless German soldiers would face an enemy fresh and ready from the sea.

The blackness of June 6th lifted, and the dawn broke on a vast armada of ships and landing craft marshaled off Marseilles, France. Operation "Anvil" was about to begin.

From out of the brightening horizon the Germans saw numerous specks appearing in the distant sea. A German reconnaissance plane flew over the convoy and radioed back: "First wave of at least 150 LSTs filled with enemy soldiers being launched. Lines of other landing craft coming in as backups to the first wave. All headed for the Marseilles shore."

The allied invasion fleet knew they were virtually free from German fighter attacks as a protective canopy of defensive fighters flew cover. Gunners on board the 7th fleet had one instruction: "Fire to miss any German observation plane."

Hastily placed German artillery, self-propelled guns, and dug-in tanks were pointed seaward from the Marseilles area, and new emplacements were being added continuously. General Von Runstedt received the message of the first wave of landing craft and he wired, "Enemy invasion began 0500 hours. Speed reinforcements". Berlin, staggered by the boldness of the attack, in turn ordered troops to be moved from the Eastern (Russian) front.

German shore batteries opened up. The 7th fleet commander gave the order to fire at suspected German gun emplacements. An additional wave of ninety-six advance LSTs filled with U.S. and British soldiers moved into silhouette as they led the attack. The first reported naval invasion force would come ashore as predicted, at Marseilles. German infantry flown in from the north waited.

"Fire!" Eighty-eight millimeter guns from dug-in Tiger Tanks sent salvos at the landing craft and the heavy guns opened up. Seventy-two millimeter German guns added to the roar as shells winged out and dropped among a confident enemy. At intervals, 12-inch shells from sea landed amongst the Germans in return.

Within half an hour the German gunners were blowing the advance craft out of the water quite literally, and the people of Marseilles wakened to war on their doorsteps. The German gunners laughed at the debacle and one commented in glee. "Ha! It's like shooting ducks in a pond." General Von Runstedt wondered why the big guns of the 7th fleet were not laying down a heavier barrage. As he suspected, the report announced that the first sea-borne invasion wave of the enemy had been obliterated. Behind the coastline there were no reports of allied air troops, but looking out from the city and environs of Marseilles, people saw the water was littered with debris and floating bodies. The enemy had failed to gain a beachhead.

But one landing craft is reported to have gotten through, and German infantry waited eagerly for their first taste of blood. As the craft touched shore the front did not fall down. Machine gun bullets ripped into its sides. As the Germans attempted to storm onto the LST they lobbed their grenades over and saw the sides bulge out and tear apart. Before the tough German infantry could go aboard for the final kill the landing craft buckled and blew apart.

German eyes perceived a hold full of wooden soldiers laying

scattered about a plywood deck and canvas sides. Two Johnson outboard motors on the stern spluttered and fell into the water. The German soldiers stared in disbelief.

Above them, unseen, it may be that the ghost of Major Paul V. McPherson of his Majesty's Royal Marines glided ashore and laughed at the Germans as he headed for his Valhalla.

On the British flagship of the fleet, the double of General Bernard Montgomery relaxed and waited to be put ashore back in North Africa following his superb role in deceiving the Germans. The deck officer inquired what should be done with the thousands of dummy soldiers cluttering the decks of the convoy. He received the reply from the Admiral: "We'll formally discharge them all when we arrive at the first port."

The 7th fleet stopped firing and withdrew. By mid-day General Von Rundstedt knew that the enemy invasion through southern France was a clever ruse that had fooled the German High Command. The order was given for three Germans divisions to stand put but that all troops and armor still on rails were to be turned immediately and rerouted back to the channel cost. In the meantime German divisions were holding the channel beaches.

In the thirty-six hours in which the crack German divisions had been lured away, the allies had been able to land on Normandy and Omaha beaches as planned on the morning of the June 6th where they eventually gained an eight-by-ten mile foothold.

The seasoned German troops from the false invasion front began arriving back in Normandy and Brittany late on the 7th of June and completed their return on the 9th.

In spite of fatigue, a tougher resistance would hinder the allied landings, but the Germans would never be able to drive the Americans, British, and Canadians back into the sea.

On August 15th the real Operation Anvil began and sixteen allied divisions landed at the areas of Marseilles, Toulon and the Riviera.

Within a month they would breakout of the Rhone Valley and join forces with the Allied Channel armies. By October that year the British and American armies with their allies would have their dagger pointed at the heart of Berlin.

Col. Williams' successful delivery of "the spy who was not" was the cue for the rehearsal of the real invasion. In the German file on the grand deception played on them, Gen. Von Runstedt had noted that the discovery of the corpse with the papers on Operation Anvil "bore the mark of the Fox" who also carried the Golden Sword.

He didn't realize it then, but one day Gen. Von Runstedt would look up from his desk in his western front headquarters and find him-self staring into the eyes of the man he dared to call "The Fox".

The Spy Who Was Not Sequel to the Mission

In addition to delivery of Major Paul V. McPherson's body into German hands, the mission assignment was to rescue a top scientist being held in a prison near Metz, France known simply by his number.

The team reached its objective, and dressed as Germans, gained easy entry to the jail. The prison night-warden was a colonel who was also responsible for the jail transport. He was, fortunately, a naturalized American inducted into the Wehrmact during a visit to his homeland in 1940. He had been trained as an engineer in the United States and was married with two children living in New York State. Upon being confronted to admit the allied team into his jail, he quickly recognized they were imposters, and after unmasking them agreed to join forces.

Thus, with a new addition to the team they simply went into the prison, freed their objective personage and marched him out behind the German/American jail warden, ostensibly to be executed. Using transport legally obtained from the jail's car pool the group sped to a nearby abandoned airfield.

At precisely 10:50 p.m., on the rescue night decided by London, they hastily placed faint flares on the runway and at 11 p.m. an English light plane landed. French Marquis filled the plane with gasoline and the team dumped the scientist on board before it departed. Thereupon, the Marquis drove the team to the Seine River where a large,flat-bottomed boat with canvas cover laid waiting. They had to get back to England unaided.

Three nights later, hiding by day and drifting by night, they reached Paris. They followed a drainage pipe leading from the river and came up inside a statue on the grounds of the old Palace Royale. It was an ancient escape route to the river for royalty. However, when the team surfaced they found they were in the middle of a German Army Service Division, whereupon using their new accomplice the team commandeered another officer's car and sped away, leaving two dead Germans.

On the 8th of June 1944 they unexpectedly came upon advance units of the invasion force. They still were not cognizant of the real D-Day landings and were surprised when intercepted by a British Infantry Lieutenant who was first amazed, then perplexed about running into a mixed lot of Germans, who underneath their outer clothes appeared to be various U.S., British, and French servicemen. The Lieutenant's platoon kept the team covered and radioed Regimental HQ for confirmation of the captives. In half an hour the team was free. Discarding their German uniforms, the real German Colonel was given a U.S. jacket and field cap. As such, the team pulled up to a landing craft and asked to board for England in their captured German car. Permission was refused to embark the car but the team landed in Portsmouth with one additional recruit.

The German colonel's story proved correct. But Col. Williams, unhappy about not returning in style, asked Gen. Eisenhower for a letter in English to be carried on the next mission ordering the allied navy personnel to transport any captured vehicle the team may have impounded. Subsequently, such a situation actually transpired.

United States historians will not divulge the identity of the scientist whom the mission freed--except to admit he was a Frenchman of German descent living in Alsace Lorraine who helped develop the firing mechanism of an atomic, 75 mm artillery piece that the Nazis intended to fire from a huge surfaced submarine on American coastal cities. The scientist had refused to participate in the undertaking because he had friends living in those cities earmarked for destruction.

In spite of the scientist's refusal to cooperate with the Nazis, such a deadly armed sub did depart from a North African port early in 1945 with a substitute armament gunner. It did reach American waters and almost succeeded in firing atomic shells for the destruction of certain American coastal cities. The story of that frightening undersea journey by selected Nazi personnel is in itself a drama of such proportions that it cannot be told in this book.
The French scientist that was delivered by Col. Williams' rescue group to the small plane in France landed in England on the night of June 5th 1944.

What the scientist told General Donovan and U.S. scientists helped unlock the key that saved two major east coast cities in the United States.

By way of human interest, the remains of Major Paul McPherson did not lay forever in a foreign grave. In 1946 (or 1947) the British government, through its Embassy in Madrid, claimed the body. Disinterred, it was taken aboard a British warship to its resting place in Scotland. On an unknown date the major was laid to final rest in Westminster Abbey. Posthumously, Major Paul V. McPherson was awarded the Victoria Cross, the first such award ever given to a body for valor while dead.

Chapter 8

PREAMBLE

THE DAY THAT CHANGED THE WAR

What was named the Battle of the Bulge was a major counter-offensive by Germany to wrest the initiative from the allies on the Western front. Massive in scope, Hitler sent four armies under General Von Rundstedt through the Ardennes. Forty divisions involving half a million troops were employed. Hitler's objective was to sever the allied forces and take Antwerp, Belgium--then cut the allies to pieces. This chapter concerns eighteen hours of the Ardennes warfare that profoundly altered Hitler's plans. Dropped behind enemy lines to spoil Hitler' victory was a team of rescuers-turned-saboteurs led by Colonel Halford Williams.

Chapter 8
THE DAY THAT CHANGED THE WAR

At first light on December 17, 1944 General Patton's Third Army tank squadron marauding deep behind German lines came upon the object of their nightlong foray.

Just south of the deserted town of Echternach, Luxembourg, on the farm of Piere Bouchardt, located on the River Sur, Commander Mike Morgan signaled his thirty-two Shermans to a full stop. Less than five hundred yards in front lay his target, an enormous mountain of gasoline covered by camouflage netting. The gasoline and ammunition dump was scheduled for shipment to three voracious armies barreling through astonished American divisions towards their first intended stop, the Meus River.

Eyeing the two million or more gallons of potato alcohol, General Morgan directed his gunner to get ready to fire a stream of liquid flame on the target ahead. He opted against using his 70 mm gun and chose the flamethrower, because it was quiet and would not alert the 212th Volkegrenadiers while he safely withdrew.

Farmer Piere Bouchardt, upon hearing the noise of the tanks, crawled up from his basement refuge and looked out at the tour de force of foreign armor staring with guns pointed at the gasoline and ammo depot sprawling over 13 acres of his valuable pasture land. Monsieur Bouchardt beckoned his wife to join him and whispered in French, "Its Americans--they've come after the Boche." As Bouchardt and his wife watched in astonishment they witnessed the six lead tanks crush the guardhouse, cross the barbed wire without resistance and scatter a dozen or more soldiers as the iron monsters bore down within firing range of the mammoth petrol depot.

Because the terrain of the farm lacked sufficient space to maneuver the entire squadron on the lower levels, General Morgan had ordered his rear tanks to hold position, cover the advance, and watch for enemy movement or weapons on higher western elevations.

Suddenly those in the backup tanks saw a lone American jeep rush out from the collection of tents below and speed recklessly toward General Morgan's lead tank. A tall man violently waving his arms overhead was motioning the six oncoming tanks to halt before they reached firing range. Unbelievably, these at the rear of the squadron saw their commander's flagship grind to a halt. It was almost on top of the jeep and its two occupants who, in spite of their danger, obviously considered the menacing tanks were trespassers.

Commander Mike Morgan and his crew could not believe what they heard coming from the officer occupant of the American jeep. The gist of the barrage of words delivered in the most precise English was as follows:

"Dammit yanks. What's going on with the mad rush? I am Colonel Archibald Scott-Fox of His Majesty's 7th Dragoons operating under the command of Fourth Army General Bernard Montgomery. We took this bloody depot at 0200 hours last night. My own men surround it. That's why you were able to get so close. Had you been Gerries, we would have blown you apart...I'm addressing the squadron commander...You're all invited at your convenience to come into the depot for a breakfast of captured German sausage, fresh eggs and real coffee."

The officer spoke in what seemed flawless English with an Oxford accent. His typically English swagger stick under the arm, the Englishman finished his dialogue.

"Be our guests for an hour Commander, and my men will gas up your Shermans while we all sit down and eat chow. During breakfast Commander may I ask your expert advice on how to blow this German depot to Hell before we all withdraw."

General Morgan touched the English observer whom he had with him, and Col. (Teddy) R.D. Wilson peered out the frontal aperture and stared at a brother English officer confronting them with an invitation to breakfast--and in essence to voluntarily lay down their arms. Then Col. Wilson asked permission to address the officer in the jeep.

As the stranger spoke to Wilson the observer in the lead tank studied the man's voice and accent. Listening carefully to every syllable, Wilson turned to general Morgan and said, "The man is certainly an officer and typically English in every respect including voice and mannerisms. He's a Sandhurst graduate and--believe it or not--he's in charge of this depot, Sir."

Then the English observer sitting next to general Morgan called out to the stranger again to give the current password. Without hesitation the officer in the jeep replied correctly with confidence and without hesitation.

Col. Wilson turned to General Morgan and stated unequivocally: "The officer before us is bona fide."

Watching from a broken window in his damaged farmhouse, Piere Bouchardt listened as the noise of the American tanks became still. He was surprised to hear a faint babble of voices when suddenly he saw the hatches of the tanks being opened and in the next short minutes witnessed about two hundred American soldiers straggle out of their machines, and leaving them unattended, head for their commander up front. Waving them all on was a tall, English officer who appeared to be escorting the Americans into huts and tents at the mouth of the camouflaged petrol and ammunition depot.

The canny farmer recalled to himself that he had seen the same English officer before, dressed as an American colonel, and of course, as a Boche.

As the farmer peered at the Americans disappearing into the huts and tents, his eyes swept back to the vacant tanks. He saw a lone hand rise in the air and heard a revolver shot. Then the hatch was closed as a platoon of Germans descended from the nearby trees, hurling grenades and firing automatics. They were almost on the tank as both motors were revved. Turning abruptly the tank mangled three or four of the enemy and, firing its machine gun, cut down the remainder of the attacking platoon.

Back at the headquarters of General Patton the unknown Captain and his crew of six told the unbelievable story of the cleverest entrapment by the enemy during the whole war.

At mid morning on the 17th, an agitated General Patton got on the phone to General Eisenhower and told him of Morgan's terrible blunder. Patton went over the head of Omar F. Bradley, his immediate superior, because Bradley had refused to allow such a mission only twenty-four hours earlier, in spite of the fact that Patton's G2 Col. Kroch had discovered the enemy depot that would provide gas and shells for Panzer divisions refitted and reformed in the critical weeks ahead.

The supreme commander, acting on Patton's information, called an emergency meeting of the joint chiefs of staff for 2.30 p.m. the same day at Allied Headquarters in London. Bradley was not informed.

Three of Patton's top officers had been captured, two British observers, over fifty-three American officers and 176 other ranks when last seen had been taken by the enemy. In addition, thirty-one tanks had been surrendered. General Morgan fell short by a hundred yards of destroying the enemy installation, leaving both he and Patton fruitless heroes. Had the General flamed the dump, he would have bogged down the big German machine in seventy-two hours, giving the badly manned American armies time to regroup and counter attack.

Evan before General Eisenhower convened the meeting of allied intelligence on how to cope with the loss of Morgan's 32-tank armored division, he instinctively knew the circumstances would require a major rescue operation. With that fact in mind, in advance of the meeting, the supreme commander ordered a reconnaissance flight over the enemy area of the disaster. Then he asked the head provost marshal to find the whereabouts of Colonel Halford Williams and his rescue team, all of who had just been granted their Christmas leave.

Thus, by 11:30 a.m. the provosts in London and elsewhere in the south of England were scouring the haunts of Col. Williams and his second in command, Sergeant Major Ian McCloskey. At 12-noon a photographic plane left Corydon Airport seeking the map reference where the tanks and men had disappeared. At 2:30 p.m. top generals, with the exception of Bradley, had flown in from Versailles and Brussels, at which time the meeting was convened. It was too early to speculate on the outcome, but all three American generals, plus Britisher Montgomery, would examine the biggest blunder of the war involving each personally, and putting in jeopardy the careers of all four of the top brass.

The photo reconnaissance plane brought back the pictures the joint chiefs needed to scan, showing both the farm buildings and recent German installations. Easily identified was a squadron of Shermans sitting on a small farm consisting of a damaged house, barns, haystacks and what appeared to be hundreds of horses. The farm sat on the bend of a river identified as the Sur, a branch of the Moselle. Alongside the farm on which the depot lay there ran a railroad, and from it a spur line was shown being built by a large number of workers. Much camouflage netting covered one particular elevation of 13 acres beside the tents and huts, and a track in the light snow led to the river.

The abandoned tanks were still in place, all thirty-one. But several hundred feet from the tanks a scattered platoon of what appeared to be American soldiers showed up. The soldiers seemingly were involved in two Quonset type huts and some field tents. Nearby there was a trench dug in the frozen ground and one aerial shot revealed several vague, elongated white dots. Within the trench lay other white marks in horizontal positions, there being a total in excess of one hundred and fifty differently shaped, white objects.

A British expert studied the aerial in detail. He had placed his three-dimensional glass on a particular spot and adjusted it to scrutinize the unidentified white objects. As his glass hovered on a group of splinters laying near a German tent, the sergeant called a superior. The non-com belted out for all to hear. "Those splinters! They're people. Some are standing and some are lying down." Then the sergeant stood up for all to hear. "They are all in their long johns. I can't believe it. The upright ones are evidently alive."

Then the man finished his explanation as others gather around. "The horizontal splinters are dead men."

Within an hour the viewer's observations and assumptions are verified and forwarded to the high command. But unanswered was the question: Why had the clothing and boots been removed in freezing weather, and were the humans Americans? And, supposing they were the missing Americans, how had the Germans tricked the tough squadron of tankers out of their vehicles to be undressed and executed without forcing a fight?

A second message coming in from Patton's field headquarters would reveal that one tank of the squadron had escaped the ambush. The tank commander was unable to provide the answer as to the outcome of those who left their tanks voluntarily.

The briefing of Col. Halford Williams and his team ended at 5:35 p.m. that day of the 17th. Final instructions were emphatic. They must all, to a man, land safely in the barbed wire enclosure--right into the arms of the enemy. Then the pilot of the reconnaissance plane explained the proposed re-routing. Drop time was scheduled for no later than 4:30 a.m. the next morning. The briefing officer asked for questions. Someone quipped, "Is there an easier way to commit suicide?"

During the briefing General Eisenhower was hooked up by phone to Patton for a coded message. Williams was not told of the conversation, but in fact, Williams noticed he had never seen General

Eisenhower in such an unquiet state of mind and concluded that both the careers of Eisenhower and Patton were on the line. He heard the supreme commander tell Patton that a "light demolition crew" would be on its way in twelve hours. "They'll rescue your officers if there are any left," he told Patton.

Apparently Patton doubted that a small crew of men could handle the mission, to which Eisenhower simply replied "We'll have to wait and see."

Now, ten hours later, Col. Williams stood in the open doorway of the light converted bomber. The English jump sergeant stood behind him. In two minutes the plane would be over the target area. The pilot had told them he'd try to make it over in one pass and hoped he could recognize the landmarks in the dark. A low ceiling of fog hung in patches as the plane left the Moselle and followed the westerly branch using visible points of contact. He advised the team they were on true course and that before them the cluster of farm buildings would shortly appear in a bend of the Sur River. He announced the target was coming up below. A gentle fall of snow had not yet obliterated the icy surface of a small reflecting pond. Suddenly the target was there. The pilot fired a cartridge that, upon contact with the ground, immediately spluttered into a spreading, low-intensity, blue-green, potassium light--barely visible. It would burn for five minutes.

The jump sergeant checked out Williams' harness. The colonel felt a hand on his back and he hurled himself out into the blackness. He felt the snap of the drag cord and got the disoriented sensation that he was floating upwards. He saw the short-time flare below and steered himself in its direction. While still praying, he landed knee deep in a haystack, surrounded by what he thought to be hundreds of huge Belgian horses. He had a natural fear of horses.

For this particular mission, Col. Williams' compliment of men had been doubled on orders of Britisher General Montgomery. Hence, behind the Williams' plane a second followed. In this plane there were six tough, experienced British commandos. These men would be dropped simultaneously with the American led mission. The

British soldiers were in the full battle dress of a German Volkeg-renadiers unit operating in the area. Two of the British team were Sikhs. The entire team generally operated in silence using the lariat and the knife against an unsuspecting enemy. All spoke German and were trained using a German army manual and German in-structors, including the goose step and Nazi salute when necessary.

The Williams' team landed in various positions with Sergeant Mc-Closkey in the worst predicament--having been blown onto the small pond and falling into a chopped watering hole near the edge. Williams removed his goggles, and replaced his own glasses.

None of the new arrivals were aware that the French speaking farmer, his wife, and small children were hiding in the basement of the damaged residence,and upon hearing the commotion so early in the morning they investigated and discovered American and English voices.

Cautiously the farmer uttered a few broken words in English. The natives were given some cigarettes, chocolate, and soap, and the farmer said he was happy they were going after the Boche. He told of the huge petrol and ammo dump and drew a layout on the snow: No mention was made of the supposed massacre, but he did point out the abandoned American tanks. The farmer told how the nearby horses had hauled the petrol and ammunition across the river on the night of the 15th and all day of the 16th of December, and that work was continuing.

The British commandoes (dressed as German Volkegrenadiers) were first to leave. Their orders were to overpower and silence the perimeter guards at the barbed wire entrance to the farm. They were to take over the posts and stop at will all vehicles coming into the depot. After the perimeter was secured, two of the English group would work inside the depot enclosure and booby trap or make inoperable the American tanks and relieve Col. Williams' men in interrogating those Germans purposely allowed through the gate.

The British team left for the perimeter posts and disposed of the guards thirty minutes before Williams took off, just as dawn was breaking. Courtesy of the British Commandos, Col. Williams' team, with the exception of the colonel himself was shortly outfitted in various German uniforms, which the British commandos had brought back to the farmhouse.

As the Williams team reached the path leading to the depot, an American jeep came into view driven by a non-commissioned officer with an accompanying General. On pretense of stopping the jeep to ask questions, McCloskey and another disposed of the occupants. Williams put on the German general's oversized greatcoat but would not find a suitable German helmet till further down the path.

Moving off in their newly acquired American jeep the team observed a number of German corpses sprawled in small groups with three or four run over by tank tracks. The tracks were those of a Sherman tank. Among the frozen corpses they found a helmet big enough for Col. Williams and then started on the last lap to their destination.

The jeep stopped as they studied the terrain before them. The dump was built on a rise above the Sur River, and beyond the dump on a higher elevation than the rest stood some sheltering trees with tracks leading into the trees. Visibility was improving and enemy troops were expected to increase. Time was of the essence. Perusing the area surrounded by rolls of barbed wire, the invaders knew there was no way of escape.

McCloskey read the letter he had taken from the German general whose coat Williams was now wearing. The letter was from his headquarters giving authority to interrogate American officers held prisoner. Reading the contents of the letter to his senior officer McCloskey and Williams both agreed that some American officers were still alive in the sprawling complex ahead.

McCloskey turned again to Williams to break the silence that had developed between them after the sergeant killed the German general. McCloskey said quietly, "I had to lasso the Gerries, even though you would have taken them prisoner. You see Colonel oppression takes many brutal forms. Witness what has probably happened up ahead.

Retaliation is the only way to fight oppression--and it must be swift and simple."

Slowly the jeep ground forward. They drove in silence toward a knot of American-dressed soldiers collecting beside a cluster of tents, all dwarfed by the mountain of supplies. Each man checked his weapon. Up ahead their eyes looked hard for the enemy stationed along the dump perimeter or for the baiting of a trap upon their stopping the jeep again. They sensed that the Germans would avoid a firefight so close to the flammable petrol and ammo. They anticipated the next action would be hand-to-hand combat.

The allied group of six surmised that part of the protecting body of troops for the depot had been those dead Germans who lay behind them and that new replacements had not yet shown up. At any rate, the team thought that the Germans in control of the dump were expecting replacements for those killed up the path and that the enemy was also confident that the other guards at the barbed wire enclosure had carefully screened the new arrivals in the American jeep. They had about one hundred and fifty yards to go.

Out of the corner of their eyes the jeep occupants saw the first American casualties, which for some reason had not been bulldozed into the trench nearby and covered over. A few bodies had multiple wounds indicating they had resisted; these were fully attired. Most were stripped down to their underwear, and those deceased men had been shot in the back of their heads. Half a dozen corpses lay sprawled naked. From a tent up ahead the team heard the scream of a man's voice in pain.

Col. Williams turned and surveyed his small close-knit group headed blindly toward the huge stores of gasoline and ammunition, the very heartbeat of the German breakthrough into the Ardennes, without which enemy Panzers would lose their blitz momentum in 48 to 72 hours. Yet oddly enough,Williams had not been apprised sufficiently of the full significance of the petrol dump. He was entirely unaware that the depot was the feeder source for those German divisions overrunning American units at that very hour with minimal resistance.

The team had gotten on sight with one objective in mind--to rescue any surviving American officers and other ranks. Williams must then escape intact with the rescued after immobilizing the remaining American tanks. The possibility to blow up the dump before departure had not been made a specific order. Nevertheless, destruction of enemy supplies was a tradition among Williams' men. But regardless of alternate military objectives, the supreme task in this case was to grab the prisoners if they were still alive, and get back through unknown miles of enemy occupied territory.

As different as they were in character, Williams and McCloskey operated instinctively with each apparently comprehending what the other was about to do. McCloskey had trained the team with one thing in mind, and that was getting the job done and finding their way home safely and intact. Sir Winston Churchill had called such a quality of bravery an "unconquerable will", referring to brave people fighting tyranny. McCloskey's trainees for the present mission had never heard of unconquerable will but each man obviously possessed it, perhaps to hide his own fears.

Col. Williams had obstinately refused to call himself a soldier, because as he often said he wasn't trained for life or death combat. In truth he had weak eyes and a damaged heart and was allowed to skip the basic training because it was too arduous. Not having taken the instructions, he was not deterred from adventure because he maintained that no one was his enemy. He would shortly be tested again.

No one of military mind would hazard a suggestion that Williams' small band of dedicated men was the only alternative available for the allies to help right the present situation. No American alternative plans had been made to impede German advances made into Luxembourg within the last 48 hours, in which 200,000 German troops with more to follow, had already driven a sixty-mile wedge through American lines. Nothing seemed able to stop the determined enemy, in spite of heroic resistance that was building at many points such as Bastogne, Belgium.

Win or lose, for the Germans the Battle of the Bulge would become their last major offensive on the western front. If they won the prize would be the port of Antwerp, inflicting on the allies a devastating military crisis costing months of delay in the planned unconditional surrender and occupation of Germany proper. And if the Germans lost this strategic gamble, they would lack the will and strength to fall back and adequately defend the Fatherland

Thus, as ascertained by General Patton and his G2 Col. Koch, the petrol depot on which Col. Williams and his team had been dropped was a critical supply area necessary for the German offensive to succeed. As daylight dawned on December 18th, the Williams team was suddenly made aware that they were approaching the heart of the dump, unannounced and uninvited. It was bitter cold. Col. Williams would later note in his diary that their arrival into that area was one of the most confusing times of his military career and engendered the worst fears in him and his men.

That the Germans had taken the allies by surprise in the Ardennes offensive was belatedly acknowledged by allied intelligence. But there was a parallel crisis involving an eighteen-hour drama more relative to this chapter that the Williams' teem had to deal with decisively each time they met it. That critical problem already evident was how to recognize the enemy that was frequently dressed as Americans of all ranks. The Nazi ruse, which had caught American troops by surprise, had shocked the senior officers and infuriated the ordinary G.I. combatant. During the first two weeks of the German offensive in the Battle of the Bulge, those U.S. soldiers who faced the initial German attacks were so utterly confused that they were easily captured by default or killed outright. Because Col. Williams and his team would soon be immersed in the quandary of double identities, it is timely to explain the German apparatus of impersonating U.S. troops.

The most reliable and authentic information on the German subterfuge comes from their archives in Bon and refers to a Colonel Otto Skorzeny, officer commanding the 150th Panzer Brigade operating under General Priess of the 1st Panzer Corps.

The brigade, called Skorzeny's Commandos, operated in American uniforms. The formation was the idea of Hitler. Himler was in charge of organization over the objections of von Rundstedt, who abhorred the idea. General Westphal, von Rundstedt's chief of staff, upon special orders from Hitler also objected but recruited the men willing to serve in the special unit. The drive began in September 1944. Those qualifying with top honors had; lived in America at some time, spoke English with an American accent, and could imitate American characteristics such as chewing gum and displaying typical American casualness as opposed to Germanic stiffness of military bearing. The operation was named "Gryphon" and their first objective in Yank uniforms was to capture the Meuse River bridges above Liege after setting up temporary field headquarters in an unexpected place--a gasoline and ammo depot on the edge of the Sur River in Luxembourg.

In all, 2000 men were recruited and sent to special schools at the Friedenthal and Grafenwohr camps. Experts checked their English/American diction. They were taught to carry and chew gum, to whistle instead of clapping, and to wear American uniforms instead of German. Then they were issued American army documents, and while cussing like good Yank soldiers, they were issued American weapons. Lastly, each was given six poison tablets.

Only ten of the pseudo-G.I.s were expert in English/American. These were made instructors. One hundred and fifty who spoke school English were sent to Limbourg and Austrian prisoner-of-war camps to polish up. The remainder were taught typical swear and slang words and a few salutary expressions.

The Skorzeny Brigade was divided into three units, one infantry and two armored. They had a total of seventy German tanks camouflaged to resemble American Shermans. Once the breakthrough had taken place, the Germans reasoned that the tanks and crews would be mistaken for a column of Americans retreating. The entire legend that grew around operation Gryphon refers mainly to the headquarters company under the command of Captain Stielau, the only one fully equipped with operating American equipment, whereas the rest of the brigade operated with German equipment more or less effectively camouflaged. Stielau's company consisted of eighty men, divided into two groups. The sabotage group was in eight jeeps, the reconnaissance group in six. The latter was in turn subdivided into four short-range reconnaissance teams and two long-range teams. Each vehicle crew generally held four men: a driver, a commander, a saboteur or radio operator, and an interpreter--who above all others—spoke excellent English.

By train, the brigade left their camps for the Ardennes between December 6th and 12th. The trains only traveled at night and were guarded by day by special Gestapo units. Stielau's company was kept apart from the main body and waited at Wahn Airport near Cologne. It would pierce allied lines with the main assault forces and attach itself to a U.S. Armored Division from the 9th Army.

On the morning of the first day's offensive, eight jeeps of American G.I. imposters operating under Capt. Stielau's company successfully infiltrated through the American lines intact. Theirs was the first penetration which would create havoc among American troops for the next week and as General Omar Bradley described it, "half a million G.I.s were forced to play cat and mouse with each other every time they met on the road," Bradley himself having been arrested three times by alert sentries.

The disturbing question that bothered Patton's G2 was where was Skorzeny? As early as December 2nd, the First U.S. Army issued a report of Skorzeny's Commandos disclosing the routes that were to be taken into American lines. On December 10th the report was repeated. Unfortunately, headquarter staffs in the various army or division units refused to take the reports seriously enough to alert lower echelons. In fact, perhaps with the exception of Patton's III Army, few commanders believed there would be a German drive into Luxembourg, Belgium. The only ones to believe their report were the Counter Espionage people themselves.

Patton's G2 officer, Colonel Kroch, was the first one to report the existence of operation "Gryphon" and he seemed to have inside information, not only on the operation but also about its Commander Skorzeny. So accurate was Col. Kroch's counter-intelligence that he knew every move Skorzeny's outfit made prior to the Ardennes thrust and he even published pictures in the American Army magazine, "Signal Corps". But the G2 had lost the illusive "Skorzeny" after the December 16th breakthrough.

Skorzeny himself was easily distinguishable. Firstly, he had been seen on most cinema screens in Europe as an enormous man, with a scar reaching from his left ear to his mouth, towering over a dejected Mussolini and looking like an adventurous cavalier. He was Austrian and an SS soldier commissioned to form allied-type commando units within the German Army having made a success of such previous raids. Anyone having met Skorzeny could not forget his size or his scarred features, with the piercing dark eyes and the stare of an occultist.

As Col, Halford Williams' team approached the knot of enemy soldiers dressed in assorted American garb, a jeep suddenly pulled out from behind a tent and stopped beside the incoming jeep load of bona fide allied soldier. Two properly dressed Britishers occupied the jeep, one a full Colonel and the other his driver.

As each jeep stopped abreast of the other, Williams scrutinized the other officer carefully. The English colonel in the oncoming jeep called over to Williams in an Oxford accent, "I say, what's up gentlemen? Who is the senior officer, may I ask?" to which Williams replied simply, "I am. Why?"

The other colonel answered directly, "Where are you headed for?" to which Williams again replied with some disquiet. "It's really none of your business, mate. Let's just say we're lost and looking for the headquarters of General Patton's Third Army."

Then the newcomer spat out, "In that case Colonel you're going in the opposite direction, because that's exactly where I'm headed."

There was a moment of silence in the knot of watching Germans up ahead as the two officers exchanged words in the most critical interval of suspense since the allied team had arrived in the German camp. Colonel Williams kept his hand hidden in his newly acquired German great coat, and he had released the safety catch of his revolver pointed directly at the English officer. Williams was a crack shot, if he had to defend himself. His entire team was also in firing position. The English officer kept his eye in the area of William's concealed hand. The manpower odds between the crews were six to two, but then there was the knot of Germans up ahead nudging closer to the drama.

Finally, to end the encounter, Williams asked the other colonel to give his ID. What Williams heard totally dumfounded his reactions. The stranger spoke clearly, "I am Colonel Archibald Scott-Fox. Then gave his serial number and the current password code.

Listening intently, Col. Williams recognized that the coded number of the officer was none other than that of a bona fide agent of the OSS, trained in the united States of America during the period of Williams' own induction. The exchange of words and challenges had been short. Williams sensed he had seen the other officer before in spite of the realistic evidence that the stranger was totally out of place as an allied officer in a German redoubt. But then, reasoned Williams to himself, so was he. The departing colonel and his driver were about to take off when he called over "Good day to you Sir," and saluted.

As the strangers face came into full view of Williams, he noticed a long scar running from his left ear to his mouth and piercing eyes that stared through Col. Williams. Williams remained unaware up to that point that the "Englishman" who was departing hurriedly in an American jeep was the crafty mastermind who had tricked U.S. Gen. Morgan and his English advisor, Col. R.C. Wilson, out of their tanks and who had methodically and coldly conducted the massacre of 156 tankers. The man's real name was Colonel Otto Skorzeny, commander of the 150th Panzers, whose headquarters was nonc other than the Quonset type building less than a hundred yards ahead. It was also the ordinance depot for the collection of captured old and new American uniforms, weapons, and related supplies.

The American tank squadron captured earlier also had been unaware that it had stumbled upon the dangerous nerve center of the German fifth column complex whose assignment, after taking prisoners, was to make them undress in the open and then shoot them without mercy. Skorzeny's barbaric code was approved by Hitler but was despised and rejected by regular German command officers and troops.

Upon arrival at the Nazi fuel dump there was no expectation by Williams' rescue team that they would meet Nazis disguised as U.S. or British soldiers. In the aftermath of the episode, Skorzeny was unable to talk his way past the tough British commandos holding the entrance to the dump, but shortly after capture he escaped. How Skorzeny was able to use the OSS code number of a bona fide agent has not been learned, but it is known that Britain's M1 Service later found the traitors who had betrayed the current password code to Skorzeny. These persons were accused of treason with the enemy and dealt with in a manner unknown, but presumably shot in Secret.

The growing knot of Germans, now swelled to over twenty-five, stood menacingly in mixed American outfits blocking the jeep-load of allied soldiers dressed as Germans. The Williams team did not yet realize that those ahead massacred Patton's tankers. In turn, the true Nazis waited suspiciously, trying to decide whether the oncoming jeep-load of apparent Germans was legitimate.

As McCloskey wheeled the allied jeep closer towards the knot of Skorzeny commandos, now about 100 feet ahead, what was about to happen had been repeated with variations dozens of times in the previous forty-eight hours, as allied soldiers met Germans disguised as Americans. However, on this confrontation the teams were matched--each side was impersonating the other. Hence, the uncertainty among all participants was; who was friend or who was foe. On this occasion the winners would be the survivors.

McCloskey moved the jeep to a full stop, jumped out and took the offensive by waving a letter of authority taken from the deceased General.

Speaking German he yelled, "My general, the G2 is mad," as he pointed to a glowering Williams dressed as the German officer in question. "He says your security is rotten. We haven't been challenged once for ID since we got into this area." The sergeant put his hands on his hips, spread his legs in a defiant stance and called out, "Who's in charge of this regiment?"

Out stepped a one star general who saluted, turning towards Williams who returned the salute. Then, addressing "General" Williams in German he responded decisively, "Sir! I'm in charge here. You may think us lax in our security but we've been busy the last thirty-six hours as you can see by the skirmish. We haven't yet buried our own dead or had time to toss all the enemy into a common grave," he said pointing in the direction of the American corpses and the bulldozed trench.

McCloskey interrupted him by first turning to Williams. "Pardon my questioning this officer Sir, but may I continue for a moment?" to which Williams, watching McCloskey's expression, nodded approval. The sergeant continued in German.

"Here you stand wearing American uniforms and not one of you can speak English." The German general turned and called out in German to a sergeant who spoke up saying, "I'm the English speaking G.I.," he stammered. "I did the interrogating of the prisoners."

"Excellent," spoke McCloskey in German. "How many prisoners are left? If you shot the senior officers, I assure you my General will have you all court marshaled in twenty-four hours. He needs to question them personally about American intentions in the Bastogne region."

The German Nazi replied, "Don't worry. We saved the commanding general, two colonels and sixteen other officers. They're lying on the ground in the first tent, tied up in their underwear. We've had some fun with those bastards. Col. Skorzeny, who just left, said we couldn't get any more information out of them. I agree. Anyway, they're nearly frozen to death. But they're back there if you want to work them over"

McCloskey turned and rambled off several sentences to Williams in German, repeating what the sergeant had said so that the German general standing at the head of the Nazis could hear his entire words. As he spoke, McCloskey interjected his sentences with unkind oaths about the enemy lying in the tent. Williams, not understanding a word of the dialogue, realized McCloskey was playing for time and consequently nodded in agreement. He realized he now must make his move or they would lose their initiative of surprise.

Slowly Williams got out of the jeep and keeping his eyes on the cluster of Nazis he pointed his finger in admonition toward the German officer. Two members of the allied team also got out and walked to the side of the enemy cluster in apparent boredom. One man, Corporal Erbstien, dressed as a German Major, whittled a piece of wood with his knife, muttering in German for all to hear. The Germans became surrounded with two men at their backs, two in front and one in the jeep who stood up on cue.

All enemy eyes looked at Williams, confused by the visitor's delay in speaking and showing consternation at his pugilistic manner of finger pointing at a fellow officer. The enemy waited for the tongue-lashing.

McCloskey looked at Williams for the countdown to move and, sensing timing was right, he hollered in German to the senior officer. "We know none of you are really Germans--you're Americans. We've been warned to watch out for you impersonators."

Suddenly in exasperation, the one star German general, confronted by Williams' silent denunciation and McCloskey's accusation, lashed back in German. "No! We're Germans also--to a man--the same as you sergeant. This is a German depot staffed by Germans. The real Americans are those prisoners inside the tent and the dead ones you see on the ground."

There was a short pause as no one spoke. Williams's intuition told him to make haste. He looked at his men. They were all in position.

Then Col. Williams turned to the German who spoke flawless English. "Swine! Order that gang of yours to put their hands in the air and no delay or we'll blow your heads off, one by one--just like you murdered our men yesterday!" The Nazi looked around and saw five automatic weapons turned toward the group. While Williams had gotten the enemy's attention from the front, his men had moved into position, and on cue from Williams, opened their coats and exposed their weapons.

The German sergeant advised his group to raise their arms. AS enemy eyes turned, they saw they were covered with automatics.

On Williams' order, the bilingual German sergeant passed on the command for the Germans to advance ten paces. Startled, they all complied, including the general.

Sergeant McCloskey and Corporal Erbstien disarmed the enemy.

From the nearest tent came moans and cries as Col. Williams and another of his team hurried under the canvas. There they found the American officers, bound hands and feet, lying on the ground with frostbitten extremities. None responded. The two rescuers removed the ropes from the victims saying encouraging words to each. As each was freed the ropes were thrown outside to bind their Nazi captors.

The task of securing the enemy was completed in fifteen minutes. Then Corporal Erbstien dressed them down in perfect German, "If I had my way," he bantered, "I'd get rid of you all, but our commander takes prisoners--even animals." The corporal continued. "My home is in New York. I'm a Jew and I hate Nazis. I was a boy of fifteen when I first found out about Hitler and his Nazis. I was visiting Prague, Czechoslovakia in 1937 when Hitler's SS goons, gangsters like you, moved in. I saw them murder my grandparents." As the Jewish corporal talked he stood over some of the prostrate enemy, now cowering in defeat. Drawing his knife he finished his tirade against Hitler's legions and boasted calmly. "My family is kosher butchers. I like working with the knife. If any of you should move a hand, I'll cut you to pieces. Try me swine!"

Inside the tent, Col. Williams addressed the Americans laying about in various stages of hypothermal exposure. There was gentleness to his voice as he said for all to hear. "We're here to rescue you at the request of General Patton. So hang on friends--the ordeal is nearly over."

A lone voice coughed out the almost inaudible words, "Say it again!" and Williams repeated the colloquial American slang, "Hang in there, man."

From the stiffened form comes the response. "That's American talk for sure."

Williams moved over to the young man and reassured him. "I'm Colonel Williams, OSS." The boyish officer was crying.

McCloskey came into the tent. Pulling out a bottle of Scotch, he lifted the soldier's head and tipped the bottle slowly to the boy's lips. Looking over the situation he said, "Colonel, let me take over here. I've run into cases like this in India."

McCloskey stoked the fire under a forty-gallon drum of hot water outside the tent. Then he found a bale of German blankets. Improvising a table as a workbench, they placed kerosene heaters in the proximity and lifted each of the helpless men onto the table and wrapped them one by one in blankets dipped in hot water. Someone found a case of real Scotch whiskey in ordinance stores, and this was administered to tranquilize those in pain. McCloskey put wet, hot socks onto their feet and wrapped each man in another dry blanket. The sergeant and another team member kept this resuscitation method going all morning. In this manner the allied officers were kept alive in spite of the languor from freezing.

The Nazi prisoners who were considered Skorzeny's men, and who had killed the Americans twenty-four hours earlier, were left on the cold ground fully clothed--in below zero weather. By 9 a.m. came the decision on when and how the allied team would vacate the depot and retreat to the rendezvous southwest of Bastogne.

One hundred and fifty-seven exposed American corpses were counted lying on the ground and in the trench. The Nazi prisoners stated that over twenty-five others had volunteered to teach Skorzeny's students a crash course in U.S. army jargon. They were taken away in a German half-track to Bitburg. These men accepted the assignment rather than be killed. Records show that when they arrived at the military school they taught the Germans words and military information that was so misleading it later implicated the Germans when they infiltrated American units. It is not known how many of these men survived the petrol dump massacre of December 17, 1944.

When Col. Williams asked the names of the commanding General, his two colonels, as well as the English observer officers, all refused to give their full names, in spite of their gratitude.

Within two hours of arrival at the depot, the English commandos came down in pairs and began immobilizing the Sherman tanks so that the enemy would not be able to use them. Taking land mines and hand grenades (potato mashers) from the ammo supplies they booby-trapped many machines. On orders from Col. Williams, three tanks and a German officer's car were made ready in which to flee.

At 9 a.m. Col. Williams spoke to his men and the British commandos guarding the perimeter. He referred to the "reality of our predicament" saying that because their presence had not yet been discovered by any of the surrounding German units, that they would not withdraw until the American officers were fit for travel and could help plan an escape route. The sergeant in charge of the British cadre advised that an armored column could never break through German lines to allied territory. Invited to join such a dash to freedom, each of the British team refused "to run the German gauntlet". However, they gave assurance they would protect the perimeter until withdrawal at which time they would strike out alone through enemy lines.

An earlier search of the entire depot had uncovered no other personnel except an NCO signaler in an operations vehicle. A nasty incident had occurred when Cpl. Erbstien and Col. Williams overpowered the signaler. The man had his choice of dying on the spot or cooperating with the allied takeover team. Corporal Erbstien was a Western Union expert in Morse code and worked a fast key. He had learned his trade in New York and served in the service at Ultra in England where the allies had broken the German code system. Hence, finding the official German codebook with all the German units listed on that battlefront, Erbstien was able to relieve the German signaler with confidence. The enemy soldier was made to quickly understand the wisdom of life versus death.

Among Col. Williams' orders that he read after arrival at the depot, under "accomplish if possible", was one simply called "G". It stated that if an enemy supply depot were located, destroy same if possible before retiring or escaping. Thus it was evident after conferring with his group of twelve, Williams had to make a major decision, stay or leave.

Consensus of opinion was to evacuate immediately but this judgment was tempered with some sober observations. One, they were surrounded by the enemy on all sides. They were, in fact, one small pocket operating an enemy depot without being recognized. They knew depot continuance was an essential part of the overall German military apparatus of 200,000 troops blitzing westward almost unopposed into allied lines. Only a few hundred yards to the east, directly behind them across the Sur River in Germany proper, were another 400,000 troops and armor moving from reserve to active positions on the new Ardennes front.

On the positive side, if it could be considered positive, there were some strong facts showing the team should remain in place. Col. Williams regarded these aspects with some hope.

For instance, the British team had replaced the original guard troops after "removing" them with lariat or knife. But their occupation as depot guardians was at best precarious; because, only being eight men, a company of enemy troops with fixed bayonets and a few grenades could dislodge them.

As morning grew, the perimeter commandos lent a couple of men to help at the depot proper immobilizing the American tanks and filling needed gaps. The two teams, divided into couples, took turns in directing the incoming petrol or ammo wagons being hauled from German train cars and tankers on the enemy side of the Sur. The delivery of these critical supplies into the depot therefore was running smoothly, indicating the horse and wagon drivers had not recognized the foreigners.

However, there was one imponderable problem that required a constant eye. A German engineering corps was building a railroad Y and spur line to the depot from the Esterback-Luxembourg main line. The sounds of steel against steel and noise of machinery grew closer by the hour. The project was currently less than a quarter mile from a depot-loading platform. Unknown to Col. Williams or his team, the spur was to have been completed and in operation on the hour of their arrival that very morning; but, because the crews had been taken off to repair a break in the main line caused by allied bombs, the spur would be one day late in being completed. This fact was considered a good omen for staying longer. At noon a dispatch rider had come in with a message that the spur would he ready for operation at 6 a.m. on the 19th of December and to expect shipments to begin. The message returned to the railway general was "All is ready."

In his final deliberation whether to stay or leave, Williams sought Cpl. Erbstien's judgment on when he would get a reliable picture of front line panzer units urgently inquiring about the late arrival of supplies. The corporal believed the supply picture at the front would be evident by nightfall. He added that between the messages arriving from rear service corps and front line units, he would be able to pinpoint fairly accurately the disposition of the enemy and mark same on the map, Sgt. McCloskey would extract and pinpoint similar information from dispatch riders and lorry drivers coming before him, filling in approximate positions of enemy fighting units.

It was 10 a.m. Col. Williams weighed the pros and cons of the dilemma, then he passed word to Sergeant McCloskey: "We hold till dark." McCloskey requested that rank be forgotten and replied, "What else is on your mind? I see you want to talk--so talk!"

Williams came right to the point in response and said, "It's a mute question if we can hold out here the rest of the day. You were right Sergeant when this morning you said, "kill or be killed." Staying alive will tax all our faculties, so I'm asking you to set aside for now my 'love your enemy golden rule' which I'm forever reminding you about. Our mission here today is the big worry at both Patton's and Supreme HQ in London. No, we are not in a big battle, but it's the most decisive undertaking on the entire western front at present. For each of us it's our own little war. To win it, we'll have to depend on one thing--gut instinct of survival."

Williams continued. "From this moment McCloskey, we can only exist under primeval law. Remember! It was you who coined the phrase. Your friends, the Brits, don't take prisoners--they've probably eliminated over twenty Germans already. They survive by McCloskey's primeval law. So, Sergeant, pass the word around."

Interrupting his officer, the Scottish Sergeant-Major asked what should be done when the heavy German trucks come in for petrol or ammo. Before Williams could reply McCloskey exclaimed, "Pardon my ignorance! I know the answer. It's primeval law. The Brits let the Gerry drivers through the gate but we make sure they never leave."

Thirteen heavy enemy lorries would arrive during the day to be loaded with gas or ammo for their units. However, it was decided that when motorcycle dispatch riders appeared with requests for delivery schedules or the depot's location, the riders would be permitted to depart with false points of reference or whatever ambiguous message was thought best. Twelve dispatch riders came and left.

Twelve noon: The camp was still intact. No allied losses had occurred. The teams of horse drawn wagons continued to move vast quantities of petrol and ammo onto the site. Williams estimated the distance between the petrol depot and the German ordinance was one mile, with the river being the halfway point. Thus, each team and their drivers were closely checked through field glasses. All seemed well.

Col. Williams asked McCloskey for a report on the American prisoners. What he heard he did not like. The Sergeant stated that the men should be hospitalized under proper medical care. None of the badly frozen Americans were able to stand or take food. The only liquid was the odd sip of whiskey. The wet, hot blanket treatment was still being applied by one of the team members. Then McCloskey threw the curve to Williams.

"The OC will not be able to drive his lead tank back to allied lines, even if they were just across the river. Neither will his two senior officers." McCloskey ended his diagnosis. "The whole bunch of Americans will be a liability to us." With that pronouncement, McCloskey threw the matter of accountability to his senior officer. "Who's going to drive the tanks and who knows how to get us out of here?" Visibly agitated, Williams replied. "I'm uncertain how to save them or even liberate us."

The Nazi prisoners were taken into one of the tents, out of sight from prying eyes and placed off the cold ground. Rebellious attitudes were noticed among two or three of the Nazis.

The cold was penetrating. River ice was tested for strength and found to be twelve inches thick. As masters of the German depot, they requisitioned dry gloves, socks and underwear to keep warm. McCloskey laid claim to the whiskey for the invalid Americans.

The sounds of the railway spur gangs grew louder by the hour, and at 2 p.m. a British commando was posted between the railway gangs and the proposed depot terminal. Creeping close to the work crews, the commando heard them say that the expected time to join up with the depot would be 3 a.m. the next morning, possibly an hour sooner.

Vigilance was stressed as tensions rose, but throughout the daylight hours the gasoline and ammo dump functioned smoothly to all appearances. During his free moments of thought, Col. Williams contrived diverse ways to affect their withdrawal. But he saw no feasible plan to vacate their salient. The young officer therefore called a short session with his two sergeants a half hour before dark to decide how to leave the depot without the Germans knowing.

Williams began, "Were all trapped in this petrol dump--although we run it there's still no way to escape. I'm trying to reach an accord among us as to when and how we can escape. I think it's best to delay our departure till later in the night," McCloskey the older soldier asked, "Have you got a particular time in mind for getting out of this bloody mess?" Exasperated, Williams uttered a courageous "No! But I'm working on it." Then he reviewed their position.

"Delivery of gas and ammo from the German supply center across the river has stopped for the day. No more lorries are arriving from front line units to pick up deliveries. Those slow-ups may be normal. But I'm worried about that Englishman who left in a hurry. He wasn't English and I'm sure he knew we weren't Nazis. Furthermore, we've eliminated over forty guards and truck drivers during the day. Their arrivals back at their units are long overdue. Questions are being asked higher up I know, and Gerry suspicions point right here to this depot. Repeat signals inquiring about missing drivers and their badly needed loads already confirm this. The only unanswered question is from where will they rush us when they attack, and when."

Concurrence of the three was not to expect an immediate assault. Sergeant McCloskey advised it would likely be launched around 4 a.m. because the enemy (not certain of the number of infiltrators into the depot) would anticipate that half would be asleep during the final hours of darkness.

The threesome determined that withdrawal preparations should commence at once. Guards were doubled on the river crossing and at the railway spur right-of-way being finished. McCloskey took charge of setting the depot for blowing at twelve midnight. Two other team members would comfort the half frozen American officers and also prepare them for the road. McCloskey and a Brit would prepare three Sherman tanks and a German officers' car for the getaway.

Col. Williams would set the escape route, which he acknowledged was the only weak point in the plan. The team had not recognized any imminent sense of danger during the day, but this satisfaction became one of apprehension as darkness set in. Succeeding incidents, reflecting a change of enemy behavior, increased the apprehension.

At 8 a.m., still alert but without sleep for forty-eight hours, the team heard screams for outside help come from the Nazi tent of prisoners. They lasted thirty seconds before the guard rushed back in and shut him up. McCloskey was also alerted and followed on the heels of the private G.I. As the Nazi was silenced he swore arrogantly at the two allied men. Loading him in the jeep, the allies drove the troublemaker down to the field of corralled horses mingling in close quarters. They pulled the protesting officer out, intending to heave him over the fence to be trampled beneath the big draft animals.

The sound of muffled whinnying filled the night air as McCloskey freed the prisoner's mouth, and they grabbed him by the ankles and shoulders. "One...two...three and." Suddenly, in German, McCloskey heard the man entreat for his life. "In my coat is a picture of my wife and children. Please, don't let me die this way! They made me do what I did. Please..." McCloskey counted one...two...and dropped his end of the victim. They took him back then threw him rudely into the tent.

Williams watched in surprise as McCloskey returned the prisoner. Williams the pacifist queried, "You planned to kill him. What happened? Did the horses kick him out?"

McCloskey barked, "I'm not the judge of his guilt," and strode off.

The time was 9:30 p.m.

McCloskey and another team member, Sgt. James Luellan, were busy searching for "explosive black powder" among the German stores when strange German voices were heard arguing nearby. Shortly, from the vicinity of the railroad spur, there appeared two German officers with hands raised striding in front of one of the team's guards. McCloskey checked their arm patches and noticed they did not belong to the Engineer Company.

The senior German officer demanded why he had been stopped, disarmed and brought in as though he were among enemies. Then he demanded by what authority was the depot "out of bounds."

"I don't like your insolence," he swore out at McCloskey. Then without warning, he made a lunge for the expert in Judo, the knife, and the lariat. The two German investigating officers were subdued. Their bodies were dragged in among the ammunition cases. Sgt. McCloskey sent his guard back to the post and reported to Col. Williams."The Gerries have made their first move to find out how many are in control of the dump. We had better speed things up mon."

At 10 p.m. a French-speaking member of the team was sent to the farmhouse inviting the farmer and his family to join the team when they departed. The man took the farmer a case of choice French wines found in the German officers' mess tent. The French-speaking farmer thanked the emissary but declined to leave through enemy lines, saying he would rather take his chances in the cellar of his own home. He was reminded that when the dump blew, the horses would stampede and besides the heat from the gasoline inferno, shells would burst at random, even into his house. The team soldier said, "Monsieur, if you stay, you realize it will be hell that breaks out." The two men shook hands and the French-speaking member of William's team said, "My commander wishes you good luck. Bon soir." They parted.

While the farm family was being invited to escape with the team, Col. Williams, who had put off further interrogating the senior officers of Patton's armored column, went into the tent and sat beside General Mike Morgan for a second occasion. Not knowing his real identity, Williams began.

"General, will you verify my rendezvous instructions as to the reference at which I'm to come in contact with General Patton's nearest outpost?" Williams showed the ailing, feeble man a map and pointed with his finger to the said map reference. The senior officer nodded approval.

Williams continued speaking quietly. "Our plans are to move out at midnight. Would you take command of the withdrawal group with your own tank in the lead?" There was a prolonged silence and a weak voice came back. "You're in charge Colonel. I'm not capable. I have confidence in you to get us through."

With difficulty in speaking, the general asked how Williams' team had been put together and on whose request. Williams told the ailing officer he had been sent on request of General Patton and the Supreme Commander, General Eisenhower. "We were flown over from England and fought our way into the depot with the sole purpose of rescuing you General, and your men," to which the general shed a tear, thanked Williams, and finished by saying, "Then you're not familiar with the frontlines?" and Williams replied, "No."

The general continued slowly and almost inaudibly. "When I brought my tanks through, the enemy had not consolidated his advances. By now he likely has. There's a shortcut to the map reference you show, but I doubt if you'd ever make it. There's a critical bridge or two to cross and by now wherever we drive the enemy will be prepared." I'm sure he's got his heavy assault guns and tank variants in place by now. It would take battle-hardened, full tank crews to get us through by direct routing."

Asked what the alternative was, the general replied that he couldn't propose a safe withdrawal. Williams rose and paced the ground.

When Williams sat down again the general told him some of the briefing information he had received from Patton's G2, Col. Koch, before leaving two nights earlier. In effect, he said that if they got away in time the safest way might be by detouring into Germany proper. He said across the river there were many divisions preparing to move into Luxembourg and Belgium and that during darkness, the allied tanks might get through in the confusion, first by going east and then south. He didn't know how to get back out of Germany, but supposed the Thionville Bridge would be the most likely escape route. Williams thanked the general who seemed to get weaker as he spoke. Williams gave orders to get the officers ready for loading. He ordered two or three pairs of dry German socks be put on each man and that each be wrapped in two blankets. Blanket bedding was to be placed in the tanks.

It was 10:15 p.m. Over fifty miles away, General Patton ordered a six-tank column assembled to search for the missing allied team from which no word had been heard since they were dropped 18 hours earlier.

Col. Williams gave instructions to his men. "We will start loading at 11 p.m. We finish by 11:30. We move out at midnight."

What's the routing?" asked McCloskey. Williams replied, "As of this moment the general direction will be into Germany. Get back into the prisoner's tent and talk to that officer you saved. Without finishing him off, find the concession going east between the two nearest German divisions. That's the road we'll take once we cross the river." McCloskey replied, "How do we cross the river on twelve inches of ice?"

There was a slight fuzz of snow tumbling aimlessly down. The breeze had died. Except for the sounds of steel on steel to the west, all seemed quiet. Williams glanced toward the river from which no wagon sleighs had crossed in over three hours. On the Germen shore of the frozen water, the land rose abruptly ten to fifteen feet through which the German wagon sleighs had cut a gentle slope onto the ice. On the side of the twenty-five foot slope, the banks still jutted up in sharp contrast. Two of the allied team had established a lookout at that point on the German side of the river to watch German activity. The lookouts could signal from beneath the steep banks without the enemy observing.

As Williams visually checked out the post he saw six quick flashes of light, a short pause, and the signals repeated. The Germans were sending a convoy of six sleighs across the river and into the depot. Williams acknowledged the signals. He realized he had no time to recall the forward observation team. He couldn't bring in his men from the railway spur because the rail line was getting too close. Cpl. Erbstien and one other guard would have to be left in place because of the German signalman. It was too late to ask for help from the Brit commandos at the main entrance. Col. Williams asked McCloskey for a defense report. Including himself and Sgt. McCloskey he had four men to stop an attack. He thought six sleighs would have at least twelve men and he was convinced that delivery of material was a secondary. The teams were bringing in Germans to recapture the depot.

Instinctively he figured the Germans would appear as friends, therefore they would not make a hostile move till they left their sleighs, What their plan would be after that, Williams could only guess. He assembled his men and waited.

The allies heard the occasional "whoa" and "giddy up" in German as the horses came closer. McCloskey had lit two six-ounce cans of potato alcohol at the entrance to the pathway leading past piles of crated ammo on one side, and the Gerry cans on the other. He stood out alone between the burning cans and raised his hand to stop the first team. Unknown to the teamsters, McCloskey was amply covered by the three other members hiding behind the crates.

It was customary to stop the teamsters to direct them where the load should be placed. McCloskey approached the two drivers of the sleigh and asked whether petrol or ammo. The reply came back that all the loads contained ammunition.

McCloskey apologized for asking if any were smoking and was answered with an oath and a statement that the drivers all knew the rules. The Scottish sergeant apologized again, explaining that there had been a serious leakage of gasoline across the track up ahead and he could take no chances of fire.

One driver in particular seemed to do all the talking and McCloskey noticed he spoke with authority and took him to be the officer in charge of the so-called teamsters. The head teamster asked, "Where are your helpers?" to which McCloskey replied yawning, "They're all getting some sleep--we didn't expect any more loads tonight." The drivers noted the lax security.

Following McCloskey's direction, the six teams drew up tightly together and each pair of drivers hopped briskly down after tying the reins. They were to unload on the left of the path. As they jumped to the ground McCloskey observed each had a weapon beneath his coat. They began to move up and form a group to unload the first wagon sleigh and supposedly would repeat this down the line till all the ammunition was placed on the ground as directed by McCloskey.

All present saw that the last team had not drawn up right. In fact, it stood beyond the burning petrol cans and the drivers were obscured by darkness. The German teamster yelled at them to move up. They didn't respond. Angered, he ran back to the last conveyance and disappeared in the shadow of horses and boxes. There was a brief interlude as everyone waited and the last team finally moved forward. The horses stopped and two drivers jumped down. Each landed on the hard ground ready for combat. Their automatic weapons were aimed into the group of nine teamsters. McCloskey, standing to one side, recognized his own men and he drew his weapon. From the crates there emerged Col. Williams and two other members of his team. Six automatics were trained on the surprised drivers.

As the Germans were made to remove their outer coats, one at a time, it was revealed they all were equipped with knives and automatics. The two allied commandos had revealed they boarded the last wagon sleigh as it came down the slope from the German side. Creeping to the front of the wagon, they had taken the two enemies, dropped their bodies to the side, and took their place. In the same way they took the inquiring teamster.

Sergeant McCloskey congratulated them and said gruffly, "Thanks, you're one up on me."

Williams lined up the enemy soldiers. They were all members of Skorzeny's 150th Brigade. Sending a replacement to guard the Germen signaler, Williams called Cpl. Erbstien from the signals truck and told him to give the Germans verbal hell. Williams went up to one of the drivers and shoved his hat back on his head. Then he ran his hand over his chin. There was hardly a beard. "How old are you?" asked Williams and the driver replied in English, "Sixteen Sir! I was drafted out of high school for this job because I have book English." Williams replied, "Curse Hitler--you're just a boy, just a boy."

Williams had Erbstien scribble out a note in German. That note, still in German archives, said somewhat as follows: "We all know about you Col. Skorzeny and what you did to Americans at this depot. I am sending this boy back to you and if any of your men are ever caught again by us we will kill them without mercy. Signed, Col. Halford Williams, U.S. Army." Williams placed the note in the boy's shirt pocket. He pointed the group to a copse of trees away from the river and ordered them to run. As the enemy started out Williams told his men to fire over their heads or behind them. The boy with the note stumbled and fell. One of Williams' men trained his weapon on him and Williams pulled it down in anger. Slowly the boy got up, found out he was still alive, and ran into the trees.

Cpl. Erbstien turned to Col. Williams and said, "Sir, you've just signed all our death warrants." With that he stamped off to the signals truck. It was 11:15 p.m.

Williams ordered the allied officers to be placed in the three tanks. McCloskey left to complete his preparations to ignite the depot. The two Sur River guards went back to their posts to watch for the next German move. The colonel sent word to the two other outposts for thc men to leave their posts at 11:30 sharp. Then he knocked on the door of the signals truck and entered.

Erbstien handed Williams two of the repeat messages he had been receiving all evening. One said in effect: "Two teamster trucks reached the depot. Failed to return. State problem. Give answer before report is made to Corps."

Williams scribbled out a message to Erbstien for transmittal over the wire. It said, "Sorry Sir, the horses are sick." The corporal read the message and looked at Williams and remonstrated. "You're not serious," to which Williams assured him he was. As the message was tapped out, Williams burst out laughing. "Don't wait for the reply," Williams finally said. "Give me the next message." The lack of sleep was finally getting to Williams, a frail man.

The German Panzer commander had asked for accountability for what he said was the last time before he called for troops to investigate the treasonable drunks at the depot. Cpl. Erbstien turned to the commander and asked what would the answer be this time. The colonel replied, "Send this: Your petrol just went up in flames." Signed, "Love, General George S. Patton," Williams laughed again. Then they all ran outside. As Erbstien cut the wires leading to the signals truck, the hands of the German signaler were tied and his feet hobbled. Then they all hurried back to the waiting tanks. Not one of the team believed Williams when he ordered the twenty-five German Nazis to be placed in the tanks. The colonel made the order clear.

It was now 11:40 p.m. McCloskey had poured the black powder fuse, and a forty foot ugly worm crawled into the depot and disappeared among the stacks of Gerry cans.

The Nazi prisoners, properly tied, were secured within the three escape tanks as well as the invalided American officers. Onto the lead tank they had attached the German officer's car, a trophy that Col. Williams had demanded must accompany their flight.

The two leaders stood momentarily beside the command tank, motors were started and preliminary instructions provided. Together, Williams and McCloskey looked around at the depot they had held since early morning, increased in volume by many tons of fresh deliveries.

Scattered in front of their vision they glanced at the unburied American dead, now covered with a dusting of light snow hiding the features of the men and the scars and bloodstains of death. In the trees beyond they were aware that more soldiers lay killed, these being Germans. In total there were over 200 corpses strewn about. Probably anticipating a remark by Williams, McCloskey reminded the officer that they had come to save the living and time would not permit them to bury the dead.

The two men mounted the tank and lowered themselves inside among sixteen other humans mostly in stages of despair or pain. Sgt. Luellan had lit the tail of the black powder worm and it squirmed and wove its way toward the depot of flammable supplies. As the fuse was about to disappear into the mountain of gas and ammo, McCloskey took one of 300 German hand-grenades he had stowed aboard the tanks. Raising himself up he tossed it deep into the petrol dump. Experience should have stopped him. What was to have been an unhurried departure, as the cans ignited slowly, became instead a roaring explosion--then a chain reaction. Almost before McCloskey could lower the hatch and secure same, the sky rained fiery metal and blazing gasoline. Before the tanks could navigate toward the perimeter, they were sitting immobile beside a raging inferno.

Up at the farmhouse, Piere Bouchardt, heard the whinnying of horses pastured nearby, saw the flames envelop the night sky, heard the whoosh of air and debris, and ran into the basement as shells from the depot began to explode.

In the commander's winter-chilled tank were General Morgan, Col. Williams, and Sergeant Major McCloskey, plus a mixture of prisoners and patients wrapped in German blankets. They had hoped the general could drive the tank but in a matter of seconds upon being deposited in the seat, the general broke down.

Williams, in exasperation took over, recalling that he had driven a tank only once in his life and that time briefly. As McCloskey pulled down the hatch and secured same, those inside the tank heard sudden muffled explosions and were aware that the tank was no longer ice cold. From the aperture lookout they saw liquid fire falling on the tank's surfaces as the interior was lit up with a beam of intense light coming through the front slit. In less than two minutes they all felt the heat.

Williams pulled back the gear lever and the tank lurched backwards to the edge of the inferno. Ill as he was and overcome with pain, General Morgan feebly instructed Williams to change gears to forward and this Williams was able to do. Now the top surfaces of the tank were further embellished with flaming debris.

McCloskey eased the general into the seat beside Williams and tipped a shot of whiskey down his throat. Still swathed in blankets and heavy socks the ailing commander showed Williams how, by turning the steering wheel left or right, the tank's direction responded accordingly. The tank literally rolled over the last wagon loads of materials brought over from Germany proper only an hour earlier. Inside the boxes was not ammunition but bales of American G.I. clothing to be used by Skorzeny's commandos in the intervening days.

Corporal Erbstien, with the help of the most able survivor, drove the second tank and another member of the team did likewise on the last one.

Increasing speed, the three desperate men managed to get their tank underway, and Williams steered it erratically down the wagon tracks toward the river. The riverbank was dead ahead when the blazing tank bore down the grade toward the ice barrier. General Morgan managed a stifled yell to raise the main gun to maximum trajectory. Out onto the twelve inches of solid ice, the sixteen-ton machine headed for the cut in the bank 150 feet away on the far side of the river.

Because of motor and tank noise no one was able to hear the cracking of the ice as the tank edged onto the river's fragile covering of frozen water. The vehicle had left the bank and was fully on the twelve-inch ice when the first reaction occurred. With a heavy jolt the tank fell through the ice shaking and scattering all the occupants. Each tried to hang onto metal. What surprised all was that the expected rush of river water through the seams did not happen.

Colonel Williams, still driving, heard from outside and below noise of pebbles and stones grinding under the metal tracks as they moved deeper into the river bottom. On top of the tank they listened to huge chunks of ice hitting the structure with loud bangs and then cascading off. One large piece of jagged ice lodged itself beneath the barrel of the gun. The motors on the Sherman never spluttered.

Like a giant can opener the projecting gun piece cut through the ice. As the water deepened, the flaming fire on top of the machine died out, and scalloped sections of twelve-inch-thick ice continued to bang and slide across the top. They reckoned the river depth in the center was five feet as Williams apprehensively kept reassuring himself the twin motors would not stall. Beside him the feeble General Morgan quietly gave implicit instructions.

The lead vehicle came up on the other shore. They were inside Germany proper. With fires extinguished and metal cooled, McCloskey opened the hatch and easily discerned the two allied sentries posted on the German side. The commander's tank ground to a brief halt and their team member quickly came aboard. The commando of the British group declined to join them and instead elected to escape with his own team. They too would later steal Nazi transport.

A reconnaissance plane sent over the dumpsite by Gen. Patton reached the area just after the allied team had left. The pilot reported the entire area lit up in a blazing inferno that turned the night into day. The pilot also reported three of the thirty-three U.S. Shermans missing from an earlier aerial count. Gen. Patton exclaimed, "Something's going on that nobody can figure out. What the H can it be?"

As Williams' tank again accelerated up the fifteen-foot cut in the bank they saw the two follow-up tanks break into the river and plunge into the path of broken ice. Up ahead, what had been darkness at midnight was all light. As agreed beforehand they headed for the first German railway cars now silhouetted brightly, the same cars from which the gasoline and ammunition had been moved to the depot during the previous day.

A mile from the blazing inferno that they had started, the explosions of the various ammo crates could be heard. Confused quartermaster store men came running out of Quonset huts but were more preoccupied with the fire and explosions than the tanks driving through their compound. Williams bypassed the rail cars and, followed closely by his two cohorts, he struck a path along the railway tracks through the opening in the Siegfried Line, formerly the old Franco Prussian forts called the West Wall. Once through the wall they had cleared the second major obstacle with the other Shermans following wildly.

The Nazi officer prisoner, whom McCloskey had not thrown to be trampled by the horses, explained the routing that should be attempted, although his comments were that none of them would make it out of Germany alive. Nevertheless the German directed them west, seeking the Bitburg/Trier Highway, intending to follow it southerly where possible. West of Tier they would cross the Luxembourg Highway, and for a second time attempt to find their way through the winding Siegfried Line of forts as well as across the Mosel River. Heading southwest while still in Germany, (if they were still mobile and alive) they would seek a border crossing into France between the cities of Chengan and Merzig. If the tanks succeeded in getting that far past impossible obstacles, both natural and man made, their next objective would be westwards to Thionville, France. However, once that far their last obstacle would be the French Maginot Line. Of course, McCloskey did not translate the complete routing to Williams for reasons of hopelessness. Williams was to remember only that they crossed the Siegfried Line twice, he thought, passed between flanks of two resting German divisions, crossed and re-crossed the Mosel River and used railway lines wherever possible.

It was soon apparent that German divisions in the reserve area through which they must travel had broken radio silence judging by the increase in small arms fire. They knew then the hunt for them was on. A German tank column preceded by half tracks and motor bikes made it necessary for the allied tanks, on more than one occasion, to bivouac and wait out passage of the enemy. Returning to the main artery too soon, they once took more small arms fire and felt the impact of heavier shells. But there was no movement of infantry. In spite of body warmth from the people, Williams would remember only the cold penetrating his 140 pounds of weight.

The sky continued bright for many miles but they were unaware that German citizens as far away as Trier, Prum, and Bitburg clearly saw the night sky erupt with bright colors, as did the French in Metz. An orderly woke General Patton at his Third Army headquarters outside of Bastogne, and the general, hurrying into the night, observed the brightness and correctly surmised the great German petrol dump south of Echternach was on fire and out of human control. He felt a justification for his action in sending the 32nd Armored Division to the depot, even though he gravely doubted the outcome of the foray. He had never heard of Col. Williams and was more concerned with the six man tank group he had sent earlier in the night to find the Williams team now believed overcome by the enemy. He presumed his latest tanks fired the dump and had dismissed the presupposition that the six-man rescue squad sent earlier had reached their objective.

Searching for the platoon bridge across the Mosel River, Williams was relieved that they'd entered a snow belt as tank tracks were quickly obliterated and visibility was near zero during severe wind gusts. Snow banks provided background drops to hide from passing armor on its way to the front.

At 3 a.m., in spite of worry that the pontoon bridge across the Mosel might be restricted to one-way traffic, they got across without being challenged. Encouraged to continue their southward trek, they passed in the vicinity of a town named Konz and along the Saar. General Morgan kept audible by McCloskey's whiskey, was able to advise due to his extensive knowledge of the German countryside in this area. On the general's instructions, Williams turned west across the French Maginot Line and sought a route across the

French/Luxembourg border to Thionville, France. Upon reaching the Thionville area the first two bridges were found to be out of commission and they all knew the Mosel at this point would be too deep to cross. The trio of tanks finally located an approach onto the rails following a departing engine, and the fugitive armor and one lone German officer's car bumped across the Mosel.

It was 4 a.m. and Williams was still driving his tank. They experienced trouble finding their way out of Thionville and left the city via a routing that took them through to Belgium, still seeking their expected rendezvous with General George Patton of the Third Army. Col, Williams would vaguely recall the road that took them past Esch-fur-Alzette and Arlon, still under German control. On the outskirts of Thionville, Williams' tank had come upon a motorcycle driven by a former Belgian Army major and a French courier carrying a dispatch destined for General Patton at his temporary headquarters. These men abandoned their motorbike and came aboard the tank. From then on the guesswork was taken out of the routing.

At first light a weary, lost trio of Sherman tanks found safety. Over a hill southwest of Bastogne, they passed U.S. infantry and rambled noisily into the path of a column of American tanks.

Anticipating a happy reunion among friends, Williams expected the meeting to be a great moment of satisfaction in spite of he and his men having been without sleep for over two full days. Williams had driven his lead tank under tension and fear for seven hours. They had been dropped onto a small plot of unknown terrain deep behind enemy lines, subdued superior forces, captured the depot, burned the German supplies before departing, escaped through enemy territory, and found their way miraculously back among-friends in cumbersome vehicles with which the team was unfamiliar--and had not lost a man.

Williams stopped the vehicle, crawled back among bodies and opened the hatch. A group of U.S. soldiers with pointed weapons watched intently as a German helmet appeared and then the shoulders and epaulettes of a German general came into view. Ignoring the confrontation, Williams carefully lowered his stiffened body to the ground and heard a voice bellow out, "Who the Hell are you!"

I'm Col. Halford Williams, special detail of general Eisenhower, Supreme Commander of Allied Forces in Europe," was the reply.

Williams removed his German helmet and opening his coat revealed his American uniform. He stepped closer to the general who had roughly addressed him and was about to speak when he was interrupted.

"I'm General Patton; the fire in the sky last night? Was it the German dump? Tell me!"

"Yes Sir! I can assure you it was the enemy depot. I'll explain in a minute, but first" Williams, having shed his German outfit, began again with all parties listening. "These are what are left of your tank squadron General. The German officers' car is mine. Three of your senior officers plus sixteen others in these tanks need urgent medical help."

In rapid fire, Patton responded with questions about the remainder of his squadron and Williams replied. ."We counted 157 bodies all shot at close range. They remained frozen where they fell until the fire cremated them last night at 12 o'clock."

Patton responded. "How many men in your outfit?" to which Williams replied, "Six." Incredulously Patton asked if they had help in burning the dump from his six tanks sent to find them. Williams simply replied, "What tanks, Sir? We held the German depot all yesterday, then blew it as we withdrew at midnight." Then Williams added an afterthought. "I hope you don't mind General, but the last message I sent the enemy was that we just blew the depot. I signed "Love, General George S. Patton." Patton beamed.

General Patton shouted an order and ambulances and trucks arrived. Third Army tankers and medics lifted the bundled officers out carcfully and rushed them to a hospital tent.

Patton saw his top general taken out, and he bent over the form as he was eased onto a stretcher. "Mike! What went wrong?" The squadron commander replied in a barely audible voice. "We were tricked. They knew our code"

Patton was known as a man of sincere emotions. He could cry or laugh or get angry without apologies. As General Morgan tried to speak, Patton shed tears as he touched the man's forehead.

The tankers were bringing out the last of the U.S. officers when an officer hurried up to Patton and broke into the reunion. "General!" he said. "What's to be done with the Gerry prisoners inside the tanks?"

Patton turned and glowered at Williams for an answer as though the two men were suddenly adversaries. "Why didn't you kill the bastardly murderers of my men?" Williams, visibly agitated at the apparent condemnation of his actions, slowly removed his glasses and, as he wiped them clear, replied, "Because General, I'm not big enough to judge who should die for their deeds."

Patton mentioned the prisoner question again. "You may not want to be judge of who dies, but I'm big enough, dammit! What are you Colonel Williams, some mamby-pamby that refused to execute those snakes?" Then Patton yelled to Major White and ordered him to provide a detail to remove the twenty-five Nazi soldiers, and he said for all to hear, "An eye for an eye." Williams did not reply.

Patton inquired of Williams how much fuel he destroyed and Williams guessed they had burned over two million gallons plus large quantities of heavy ammo and other stores, including American clothing for use by Nazi infiltrators.

The cavalry general reflected on this astounding information, and immediately the anger in his voice was gone. He proclaimed, "You've slowed down the German offensive in the Ardennes if what you say is true. Before 72 hours I estimate their first panzers will feel the pinch. Furthermore, the Germans must replace that stuff right away, at all costs, or their front line armor can't move.

Colonel, you may have shortened this war by six weeks."

General Patton repeated. "We've got to make use of that delay you've created."

At this point Patton did not recognize that he had offended Williams by calling him a mamby-pamby for bringing in the prisoners. Williams' ego had been badly bruised by the remark made for all to hear. He was stung by the belittlement in lieu of praise.

Patton ceased his reflections on strategy and recognizing Williams' presence again asked matter-of-factly, "Colonel! Your looks deceive me. You remind me more of a bookworm than a saboteur. What prompted you to put that German dump to the torch when you could have gotten in and gotten out once you found my men?"

Williams, waiting for a chance to repay Patton for his trite description of his calculated bravery and colossal achievement, retaliated slowly with an enjoyment that Patton failed to discern. "Well General, I set fire to the dump mainly for one reason. I didn't want your G.I.s to find all that good potato alcohol and drink themselves into a regimental stupor while half a million enemy troops poured through your lines."

Patton hardly waited for the sentence to end; he called out, "Damn it, what a stupid remark. You can't even be half serious. You should get yourself involved in temperance, not war."

"Right on both counts General," replied Williams. "I was never more serious," the younger man responded with mouth turned down to look more adamant.

General Patton let out an oath and turned away in disgust.

Col. Williams enjoyed the parting moments but hid his delight.

During the abrupt interlude of information exchanged between the rescuer, Williams, and the Third Army commander, Sergeant McCloskey and the aids hauled off the German officer's car to be refitted with wheels, tires, and seats if they could salvage parts from a nearby German vehicle dump. As the German car was taken away, Williams turned to General Patton, informing him that his men and he were going to drive that car to the nearest port. They intended to see Paris before Christmas, and then head back to London. "We'll make the trip a kind of Christmas holiday," said Williams to the general.

General Patton stared at Williams in disbelief at the remark, and then insisted they be taken back to headquarters in his plane. Williams politely refused. General Patton did not make his offer a mandatory order. However, he cautioned them to avoid going to visit General Omar Bradley on the way back. Col. Williams did not understand the reason for the caution.

"I have a favor to ask you General," said Williams. Pull out two of those Nazi prisoners right away and get them over to your G2 because they have valuable information, along with my Corporal Erbstien, on the position and movements of German front line troops." General Patton gave the order at once.

As McCloskey and Patton's men were scavenging the dump for the replacement parts for the damaged car, Col. Williams had already been taken into a tent on orders of General Patton where he was being made ready for a hot bath and clean clothes: The team was scheduled to sit down for a hearty breakfast in less than half an hour, in spite of their fatigue, when the headquarters heard a volley of shots.

Hurrying to the source of the shots, McCloskey was speechless in disbelief. The remaining twenty-three German prisoners had been executed. Among the dead men he found the body of the Nazi officer who had helped them all to find their way back to allied lines. He had never asked the officer his name. He reached into his pocket and withdrew a picture of the man's family.

Turning to the shooting detail, McCloskey hollered, "You S. O. Bs! You're no better than they." Then he stalked off to find his commanding officer and register a complaint.

On hearing the sergeant tell of the perfidy, Williams tried to calm McCloskey and replied sadly. "I never thought the general would really order it."

"Strange thing about good and evil bastards," spoke McCloskey, "you can't tell them apart." Someone replied, "Don't look too far."

In justifying the killings, Williams added, "Should we judge the executioners? If I were they, knowing those Nazis had killed 157 of my men with more to follow, I wouldn't take time to reason whether I shot them because of righteous anger or retribution."

Sgt. Luellan joined in. "The Nazi prisoners were doomed to die just as sure as our role on this mission--to date--is to live. Perhaps they were chosen to pay for the retribution of good Germans like Dietrich Bonhoffer and other sufferers who paid with their lives under the Nazis." Someone asked who the guy just mentioned was and the reply was "never mind. "In the end we're all accountable, foe and friend," Luellan replied.

McCloskey said gruffly, "Whether we're the punishers or not, the whole business of rescuing people has become rotten, because we end up killing others to rescue the few. It's made me hate myself more every day. I hope a higher power can cleanse my own soul. Maybe the supernatural experience we had in that French cave was given to remind us that a world of spirits is watching our actions under some supreme force keeping score on our lives."

Williams soothed McCloskey by adding that his own deeds involving the death of others, no matter who pulled the trigger, were also accountable. Then Williams added philosophically, "The perfect name for war is hell, because in war those who run the nations involved in war suspend all moral laws."

Someone asked what moral law had to do with the question of accountability, and Williams attempted an answer by saying, "It's your conscience telling you what is right and what is wrong."

McCloskey joined in again, "Then my conscience tells me that war is wrong, even though I have a fighting instinct of survival. I dinna ken know how they ever attached the words honor and glory to war. Sacrifice, aye! They should have outlawed war long ago, even though differences perhaps should be settled with a good fight."

They all laughed and someone yelled that McCloskey was crazy, but Williams ended the conversation by agreeing with his sergeant. He said, "You're right McCloskey, bet it's too late for our generation to outlaw war, and a thousand generations before us no doubt. But when Christ comes back as he claimed, he'll outlaw war."

"And just when is Christ coming back?" someone said rather derogatorily, and Williams answered simply, "The timetable hasn't been posted."

The beef session ended in the tent where Williams was finishing his bath. They had just concluded that; war, in spite of evil would probably make heroes of them all. An orderly entered and called out, "Breakfast for the heroes." Word had gotten around about the dump explosion.

When the short stay at Patton's temporary headquarters was over, General Patton accompanied them to the departing car. He tried to warn Williams not to make the trip, reminding him they still had to travel through German lines, and territories occupied by Free French, and the U.S. Knowing he could not convince Williams to fly, he handed him a letter of safe passage to the port of Cherbourg. As for getting through German lines, he left that up to the ingenuity of the rescue team.

As they parted, Williams and his team heard the motors of many tanks start up as General Patton said his finale.

"Colonel, I can't figure you, nor how you pulled off that depot fire and got back here as a green horn driver. But what you've done has given me the greatest damn dose of optimism in all my military years."

Williams was unaware at the time, but by delivering the German armies such a setback at the petrol depot, and by supplying General Patton early intelligence information on the resulting handicap to Nazi fighting units that depended on the petrol and ammo, he had done much to move Patton's army into subsequent attack positions.

Three days later, a German officer's car was driven onto an LST at the port of Cherbourg. The team explained their German dress to the British military upon arriving in Folkstone, England, and after removing their German outfits McCloskey took the wheel of the trophy and drove to London. They all were still intact, without a scratch, just as they were four days earlier when they were dropped on the German target.

The oddity of allied soldiers driving a German officer's car perked up the sentry guarding the Supreme Allied Headquarters. Asked to fetch out General Eisenhower, the sentry got on the phone and stated ponderously that Col. Halford Williams and fiends had just arrived from Germany and request an audience with the supreme commander.

A small crowd was gathering as General Eisenhower hurried out and, with his famous smile, he took the salute of Col. Williams, who said modestly, "Mission completed okay Sir." Then he added, "May I present you with a Christmas gift Sir! Compliments of the Nazis guarding the late petrol depot."

They put Williams to bed on the 21st of December and he was not told that Gen. George Patton that same night would undertake the fastest and most daring redeployment of allied troops in World War II, and as a result, would eventually block the Nazi offensive to Antwerp and hasten the end of the war.

When General Patton later visited the dumpsite, he wrote in his diary that he had never seen such destruction of military supplies. In recommending Col. Harry Williams for the Congressional Medal of Honor he wrote, "Never in his military life had he seen such an outstanding piece of bravery in which one man and his team of five so completely destroyed one of the enemies biggest supply dumps and at the same time brought in so many prisoners."

Col. Williams was also awarded the Victoria Cross from Britain for his action in the Battle of the Bulge, as was Sergeant McCloskey.

The tank commander, a captain in the 32nd Armored Division who escaped with his crew of seven from Skorzeny's trap and brought back details of the entrapment to Gen. Patton, received the Congressional Medal of Honor.

General Mike Morgan was flown immediately to London for hospitalization. Later he was given an opportunity to serve in the Pacific in lieu of a court martial. He chose the Pacific where he was killed in action.

One of the surviving top U.S. officers captured at the depot was found in 1984 in a veteran's hospital in California, and he verified the information on condition that his name was not mentioned.

Whereabouts of the other sixteen U.S. junior officers captured at the petrol dump was not sought, except that they were all shipped immediately to U.S. military hospitals in France.

Colonel Otto Skorzeny escaped allied detection on at least two other occasions, one when a group of 206 Germans led by Skorzeny infiltrated Paris and Versailles to assassinate General Eisenhower. All were caught except Skorzeny. The second occasion in which he was not recognized was when he surfaced from a sunken German submarine in May 1945 off the Florida coast, U.S.A. He came ashore, was placed in a prisoner-of-war compound and eventually repatriated to Germany. After the war, Skorzeny settled in Spain according to U.S. military intelligence reports and was tried for war crimes at Nuremberg, but acquitted.

Chapter 10

THE MISSION TO FIND ADOLF HITLER

It was autumn 1944, Allied Headquarters, London, England. Documented reports coming in regularly from allied agents consistently maintained that a major happening of political/military importance had occurred inside the German hierarchy. Adolf Hitler, Chancellor of the Third Reich, had been replaced by a permanent double. Had Hitler gone insane or was he dead, the Allied Chiefs of Staff pondered.

Classified information had already told the allies that should Germany lose the war an alternate plan had been prepared for a certain elite part of the upper echelons to vacate the fatherland and begin life anew in another area of the world. Proof that such a master plan of German intentions had been formulated and put into effect since 1943 had already reached the allies via the French underground. London had been advised repeatedly that long passenger trains traveling by night loaded with German troops and special technical personnel were headed for Spanish ports of embarkation. There the troops and associates departed on surface vessels and mammoth submarines.

Hence, a special message from a Spanish agent to London intelligence did not surprise Gen. William Donovan of the United States OSS that a disguised Adolf Hitler may have vanished in 1944.
He had stopped at Zaragoza, Spain with Eva Braun, a boy of four identified as Adolf Hitler, II, and an older adopted boy, the agent report stated. The trio was said to have left the port of Aymonte via submarine.

Twelve allied agents, five of whom were American, were infiltrated among the German rail evacuees through Vicky, France and Spain. They verified French reports that a systematic removal of key Germans and entire troop formations was taking place. Allen Dulles (to become future director of the Central Intelligence Agency) was one of the American agents planted among the enemy.

According to the confusion and gossip surrounding Hitler's whereabouts, however, was another conflicting report that Christina Edderer, Hitler's private pilot, had flown Der Fuehrer to Norway for submarine passage to points unknown.

Of major consideration in trying to solve the puzzle of Hitler's existence, allied intelligence finally put emphasis on a detailed account of a secret Nazi meeting held in Strasbourg on August 10, 1944. At that meeting the rulers of the Nazi party agreed to remove Germany's gold and precious metals for overseas shipment. Accompanying this bonded shipment would be Hitler's most trusted deputies. British agents tracked the underwater carrier from a Spanish port to Alexandria, Egypt and through the Straight of Gibraltar into the open Atlantic.

The Allied Joint Chiefs, alarmed by this growing influx of convincing information, were concerned that indeed the enemy was evacuating key Germans to colonies known to exist already in South America or beyond.

Therefore, it was surmised that Adolf Hitler and his retinue of loyalists might have been required to join that exodus.

In February of 1945 allied intelligence, uncertain of their agents' assertions that Hitler also had disappeared, made plans to sharpen their own persuasion. It was decided to verify in a personal manner if Hitler was still in charge of a dying empire, or had left his post.

The plan was to pierce Hitler's Reichstag in Berlin and obtain a first-hand report by spying on the person who occupied Hitler's private quarters. Was it he or was he a double?

The man chosen to lead that mission impossible was Colonel Halford Williams.

During the last week of February 1945, General William Donovan matter-of-factly summoned Col. Halford Williams to attend a special briefing session to last three days at a secret location. Donovan simply said to Williams, "We have found a way to get into the belly of Berlin."

But Donovan's order had reached Williams at a time of depression brought on by his unwanted role as leader of a team of commandos sent on such suicidal missions that his own life had become an expendable resource. Williams, the man, came to believe this attitude prevailed among most of the Chiefs of Staff, including the Supreme Commander, General Dwight D. Eisenhower, and Britisher General Bernard Montgomery in particular.

Upon constant reflection of the dilemma, Williams did not feel anger or bitterness toward the high brass for their willingness to sacrifice him and his team. But nevertheless, he was confused.

The tranquility, which was the mark of his personality when he was twenty and free from the realities of war, was gone.

But now he despised his role as the leader of a commando team who had to kill to escape, who had to live like animals to survive each mission. And as to the glory due for his role in the espionage endeavors, Williams knew none would be forthcoming, for he was sworn to eternal silence.

Col. Williams had heard the names they called him: The invincible soldier, the one who loved to defy death, a freak, a loner, a hero, a fool--almost every oddball description of his personality was voiced at allied headquarters.

Williams wished he had the moral depravity to hate the Chiefs of Staff and their planners who didn't mind devising schemes by which he was the catalyst leading others into new realms of death on a weekly basis. But hate them he could not. At times he recalled his indignant mother calling this personality trait a weakness that someday would make her son an easy mark for others to exploit.

Hence, Col. Williams reluctantly went to the briefing session ordered by Gen. Donovan after a typical forty-eight hour bout of guilt and fear, including terrible nightmares and delirium.

At the briefing session Williams managed to compose his random thoughts of rebellion against the system and allow him to be introduced to those experts who would familiarize him with the hazards of the new assignment. The first expert was a tall, slim, elegantly dressed Englishman of about thirty, sent over from Britain's Ml Intelligence Service. The man's real name was not mentioned for security reasons. All Williams could ascertain was that he was an engineer, his expertise being underground drainage and sewage systems as they related to espionage. That the gentleman was cognizant of the vast underground engineering conduits and tunnels of Berlin was soon revealed.

Before giving Williams precise instructions the Englishman chose to get better acquainted with the young American, so he asked, "Are you aware Colonel, that all major buildings housing regal or politically important persons have secondary underground escape routes by which their leaders can disappear? Such tunnels have been used for ages when it became necessary to save the leaders' lives or simply as a means for them to get away from their abodes without being detected by friends or enemies."

Col. Williams was intrigued by the subject matter of escape tunneling as used by knights and monarchs since the Middle Ages. Then the visitor brought him up to date by references to life in the present century.

"Rest assured Colonel, the American White House has escape tunnels and Buckingham Palace undoubtedly has also. We know for certain the Kremlin has used them since the time of the Czars and it would be unwise to wager that even the Vatican hasn't at least a few. So, you understand Colonel that while mining or tunneling was done in ancient days to gain access to castles or other structures, in our time the tunnels have evolved principally as escape routes.

After gaining the attention of his rapt listener with a condensed history of tunneling, the instructor then produced two distinct sets of maps. The first set was a scale drawing of the sewage system of Berlin--or as he himself expressed it--the German Reichstag and it's location related to the city's underground drainage system.

The second set of maps the instructor was to etch later into the photographic mind of Williams was the secret escape system of tunneling which emanated from the Reichstag's Chancellery and connected itself to the city's deep underground drainage system. The English person labeled those tunnels as a thoroughfare built to enable Der Fuehrer to escape in times of unparalleled danger to his life. The Englishman told Williams that Adolf Hitler carried around his neck at all times the key that opened the secret door to those escape tunnels.

It was inferred that one of Britain's master spies in the 1930's had either obtained the map of the tunnel escape plans leading from Hitler's private apartment or else the spy may have descended Berlin's underground drainage system and scouted the routing in reverse, right up to the walls of the Reichstag. Col. Williams believed the man giving him the secret instructions might have been that daring Ml agent.

The two men spent a single day studying the Berlin drainage system with particular emphasis on the huge collector running nearly six miles from the Reichstag to the river.

The visitor made sure that Col. Williams was familiar with every foot of the main collector pipe, including the openings of the connecting arteries and each distinguishing mark along the route.

The visiting instructor taught Col. Williams all he knew about the Berlin underground drain and the secret escape tunnels coming out of the residence of Adolf Hitler. But Williams was carefully warned of precautions. He found out the danger of flash flooding that could turn the main channel into a raging underground river sweeping everything that lay in its path to destruction. Therefore, when the subject mission takes pace, Williams was warned the weather probabilities over Berlin must be without rain.

The refined English gentleman folded his maps, placed them in his briefcase and departed. Col. Halford Williams was expected to have memorized them in detail.

On the third day of the briefing sessions, Williams was introduced to a journalist with intimate knowledge of Berlin's surface streets above and in the vicinity of the main underground drainage course. Again, the man's identity was not acknowledged, but Williams believed he recognized whom he was. The journalist immediately warned the young man it would be safer to stay underground in the sewage or drainage system than to venture up to the surface. By the use of films and commentary, Col. Williams was shown; sections of ruptured streets, the debris of bombed or shelled buildings, and the apparent surface agony and anarchy prevailing in Germany's capital city during the dying days of the war as Soviet armies began to penetrate its outskirts.

On the final afternoon of the session, Williams and his men were shown films and still shots of Adolf Hitler taken over a period of years. Pointed out to the viewers by experts on voice and mannerisms, were the body movements and idiosyncrasies of Hitler.

When the moderator of the films asked for an appraisal of what they had seen, as it would relate to the forthcoming mission, Sergeant McCloskey summed it up on behalf of the team. "I believe you've captured every antic of that domm dictator bastard except perhaps one: we never caught him picking his nose in public." The meetings broke up in laughter.

General Donovan spoke to Williams as follows: "Rest up over the weekend. Weather permitting, you will move out on the mission early next week. It will be a night-drop behind enemy lines after which you will steal transport to reach the objective. Prepare to penetrate the belly of the beast and spy on Adolf Hitler!"

Col. Halford Williams reviewed the briefing instructions on April 3rd, 1945. They had parachuted safely behind enemy lines and stolen a German officers' car about twenty-five miles from the first objective. They were two hours behind schedule when they arrived at the bank of the river, immobilized the stolen car, and moved off across the river in an inflated rubber boat. On the east shore the boat was hidden and they faced the first challenge. Iron bars blocked the entrance to the huge drain. The sun was just rising behind them.

Prepared for such an eventuality, Sergeant McCloskey produced a hacksaw with six steel-hardened blades marked "Made in Germany". He cut out an opening large enough for all to get through with their variety of equipment. When the team of five men was inside, McCloskey taped the cut bars back in place to avoid detection from the river. They then unfolded a collapsible cart and began the long hike to their destination. Hurriedly, they moved into the darkness of the drainage sewer before the first rays of day could catch their silhouettes and betray their presence.

The march in the storm sewer began. Having arrived late, Col. Williams adjusted the pace to double-time. The eyes of each gradually became accustomed to the darkness. The colonel took the lead, the top sergeant the rear. No one talked as they walked on special rubber-soled boots. Chief worries of Col. Williams were if the rubber boat were to be stolen or the car towed away. If all went well he thought they might be able to spend about eight hours at the objective and two more hours retracing their steps back through the sewer system. Each checked their flashlights.

The team had gone about five miles in silence, keeping pace. Up ahead they saw another large connector opening into theirs. Williams had been told this was a section where he could go wrong. Pausing to envision the map he called for a halt. He took a compass bearing. From somewhere far away they thought they heard voices and surface noises. Suddenly there was a violent explosion from above. The noise echoed down the subterranean corridors.

Sgt. McCloskey volunteered to walk along an intersecting drainage thoroughfare to determine which of the two they should take to their objective. Fifteen minutes later he returned, and Williams asked, "What's up yonder?" McCloskey replied, "Same size corridor for approximately 1500 yards, then it narrows." His commanding officer replied. "Wrong way--we stay on this routing."

All munched on hard rations and drank from their canteens as they moved off in single file. A member broke rank and the marchers halted.

The soldier went over to the wall as he reached into his jacket for a piece of blue chalk and scrawled a ludicrous-looking face with four or five strokes.

Colonel Williams was not amused as he turned and heard the ordered silence broken by audible chuckles. He flashed his light on the caricature, and breaking silence himself queried in a lowered voice, "What may I ask is that goofy, spaced-out idiot you just drew and why?"

The soldier replied, "He's a relative of us poor GI Joes. His name is Kilroy. If we get mixed up at this intersection on the return trip, Kilroy here will show us the corridor we must take to get out of this damn trap."

The soldier remarked that the Gerries would never guess the meaning of Kilroy's picture. Neither did Colonel Williams. The attempt to create humor had relieved tensions as the march resumed.

The mission was an hour and a half inside the drainage sewer and had marched less than thirty minutes more when Col. Williams called for a halt. Using his light he spotted the main clue he had been searching for. It was an iron grate of ordinary door size some feet above the drainage canyon's floor. He saw the padlock on the grating and called for Sgt, McCloskey to bring out the acetylene cutting-torch. The lock was severed and a member shoved the grating inwards. Within moments each man and his equipment were hoisted through. They closed the gate.

This was a small corridor estimated to be about seven or more feet high. It rose steeply for a distance of three city blocks when Williams spied a metal ladder extending through a large opening in the tunnel. Leading the group for the climb, McCloskey ascended about fifty feet. He disappeared into a large-sized manhole above his head and found himself in an upper room that was the hub of three more tunnels going in different directions. Signaling to those below, the team followed the Scotsman and assembled on the concrete floor of the room above. Laid out beside them were the two-wheeled cart, the portable welding kit with tanks, a movie camera, and sound recorders with built-in batteries with a life of three hours. The team had been less hindered because they carried no heavy weapons or ammunition. But they were still short of reaching their objective, that is, the foundation walls of the Reichstag itself.

Col. Williams stood in the center of the vault and took out his compass. He knew in advance he was in the prescribed hub and what degree would match the tunnel through which they should continue in from that point. Quietly and cautiously the team advanced into a smaller passage. In a few minutes Col. Williams, in the lead, reached an iron stairway leading upwards. They could go no farther.

Flush against the wall was a steel door. If Williams had memorized the sewer directions properly, they were in front of the private apartment of Adolf Hitler in the German Reichstag. The wall behind that secret door was five feet thick. And inside the thick foundation walls behind the steel door were the secret passageways engulfing the private apartment of the world's top dictator.

A little over two hours earlier the allied team had confidently crossed the river and broken into the first of many corridors leading to their present position. Now they were just outside the nerve center of the entire German command. Each man knew that retreat alone through the maze of tunnels to outside freedom was impossible. And each knew this trip was especially eventful because they had been denied the firepower for defense.

As the locksmith began to work on the steel door at the top of the short flight of stairs, Col. Williams backed off and called for a huddle. The team squatted in awkward positions to hear the final orders. The officer whispered, "Allow me to review for a minute or two what to expect on the other side of that door!"

The colonel got no further. A team member interrupted, also in a low voice. "Let's review a few things about us for the entire team. Each has his knife and the Sergeant his knife and lariat. With this big arsenal we're supposed to go into those dark passages between walls lurking with Nazi guards familiar with every inch of the floors? Before we even get adapted to the light changes we'll all be dead men. Count me out of this suicidal break-in."

McCloskey grimaced at the complainer. None carried ID's and none answered to their right names. Using the code calling, the Sergeant spat out the name Benson.

"So, you won't go through that door? You have two choices: One, to bite your cyanide capsule right now, and nae foolin mon. Two, we'll execute you before the rest of us go in, for being a cowardly deserter. That leaves only three of us left to do the job but we'll do it." Benson said no more.

A second man questioned the mission but without Benson's defiant attitude. Shifting nervously on his haunches, he addressed Col. Williams. "Sir, do you think we can really avoid an encounter inside the passageways? Remember, we're on the enemy's turf like Benson said. This won't be an open, free fight. It's got to be hand-to-hand conflict with vague forms."

McCloskey interrupted. "We've had several days of training for this job. I taught you birds everything I know on how to defend or kill quickly in close quarters. And not one of you was able to throw me. Yet, I could have gotten each one of you. All I can say is that you were shown the right techniques. Use them domm it. Use them or die."

Col. Williams interjected. "Let's sum up our present position. Our combined strength is tied into each individual weakness. If anyone of us fails, we're all goners."

The unquiet teammate was not placated by the last summary of their present no-win environment so he said to his commander, "They tell me you've gone on close to sixty missions and the Sarg about forty. Me, I've done about a dozen of what seemed normal actions against the enemy. But this one is different. I've already got claustrophobia in these rabbit holes. I can hardly stand the feeling. I'm scared. My legs are woozy. I can't help it, Sir."

Williams turned to the dissenter. "You've got to go forward from this point. Sure you're frightened. We all are to a degree. But the mechanism of self-defense will take over when you find yourself up against an enemy who has only one purpose--to kill any stranger he sees inside those passageways. And he won't ask a single question before he strikes."

"Now, if you function as Sgt. McCloskey has trained you, you'll survive. If you have any guilt feelings about killing again, save them for the padre when you get back to London."

Williams continued. "I know your deep-down thoughts. Do I have to kill again just to save my own life? How did I get into this jam? Or perhaps you think you'll allow yourself to become a sacrifice and let them cut off your young life. You won't be the first to consider that option either. You see, for a just cause that would be the noblest of admissions. But in war no one becomes a martyr by decision, or he dies. You must fight to live. On the other side of that door there is no turning back."

The young soldier apologized by saying to his commanding officer, "Let me take one more shot at the problem Sir, and then I'm through. You Sir are a pacifist they tell me. You will use your weapon only in self-defense, even with the golden sword they say you've sometimes carried."

Williams interrupted. "I've just told you the facts of survival, man. What you do inside those secret alleys of the Chancellery will be in self-defense. Act accordingly or you won't see London again. And because of your sudden timidity you might knock out the home trip for all of us. What happens to your conscience during the next hours will be up to each of you. Perhaps all of us may carry back a guilt complex for killing in order that we ourselves survive--or the worst of all disorders--cowardly shame for letting down your team. I would think the shame would hurt worse than the guilt for the rest of your life.

McCloskey listened attentively. Col. Williams glanced at his face. He knew his sergeant had deep anxiety about his men being able to function as a unit. Williams heard McCloskey mumble that perhaps the colonel had made a mistake in choosing the present fighting men for this occasion.

The team suddenly heard the rumble and vibration of falling bombs from somewhere on the charred surface of Berlin. The detonations increased. Col. Williams realized a daylight raid of American super fortresses was taking place.

The locksmith signaled and the dissidents in the huddle reverted to warriors again. With McCloskey, the master of the lariat leading, they mounted the stairs and one-by-one vanished into the passageway inside the Chancellery of Germany's Third Reich.

The steel door closed behind them.

In the passageways extending to their left and right, the commandos sensed an eerie aloneness except for the muffled sounds of bombs falling on the surface of beleaguered Berlin. The conglomerate of spies was soon thankful to find themselves identifiable to each other and bathed in a dim light. As forewarned, they paused and adjusted their eyes and ears to the gripping confinement of the enclosure. The first thought of the officer in charge was that they were in a labyrinth of twisting corridors. Then he rationalized that the architects of these underground bunkers would be more concerned with a simplistic design. As each man fixed his eyes on the others it was evident that each was standing in readiness for combat with hands on their weapons in a narrow peephole gallery built around a series of rooms designed to guard and protect Adolf Hitler, master of the Third Reich. The allied team was at a point of no return.

Without speaking as agreed before entry, McCloskey and another moved to the left corridor and two others advanced to the right making two spearheads of encounter. Col. Williams kept the movie and sound technician with him and followed in the direction of McCloskey. The colonel's objective was not to seek an adversary but to locate the strategically placed openings that would bring into view the occupants of the apartment on the inside of the wall.

After careful scrutiny of the inside wall Col. Williams noticed a pencil gleam of light. He knew his left flank was protected by his sergeant and another teammate, and to his right, if all was well; two other team members controlled the corridor. So far so good, thought the colonel. But he was unaccustomed to the absence of noise or scuffle.

Placing his eye to the slit in the wall he was able to see across a room into a wall mirror. He realized at once the mirror reflected a painting on the reverse side of the room. Williams caught the connection. His present peephole was somewhere within the painting.

As he stared intently at the mirror he knew he had come upon the key to the pattern of surveillance. Looking forward and down at the mirror in question, Col. Williams found his gaze locked in amazement at not one, but two Adolf Hitler's. Immediately Williams' mind regressed to the week before when he was watching the film clips of the German leader. He recalled; the lock of frontal hair falling over the left temple, the Charlie Chaplin moustache, the fiery glint in the eyes and emotional pitches in the voice. But most of all, Williams' eye fixed on the shape of the face, the bone structure and ears.

One of the Hitlers in Williams' view sat at a dressing table carefully putting on his makeup, kneading and pulling the skin as he applied cosmetics. The other Hitler apparently had completed his face. At first Williams wondered if the one standing was the real Fuehrer. He didn't have long to wait for the answer.

From across the room in an area not covered by the existing peephole came a busy-looking man. He was seen to examine the features of both men, touched up the face of the man sitting at the dressing table, and then the makeup artist brushed the hair of both men and set their coiffures perfectly in place.

The allied technician took his place at the peephole. Quickly he discerned the scene in the adjoining room. He checked the size of the opening, adjusted the camera and placed the specially made lens opening to the hole in the wall. Silently the movie scanner was filming movements of the occupants while a small, powerful microphone recorded the Germanic voices. As the technician concentrated on his work, Col. Williams turned and watched in both directions for disorder or even an attack. He was uneasy because none of his men had revealed their whereabouts. The rule of strict silence was working.

Perhaps five minutes later, the technician touched the colonel and Williams placed his eye against the peephole again. One of the completed Hitlers was seen to pull asidea chest of drawers. He disappeared through the wall.

From the surface of the city the team again heard the rumbling of falling bombs. Williams estimated the hits were nearby. The concussions grew heavier and the vibrations surging through the massive concrete and steel structure made Colonel Williams apprehensive. Looking through the peephole he was startled to see a red light appear on the wall of Hitler's apartment. Quickly the occupants vacated the premises. An air raid was in progress.

Williams touched the movie man and they headed in the direction where Sergeant McCloskey was last seen. A few feet down the corridor Williams was surprised to see the outline of a door stenciled on the inside wall. He studied the outline for a moment then shoved on one side where the knob ought to be. That section of the wall gave way and turned on a central pivot. Williams and the technician stepped gingerly from behind a bookcase into the private bedroom of Adolf Hitler. The red light still glowed. The air raid was continuing unabated.

The rooms were littered with clues that they were seeking. The two men entered the bathroom, examined in detail the vanity table and scrutinized the bedroom. Opening a closet door they found four sets of Hitler uniforms, completely authentic except for one discrepancy. Each was marked by a different size, including the four pairs of neatly placed shoes beneath each set of clothing. Were there four doubles, thought the Colonel? Obviously.

On the dressing table where the fake Hitler had made up his face moments before, were smudged life-sized portraits of the real Hitler to be used, no doubt, for comparison.

The clever technician then busied himself with the use of a portable fingerprint kit and dusted several places and items that were generally handled by the occupants. Then he took a dozen still shots with a miniature camera.

Before departing, Williams pulled out the chest of drawers behind which he had seen one of the doubles disappear earlier. On the backside of the chest he sawa spiral staircase. Venturing in, he descended several circular steps. As Williams hesitated on the steps the technician hissed at him from above. The red warning light had gone out, signifying the air raid was over. Together, the two men hurried back into the passageway and closed the bookcase door behind them.

Williams immediately wondered where McCloskey and the other team members were holding out. A hazy form glided soundlessly toward the two men, and Col. William's stood transfixed. Before the form reached him at arms length, a voice whispered. "Hoot mon, is all well Colonel?" Williams breathed a sigh of relief and replied, "Indeed it is Sergeant. How goes it with you?"

Sgt. McCloskey led his colonel and helper along the passageway. Laid out head-to-toe on one side were three bodies. All helped drag the corpses to a small storeroom in the wall. There the elite guards of Adolf Hitler were dumped.

McCloskey spoke to Williams, "I had nee time to ask them when the next shift would take over. Therefore, we must be canny from now on!" Then McCloskey took Williams and the technician to another peephole located downward in the labyrinth. From that vantage point they watched activities in the underground bunker for almost an hour and were able again to study and film the Hitler double who had descended the spiral staircase seen earlier by Col. Williams.

The colonel checked his watch. It was almost 6 p.m., time for exit. The locksmith was outside the steel door waiting their return. As the team departed, the smithy locked the entrance door again. Leaving the tunnel system, they retraced their steps into the deep underground sewage pipes. It was a more contented group departing from the belly of Berlin that still rumbled with occasional sounds of surface explosions. At 8 p.m. they were on the river where the acetylene paraphernalia and cart was dumped. On the far shore they found that thieves, or curious soldiers had not tampered with the car. McCloskey replaced the distributor cap and reconnected the spark plug wires, after which they drove off. Eventually they passed through German lines and crossed to the allied side under a flag of truce. Allied front units had been told to watch for such a situation.

London was happy. Many of the fingerprints matched those of the real Adolf Hitler indicating his presence in the rooms recently. The voice recordings were definitely not those of the real Hitler, and the movies which showed the doubles being made up revealed there was a great subterfuge hoisted upon some of the German general staff and the population at large regarding the person and location of Germany's leader in the final days or perhaps months of World War II.

When General Donovan addressed the next meeting of the Allied Chiefs of Staff he said in a cryptic voice: "Since the successful return of the last mission into the Berlin Chancellery of Adolf Hitler, it has been ascertained that there exists at least four doubles in Hitler's place. The one or ones masquerading as Hitler made us all believe Hitler had gone mad. Whoever those doubles may be, they are imposters under the control of others. I categorically make this assertion."

"Hitler is alive!" Those were the first words Joseph Stalin said to President Harry Truman and Prime Minister Churchill when a discreet moment was available at the 1945 Potsdam Conference. "The body in the bunker was not that of Hitler," said Stalin. "The hair, teeth and fingerprints do not match."

Then Stalin gave the complete autopsy details to the Prime Minister of Britain and the President of the United States.

CHAPTER 9

VISIT TO GENERAL VON RUNSTEDT INSIDE GERMANY

Before the Battle of the Bulge ended, the ultimate defeat of Germany was evident to their General Staff. Their last thrust through the Ardennes into allied lines had failed, and hence prevented the Germans from regaining the military initiative. Allied Intelligence had been grossly negligent in not foreseeing German intentions, and were it not for General George S. Patton's Third Army, ultimate allied victory may have remained illusive for several more months.

Patton had shown himself to be the most daring strategist of the allied commanders, but was disliked by most compatriots, mainly because of his truculence and independence--and his outspoken tongue.

General Eisenhower had spent much of November and December in his French headquarters smoothing the ruffled egos of his field commanders, particularly Britisher Montgomery who eyed the combined northern command at the expense of allied unity, and the career of General Patton in particular. Hence, as the old year ended, allied Chiefs of Staff were somewhat preoccupied with internal envy while busy consolidating their efforts to stop Germany's military gamble into Luxembourg and Belgium.

By January 1945 on the western front, the Germans were left holding defensive positions in all sectors. They had formulated no further master design to dislodge the overpowering allied armies from the continent. Germany's towns of Trier and Bitburg were about to be arrogantly breached by General Patton, and the Germans would groan at the first pain of foreign tanks tearing into their vitals.

General Eisenhower professed to be optimistic about the new year. He had made his major decisions regarding revised battle strategy, had settled the field dissensions among his commanders, and as a result was encouraged to get on with the business of concluding the war. At the same time his counterpart in overall U.S. intelligence, head of the OSS, General William (Wild Bill) Donovan, was able to concentrate on supervising important intrigues beyond the battle lines of the fighting men.

In such an atmosphere at London Allied Supreme Headquarters, Col. Halford Williams was ushered into the presence of the Supreme Allied Commander early on the morning of January 17, 1945. General Ike rose and took the salute, then asked Williams to be seated and offered him a cup of hot tea. With the tea offering, Williams knew there was something afoot.

The two soldiers discussed the latest Williams mission into the Ardennes forest where he had blown up the major stock pile of petrol intended for use by the German Panzer divisions in Hitler's presumptuous drive toward channel ports. The General personally complimented Williams on his success. He told him that General Patton had stated unequivocally, both orally and in writing, that the blowing of the German supply dump had shortened the war by many weeks and foiled the German thrust to Antwerp, Belgium.

Col. Williams listened quietly, speaking only when a direct answer was required, adhering to an embarrassing politeness for which he was known. Before arriving, Gen. Eisenhower had read and re-read Williams' account on how he and his team exploded the enemy's main petrol ordinance dump. General Ike had thoroughly enjoyed Williams' narrative description of Patton's reaction when Williams goaded Patton, saying the dump of synthetic potato petrol had been destroyed to prevent future drunkenness among Patton's G.I.s. Eisenhower chuckled each time he thought of Patton, the connoisseur of good whiskey, becoming enraged while believing an intruding colonel had set himself up as the divinely appointed temperance advocate in Patton's army.

Patton had seen Williams only that one time in December of 1944 but, unlike Eisenhower, he had failed to notice that Williams had a straight mouth, slightly down-turned at the ends, with no distinguishable laugh line even when amused. One had to closely observe his eyes to recognize a reaction. Eisenhower had learned to focus on Williams' eyes for subtle emotional changes rather than watch the cut of his mouth. Thus, when Eisenhower again brought up the blowing of the German potato gasoline dump, he carefully noticed Williams' eyes sparkle with amusement at the conversational trick he had pulled on General Patton, despite the tongue-in-cheek joke being so uncharacteristic of Williams.

Waiting to get on with the real purpose of the meeting, Gen. Eisenhower toyed with an urgent dispatch from Gen. Patton--the memo being the reason for Williams' presence. The memo, still among Patton's personal papers, read as follows:

"Ike: Can you send me that silly, stupid bastard who tried to make me believe that he destroyed the big German fuel dump to keep our soldiers from drinking it? Here he did the allies a great favor and then killed his credibility with me with that silly excuse. I need the silly bastard to take my reply to Rundstedt, as he is the only one that I know who is just stupid enough to get through and back in one piece."

Prior to arrival of Williams that day, the Supreme Commander had already replied to Patton as follows:

"January 16, 1945: Ike to Patton: George, I have asked that "silly bastard" be sent, and he will meet you in Paris tomorrow morning by plane. Do not underestimate the man, as he is probably the ablest and the greatest allied intelligence agent to come out of the war. He may seem a bit odd, as do all OSS men, including General Donovan, but give this man a difficult job and he will always come through with flying colors. I can tell you that this man never touches any kind of hard liquor and was probably horrified at the thought of the thousands and thousands of stacked cans of good German potato moonshine being left there for our soldiers to drink and thought that he was doing mankind a great favor by destroying it. It is also estimated at H.Q. that he shortened the war many weeks by blowing up the entire dump including the motor fuel."

Ike was grateful he wasn't required to show the young teetotaler Patton's memo expressing his displeasure regarding the gasoline confrontation, hence the Supreme Commander simply said "General Patton sends his regards and wants you for another assignment."

Conceivably, the allied chief had considered Patton's letter an ignorant affront to OSS planning and to Williams' bravery that had saved the lives of three of Patton's top officers. The mission had also changed the course of the war as it developed against the Germans in Hitler's final thrust in the Battle of the Bulge. For as Ike realized, had it not been for censorship Patton's untimely probe into the German beehive of activity and capture of his ablest officers might have destroyed forever Patton's image of invincibility.

Williams as usual was a bit nervous before the Supreme Commander. Finally he asked the purpose and place of the mission. He showed some discomfort by the habit of rubbing his right fist in the palm of his left hand as his mouth turned down at the ends. Ike pretended not to notice. He simply told Williams he had been given a new mission and was expected to move off in less than two hours; he would receive full instructions en route. Williams glanced for a sign of admiration from the general, or another complimentary word or two about his amazing triumphs. None registered on Eisenhower's countenance. His eyes had turned stern. Williams surmised the senior staff officers would forever keep a lid on the hidden debacle of the Ardennes Battle. Saving face for the allied brass would override all other considerations. Before Williams could register any further response, he heard himself being dismissed with a candid, "Good luck."

Later, within the hour he had put on his full dress uniform and golden sword, and upon leaving he was handed a special envelope addressed to Gen. George S. Patton. By noon he was at Orly Airport, then a military field outside Paris, having been flown over in a two-seat plane. A military escort picked him up as he deplaned, and Williams followed the colonel to the second floor dining room of the airport. As he entered, General Patton, in rumpled battle dress, came over and shook his hand.

Patton blurted, "I asked for you in spite of the rotten gasoline joke when you played temperance advocate and made me look stupid. Also, in spite of your refusal to accept my offer of a plane ride back to London last month. I have since heard about your idiotic Christmas holiday ride in that captured German car right through enemy lines as though there was no war going on. At least you obeyed one of my orders. You stayed away from Bradley's headquarters."

Patton continued to get his beefs off his chest, pulling rank to keep Williams at attention. "I'm told you and your gang visited Paris on the way back to London. They tell me you even demanded passage out of Cherbourg for your German car. We all know you delivered the trophy personally to General Eisenhower, and now they say he's driving the damn toy all around London."

Williams rallied from the frontal attack and feebly raised his hand in protest. He asked permission to speak. Then he ended the escapade of the German car safari with a smile and confided to Patton with mollifying words.

"After all General Patton, that toy was the Big Chief's first Christmas present. It made him very happy--and we all need a happy commander-in-chief, don't we?"

This time on summing up the earlier confrontation, Patton caught the sparkle in Williams' eyes, and they overcame their registered resentments towards each other by laughing. After all, the two men were main actors in the scenario leading to a realignment of world powers, which was expected to follow.

(The captured German officers' car today is among the wartime belongings of Col. Halford Williams in storage at the Smithsonian Institute in Washington, D.C.)

The evidence clearly suggested that these were two extraordinary men, undoubtedly the greatest U.S. heroes of World War II. But different they were. Patton was a five-foot-ten rough swearing, cigar chomping, and hard drinking officer graduate of West Point who was instinctively a soldier. He often insisted that he was familiar with Europe before arriving in this life having once served in Napoleon's French Army. His Third Army G2, Col. Koch, had foreseen the German plan in the Ardennes sector along the fifty-one mile Luxembourg front; therefore, Patton alone of the Allied Commanders was prepared for the German thrust. Furthermore, it was his armies that kept the Nazi push off guard before finally stalling them by January 11th.

In front of Patton sat another military man who disliked being called a soldier. Halford Williams also had an instinctive ability to make the right decisions for self-preservation in times of danger. Six feet of slow-moving body mannerisms, he had a changeless, somewhat somber facial expression, meek character, and he looked out of place in a skirmish or fire fight with the enemy, or for that matter in a saloon. He, unlike Patton, never ordered his men disciplined for disobeying an order or turning coward in battle, instead refusing to press charges. He didn't swear, seldom joked, and acted much like a grown up Eagle Scout, uncomfortable in an adult world.

Col. Williams sat down to his cup of tea and French rolls in the Orly Airport restaurant, ignoring Gen. Patton's advice that the tannin in the tea would someday poison his kidneys. Williams attempted a smile as Patton ordered a double whiskey and asked Williams for the special letter from General Eisenhower. Opening the manila envelope he scanned the contents addressed to him and then handed a wax-sealed envelope to Williams with an accompanying letter addressed to Field Marshal Karl Gerd Von Runstedt, Commander of the German Forces on the Western Front.

Col. Williams was still ignorant regarding the mission that he had begun alone. Patton however was cognizant of all the preliminary happenings, the first of which had begun on January 14th while he was at his headquarters in Luxembourg City. On that day a German officer named Col. Wilhelm Von Strauss had arrived with a flag of truce bearing a letter to Gen. Patton from General Von Runstedt. Gen. Patton placed the German truce bearer in the Kons Hotel and immediately sent word to General Eisenhower and General Montgomery, as well as to authorities in Washington and London. The Von Runstedt letter read as follows:

"To General George S. Patton, Jr.

Commander, Third American Army, Luxembourg City

My General:

Here we are destroying each other in a senseless war when our real enemy, Russia, is lurking in the background ready to pounce on the loser. Why don't we get together and form a truce, then combine as one army and drive the Russians back to their borders. Otherwise you in the future will face this black-hearted foe alone.

I propose that we meet on equal terms in Bern, Switzerland within the next three days to discuss this.

May I await your reply? My messenger shall wait.

Signed: General Von Rundstedt"

After twenty-four hours of heated discussion and debate among the allied leaders, both politically and militarily, Patton was authorized by General Eisenhower to reply that he could not meet with Von Rundstedt on such short notice but that within three days he would provide an answer to the German's suggestions. Patton had told Von Rundstedt in the initial reply that he personally favored such a meeting also since it would no doubt shorten the war and lead to a possible armistice if other terms failed.

Now on the 17th of January, the allied reply to the German letter indicated the high character of the forthcoming meeting expected between Williams and Von Rundstedt. He complimented Williams on his excellent attire and told him he was aware of his photographic memory both oral and visual. The general glanced at Williams' Sam Brown belt and sword, but made no disparaging comments.

Next morning, on the 18th, a winter snow covered Basil, Switzerland as the OSS colonel studied the big Swiss diesel at one end of the station. Attached was one railroad car of the Third Reich. On the roofs were Swiss markings showing a cross resembling the cross of Lorraine, Williams guessed. The idling diesel engine was piping heat into the German railroad passenger car.

As Williams boarded, a German captain, whose name he did not catch, met him. It was the German captain's duty to escort the American Colonel into Germany proper. Now, accompanying the American officer stood a black, master sergeant about five feet seven, trim in shape, carrying a rolled up flag of truce which would be displayed once they left the train inside Germany. The three men entered the German car, and as far as Williams could observe, there was no other occupant. Slowly the car moved to the German/Swiss border check point without stopping for customs, the one-car train rolling slowly into Germany carrying an American Colonel attired in full officers dress uniform with a golden sword at his waist.

Col, Halford Williams, the terror of the German Gestapo and their SS troops, was visiting Germany in his best dress form, the first official journey he had taken into enemy territory since he began his illegal infiltrations sixty missions before. And he was going first class with $300,000 in gold still on his head, dead or alive, the original amount long since doubled or tripled.

The first unpleasantness occurred when the German captain approached Col. Williams and insisted politely that he be blindfolded. The German captain did the same for Sgt. Meeks, the carrier of the truce flag.

An hour into the Black Forest, Williams heard the German Captain pull down the train blinds. Then he returned and removed the blindfolds to break open three box lunches and lemon drinks, all purchased at the Basil railway station. Moving slowly, it was obvious the tracks had been recently repaired due to allied bombings and Williams guessed, as they ate the sandwiches, that they had traveled less than fifteen miles. He remembered the German captain being courteous and speaking excellent English. The black American sergeant sat quietly nearby and Williams noted that the several swatches on his sleeve showed he had been a reservist before the war.

During the lunch Col. Williams looked across at the American sergeant and tried to strike up a conversation. Not responding to small talk, Williams pulled rank and asked the sergeant who he was and what was the military basis entitling him to be the carrier of the truce flag on this trip behind enemy lines.

"I'm Master Sergeant Meeks, stationed at Third Army Headquarters. My unit is the 110th Texas Cavalry, since 1931," the black man replied.

"But who's your commanding officer?" insisted the Colonel, and Sgt. Meeks replied, "I am the driver for General George S. Patton."

Williams was somewhat astounded at the disclosure. He thought this is really Patton's show. Finally, recovering from the introduction of the black sergeant, he asked how he had risen in the ranks and how long he had been associated with Gen. Patton. He was surprised at the short, laconic reply.

"I began as a stable boy when Gen. Patton was a cavalry officer in Texas. The general's great love was horses, same for me. In 1935, while his military stable hand in a camp near Abilene, Kansas, I was picked up while in town by about thirty whites that accused me wrongly of raping a white girl. Word got back to Gen. Patton and he hitched up teams to two artillery pieces. He arrived in town just as the mob was about to lynch me. When the general appeared, thank God, he fired warning shots over the mob's heads and told them he'd level the town if they didn't cut me loose at once. As you can see Sir, I'm quite alive and have been with the general ever since, and I'11 stay with him till he retires."

Williams wished he had not pried into the sergeant's past.

The German captain listened in apparent awe at a way of American life that had lingered into the pre-war years. Neither men asked questions when Meeks finished. The trip lasted two hours and then came to a stop.

From the station the three-man group was picked up in a military car and began the ascent towards their rendezvous. Fifteen or so minutes later, in mid-morning of January 17, 1945 the blindfolds were removed from Col. Williams and Sgt. Meeks. Straightening his clothes, Col. Williams marched briskly beside the white flag of truce held aloft by the black American sergeant to the headquarters of General Kurt Von Rundstedt, the most respected German military person facing the might of the western world. Williams chuckled to himself. All we lack, he thought, is a Scottish highlander playing the pipes.

He scrutinized the faces of a few members of the enemy headquarters staff. None he recognized. Then as the escort paused before Von Rundstedt's door, Williams briefly glimpsed a hawkish face with piercing eyes staring at him through the doorway of an adjacent room. The tall, slim, dark-haired man wore the uniform of the S.S. A scar went from his left ear to his mouth. Then Williams remembered. In his mind he saw an English Colonel driving away from the Asternach petrol depot on the fateful morning of December 18th. One glance at the same man told Williams he was near the presence of a hard core Nazi who had infiltrated the U.S. espionage system and was perhaps at one time a double agent. Williams wondered if he had walked into a trap. He had been told that the price on his head had gone up to $300,000 in gold, dead or alive. He reasoned that the cunning of Otto Skorzeny would be engaged on how to collect the ransom during the next few hours.

The door opened and Von Rundstedt rose from his desk sitting before a big fire in the hearth. As Von Rundstedt returned Williams' salute, avoiding the Nazi arm stretch, he resumed his seat, and Williams looked out the window at a ribbon of water below the Bavarian mountaintop on which the chalet stood. He sensed he saw the beginnings of the Rhine as he moved before the General's desk and stood at attention. The black sergeant displayed his flag of truce and subsequently was dismissed to the orderly room. For the moment, all the military bearing of each officer would be evident; the proper officer stance of the younger 26-year-old American, and the confident, wiry, middle-aged German officer before him, trained in the old pre-Hitler army school of discipline and obedience.

Von Rundstedt was Prussian to the core. His officer's sword and belt hung on a coat rack beside his desk indicating the general wore the sword frequently. To Col. Williams, he was the archetype of old German militarism that he respected. Beneath the older man's stiff bearing, Williams saw in his face a lifetime of soldiering. Yet below the visage there was friendliness in spite of the attempt to be over courteous. The general offered Williams a cigarette and was refused. In declining the cigarette, Williams saw the eyebrows of Von Rundstedt raise, and he first observed his wrinkled skin beneath a monocle that added nobility and hauteur. It was plain that each man respected the other.

"Stand at ease Colonel," began the German officer politely. Then he painstakingly studied the American. The general removed his monocle and finally spoke directly to the emissary.

"You are most certainly not English. This is the first privilege of meeting you, Colonel Halford Williams." The general lingered on the name, Halford Williams, and repeated it. "Williams is your code name, I presume."

The German general inhaled a breath of smoke, tapped quietly on his desk as though contemplating the pieces of a jigsaw puzzle, then released the smoke. He looked up and said, "We Germans all call you the American Fox because your rescue missions are legendary inside Hitler's occupied lands from Norway to the borders of Russia. They say you are invincible--that you can't be killed. It is also reliably reported that you have been dropped or appeared suddenly inside Germany dozens of times, perhaps as many as sixty over the last two years alone."

The German's eyes lighted with admiration as he studied the waist of the American colonel standing before him. "All the stories say the same thing. They say the Fox at times carries a golden sword to direct his five or six-man band. Imagine such a ridiculous medieval symbol of authority. Of course Colonel, you don't need your sword on a mission like this where only diplomacy is necessary, do you?" The general's tone was not sarcastic but quizzical, asking for a response.

The young American colonel still stood silent. Then the interrogation continued. "Can you hear me Colonel?"

"Yes Sir!" the younger of the two replied.

The general continued. "Hitler's reward for delivery of the Fox, preferably alive, now exceeds $300,000 in gold. Perhaps I should tear up this letter and collect the reward."

The American Fox smiled defiantly. Von Rundstedt went on "I know deep within me that you are the Fox. Eisenhower would not send anyone but his bravest and most trusted for this mission, because he had to be certain the message reached me."

Col. Williams interrupted. "And General Eisenhower also had to be certain that the man he sent knew how to get back safely in spite of enemies like the scar-faced SS officer outside your door."

General Von Rundstedt responded. "Have no worry Colonel--remember you are my guest." But even allowing yourself to be blindfolded under German guard, I think you knew quite well that your destiny was not to die--yet. Although, should I not consider turning you over to that despicable man you refer to lingering outside in the corridor? Please reply Colonel."

As though unmoved by the penetrating analysis, the American agent answered, "Sir! Even if I were the one whom you call the Fox, I should not worry. Among the allies General, your name too is legendary. You have been tagged as a gentleman with honor--an enemy to be respected. Even if your Fuehrer ordered it, you would not keep a bona fide courier as a negotiable instrument of blackmail."

The general nodded almost imperceptibly. "May I suggest that we now proceed with the order of business? Do you have a letter for me?"

Col. Williams withdrew the letter from Gen. Patton and handed it to the senior officer, who upon receiving it directed the young American to be seated and then proceeded to break the seal of the envelope and read the contents. The letter was on one page in duplicate.

Patton's letter is not reproduced here but in effect the contents were as follows: "I am sympathetic to your proposal that we join forces against the Russian armies. I request we meet at the Wolfgang Bar in Berne, Switzerland on January 26th with your most able staff officers. I hope we may concur in changing allied strategy favorable to your recent German peace overtures, subject to approval by the Allied Commander-in-Chief, General Dwight Eisenhower." The letter added that any joint agreement would be made also with the political acknowledgement of President Roosevelt and Prime Minister Churchill.

Von Rundstedt glowed as he read Patton's letter. Then he stood up and asked Col, Williams to take breakfast in the officer's mess while an answer was prepared. The general said that if time permitted they would resume their informal talks after the colonel had eaten breakfast. He advised Williams that expected departure time would be after dark. Williams wondered if Skorzeny would wait for him in ambush when he was marched back to the train in blindfold.

The American colonel sat in the officers' mess eating a breakfast of Bavarian rolls, jam, sausage, and tea as a number of German army and air force officers passed in and out of the room. He considered the presence of civilians plus several different military officers representing the three services. It was unusual and wondered why they had come. He reflected that Germany was closer to recognizing the end of the war than most allied leaders realized and that the chalet was a key lodging on an evacuation route out of Germany.

One face that he noted carefully he was to see twice again. This was a Wermacht Air Force idol of reddish face and hair that had shot down thirty-three allied planes. His name was Kurt Von Schusnick. He was a top enemy ace whom the English, up to Churchill, respected for his audacity and combat ability. Williams also caught sight again of the tall, piercing-eyed Skorzeny as he looked briefly behind him at another table. He was agitated that Skorzeny was nearby and wondered if this enemy killer was studying him for a reason regardless of the mission being one of trust and truce.

The American had never been so vulnerable, and he was relieved when the General's Aide De Camp, Felix Von Rattenwell, came in and invited him to return to the warm fire and comfortable chair in Von Rundstedt's office.

He was asked to sit down and relax by the general who told him that he had accepted the conditions for a forthcoming meeting with General Patton. An additional document was being typed in English that was to be studied by the allies prior to the scheduled meeting in Berne.

The records show that Von Rundstedt had penned his acceptance to Patton's letter of invitation to meet and had signed and dated it. In addition, there was an attachment of a German proposal for the allied and German armies to meet and unite within Germany and march towards Moscow. The plan as proposed by Von Rundstedt and his staff did not have the concurrence, and would not include the presence of Adolf Hitler. While waiting for the document of proposal for allied and German armies to unite against Soviet Russia, General von Rundstedt left his desk and drew up a chair beside Williams. "I seldom get an opportunity under the watchful eyes of the Nazis to talk man to man."

Williams saw the stern countenance of the general change to one of introspection and he waited for a thaw in the man's formal bearing. The German drew a smoke-filled breath, exhaled, and quietly reminisced out loud.

"I'm certain you're aware Colonel, that twice in your wartime career you prevented Germany from winning major campaigns. As a result, our failures left us, up till now, unable to negotiate an honorable peace."

Williams was flabbergasted by the direct confrontation. "That's a puzzling statement Sir," answered Williams.

Von Rundstedt lowered his voice and continued. "The Battle of the Bulge is the most recent case in which you were largely responsible for denying battle triumphs to Germany. As you know, we lost the campaign in the Ardennes, and you, Colonel, brought about the contributing incident. Have patience and follow my military logic for a minute!"

Von Rundstedt continued. "My paramount belief is that your armies never could have stopped us in reaching our objective, Antwerp, if you and your handful of infiltrators had not blown up our Esternach petrol and ammunition depot. We relied almost exclusively on that depot to maintain front line momentum for our panzer divisions, particularly during the first critical week of the blitz. Had we reached our goal we would have cut enemy divisions to pieces and changed the outcome of the war.

Colonel! Because you totally destroyed our initial stocks of petrol and ammunition, we fell short of our goal. We slowed down so much that in forty-eight hours my fighting armor began rationing its petrol and consolidating gains, when it should have been assaulting enemy lines.

During that delay, your able General Patton's follow-through stalled us long enough to spoil our plans to take Antwerp. I personally consider Patton's redeployment of his troops against us in the Battle of the Bulge to be the most masterful counter-attack on either side in World Wars I and II."

The German general concluded. "Because you blew up our supply depot, Germany lost the last battle on the western front and an opportunity to negotiate a conditional peace.

"Williams quizzed the German general and asked why he portrayed his guest as the man responsible for blowing the petrol dump to which the old warrior replied, "Over twenty of our people that day reported a tall, thin, bespectacled, young man as the leader. They also made another penetrating observation--the young man spoke not a word of German. Von Rundstedt paused a moment and continued, "The most reliable assurance I have, however, comes from the SS colonel across the hall. He verified who you are only half-an-hour ago."

The general butted his cigarette and smiled in fatherly way at the young stranger. Williams reflected on the general's profound critique of the Battle of the Bulge and pondered the officer's intentions as he methodically placed another cigarette in the holder and lit it. Speaking carefully, Von Rundstedt continued. "May I tell you of another occasion in which the American Fox helped steal a victory from Germany and drive Hitler into a mad rage for two days?"

Williams answered the query saying, "How could a stranger, unknown to Hitler, add to his insanity?" The German general seemed to enjoy the ad-lib. He answered in a low voice. "That stranger--whom I instinctively feel is you Colonel--was instrumental in splitting our defense forces guarding the English Channel on 'D Day.' You, the American Fox, are the one whom I believe delivered into our hands false information that changed the outcome of the war in Europe and made the fatherland the loser." Von Rundstedt, ignoring the younger man's contrived naiveté, spoke cautiously and adjusted his monocle as he scrutinized Williams for a reaction.

He then said: "On June 1st, 1944 I believe, a dead British courier with the false plans of an imminent June 6th invasion of Europe through southern France was found washed up on the Spanish Mediterranean beach. German intelligence procured the elaborate documents planted on the dead courier, and Berlin experts examined them. I was present at that high command meeting and, against my better judgment the Fuehrer decided the invasion plans were authentic. He ordered us to pull twenty-seven divisions of battle hardened troops from positions on the English Channel forts and divert them hurriedly 500 miles south to the French shores of the Mediterranean, for what was expected to be the forthcoming invasion of the continent.

"But where did the real invasion take place Colonel? On the beaches of Normandy and Brittany of course! And when did the real invaders assault us? On June 6th naturally.

"Let me tell you Colonel! If we had left our twenty-seven divisions on the English Channel, 'D Day' would have meant disaster day for Eisenhower and his overall strategy to occupy Europe. Even so Colonel, your armies almost failed to get a foothold on the continent, notwithstanding half our fighting men and their weapons were lured away."

The general uttered the next sentence with forceful but low tones. "If I had not been forced to divide my armies on 'D-Day' and lose our defense advantages, the war would have been over long ago. And many months ago we would have made an honorable peace."

Pointing his finger at Williams in a non-menacing way, Von Rundstedt finished by saying, "Yes Colonel Williams, our intelligence knows you have been London's principal agent used over 60 times to embarrass Hitler's Socialist Republic of Germany. And you are the Scarlet Pimpernel who cheated us twice in winning major battles."

Williams simply replied, "That is a sobering thought General, but every man to his own opinions. Of course I can't comment on your theories, but I will say that it seems ironic that we both are engaged today in a similar role of trying to end the war honorably for both sides."

The general smiled.

A cup of well-brewed tea was brought in for Col. Williams, and as he sipped the beverage the German general ventured to ask Williams how he bad kidnapped the entire headquarters of the German 14th Army shortly after "D Day." Williams denied he had participated in the disappearance of the headquarters staff including General Von Bock, but when questioned he did admit that General Von Bock was doing well under house arrest in an English seaside town. The American officer corrected the German general in his use of the English word kidnap and asked him to regard the removal of the headquarters staff as an accidental abduction carried out in the most humane manner. The older man smiled and ended the voluntary interrogation by saying, "Thank you for news of my esteemed friend."

Williams had not become annoyed with the general's direct assumptions. On the contrary he had grown closer to the stranger, and his respect showed. They both had become fallible in searching for the reason for the war and the role of their respective nations. Williams thought of the simple explanation offered by Von Rundstedt on why Germany lost the two decisive battles to which the general referred. And wondering about this aspect, he ventured to speak about the metaphysical, the unseen forces affecting mankind. Hence, he undertook to say, "General, irrespective of the misfortunes of war which you partly attribute to my actions, it was not the loss of those two battles you mention that will cause Germany's ultimate defeat. The outcome of this planetary clash is deeper than two human armies pitted against each other.

"The real antagonists in the fight are supernatural forces of good and evil, and men are the pawns who follow whichever force they choose."

The general quickly responded and asked, "Strange, you should mention that. Are you identifying the evil force with Germany?"

The younger man, who as a boy had witnessed the supernatural, answered. "The evil cancer in Germany has been Hitler and his Nazism since pre-war days, that's the point I wish to make."

"I agree about Hitler and his cultism," replied the general, "but are you saying the allied nations fighting against us are not evil?"

"I'm not inferring that Sir," spoke up Williams. "I'm saying only that the lesser of the two evils lies with the allied nations, and that in the case of World War II, the higher forces of good will triumph. I am also prophesying that this will not be the last confrontation between supernatural forces of good and evil in which men will fight the battles. There will be another war I think greater than this one, and I doubt if Germany will be the antagonist against us."

The general responded an acknowledgement. "I don't know who will be in the next war. If it comes, I won't be here, no matter whose side Germany takes. But I agree with you my fine young Colonel, let's hope the forces of good in the whole world will overcome the evil."

As General Von Runstedt indicated the talks were finished, Williams added his favorite theme that "war would be no more."

The top German commander offered his parting advice. "Do not be concerned about the return train trip to the Swiss border. You and what you carry are too important to fall into the wrong hands. During our confidential talk I made sure that neither of two SS officers attached to my headquarters overheard us. Of course, you already know Col. Skorzeny, but my officers also are making sure that SS officer Col. Wurzack, stationed here, is also kept preoccupied. Furthermore, I assure you neither will attack you on your way back. For that reason I have ordered your rail car guarded by well-armed soldiers loyal to me"

The next morning of January 13, 1945, General George S. Patton met Col. Williams and Sgt. Meeks at the Swiss border. He accepted the written German proposal for ending hostilities against the allied armies in Europe and studied a proposed plan by Von Rundstedt and his staff for the combined forces to march on Moscow.

Eight days later the Wolfgang Bar in Berne, Switzerland was the scene of a strange meeting as American Colonel Williams witnessed the ever so correctly dressed Von Rundstedt sweep into the bar with two staff members including the air ace, Kurt Von Schusnick, whose face he had seen in Von Rundstedt's mess.

Minutes later the bar door swung open again and General George S. Patton stomped in, dressed in helmet, crumpled field dress, and high boots. Patton led his group over to the table whereupon the Germans stood up, exchanged formal greetings, and the ensemble sat down and ordered drinks. Von Rundstedt asked for scotch and Patton, bourbon.

Setting down their glasses after a quick toast by one of the American staff officers, General Patton rose, ordered another round and while still on his feet, gulped his bourbon down in one swallow. He looked directly at Von Rundstedt and exclaimed, "Hell, General! What are we fighting each other for when the worst bastard in the world is that S.O.B. Stalin?" Those opening remarks set the tone for the meeting, the rest of which is still classified.

But the military plans agreed upon at that secret rendezvous between the leading allied and German officers were to be held in abeyance--forever.

Two weeks later a disappointed Von Rundstedt, back at his headquarters, told his officers that the plan proposed by he and Patton at Berne had been vetoed by President Roosevelt, even over Churchill and Eisenhower's objections. Von Rundstedt said there was no hope to end the war except to fight till the final surrender of the German armies.

Aside from the military aspect of the war in Europe, the forthcoming Yalta Conference scheduled secretly for February 1945 would inflict a political disaster for Germany more insidious than five years of military losses. Following the Yalta Conference, when the subterfuge of Roosevelt and Stalin was revealed, Germany's peace terms would prove bitterer than the Treaty of Versailles of World War I.

No Doubt General Von Rundstedt was disappointed at the failure of the allies to march collectively with him against Soviet Russia. Perhaps he reflected on Williams' words that, "in the end good will triumph over evil." He may have asked himself the ironic question: If the forces of good won the battle to free Europe, why was the victory divided with the forces of evil? Perhaps, as Williams had prophesized, it would take another war to banish the forces of evil from this planet.

Chapter 11

RESCUING THE SACRED RELICS

It was April 6, 1945. The war in Europe was winding down. The solidarity of the German armies had been broken as Russian troops from the east and allied soldiers from the west overran pockets of isolated German resistance.

Inside the Hungarian border and approximately two hundred miles from the allied front headquarters in Vienna, Austria, Col. Halford Williams and his team of five waited in a defile along a narrow country road. It was 10 a.m.

The group had just placed a concealed chain with attached grenades across a cut in the dirt road and secured the chain at both ends. In the four hours since their air drop from an American plane piloted by Lieutenant Commander Ted White (U.S. Navy), the team had surveyed the area, buried their chutes and located a small cave close to the road in which they had hidden their gear for this particular operation. The necessities included seven days of K-rations for each man, blanket, ground sheet of canvas for sleeping or use as a stretcher. Each man (except the commander) also carried a knife, snub-nosed machine gun with 200 rounds of ammo, and his 45-revolver.

The intruders waited silently since 8 a.m., three on each side of the road, ears tuned for the sound of approaching vehicles from the northwest. They had taken positions near a recent firefight between Germans and Russians indicating they were in a Russian controlled area.

Radio operator Soitzman had picked up Russian military on a frequency which revealed that somewhere in the general area there was a large body of Soviet troops with more expected to arrive the same day. The team became sensitive that there must be some important objective suddenly drawing Russian troops into the same vicinity. They would soon find the answer.

Allied briefing had told the commandos that their objective was non-military but concerned only the capture of a single box about 18" x 30" x 12", the contents to which they had not been made privy. The mystery box was expected to arrive along this same deserted road in a convoy of three German officer's cars. The convoy would be coming from the northwest, and its ultimate destination was a castle in Hungary. Beyond that information they knew little else. It was almost 10 a.m. as the team waited on either side of the road, full of expectation and tension. The crisp morning air had warmed and the birds began to sing.

The country road twisted through hills and valleys into the interior of Hungary. Within this locale at mid morning, the team heard the faint mechanical sound of approaching vehicles. Each of the men held an elevated position for the ambush, which assured advantage in firepower and observation. Nevertheless, Col. Williams expected the enemy would likely out number them four to one and probably was prepared to hold out to the last man. They had been told to expect the object of their mission to be located in the middle car and to avoid damaging that vehicle or firing directly into it. Hence, the plan was to knock out the first car and in so doing, stop the others in their tracks.

The oblong wooden box in question had rope handles on each corner. Williams figured the box would be easily confiscated, but it was assumed that one or two of the guarding Germans would have knowledge of the box's contents and would not yield the prize without a tough defense.

Unknown to the colonel the contents of the box had been fought over, stolen, purchased, and had been the focus of battles through all generations since the time of Christ. Perhaps most significant to those who claimed the contents of the box was the spear head, a holy relic said to have pierced the side of Jesus after he succumbed on the cross of Calvary. Over forty kings and conquerors were credited with having held the spear point in their possession and had been undefeatable till the holy artifact was taken from them. Also, considered less holy but held in great esteem, was the sword in the box which history had said was wielded by Roman Centurion, Gaius Casius Longinus to defend the body of Jesus when it was removed from the cross. Gaius Casius was also said to have owned the shield that Col. Williams and his team had come upon sixty-one missions earlier in the French cave. As happened on that previous mission, the young soldier also was unaware this time of the existence of the sword or spear. He would soon be caught up in the historic drama. But he had never read von Eschenbach's romantic Parsival, or visited the Hofburg Museum in Vienna, or wetted his interest in the so-called legendary tales of King Arthur. The third item in the box was the jeweled iron crown of St. Stephen of Hungary.

The day before in Paris, Gen. Eisenhower had called Williams in and announced the assignment authorized by General Donovan, OSS Chief. Williams was asked if he wished to refuse, but he declined. He had handed the general a list of the five men he wanted, went to bed, and when he woke at midnight, his team had been assembled, ready for final briefing.

The three cars came into view less than a quarter mile distant. Their speed was about forty kilometers per hour, four to five car lengths apart, and each carried eight soldiers with drawn guns. The cars came abreast of the allied team spread out on both sides of the cut as the lead vehicle crossed the hidden chain. The explosion blew the car's front end into the air, and falling back it caught fire. The drivers following braked their cars as the enemy jumped and ran for cover.

Five allied Tommy guns opened up crossfire on the running men. The allied commandos, still firing, exposed themselves in order to broaden the field of fire again retreating targets. Upon seeing that the ambushers were not Russians, those Germans not hit or who had not escaped raised their hands whereupon Colonel Williams signaled cease-fire. Sgt. McCloskey recognized the first words, "Americans? Americans? We surrender."

Less than half an hour later two German officer's cars were turned around and headed back in the direction from which they came. Five unarmed German soldiers clung onto their seats in the wild ride along Hungarian roads that were expected to lead to Vienna. In the first car rode Col. Williams, Sgt. McCloskey, and the oblong box of treasures. And watching the box steadfastly sat a German army RC chaplain who had refused to run when the attack took place.

Williams had hurried to the center car and confronted the unarmed, obdurate guardian of the box who had remained defiantly seated. The two officers had exchanged words in English. Col. Williams checked the ID of the 45-year-old refined German as the officer cleric stared intently into the face of the younger scholarly-looking man. Williams heard the chaplain say, "Sir, something within tells me that you are the proper custodian of this box. My instructions were to transport it to a nearby castle in Hungary where it was to remain hidden till after hostilities at which time it would end up in the Vatican."

Then the priest told Williams that the box contained unspecified holy relics, which were authentic. He said there were at least two other imitation sets of the same relics in existence elsewhere in Europe. Williams had listened in rapt silence, as he recalled the final words of General Eisenhower when departing on the mission the night before.

The general had cautioned Williams. "I will not reveal what you're going after, except to say the Germans possess it, the Russians want it, and we're determined to steal it. In spite of the three to five thousand Russians already deployed in the search, I want you Colonel, to be the first to find the box of objects and bring them back to Vienna."

Eisenhower added these words, "Soldier! We've sent out at least one other mission to find the same thing you'll be looking for. We're making sure the Russians know about the other mission because that one is after an exact replica of what you're seeking. We'll leak the information on that diversionary search later on, but your mission is top secret and the Soviets must never know of it." Williams asked the general how he would know if he was to find the real object, and his commander replied ambiguously. "You of all people will know if the object is the true one or not." Perplexed, Williams was dismissed. His final instructions were that if they recovered the box and ran into Soviet troops while escaping, they were to bury the prize and remember the spot.

As they relate to this chapter, the contents of the box, i.e., the sword and spear are first identified in the year 1938. On that date in history of the modern world the sword and spear lay undisturbed on a purple velvet dais encased in glass in Room #10 of the Hofburg Treasure House in Vienna, Austria.

In the same Treasure House about thirty years earlier, a young man of slight stature, with a shock of dark brown hair hanging on one side of his forehead, and sporting a Charlie Chaplin moustache stood looking at the objects. Around his neck there hung a gold cross with two different length bars known as the cross of Evil.

He had longed to hold the spear and sword relics about which he had read in his spare time while selling water-colored paintings on the streets of the city. His name was Adolf Hitler, and later in his life his German armies would march into Austria and annex it.

Hitler never forgot his desire to hold the relics of Christ's crucifixion still exhibited in the Hofburg Treasure House in 1938 when his storm troopers took Austria. Within hours of Nazi occupation, Hitler demanded immediate access into the museum. After visiting hours, once again he stood in awe along with the museum attendant, staring at the spear which had pierced the side of Jesus Christ and which legend said gave power of conquest over one's enemies. Such a talisman Hitler needed to embrace--and confiscate.

On the first step of that road to world power, Hitler had already nurtured an evil spirit of hate and anger. He had become a mass murderer of friends and enemies in the years since becoming head of the German state. Now this man of sinister purpose, who would rise to greater heights on the dead bodies of millions, stood in front of the two artifacts that he most envied in life.

The gloved attendant opened the glass case and stood back. The ancient weapon was made of thin strips of white hot Damascus steel hammered together to form one blade about twenty-six inches long. The sword was not curved and had no blood groove. Its small, notched handle had probably been covered with an outer casing at one time.

Adolf Hitler, the man with satanic dreams of destroying the Jewish race before achieving world domination, reached into the display.

Hitler lifted the weapon carefully from the dais as the custodian watched uneasily. The dictator jumped up as voltage seemed to surge through his entire body. Undeterred, he tried again to hold the weapon and was lifted into the air unceremoniously. This time he dropped the weapon and winced with pain. Along the fingers and thumbs of his right hand and across the palm of the other were severe burns where his flesh had touched the holy relic. He looked in anger at the attendants then raised his hands to his face and peered at the burns.

Moments passed as the Nazi leader recovered from the shock. With his damaged right hand he again reached into the glass case and his arm hovered hesitatingly over the spear which 2,000 years earlier had pierced the flesh of Jesus Christ following his crucifixion. It is doubtful if Hitler had thought seriously about the thrust of that spear point into the God man's heart twenty centuries earlier from which there gushed out blood and water symbolizing the new covenant between God and man. But Hitler picked up the spear with his right hand and clasped it to his breast.

Suddenly the dictator let out an anguished cry. The curator saw Hitler's right arm extended and come crushing against Hitler's chest. A repeat thrust was imminent as the possessed spearhead was prevented from delivering the fatal thrust. One of the Austrians grasped the weapon and pried it from Hitler's atrophied hand as the Fuehrer fell immobile to the floor. He did not rise.

Quickly replacing the spear in the case and locking the glass door to the enclosure they carried Hitler out and summoned Himler, Kaltenbrunner, von Siervers, and Buch stationed outside the Hofburg. The well-laid plans had fallen amiss for Hitler's henchmen to provide him a private audience with his ancient idols of power. Only two days earlier Hitler's 8th Army had forced the people and police of Vienna to accept the German occupation of Austria, but in only a few revered moments the ancient artifacts attached to the death of the Judaic reformer and world savior had rejected him.

The man who would hold and claim the sacred relics was not revived even after a doctor worked on him. A Catholic priest was urgently brought in and the usurper of German power was finally resuscitated by the power of medicine and the cross. The record of that Hitler-versus-spear encounter is held in the British Archives, the written account having been transferred to London from Vienna after World War II.

If the spear were an indication of Hitler's ordained future power, he was never destined to unite the Germanic tribes of Europe. But the following day the sword and spear and other regalia were removed from their case and taken to Nuremberg, the old capital of the German Empire. Sometime in 1941, after Hitler had; begun his intensified purge of the Jews, had overrun Poland and Czechoslovakia, and had killed most of his adversaries and countless Slavish people, he had the spear and sword brought to him from St. Katherine's Church in Nuremberg to the Reichstag in Berlin.

Calling in his trusted confidant, the Chancellor confessed, "I cannot as much touch that old spear or sword they're so dangerous. Can you get the spirits out of them without them casting a curse on me?" The two relics were taken to a workshop where each was so duplicated that it would pass visual inspection. The replicas were returned to Hitler who happily examined them and believed the following explanation of how they were dispossessed of anti-Hitler spirit forces.

The occultist dictator was told it had been necessary to nickel plate the sword blade and in so doing, the electrolysis had removed the spirits of burning. A new handle gave the sword beauty. Hitler was grateful regarding the expunging of the spirits that had harmed him, and he picked up the sword and beamed with delight, immediately attaching the scabbard to his belt. He never learned the sword was a cleverly made replica.

Concerning the spear head with the embedded copper spike in the center groove, which once had helped fasten Jesus to the cross, Hitler also examined it carefully. Picking up the duplication he cautiously discovered he could maneuver it without an external force usurping the movements of his arm and hand as was done at the Vienna Hofburg three years earlier.

Inquiring how the change was affected, he was told that a powerful electromagnetic force had been applied to de-energize the adversarial force surrounding the spear. Thus, Hitler believed he was on his way to world conquest.

Upon being interviewed later, the German artificer who had duplicated the weapons confessed he had received a revelation that a White Spirit Order, being the highest realm of good in the spirit world, protected the original pieces. It was also revealed to the craftsman that Hitler was under the influence of the Black Spirit Order, representing everything evil.

The person who duplicated the relics and fooled Hitler was interviewed twice in 1985 and verified that Hitler, after that date in 1941, never saw or touched the true relics again. The originals were given to an anti-Hitler officer in Berlin who was responsible for their hiding. Their presence remained unknown to the public until Col. Halford Williams became the temporary custodian from the unknown Catholic chaplain on April 16, 1945.

As the mixed team of allied and German men drove west through the Hartz Mountains of Hungary, they realized they had landed in a constricted triangle of land close to the borders of Czechoslovakia and Austria. The compass kept them on a westerly course as

Col. Williams conferred with the German priest who believed they would cross the winding Raba River later in the day. To the south lay the town of Gyor that Williams avoided, speculating it was occupied by Soviet troops.

Sgt. McCloskey was more worried about the German presence among them, but Williams insisted the disarmed Germans presented no immediate problem. "Why did you bring the Gerries along," asked McCloskey? "The priest acts like he owns the box; he won't take his big loafers off it." Williams explained his thoughts. "It's okay! He's so dedicated, it leaves me time to find a safe way back to Vienna."

Checking a map the colonel identified their secondary road and was certain they eventually would come to the Raba River where there was marked two bridges, either of which they could use."

"Let's hope the Ruskies aren't guarding the bloody bridges," spoke McCloskey, who then heard his OC say, "Don't count on it! I have a gut feeling they are expecting us."

It was dusk when the two cars reached the Raba after having avoided Russian patrols and detoured their roadblocks. At long last they sighted the first possible crossing and cautiously drove up, only to discover the reason for the absence of Russian guards. The bridge had been blown. After checking the disabled crossing, Sgt. McCloskey advised that the bridge had fallen in the last twenty-four hours. It was apparent they were being hunted and that the Russians, knowing they were in the area, were severing all escape routes to the west and north.

That night they bivouacked in tree cover and shared their K-rations with the German prisoners and established somewhat of a survival relationship. The second possible bridge was located the following day after circuitous detours and enforced concealment from Russian troops that grew more abundant in the area. Williams knew the net was tightening when they found the second bridge also blown. On the morning of April 18th, the third day of their mission, the team came to the realization that the Russians were gradually corralling them, and the main corral was the town of Gyor. The unwelcome alternative was to abandon the cars, carry the box and head west on foot.

Williams called the entire group together including the Germans. They gathered around in silence, and the colonel--not given to overstating a situation--made the sparse announcement: "We're going to town." Then he added, "The Russians won't expect us to oblige them, but we have no other choice."

The cars were loaded and they took off toward the main highway into Gyor. At 7 a.m. on the outskirts of Gyor they met their first welcoming committee; a roadblock set up for them of six well-armed Russian troops. Slowing down and coming to a halt they waited for the enforcers to make the first move. They did.

Two Canadians had volunteered for this mission. One whose name is not recorded spoke Russian fluently, and the other had the given or assigned name of Bruce Black, RCAF. As the cars came to a halt, the Russia-speaking Canadian affably engaged the first adversaries, two Russian officers and an NCO with drawn guns, while in the background stood three other covering soldiers. In a couple of minutes the Canadian interpreter captured the interest of the Soviet officers who began to relax their guard. Williams handed the Canadian a blanket pass written in Russian and signed by the Soviet commandant of Vienna. Its authority was meaningless two hundred miles from Vienna, but the Russian officers began examining it, still confused by their first encounter of a mixed bag of allied troops beyond their lines who had just captured some Germans. As they conferred about the paper, the Russians asked permission to examine the vehicle. The Canadian sergeant interpreted slowly for Williams seeking a delay, and meanwhile, the other Canadian, Captain Black got out of the rear vehicle on the left and stretched his legs and arms to distract the Russians. On cue, Sgt. McCloskey did the same in the front car dismounting on his right. He told the Canadian to tell the Russians he had to relieve himself at a nearby tree as he carelessly leaned his Tommy gun against the car for the Russians to observe and dispel their caution. As the Scotsman reached the tree adjacent to the Russian soldiers in the background,

Black began some calisthenics to further distract them while the Canadian interpreter engaged the officers more candidly as to why they should inspect the cars.

The scenario was the same one often repeated by the team--distracting the adversary with a harmless amateur show of goodwill. The Russian officers never saw McCloskey get two of the backup men with his lariat, but in less than three minutes, they were laying dead on the ground.

Sgt. McCloskey hollered to get attention. The Canadian interpreter pointed to McCloskey and the Russian officers turned their heads to see two fallen comrades and one with an American 45 revolver at his head. As each startled Russian returned his gaze to the jeep occupants, they were confronted with five Tommy guns aimed directly at them. On orders from Col. Williams, Capt. Black disarmed the Russians and the German soldiers tied each to trees and stuffed gags in their mouths. The allied commandos then added six more loaded weapons to their meager arsenal.

The job finished, Col. Williams surveyed the desecration, and said with relief, "Let's get out of here and into town. We must find the main railroad. Like it or not, we'll try and drive these cars west on the rails until we come across the first usable auto road to the next main town, Sopron."

Asked where Sopron was located, Williams replied, "Half way to Vienna which is two hundred miles from here by rail." Said the commander, "We've got a long way to go to get out of Russian territory."

At that point the Canadian interpreter who had talked to the Russian officers revealed that the local Russian troops were part of a 3,500-man contingent sent into the area to locate an important war booty hidden in a box or boxes carried by Germans or perhaps allied troops. No matter who had the boxes they were to be taken. Taking to side streets to avoid Russian patrols the cars passed the occasional single to threesome of Soviets, but were not challenged. Less than four miles from the last roadblock was the main railroad line from Vienna to Budapest. Moving carefully in a southerly direction, the two cars penetrated town center where they expected to cross the railroad line emanating from the station.

The air was still crisp as they bundled up and passed odd Russians in full battle dress. The sky above the town of Gyor had shed its occasional fleecy cloud as warmth from the buildings ascended into the lower atmosphere. The team was surprised there was so little motor traffic and realized there was a strict curfew imposed by the new conquerors. Col. Williams felt his two Nazi cars stood out so plainly they would be targets of a sudden Soviet fusillade; therefore, except for the drivers, all men were ready to defend the little convoy.

High above the Hungarian town a lone reconnaissance plane narrowed its spiral pattern as an allied airman with spotter field glasses kept his searching eyes fixed on two lonely German military cars groping their way through the town. He watched them bypass the main intersection and take a secondary street past vacant warehousing and come abreast of the main line of the railroad track. He witnessed the German cars come to a halt as if surveying the scene in front, and then move across the tracks less than a block from the town's railroad station.

The spotter let out an oath and spoke to the pilot in the intercom. "I can't believe it! Those idiots in the cars below! They're about to take on the whole Russian Army." Sweeping his vision to the left he shouted into the intercom again. "There's a whole trainload of Russian infantry down there. I count thirteen cars. Heads are poking out of train windows and the station is surrounded with milling troops."

The pilot turned his radio dial and began to broadcast. The plane was equipped with a scrambler and the pilot spoke in English. "Believe we have agent XX0-6 still in sight. Allied occupants are riding in two German staff cars approaching railroad station in town of Gyor. Mission is about to expose itself to a thirteen-car load of freshly arrived Russian troops from the east. Don't understand purpose of confrontation. They haven't a chance."

The American G2 sector in occupied Vienna picked up the scrambled message from the spotter plane. The radioman handed the message to the officer and commented, "This reads like a suicide note."

The reconnaissance pilot informed the observer that the red light had come on the gas gauge. They would have to depart the area in less than five minutes if they hoped to get back to Vienna. The reply he received was fatalistic. "That's all the time we need to witness the end of this mission. They either have to take on all that Russian infantry or steal the entire troop train with a thousand or more unwelcome travelers. Either way it's a no win."

It was not yet 8 a.m. The two-car convoy stopped and they saw the main tracks of the railroad ahead. Col. Williams raised the field glasses and saw a train sitting at the station with its engine idling with boilers at full steam. What he observed was a saddleback mountain locomotive with six drive wheels and an oversized coal tender. The train included a baggage car and thirteen coaches. Half the coaches had Russian soldiers leaning out of windows and doors, and half the soldiers had disembarked around and within the station.

With glasses still to his eyes, Williams spoke so McCloskey could hear. "That locomotive has a full head of steam. It's pulling a Russian troop train. By the unloaded baggage it looks like this is Ivan's destination. I think they've just taken on water for the boilers. If we commandeered that train we'd have a straight two hundred miles or so of free passage."

Williams' binoculars showed the conductor getting orders from a Russian commander. The colonel estimated the station building was 500 feet or more from the front of the train--the engine and the street on which the allied team had stopped. Halford Williams thought about his student days when he worked in a roundhouse in Miami, Florida shunting engines back and forth--and he recalled one summer in Costa Rica as fireman and occasional driver of a narrow-track banana train from San Jose to the port.

McCloskey interrupted Williams' thoughts. "Forget what you're thinking. I know already what's on your mind. You're figuring how to steal that troop train and make our getaway on that instead of these cars." McCloskey continued, "My advice mon, is a flat no! Because who's going to run the engine, who fires the boilers, and how do we get rid of the Russians? And if we did manage to get going, who'll keep the switches open between here and Vienna?" Williams politely ignored McCloskey.

Turning to the German prisoners he asked if any had ever been railway men and he received a prompt reply that one had been a brakeman before the war. He volunteered information that identical couplings joined all European train cars.

Williams hardly waited for the German to finish. "Could you uncouple the coaches from the baggage car?" The answer that came back was, "Yes Colonel, if somebody could shunt the engine."

Williams smiled. He started the vehicle and the two autos moved leisurely down the street across the railroad tracks. As the second car passed the big engine, the vehicles were out of sight of the troops and trainmen standing at the station five hundred feet away on the other side of the train. McCloskey pulled the lead car off the street alongside the steaming locomotive and the second car followed. The instructions were simple and told once.

"Myself and my sergeant will take the engine. The German brakeman will station himself behind the baggage car with a machine gun trained on him in case of desertion. The remainder will board the baggage car and open the one side door. Black and the German padre will stay with the object in the car until ordered to hoist it aboard the baggage car when the doors are opened." That left three of the team in the engine, one guarding the German prisoners in the baggage car and one to keep his gun on the prisoner who claimed to be a brakeman. Col. Williams got out of the car and mounted the ladder to the engine, followed by McCloskey.

As the two allied team members entered the mountain locomotive they were surprised to come upon the engineer and a fireman.

First observation was that each man was in civilian clothes and had a hammer and sickle armband. They were good Communists, obviously. Just as the allied commandos scrutinized the trainmen, Williams and McCloskey were watched in return. None of the four liked what they saw. McCloskey pulled his 45 and Williams ordered the man to follow new instructions. The engineer refused commands in both German and English. Seconds flew by. At any moment the conductor would bring back the orders. McCloskey grabbed the engineer and struck him a blow on the face. As the engineer tried for McCloskey's weapon, the Scotsman hit him again, and the one who would operate the train fell out of the cab onto the ground. He was stunned by the tumble. They had lost the engineer. Williams took his place at the controls. He hurriedly examined the levers and gauges. There was a full head of steam he thought. He yanked open the fire door and saw there was a bed of coals, with a blue-white flame on top. He noted the fire was stoker fed from the tender, and he also noted a husky fireman on whom no one would want to turn his back. Examining the Johnson bar, Col. Williams realized remotely he was familiar with the engine's operation, but totally inexperienced.

Adjusting himself to the engineer's seat, Col. Williams cautiously pulled back the reverse lever hoping the brakeman was ready. There was a second-or-two interval and then the long train slowly shuddered and inched backwards. Underneath and between the baggage car and first coach of Russian troops, the eager German who had professed brakeman ship, flipped the coupling link. Quickly the man jumped out clear of the cars knowing that once the link was flipped the reverse lever was expected to be thrown forward by the stand-in engineer, and the big six wheeler would move off carrying only the tender and baggage car. The German fell backwards free of the wheels as the forward part of the train separated itself from the standing coaches. The team member guarding the brakeman picked him up and together they ran alongside the forward moving baggage car toward the open door. Willing hands pulled them both aboard. Apprentice engineer, Halford Williams shoved the Johnson bar further forward and the stolen train accelerated away from the Gyor station while hundreds of Soviet troops ran and fired at the fugitive engine. The men in the baggage car hit the floor.

High above Gyor, the reconnaissance plane and its crew were witness to the action. They saw the front of the train separate and pull away from the station as an enlarging crowd of figures chased after the runaway. Over the intercom of the plane the observer called excitedly to the pilot. "Can't believe it. Front of train is pulling away from the rear! Soviet troops are stranded. It's a runaway and it's gaining speed."

At allied headquarters of the three occupying powers in Vienna, the American section received this scrambled message at 8:43 a.m. "Mission under our surveillance has stolen front section of Soviet troop train. Train gaining speed--headed west towards Sopron."

The Americans relayed the message to the British who controlled the master electric relay switches from Vienna to Budapest. The British engineers immediately ordered the main line between the two cities to be cleared of all other traffic. A Russian train heading east to Gyor entered sidings and waited for the "special Soviet train" to pass, on its priority run to Sopron.

But paradoxically, Williams and his rag-tag crew thought the Soviets controlled the switches going west from Gyor. Consequently they took evasive action to prevent the Russians in Gyor from alerting the westward stations to close switches on the main line. Five minutes out of Gyor, Williams stopped his flight while McCloskey scrambled up the pole and cut the telegraph wires. The novice engineer was relieved to sight green (go) signals on all switch boxes as they traveled west. He never learned his runaway train had track priority.

With the tension of breaking away from the pursuers over for the time being, Williams turned to new worries as he fled with flues open and belching black smoke. Worry number one! Odds favored an oncoming train as a possibility of a terrible collision became more probable minute-by-minute. Second worry! The Russians somehow might send word ahead by radio, road, or plane and the stolen train would be switched onto a siding for a showdown fight. So, in case of an impending collision, Col. Williams sent word back to the baggage car for everybody to abandon the train at the toot of the whistle. Switched to a siding they were to fight. At the same time it was necessary to send a team member up front from the baggage car to keep a gun on the belligerent fireman whom McCloskey had to relieve intermittently.

To the pre-war tourist traveling the route by rail, the beautiful mountain scenery would capture complete attention as the train moved leisurely along. But to war-time engineer Col. Williams, the road ahead required all his attention as he drained every bit of power from the panting boiler. The local population could see the megaton monster for miles as the sun came up behind the fugitive train in the eastern sky. There were long stretches of well-maintained track and a preponderance of well-banked curves. Williams seldom altered speed except in tunnels, pulling back gently on the Johnson bar for the curvatures and riding full steam ahead on the straight stretches of track. As he remembered the escape trip, Williams thought the elevations were gentle and these gave little concern.

When not looking at the gauges and adjusting his touch to the sensitive Johnson bar, Williams' standards of safety were often in doubt. He was continually entranced by the fear of coming upon a blown trestle bridge spanning a deep ravine or waterway. Also worrying him were the many dark tunnels through which they fled. Williams believed that each tunnel held its own danger of an oncoming train or a hidden obstruction. He had decided not to turn on the big head lamp in the tunnels nor pull the whistle cord except in an emergency, in order to save steam. His one cry to the tender was: "Pour on the coal."

He remembered passing three standing trains on the sidings not knowing one was a Russian train carrying reinforcements to Gyor to search for the box.

For a second time they stopped in a wilderness area and McCloskey took his Tommy gun and blew off the insulators and wires. They were nearing Sopron, running over 100 kilometers per hour, flues open, with the stack belching black smoke. As the wild train bore down on hectic activity at the rail crossing of a major highway, a long Russian convoy of trucks stretched on either side as the train roared by. The blockage failed to materialize as drivers scrambled their trucks off the tracks.

Hardly recovering from the highway incident, Williams found himself coming upon an unexpected curve. The baggage car swayed as Williams applied the brakes to reduce speed. Again he thought, "I was saved by a well-maintained road bed." But he was also joyful to realize they had covered half the course. Sopron now lay behind them to the south, and less than one hundred miles ahead was their goal: Vienna.

Williams' last anxiety attack over took him as they approached what appeared to be the Lietha River as shown on his map. His engine was on the bridge trestle before he was aware a large object lay in the center of the bridge in between the tracks. Too late to apply the brakes the huge engine tossed the unknown object aside with a shudder but the impact left the tracks and ties undisturbed. The fight gave Williams time to reconsider his reckless flight and accordingly he reduced speed, concentrating on their arrival in Vienna. But what Williams did not know, the Vienna yard was in Russian hands. He was unaware that having accomplished the mission, the prize could still be snatched from his grasp at the end of the ordeal.

Ahead lay a long finger of water that he observed as the elevation dropped to the river flood plane. Stretching across the water he spied what looked like a metal brace. He reduced speed and slowly applied the brakes. The train swayed slightly as they hit the bridge across the Danube leading into the switching yards of Vienna. From the baggage car came a muffled cheer.

Gradually Williams realized his train was being guided to the right as he slowed the mountain locomotive to a crawl. Leading from the marshalling yards he saw a footpath on the other side of which he had observed a road. The baggage car occupants heard the single toot of the whistle and in moments the crew of the runaway train were on the ground and following Williams and McCloskey along the path to the road. In the middle of the group, four men including the German padre were carrying the box of relics. None of the crew was aware at the time they abandoned the runaway train that the British had switched them out of the Russian zone into the American, and that eight American jeeps were patrolling the roads adjoining the tracks waiting for the train to stop.

They had no sooner hit the road than an American jeep appeared. The allied team piled into the jeep, along with the German padre and the box,

The first question Col. Williams asked the driver was how he knew "we were on the road and needing a lift." The driver replied, "Three armies are looking for you birds, Colonel. I'm glad we beat the Russians." Williams asked the driver to radio for help regarding the stranded Germans left behind and to take by force the reluctant fireman.

Reading the file on the mission, it was noted the name of the commandant whom Col. Williams was taken to is inked out of the report, as is the name and rank of the German R.C. chaplain. Nevertheless, it goes without saying that Col. Williams and his entourage carrying the objects were ushered into the presence of the senior American officer. The team was dismissed, but the chaplain insisted on staying with Williams. The box of items was placed on a table and the chaplain, withdrawing from his pocket the key to the chest, proceeded to open it and reveal the sacred contents for those present. It was 1 p.m. on the third day of the mission. The hunted had outrun the hunters for the 61st time.

The conscious mind is a moving picture of current happenings, events and people. The abstract, the philosophical, the religious is prodded out from deeper areas of the brain. To Col. Halford Williams, as they opened the box his conscious mind was still displaying fretful images of his exodus from recent trouble. He wanted to dismiss that adventure, and rest his exhausted self.

But as the German army chaplain removed the cloth wrappings from the leather-lined interior of the box, Williams' mind, tired as it was, bounced back to the activities of the moment. Fascinated, he watched the chaplain carefully set aside the outer wrappings removed from the objects, and he was acutely aware of the respect bordering veneration with which the chaplain handled the contents. First the chaplain removed the iron crown of St. Stephen and respectfully sat it back in place after quickly passing it to the other participants. With profound deliberation, the chaplain then unwound the two outer wrappings from the spearhead and placed it back in the chest.

Finally he began to expose the ancient Roman sword. The Commandant noted, as did Williams, that the chaplain was careful to avoid making any contact with the sword using his bare hands, and he insulated them with the inner chamois wrapping each time he moved the weapon. It was apparent that the chaplain was familiar with the contents of the box and had handled the objects previously.

Impatient of the chaplain's reverence for the objects, the U.S. general reached into the box and grasped the sword blade intending to lift it out and scrutinize it. Suddenly the man let out an oath and the sword fell back in place. Turning his head to Col. Williams the commandant exclaimed, "This thing has the curse of the Hapsburgs on it," and stared at his hand. Inadvertently the chaplain touched the sword without the chamois protection, and he too was burned. He withdrew his sore hand and said nothing.

Williams raised his eyebrow in perplexity and his mouth turned down showing inner concern. He listened as the commandant asked the cleric if he too had burned his hand on touching the sword momentarily, and the man confessed he had. Then he spoke with profound authority.

"There is a legend connected with the sword which I'm inclined to believe, and it is that he who can pick up the sword and not be burned is a chosen one whose mission (and that of his descendants) will be to unite the German tribes and their confederates in Europe in a new age of good against evil."

Col. Williams was listening only superficially to the conversation after the chaplain's last remark. Ignoring the Sword of St. Maurice, he reached into the case, and as if in meditation, casually lifted out the spear.

Williams was not an initiate of any religious order, holy or otherwise, and had never been involved in Christian or occult rites, except for three months he had spent in a Tibetan monastery in 1937. He was unlearned in the catechism of the bible, did not know the apostles creed, nor had he the charismatic experience of being filled with the Holy Spirit. He was aware of Christian Science principles, but in retrospect, he was untrained and unprepared for his present role of discovering his new identity.

He had no prior knowledge of the spear's history or the history of previous handlers. He considered holding the spear and giving it a cursory examination, therefore, to be a purely temporal act without significance. As he inspected the spear by sight and touch, the German custodian did not advise him of the object's metaphysical chemistry that emitted a cosmic discernment of those it preferred and those it rejected. To Williams, the spear was just an object, which did not intimidate him by vibrations of either good or evil. He did not address the spear or utter a silent prayer. Thus, without warning or pre-suggestion, upon holding the lance he instantaneously departed in spirit from the reality of the picture which unfolded in his mind, and his discernment was as follows:

Before him was a huge panorama of a changing scene outside a walled city involving brutal executions. Subjectively he watched a Roman foot soldier rushing up beneath the body of a victim stretched on a high cross of at least ten feet, between two others on crosses. The soldier carefully aimed the spear and thrust it up and through the ribs of the crucified sufferer who apparently had succumbed.

Col. Halford Williams, the modern day warrior, sorrowfully watched blood and fluids gush from the slain person's side. In spite of the horror and anguish he felt, a purifying surge sweep through his mind accompanied by a sense of peace, like the lifting of a burden.

Compassion told Williams that the one on the subject cross was a righteous man. The American officer's mood suddenly changed again, and he was awed by the thunderous and blackened sky streaked with flashes of lightning. The earth beneath the crosses shook. To Williams the calamity of the elements portrayed the anger of Nature writhing against those executioners who had cut short the mission of a Godly emissary to Earth. Unknowingly and without reason Williams viewed the cross as an evil curse representing the worst kind of death. But in the next instant he began to regard the cross as a symbol of mercy, mainly because a divine power had withheld total judgment on the man's killers and their accomplices. He comprehended also that he who had been sacrificed had been eliminated because he had challenged the established religious order of his day.

As Williams' astral eye moved across the scene it was revealed to him that he had witnessed a colossal struggle, not so much of human forces, but rather unseen principalities of good and evil, each struggling to put their stamp on a future world. The human mob, led by clever men of power, represented the old formal order of religiosity. The sacrificed one on the main cross represented the new order; not so much of law, but of God incarnate in man through Love.

Williams later would refer to the scene as the crossroads to the future of the world--a future with either acceptance or rejection of universal peace and justice. As Williams watched the scene he queried: Has man's religious intolerance changed any in 1900 years?

For Williams in the mystique of projecting his mind into the past, he was left momentarily sad as the ancient scene faded from view. His last image was that of a dead man whose proclaimed Godliness had been defeated by the ceremonial order that he had challenged. And Williams' inner being wondered sorrowfully how victory could ever rise out of such a tragic but noble ending. Or was it the end, he thought? Because, as he returned to the present he envisaged his own name spelled out on the cross along with that of the emancipator. He accepted that anyone who looked at the cross and believed would find his name there too, and in believing he would be purified in his soul.

These thoughts burned themselves into Williams' mind.

Replacing the spear he felt somewhat repulsed in the conscious mind, and he gasped a deep breath of relief even as revelations of the historical drama continued to filter into his mind. Hesitatingly, he picked up the sword. At this moment in his life, Halford Williams was uninformed of the sword's mute intolerance that had burned the hands of so many humans for two millennia. Lifting the object out of the box, the pacifist ran his fingers across the sides of the blade and carefully felt its edge. The General watched for reaction not knowing that the younger man had already regressed into history seconds earlier and that it would happen again. The chaplain looked on with anxiety.

Holding the blade, Williams again became oblivious to the present and his mind slid back into time again. His present body senses of sight and sound were immersed in a vacuum. The now became then and he was a witness to a continuous episode that began when he held the spear--watching men and women in strange garb, acting as adversaries in a tragic drama that would change the world. Williams' mind became again the screen on which a time camera began focusing images of the past. The result was a catharsis of his entire being--cleansing his present conscience as he became a witness to the past.

In the new scene the focal point of the drama remained the high cross. On it there hung by three spikes the limp, bloodstained, body of the same God/man. Immediately he recognized the being; he was the same one seen in the two years earlier, first while in the cave beneath the French monastery. It was the same face who had foretold the future of the world and whose power had later stilled the waves and saved them all from death.

In the new images the sky remained overcast. Intermittent bolts of lightning starkly lit up the clouds. Claps of thunder resounded agonizingly across the heavens outside a walled city.

An unsteady ladder stood against the high cross and a Roman

soldier maneuvered a long rope around the armpits and over the chest of the victim. Finally, the rope was looped over the crossbar on which the wrists had been spiked and tied on either side of the upright post. Then they began to lower the body to the ground as the freed arms fell slowly down. A Roman foot soldier on the ground (the same who had thrust the spear into the man) released the rope ends and eased the body down onto the rocky ground; face up, beside the cross on which he had died. Two centurions stood by supervising.

Gathered before the crosses were three distinct groups of people. Those of the foremost group in control were two Roman centurions standing nearest the center cross in charge of a platoon of soldiers on foot. The Romans wore daggers and swords and carried spears and shields. Two fretful horses were tethered at posts.

The largest, most noisome group numbered over 300, and the Romans who watched them as they pressed forward kept these back. A burly man dressed more ornately than the others led the group. He carried an open-arm shield and his sword was unsheathed. Accompanying this leader and directed by him were eleven other guards with similar armament but attired more plainly. Following these twelve guards were a mixed lot, mostly men, in varied appearance.

To one side and close to the protection of the Roman soldiers were assembled a disjointed lot of men and women numbering less than thirty. The central front of these persons was a small pocket of women. Many of this pitiful group stood with bowed heads, and from them came no calls or clamor except the occasional moans of their members. They displayed no weaponry.

From the smaller group a man of authority directed two others to the foot of the center cross. They carried a crude stretcher and as they reached the body in front of the center cross they laid down the conveyance and prepared to carry away the crucified one. No sooner had they attempted to lift the body onto the stretcher than there arose a cry of abuse from the much larger, rival group, whereupon the leader of their armed guards rushed toward the body intent on preventing its removal.

The older centurion of the two reacted quickly. Withdrawing his left arm from the round shield he immediately placed the protecting armor over the head and upper torso of the deceased figure. Placing his right foot on the shield to help keep it in place, the old warrior was in a pivotal position before the oncoming leader of excited men and women as they neared the body.

The burly priest was first to swing his sword and before it could cut, the old, experienced centurion parried. Not waiting for the attacker to swing again the centurion knocked the shield from the offender. In a flash the Roman blade was driven into the middle of the charging man and he fell to the ground. Moments later, the opposing forces rushed the lone centurion. He leaped between the attackers and the inert form as he held his stance. With a dagger in his left hand cut opponents who got in too close as his right arm worked the sword in a wider reach. Seeing his comrade outnumbered, the remaining centurion rushed over and joined the close combat, as did two of the Roman foot soldiers. With superhuman speed, the old pagan centurion, standing in majesty over the corpse, led his men in the conflict to prevent the mutilation of the crucified body.

Even in the clash of swords, the leader of the attackers rallied. He managed to raise himself to his feet in spite of his wound. As he rose with dagger in hand, a single bolt of lightning struck him and he dropped dead. The electricity deflected among the shields and swords of those fallen, but it did not find a path to the shield covering the dead man. Following the lightning, awesome claps of thunder again exploded and earth tremors shook the ground. Faced with the loss of their leaders and the fearsome revolts of the natural elements, the large, shifting crowd turned in panic and fled toward the city gate. Roman foot soldiers pursued them.

The centurion dragged the fallen bodies away from the corpse and the older of the two retrieved his shield off the unmarred visage of him who lay helpless in death. On a motion from the centurion, the two litter bearers rallied, and returning to the affray, carried their fallen comrade away toward a small stone building nearby to prepare for his burial.

Looking up steadfastly at the changing sky, the centurion wiped his sword and realized something had happened to him. He had not received a cut or scratch on his entire body, even without the protecting shield which he had forfeited to save the dead one from disfigurement or decapitation. But most amazing of all, the old pagan knew the film over his eyes was gone and that he could see again like a young man. Glancing across at the younger centurion, the older one noticed that the scar across his face was no longer there, as he saw the man rubbing his cheek in bewilderment.

Col. Halford Williams of the 20th century also knew without fore-knowledge that the older centurion was Gaius Casius (Longinus) and the younger of the two was called Ottaganus and that the latter was Germanic in origin. He also understood without knowing that the leader of the insurrectionists was a priest of the temple. And Williams clung to a conviction that the crucified one was Jesus the Christ and that his name on the plane to which he went, and from which he had come, was Messiah and Emmanuel, and the only Son of God.

As the commandant brought Williams back to reality by his raised and worried voice, the chaplain joined in, “I was right Colonel. The sword and spear belong in your custody.”

The German RC chaplain continued. “You did not even grimace when you held the sword. Show me your hand please!”

The chaplain took the hands of Williams and carefully examined them. “Sir!” he exclaimed. “You have no burns. Who are you, may I ask.” to which Williams confided that he was Austrian on his mother’s side.

“That explains it,” said the chaplain, obviously a historian. “Three Hapsburgs in recent history including Emperor Karl, Franz Joseph, and Maximilian were never able to handle the sword. But Francis The First was the last reigning monarch to do so without being burned. It was revealed to me that at the end of this war I would meet the true Hapsburg heir who would be able to handle the sword, as did his ancestor. You Sir, or your descendants, are the chosen ones of God to lead the German people into a new age," to which Williams replied. "Wrong chaplain, keep looking for your man. I've served in one war that I didn't want, and nobody is going to draft me for another--be it as soldier or king."

The older man ignored Williams' rebuttal and answered quietly. "You were born of destiny and are not its maker." Then the chaplain asked Williams to sit while he placed the heavy crown of St. Stephen with its ruby-topped cross on the young man's head as though being crowned. The crown sat placidly. Then he placed the crown on the head of the general, but each time he tried to set it in place the crown lifted mysteriously off the general's head.

The German explained, "In 1859 Emperor Francis Joseph of Austria, while being crowned with this same crown, had to have it held on his head by others during the ceremony because the inanimate object continued to lift, not fall off. Later Austrian Emperor Karl went into the cathedral with his revolutionary forces and proclaimed himself King. The crown refused to sit on the head of Karl according to Hungarian witness Admiral Hoarsey.

The chaplain and commandant left the room, and each had their hands treated and dressed for painful burns. On return to say goodbye, the cleric asked Williams to take the sword once again and touch his burned hand. Williams complied and instantaneously the sword in his hands became a rod of healing. The bandages were removed from the man's hand and it was whole again. The American general refused saying "No more hokus pokus."

Williams confided in no one at the time that an inner voice had sworn that further historical evidence of that crucifixion event he had witnessed in spirit would be rediscovered before the turn of the century in ancient scrolls hidden in four places of Europe. And the revelator told him where the scrolls would be found.

In spite of his experiences in the realm of the metaphysical, Williams' self-appraisal was that he was less religious in nature than scholarly; he was more of an adventurer than a soldier; he was more of a commoner than a king. Hence, the un-rhetorical young American kept his own counsel that day and prayed repeatedly the plea, "Why me Lord? Why me? I just want to go home."

The other team sent by U.S. Intelligence to find the box of relics did locate what is believed to be one of the two known sets of replicas of the sword and spear. These U.S. soldiers were Capt. Walter Thompson and Lieutenant Horne. They are said to have recovered the replicas in Nuremberg, Germany on April 16, 1945 after which they were returned to Austria under orders of Gen. Dwight Eisenhower. Sometime between August 1945 and mid January 1946, the true sword and spear rescued by Col. Williams' team replaced the replicas and again the true historical relics are displayed in room number ten of the Hofburg Museum in Vienna. The crown of St. Stephen of Hungary was in U.S. custody till 1970.

Chapter 12

PREAMBLE - THE FINAL MISSION

The World War II armistice was being negotiated secretly in April 1945, when the commando team of Lt. Col. Halford Williams and his six men were dropped for their last assignment of the war. The site was onto the grounds of an infamous Nazi torture and execution prison in Poland. The task of the allied commandos was to break into the prison, rescue a famous hostage about to be killed, and bust out.

But the team's morale to survive intact had fallen when its leader, contrary to instructions from allied headquarters in London, insisted on freeing not one, but five important personages that had been chained by their necks to dungeon walls. Once free, the plan was to make an orderly escape with the added human burdens through three hundred miles of hostile territory.

The allied cohorts did not go far after rescuing the five celebrities. So close were their pursuers that the combined group of thirteen escapees was forced to hurriedly hide in a concealed hole on the grounds of the notorious prison. The hunted allies were only minutes from being gunned down as they tried to vanish from their pursuing jailers, garrison troops, and tracking dogs.

Chapter 12

THE FINAL MISSION

A light snowfall laid a blanket over the pocket of briars and thorns on the grounds of Prison "X" in the province of Silesia, Poland. The giant oak tree under which the allied team had taken refuge stood majestically on a remote area of the grounds overlooking the thorny acreage. Its sprawling limbs, bare from a long winter, resembled girders holding up the impoverished plot of land beneath.

As prison guards patrolled the immediate area, German shepherd dogs sniffed at the base of the old oak. A volley of rifle shots blasted its upper branches engulfed in the blackness of night.

A half-track loaded with armed searchers pushed its way through the outer perimeter of the forsaken acreage, the driver unaware he was approaching a terrain of sharp rocks scattered about by nature. Crushing the bushes as it moved forward, the half-track snagged its front end on a rock outcropping. A curse was heard coming from the cab followed by a burst of machine gunfire sprayed into the interior of the briar patch. The half-track was reversed and backed into the open.

Two non-commissioned officers with their canines continued to search. The dogs were urged to enter the thorny area following the matted path made by the withdrawn half-track. Suddenly one of the dogs began whining. Its whine turned to a sharp yelp. Evidently the prickly thorns had pierced its snout or paws. The animals would venture no further.

An infantry platoon had moved up to the edge of the wild acreage, stopped and fired another volley into the thicket and again up into the darkness of the old oak. Sergeant McCloskey listened carefully from the concealed hideout. When the firing had stopped, he heard a voice call. "An animal wouldn't hole up in this place."

The combined military searchers and guards departed. It was still dark as the noise of men and machines subsided to the relief of thirteen bodies hiding in a temporary scooped-out hole in the earth, whose only defense was simply a barrier of thorns.

Daybreak of April 7th slowly penetrated the improvised cloth-and-snow-covered hatch of the dugout. None of the escapees had been hit by a stray bullet. But the original group of seven was now thirteen. They included two basket cases and one captured German, the jail guard "Fritz" who had willingly accompanied them in their escape from the prison. Col. Williams believed Fritz was not the petty guard he pretended. The wily Sergeant McCloskey was also doubtful and had warned Fritz that a knife was ready for his heart if he broke silence and gave their hiding place away.

Thus, at daybreak Sgt. McCloskey divided the team's three days of K-rations with six additional mouths. There was food for only a day and a half. Heat pouches were opened to warm up the damp, cold earth as day one found the escaping pilgrims without sunlight, hungry, and shivering in spite of their own thermal warmth. In the distance the barking of dogs and sporadic gunfire made them all aware they were still being hunted and were unwelcome guests in a foreign land far from home.

After rations had been doled out, strict toilet routine was ordered. A detail was formed to enlarge the hole under an adjoining flat rock and to this spot each crawled when required. The basket cases were helped.

As the sun rose on the morning of April 7th, the snow turned to rain, increasing the group's discomfort and fears of detection from above. The men slept fitfully with one person placed on constant alert. As the snow melted Sgt. McCloskey went topside and added more branches to camouflage their dungeon. His hands were badly scratched from the work.

Tensions rose due to strict rules that forbade talking above a whisper. On the second day, April 8th, by faint light, a team member produced a deck of worn cards and all played rummy except the colonel, the unknown boy, and the sick scientist. When Beria, the Russian, made a snide remark about the attention Colonel Williams gave the manacled boy, Sgt McCloskey demanded a translation and passed word to the Russian hostage that if he made one more off-color remark he would get his commie teeth pushed down his commie throat--a blessing for all. This threat restored a delicate balance of command. The boy remained mute and gave no hint of identity or origin. The German scientist slowly began to function as a team member in spite of his infirmities from being tortured.

On day three of their confinement McCloskey summed up the predicament of thirteen people crammed together in the hideout.

"Mon, I knoo hoo ta keep discipline on a route march or in battle, but I dinna ken knoo hoo ta keep sane in a stinking oothoose like this." Col. Williams smiled at his brogue.

In the meantime, allied reconnaissance planes out of Vienna flew non-stop during daylight hours of April 7, 8, and 9. They had reported no sign of the fleeing team and their willing hostages. It was concluded by London that they most likely had perished in the prison.

Before midnight of April 9, Sgt. Stobel, the enlisted Royal Canadian Mounted Policeman, volunteered to venture out. He pulled himself up onto the oak tree limb, crawled to the massive trunk and set out to explore. He returned in less than two hours. Enthusiastically he reported his findings. There was a motor pool stocked with vehicles including officers' cars nearby and apparently unguarded. He reckoned the getaway vehicles were ripe for the taking. There was unanimous agreement to vacate.

Recharged with hope, the internationals pulled themselves together with a single purpose. Each climbed out of the odious shelter, stood one-by-one beside the hole and discovered their land legs again. The prostrate boy whom most argued to abandon was still in shock. He was carried out across the limb on the improvised litter. Silently they all formed up and with Sgt. Stobel leading in Indian file, they began a two-mile trek towards the German motor pool. The Russians rotated in carrying the stretcher. Col. Williams aided the scientist.

It was 0345 hours when they reached their objective, subdued a guard, singled out two officers' cars, and requisitioned additional Gerry cans of gasoline. The vehicles were pushed down an incline where the motors were started. By 0400 hours nearly three hours before daylight of April 10, the final mission was on its way home. Happy to be free, someone hummed, "Heave ho, we've only three hundred miles to go."

The allied team believed that the enemy had not watched them. But they were mistaken. Within two hours two carloads of motor pool personnel, with their military insignias removed, took after the fleeing escapees. The pursuers believed they were on the trail of the saboteurs who had broken into the impregnable Nazi fortress and stole the most valuable hostages of the war.

What appeared to be an easy steal of transport for the allied team was to become a one-way escape into a worsening realm, particularly for Col. Halford Williams. His long string of over sixty missions without a casualty was about to end.

Capt. Johnathon C. Wilson, U.S. Army/Air guided his two-motor reconnaissance plane out of Vienna over the grounds of Prison "X" on the morning of April 10. He arrived at first light and noted that the hectic activity on the grounds that he had photographed earlier in the week had simmered down. The German pocket of strong resistance still held against Soviet onslaught. The prison complex remained undamaged except for the gaping hole blown in one corner of the main building.

Banking his plane over the motor pool stockade, his attention was caught by two German officers' cars being loaded with extra five-gallon tins of gasoline. Spare tires were being strapped before, on the sides, and aft of each car. He observed he was watching a hurried exodus. He waited several minutes as the two cars sped frantically away from the stockade and journeyed westward toward the connecting highway; the same routing which the allied commando team--unbeknownst to Capt. Wilson--had taken earlier the same morning. Capt. Wilson made a mental note of the distinguishing marks of the two vehicles in case he spied them again. He hoped to he able to track their progress for no apparent reason. He presumed any lead, however insignificant, would help him construct an explanation as to the total disappearance of the valuable missing allied team.

Meanwhile, the allied commando team and their hostages in the lead cars were not aware that the enemy had caught on to their clever escape plan and would attempt to overtake them.

The cat and mouse drama began at dusk the same day as the allied team sought its next safe harbor. Seeing another closed farm gate leading to buildings well off the road for protection during darkness, Sgt. McCloskey pulled the lead car over and stopped. The pursuit cars that had kept behind now were obliged to pass or take the offensive. They passed.

Capt. Wilson in his recce plane had one task the day of April ll. He would continue to fly the likely escape route that the lost allied team was to take, observing more closely the traffic pattern, most of which indicated German withdrawal from the Eastern front. Capt. Wilson knew what he was seeking. If the allied team were on the road below, they would have taped the roofs of their stolen transport with distinguishing black and white stripes. But no such vehicles could he find.

His hypothesis exhausted, he was forced to rely mainly on a hunch that the team might still be alive, or at least part of it. He shortened his traffic patrol to seventy miles. On one occasion he noticed a broken-down German officer's car on the left side of a cratered, muddy patch of highway. He perceived a German-dressed NCO and civilian scavenging tires from another abandoned vehicle. Wilson noted a second stopped car following in tandem and a motley crew surrounding both vehicles, sprawled about like monkeys in a tree he thought.

With foreknowledge of briefings from London headquarters, he decided there were too many occupants in those two conveyances to be the object of his search. He envisioned no more than eight people in the allied team. Undaunted, the captain tirelessly scoured the roads throughout the day confident he would discover further evidence below. His ensuing time in the air was fruitless.

There remained about an hour of daylight as the recce pilot set his sights again to relocate either of the two German cars with which he had made himself familiar. Finding the object of his search, he zeroed in on the two-car convoy occupied by what he referred to as the motley crew, somewhat out of place even in the pattern of retreat. This time the two cars were about to leave the road and venture into a deserted farm. Wilson observed their careful exit and particularly the variety of dress at which time he made a major decision. Although some appeared to be enemy troops there were also a mixture of civilians. Wilson's prolonged scrutiny of the occupants walking beside the vehicles led to two assumptions: one, the people in the cars were either disguised; or two, they were enemy soldiers, some of who had shed their military uniforms for civilian dress to escape the oncoming Russian sweep. If the people below were in disguise, could they be suspected as the missing allied commando team?

Departing the scene for his Vienna airport, Col. Wilson got a second break in his observations. He spied the two cars he had seen leaving Prison "X" two days earlier. They were parked a mile down the road from an elevation on which they could watch the nearby farm and its recent overnight occupants.

Capt. Wilson, short on fuel, determined he would be back on the interesting locale at first light.

April 12. The missing allied team had been three days in the dugout and now were beginning their third day on the road, still unrecognized from the air. The night before they had harbored, caught, and butchered a pig and roasted the cuts under supervision of McCloskey. Then they had bathed and slept peacefully in the house and barn. Feeling refreshed and renewed they hit the road again. They had gone less than sixty miles.

The overcast sky began to brighten as the group left the safe harbor at 0700 hours. As they moved onto the main road they noticed two German cars similar to their own. They passed them without provocation.

In the meantime, an emergency meeting of the Joint Chiefs of Staff was being held in London. The plan devised was to storm Prison "X" and come to the rescue of the allied team--whether dead or alive.

Col. Cromosky already had departed from Vienna along the lost team's proposed escape route. His relief column would get only thirty miles before blown bridges would halt their advance.

On April 12, Captain Johnathon C. Wilson left Vienna before first light, heading for his coordinate in Czechoslovakia. His was a rendezvous with two suspicious looking automobile groups, each group carrying about a dozen men he reckoned. He speculated that one pair of cars contained the hunters and that the other pair of autos held the hunted. He based his premise on the fact that he had witnessed two of the cars depart Prison "X" and overtake the second pair of autos. Capt. Wilson reasoned that if Prison "X" guards were so positive they had found their quarry, that quarry possibly could be the allied commando team which, unknown to London, had vanished for three days and then escaped from the region of Prison "X". He felt the mystery of the vanishing allied team was beginning to unravel. It had to, inasmuch as Capt. Wilson had only forty-two hours to solve the plot. At that time the allies would launch a massive airborne contingent to take Prison "X" and complete the undertaking on which Col. Williams and his team had apparently disappeared.

April 12 - Last night. In the lead car parked by the farm gate where bivouac had been decided, sat Sgt. McCloskey along with the darling of the team. He was Corporal Frederick Grimes, twenty-two years of age, handsome and sure of himself. If there were a favorite, Cpl. Grimes could be considered the favorite of Col. Williams in particular. They had known each other back in their hometown, had gone to the same military academy, and were graduates of the same high school. Furthermore, Halford Williams was the idol of young Grimes. This was their sixth mission together, Grimes having asked to be assigned to Williams' charge to gain field experience prior to attending West Point Military Academy back in the United States. McCloskey disliked Grimes initially but came to acknowledge his charm and wit. Even the Russians lit up when Grimes talked with them. The only one among them who failed to respond was the boy taken from the jail, still carrying heavy manacles and chains around his neck and both ankles. Grimes, the product of a broken home, wanted most of all to be well liked by each member of the group that was reflected in his outgoing personality. None knew that his mother, a career woman, never had time for him as a son, or that his father had left the family when Grimes was a boy needing a father's affection.

When Beria failed to respond quickly enough at McCloskey's command to hop out and open the gate, Cpl. Grimes, eager to please, jumped out of the lead car and ran up to the gate leading to the long farm lane. The aspiring young officer candidate grabbed the chain binding the gate, unsnapped it and dropped it over the adjoining post. As he did, he shifted his feet.

The land mine or mines buried below the surface and carefully concealed exploded. Sgt. McCloskey was first to react after the explosion. He restrained Col. Williams, refusing to let him out of the car as blood and body fragments splattered the windshield.

Col. Williams had just lost his best and perhaps only friend, and he was overcome with shock. On this sixty-second mission his spirit would be broken as he faced the death of one for whom he had developed a brotherly affection. Since discovering the Christ relics nearly two years earlier, this had been their first casualty during a time when Williams had witnessed perhaps two thousand of the so-called enemy die in their raids. No one spoke as they wheeled the cars off the road and around the gate which moments before had become the take-off point into eternity for Frederick Crimes.

Sgt. McCloskey took command of the team without objection from Col. Williams. They moved cautiously thru the open field on foot followed by the cars, toward the abandoned farm buildings. The cars were driven into the barn as was done the previous night, but this time no one brushed the tire marks from the ground. They searched the deserted buildings, mounted guard, bedded down and spent the night. There was no small talk.

The night temperature had warmed to about forty degrees Fahrenheit and the drizzly rain and wind had ceased. Overhead a canopy of stars twinkled in a crisp sky. With two cars hidden in the barn and everyone turned in for a night's rest, Sgt. McCloskey beckoned to Col. Williams. Together they went outside.

Leaning on a wagon McCloskey spoke in low tones "Colonel, have you noticed the two carloads of Krauts following us," to which the American colonel replied he had not.

"Believe it or not," spoke the Scotsman, "those cars have corresponding numbers to the two we confiscated from Prison "X". McCloskey paused and added a warning. "It means we're being followed. They've bivouacked up ahead of us the last two nights. Somehow I connect those carloads of Gerries with Fritz who joined us in the jail. He's no ordinary guard, mon. I've trained men like him. He's a high ranking officer--quite surely."

Jarred from his grief over the death of Cpl. Grimes, Colonel Williams replied. "What's their object--these guys following us but not trying to take us over?"

McCloskey answered. "I reckon they will make their move tonight, or tomorrow at the latest. They've sized us up by now, and they're certain who we are. Each time they've passed us they have tried to peer through the side curtains on our cars to estimate our probable firepower."

Col. Williams asked in a frustrated manner, "But what's their object?"

McCloskey replied. "Their plan at first will be to confront us in a friendly way--supposedly. They are probably intimidated by how we tore in and out of that jail leaving so many dead men behind. And I also think they realize we have Fritz, whoever he may be."

McCloskey leaned closer to Williams. "The real reason for taking us over may be something more sinister. They want the hostages--the Ruskies. Hoot mon, these Commies are worth millions to the Nazi remnant still operating from Berlin. And Stalin would give half the bloomin Kremlin to get back his cronies."

The older solider replied. "You're just a lad Colonel. Me, I'm past forty. But together we must get this outfit home to our lines without another casualty. I've posted guard at the main road and ordered our men to keep their weapons handy tonight. I've got my eye on Fritz."

Col. Williams pulled the collar of his German greatcoat around his neck and withdrew, to be alone with his thoughts.

In the morning they washed the cars and waited till the ground haze had lifted. With as few commands as possible the speechless boy was lifted into the car followed by the three Russians and the German/American scientist who had improved much after nourishment and recognition that he was among friends. On direct order from McCloskey, Fritz, the German jail guard, led the way on foot in case of other land mines. With expertise surprising to all, Fritz dug up three more mines. The two cars left for the entrance to the farm again and had almost reached the gate.

High above, the same aeroplane that the day before had spied car tracks going into the barn, had returned to the scene. Capt. Wilson, the pilot, turned his plane in smaller circles and watched the two vehicles come out of the barn and move slowly toward the road. He saw them stop long enough for the tops of the two German staff cars to he covered with striped bars of black and white silk. His hunch had paid off. Feeding his message into the scrambler he called out, "Made certain contact." He was somewhat embarrassed to hear the reply. "Made contact with what?" Capt. Wilson smiled and broadcast the discovery in detail.

It was the seventh day of the mission. When the pilot's message was verified beyond doubt, the allies would harden their negotiations by insisting on unconditional surrender of all German forces. And for the leading Nazi hierarch who had masterminded the gruesome plot, their last hope to save their own hides had vanished when Col. Williams and his team of rescuers escaped--unless perhaps they were to be recaptured.

The allied team and rescuers stopped near the broken gate where Frederick Grimes had died. Waiting for Fritz to clear a path, Sgt. McCloskey endeavored to make his commanding officer respond before they started out again on the long journey. Consequently he remarked "That booby-trap was not meant for Grimes. The Gerries set it--for Russian looters." The sergeant turned and glared at the Soviets whom they had been so careful to protect and preserve.

McCloskey continued. "The farm family may return and discover an American was killed here and they'll always wonder why. Grime's spirit might linger long after we're gone. He'll probably open and close that bloody gate forever, expecting us to come back and get him."

The wily Scotsman heard the rebuttal he had expected. "Shut up if you don't mind," came from the lips of Williams.

But McCloskey's verbal meditation had released a torrent of unspoken thoughts that had been bundled up in the minds of the team all night. Relieved by William's blunt reaction, McCloskey, wanting the last word added, "I was trying to jerk you back to reality, mon. You didn't die with your buddy. Remember, you're alive and command this operation."

Williams resented the intrusion into his self-imposed lament and raising his voice said, "I'm not a soldier--I'm a man with feelings--war or no war." Everyone within the sound of his voice knew he hurt inside.

Soitzman butted in a comment of stark reality. "Is this some kind of graveside service to honor the dead? There isn't even a shovel full of him to be picked up. So let's get the h--- out of here."

As if to soften Soitzman's harsh vernacular, Sgt. Stobel spoke quietly. "He didn't even give us a chance to wrap him in his own blanket."

Someone added, "Everyone will miss Grimes except the dumb kid. This rhetoric brought Williams back into the conversation again.

"Dumb kid? He's not dumb may I remind you. It's just his outer shell that cracked. Inside he's still intact," Then turning to those assembled, Williams added in a chiding way, "If you so-called people would talk to him as though you cared he was a human being who needs love, he might recover and tell us who he is and where he came from. None of us know what this kid has been through in the hands of those monsters back there. As far as I'm concerned, mind you all, he's one of us on this trip even if they temporarily destroyed his mind by psychological torture and worse."

One of the Russians, believed to have been Gromyko, came up to Williams with two pieces of branch tied together. Intervening, McCloskey asked the reason for the crude woodwork and Andrei Gromyko replied, "It's supposed to represent a cross, I put it together to mark the spot where Grimes took off," to which the Scotsman queried with a stinging retort, "An atheist...a cross...a Christian memorial. What's the connection? Politely the Russian simply responded, "We all liked Frederick. It seemed the right thing to do."

A fragile bond of comradeship emerged within the non-compatible cominglers.

From above they all heard the sound of an aeroplane zeroing in and saw the plane's wings dip as four small parachutes fell out and billowed down with meager supplies. Attached was a note. "Thought you guys could use these." The striped roofs had paid off.

The cars left the farm and turned southwest again. Before leaving the premises all had noticed two other similar vehicles move slowly past the farm entrance and over a hill in the direction that the team intended to take. Now, having resumed course, the allied team was soon to overtake the new arrivals. On the crest of the hill the team found their track barred. McCloskey, whose military tactics never varied and knew that he who takes the offensive controls the situation, pulled his lead car to a halt on the shoulder of the road. He stopped beside the first road blocker.

At first glance none except perhaps Fritz noticed the similarity of the markings on all four cars. And no one except Williams heeded the look of familiarity on Fritz's face when he eyed the challengers. None of the team except perhaps Fritz and McCloskey had been aware that those who now blocked their progress had scouted them for the last forty-eight hours.

Some of the intruders had seen the allied commandos subdue the guard at Prison "X", steal the two cars and shove off. They also had detected that the clever auto theft was carried out in hushed English voices, not Russian or German. The newcomers also realized they were a small section of a thousand Germans combing the land for the escapees of Prison "X".

At the point of interference none of the allied team comprehended with any certainty the intentions of the newcomers--whether the connection was retaliatory or simply to commandeer the allied cars for their own use. And none except Col. Williams, his sergeant and the German guard, Fritz, suspected a possible kidnap of all or part of the allied group, to be whisked away for malevolent purposes.

At the last minute, McCloskey motioned to "prepare for action." The team was outnumbered two to one. The stakes were high against them.

Action, long borne of practice, followed. One of the team held a knife to the back of Fritz and whispered a threat. Meanwhile the Nazi interceptors saw a muscular man get out of the lead car they had forced onto the road's shoulder. He walked with a swagger to the front intercepting vehicle to get their attention. When all enemy glances were riveted on him, they perceived his outer garment was that of a German sergeant, but his trousers and boots were foreign.

McCloskey barked out just one short sentence in German to the aggressors. "Hello fellow soldiers of the Fatherland! What can we do for you?" As he spoke he threw up a stiff Nazi salute.

As the new arrivals stared at McCloskey, six British Tommy-guns appeared over the sides of the two allied cars, the stunned arrivals from the death camp blinked at the audacious maneuver.

Sgt. McCloskey and another disarmed the occupants of the two cars, took their weapons, removed the ammo and searched the cars for additional weapons. They found none. The officer in charge of the newly arrived enemy claimed they were deserters from the Russian front and asked to join the allied team who also were escaping. The convoy now fleeing west numbered four cars, twenty-five men and a boy.

High above was the allied reconnaissance plane piloted by Johnathon C. Wilson. He photographed the episode and watched the occupants of the two cars overcome the new arrivals and disarm them. Also photographed for London's G2 branch was the departure of the enlarged convoy with the new arrivals covered by a Tommy gun from the second lead car. But what worried the observer above the drama was when and how would the former death camp wardens make their move to take over the allied team and its valuable hostages. Based on the radio communiqués and subsequent photos taken that day by Capt. Wilson, the Allied Chiefs ordered a "stand down" of the planned assault on Prison "X". The relief column commanded by Lt. Col. Cromosky was not recalled.

The convoy covered only a short distance that day without incident. McCloskey doubled guard and placed Fritz under constant watch.

Next morning the recce plane reappeared and dropped a note to the officer in charge. Attached was a box of English tea. The note requested immediate reply. Col. Williams, out of sight of his vehicles, spelled out on the ground with an assortment of material, XX0-6. The plane dipped its wings and flew west. Capt. Wilson was beaming.

On arrival in London that night, the allied G2 deduced the following from the aerial photos: The two cars that earlier had left the abandoned farm, definitely were driven by the lost allied rescue team of Col. Halford Williams, Agent XX0-6. And Williams was still alive. It was also considered probably (without understanding the deep intrigue involved) that he had accomplished his mission, but where they had cunningly disappeared for the first three days and nights, no one could conjecture. The cars with the dozen German occupants that had overtaken the Williams team and their rescued had been artfully disarmed by the allied commandos. One set of pictures showed the enemy guns being stacked off the road (later to be discovered by advancing Soviet troops).

But one bewildering question bothered London Intelligence and General Donovan in particular. Their constant question was: Had the interloping enemy attached themselves to the Williams team with a pre-planned purpose to eliminate them or to return them as prisoners, along with their famous hostages, to a Nazi stronghold still intact? That was the sting.

Or was the join-up of the two disparate groups of military without sinister purpose on the part of the newcomers? That was the quandary.

Aerial photos revealed these additional persons started their pursuit at the crocodile prison (Prison "X"). It was obvious to London that Williams and company apparently did not realize the connection or McCloskey would have precipitated a shootout with the new arrivals at once. Nevertheless, it was established the pursuers had singled out their quarry, and the worst was yet to happen regardless of who won the first round.

Word was dispatched to Moscow that the allied team had been located. Allied intelligence already had intercepted a coded Nazi message from Prison "X" to Berlin that the commandant of the prison was missing and the three Soviet victims had been freed. No word was mentioned about the mute boy, but the German scientist was said to have disappeared.

Moscow was asked (and agreed) to let the allies handle the link-up with those concerned. Moscow was also asked (and agreed) to keep its advance troops ten miles back from the escaping team in case the three Russian hostages might be shot by angry Germans if surprised by Soviet troops. But the Russians did not intend to keep their promise.

April 13. The lost team, their rescued hostages, and a retinue of twelve new German arrivals whom they had reluctantly accepted, resumed the journey. Allied lines were about two hundred miles away. The same day the secondary road merged onto a major thoroughfare and the first miles indicated a fast trip to Vienna.

But team optimism began to falter when at intervals the superb highway became a slow track peppered with bomb craters. Suddenly ahead of the small convoy of four cars there loomed a deep cut in the roadbed. Coming to a halt there lay in the gorge below the mangled remains of a once formidable bridge structure.

The disarray shocked the occupants. As motors idled and all stared ahead, they were slow to realize they were being surrounded by a roving gang of enemy soldiers. The allied team was about to become prey to mob violence. The motivation was not enmity or military aggression. It was to sack the latest car arrivals for the one life-giving commodity--food. Col. Williams and his team had arrived in an area where existed but one law--survival of the fittest. The surge of ex-military personnel turned scavengers and looters pressed against the new group of confederates. They pulled open the side curtains. Hands reached within.

Sgt. McCloskey at the wheel of the first car sensed the inevitable--bloody hand-to-hand combat. In a moment he knew they all would be overpowered unless his team took action. Then it happened.

Throwing open the car door, Fritz, the supposed jail guard from

Prison "X", leaped onto the ground in the midst of the desperados. He landed with a one-word challenge:" Listen!" He became the center of attention. The roving eyes turned from surveying the auto occupants and fixed their eyes on Fritz. He spoke.

As Fritz addressed the freebooters, Col. Williams witnessed the calming effect on the listeners. Fritz had held their attention for about three minutes when glancing back at the car occupants he saw Sgt. McCloskey unmistakably prepare for offensive action. Rushing back to the lead car, Fritz changed from German to English. He pleaded as he whispered to Col. Williams.

"Colonel! Don't order a move or we're all dead men. I've just got us some breathing time. Told them you were Americans and Britishers of high rank. You were on a secret mission into Poland. Also told them your outfit had three Russian prisoners and we were all racing to get back to allied lines on orders from the western armies'commander-in-chief."

Col. Williams heard the statements made by Fritz and lost his poise. "Mister," said Williams, "you are in deep trouble for disclosing our identities and mission. In fact you're a traitor. Now, your Kraut buddies will surely waylay us."

Fritz simply said, "Think what you may Colonel! But my presence before these outlaws had changed their minds from taking us over. Instead they are backing off. They might even join us. It is possible they would surrender--en masse."

As Fritz explained the tactics of his intervention, McCloskey was about to give the signal to charge the menacing German troops. He felt a nudge on his arm from the colonel. He was stunned at the words. "I've appointed you spokesman number one for our outfit. Hop out with Fritz and try to get control of those cut-throats!"

McCloskey had heard Fritz ask for time. He also understood him. But now his colonel had ordered him to follow-up on the statements of Fritz who had spoken so eloquently. Still, McCloskey wasn't fully convinced Fritz' remarks had swung the enemy vote to the side of the allied team. The Scotsman would have to bide for time. He knew he was out of place appearing as a reconciler. A diplomat he was not, and his German vocabulary was limited. Hence, he began.

"German officers and men: Let me speak plainly. In a way we're all in the same boat...trying to get as far west as possible ahead of the armies of the Soviet. As your countryman said, we in the cars here are a mixed bag of Americans and Britishers with prisoners we picked up in Poland. That was our assignment. We began as an allied group of seven people and have been joined by a couple of carloads of men who say they are German troops deserting from the eastern front. Our objective is plain. We must get to Vienna as soon as possible.

Our German friend here says you people want to join us, or even surrender. Frankly, we don't want prisoners. You'd slow us down and might take us over, since we're less than a platoon in size."

Fritz interrupted McCloskey. "Speak friendly to them!" McCloskey began again. "If you men were to join us--of your own free wills of course, it would be purely voluntary on your part. Once we all got to allied lines you could surrender there to authorities." McCloskey's blunt proposal got a mixed reaction.

The German troops turned outlaw, began to mumble among themselves. Watching the questionable looks on the faces of those before him, McCloskey took the advice of Fritz and changed his harsh tone to one of conciliation.

"Soldiers! The first condition in joining our march to freedom would be for us to share our rations with you. If someone could find a bushel of potatoes we have enough sauerkraut and freshly cooked pork to last for three good meals."

The Scotsman knew he had just bargained his team into a strong advantage by appealing to the appetites of his adversaries. "So, for sharing our food till we get additional supplies, and accepting our guarantee of protection as bona fide prisoners of war when we reach Vienna--you men would be expected to pitch in and help. You would have to rebuild bridges, fix roads and keep the cars and other transport in working order. And everything you did would have to be half time--to keep ahead of the Russians." McCloskey knew that every time he used the word Russian he put fear into the listeners. After translating the gist of his remarks he introduced Col. Williams who at once became the center of attention.

McCloskey translated as Williams spoke. "Good day German troops! Your coming with us would indeed slow us up many days. Yet, your presence among us could also be helpful if you decided to join us as escapees like ourselves. But my military logic tells me you would first have to give up your weapons; otherwise Vienna headquarters and we would have to consider you still hostile. If you could agree on that requirement, you would have to help us solve our next problem. We lack manpower so you would become our work force, a sort of engineering company to get us across the blown bridges and around craters. The problem that is ever present is: Can you keep us ahead of the Russians? If you all agreed to these conditions I believe I could request General Eisenhower to send food supplies for the long journey ahead."

The colonel studied his audience then added, "German men of war, these are instructions only; they are not orders. Join us if you will. Its up to you."

Silence reigned throughout. Then a German major stepped to the front. He saluted Colonel Williams. "Our only hope Sir lies in the west. I vote we follow you."

Over sixty additional German troops joined the team that day and the incident was typical of others to follow. McCloskey and his men took their weapons, removed the ammo, stacked the guns and put the Germans to work--after giving them the first meal they had in days. In less than twelve hours the first of over forty future travel disruptions had been overcome using the trained skill of the German army, some of whom were bona fide engineers.

The Germans studied the space where the blown bridge once

stood. Then, with an outstanding work ethic and pure manpower, they tumbled all the disabled and smashed cars into the gorge for foundation support of a temporary bridge. On one occasion they left the scene en masse and later appeared with over 500 feet of heavy rail. They tore a nearby barn to pieces, and when finished, a single plank roadbed for automobile wheels spanned the gorge. The team drove their cars across followed by the new parade of men and machines. As they were leaving all heard the frantic train whistle and the crashing of metal as a passing train was derailed--due to missing steel.

Progress for the allied team was now reduced daily. Meanwhile, the group increased to over a hundred; some young, some old.

The prisoners, or fellow escapees, whatever they called themselves, initially had to forage for their own additional food and water supplies. But within thirty-six hours, allied aerial reconnaissance had made arrangements to drop more K-rations and this food service kept up morale among the newcomers. To the Germans weary of a Spartan existence on the eastern front, they gobbled up the K-rations with contentment. McCloskey appointed German sergeants to minister rations and needs. From a bare survival before the Williams team came along, the fleeing German troops were reveling in canned bread and butter, meat, vegetables, jam, chocolate and soup. They also found sewing kits and shaving needs as well as American cigarettes. This food was the catalyst that kept the German troops in line and able to work on the roads and bridges.

German engineers reconnoitered each ravine or gorge to be spanned. Temporary crossings were then rebuilt after a fashion considering the required weight factor. Where possible, the cars were winched across. In like manner the Germans drew gasoline from abandoned or shot-up vehicles and kept the first two cars in running order. Vehicles with mechanical breakdowns or out of gas were towed. Sick or disabled German troops were loaded on these and tended by medics. Brute shoving power was used for steep inclines and hand-pulled winches for defiles.

Williams and McCloskey depended on opposite methods of diplomacy to deal with the former enemies. The colonel promised them safe passage to allied lines, and thereafter if they cooperated. Sgt. McCloskey used different tactics. He railed at them frequently assuring those who didn't participate that they would be shot. He told them he would call for Russian support (which was gaining daily on the escapees) to get rid of them all if bridge and road maintenance was not carried out swiftly. Thus the strange convoy moved slowly across the countryside.

At the end of the second week on the return route to Vienna, the allied team had traveled approximately 200 miles according to their car odometers. They had crossed over thirty destroyed bridges and filled in hundreds of craters or had improvised detours around them. As they passed groups of German soldiers without command who were also fleeing from the Russians, these were allowed to join. From the second of the team's cars, a machine gun was kept trained on the former enemies, particularly at the first twelve who had been overpowered by McCloskey and his men. The machine gun reminded the German troops that the route march was deadly serious. There were casualties: fatigue, sore feet, worn boots, sickness, all these problems began to increase as miles were added. Sgt. McCloskey, on orders from Col. Williams, made sure that none of the men were left behind and that carrying these human burdens was a job distributed among the prisoners themselves.

For the Germans the constant fear was that the Russians would overtake the column, and hope of refuge in the west would be lost. Each morning as reveille was called and Col. Williams awoke, the team would discover new arrivals in addition to the regular contingent of the day before--from where no one knew. The newcomers, the losers in war, joined because they recognized there was no hope of escape. They obviously discerned a purpose in joining the strange column of defeated men like themselves, being led by a handful of allied soldiers walking ever toward the western front--and safety.

Among the German arrivals, word had quickly spread of the quiet, scholarly, bespectacled, young colonel who led the American group and who was obliging towards the care of his adherents. Word also went the rounds about the older, tough Scotsman who cracked the whip for the colonel and bided no disobedience. The common German soldier understood this discipline and buckled down accordingly. They soon were aware that McCloskey had established a loose regimentation among the various German units, and those responsible for keeping order had to answer daily to the Scotsman.

It was customary for Sgt. McCloskey to wander among the former enemies and check them out for needs or failure to cooperate. Sanitary fresh water and mess details were organized, as in the British Army and those in charge were answerable to the Scotsman.

On the 23rd of April, eighteen days after the mission began, two German officer's cars occupied by agent XX0-6 and his team, now traveling in leisure, could be seen moving slowly along a paved highway in western Czechoslovakia, near the border of Austria. They had traveled almost 250 miles from the crocodile prison with all those rescued intact. They had begun the trek in Poland, covered the length of Czechoslovakia and were about to enter their third country and presumed destination. Behind the two-car convoy marched and rode an endless line of Germans who wanted desperately to become prisoners of war to the allies in the west. They were no longer rag-tag; they were a new army.

At 10 a.m. on the 23rd under a warming sun, there strode backwards in front of goose-stepping German troops, a sort of sergeant-at-arms music man, waving his hands as though he were conducting a mammoth chorus. The man who loved the music of bagpipes most had to do without them that day. To his own version of Old King Cole was a merry old soul, Sgt. McCloskey was conducting the POW's-to-be in a sing-along of the song. Along with the Scot, the German troops were singing "Dirty old Hitler was a wicked old soul and a mean old soul was he; He called for his friends and en-em-ies and shot them one, two, three." The chorus swelled louder as the Germans made up their own unspeakable versions. Sgt. McCloskey smiled and got back in the lead car. With Col. Williams now driving, he commented as he sampled a confiscated bottle of

German schnapps, "Singing soldiers don't make trouble."

Between them sat the speechless, manacled boy, now half-sitting on his own. The two men still dressed in German greatcoats and helmets instilled in the boy an abiding fear that his rescuers did not realize.

On the 25th of April the German column was over two miles long and numbered 3000 officers and men, part of which was motorized. A general who had sworn obedience to Col. Halford Williams and his six-man team led them. But the general (as did over a hundred other fellow officers) had removed his insignia on the orders of Col. Williams and had hidden them in his pocket.

Not only was McCloskey concerned with morale, but so was allied command in Vienna. Believing there was safety in numbers, orders were issued to bombard them with K-rations and medical supplies daily. As for the twelve suspected kidnappers, they were not given the chance to make a move, so carefully were they watched.

On the 25th of April, Col. Cromosky and his relief column had advanced less than fifty miles, having been slowed to a crawl by blown bridges and detours. Rounding a bend on the 25th, they heard a familiar tune and suddenly saw moving toward them a column of German soldiers over a mile long. Leading the Germans were two officer's cars with a lone machine gun sticking out a rear window.

Col. Cromosky speeded up and stopped beside the first German staff car. He got out, saluted the German dressed officer in charge who obviously was not German as his under jacket showed. Col. Cromosky said, "You Sir must be Col. Williams, the ninety-day wonder I've been sent to rescue. I'll take over and escort you back to allied lines after you scatter those Gerries you picked up along the way."

Col. Williams reacted. "We've had a fairly pleasant trip up till now. But let me tell you Sir! Nobody escorts us back to Vienna on the last dogleg of this expedition. Instead, you will provide two of your vehicles to transport my team and the rescued hostages.

And you, Colonel will stay with these Germans and make sure you don't lose one of them till they're all safely behind allied lines just as we promised.

That initial altercation was the beginning of disagreement between the two officers. In the end Col. Williams won the argument by suggesting Col. Cromosky get Vienna on the radio and patch him into London so he could talk to his friendly advisor, General Eisenhower. The ruse worked.

The rescue team drove off in Cromosky's vehicles and arrived in Vienna a day later.

The Russian politeness disappeared, as they demanded that the first stop be at their headquarters. Williams refused. They were delivered to the American Commandant and then Williams took them to the Soviet building. Returning to Allied Headquarters he found that the American/German scientist had been taken care of and would soon be on a plane to Los Alamos, New Mexico. Williams had the boy admitted to a U.S. military hospital for observation, and then he and his team went to sleep in comfortable beds.

Seventy-two hours later an orderly awakened Col. Williams. Beside his bed was a cup of hot tea, clean underwear, new uniform and officer's cap--all with proper insignia. Nicely shined boots sat beside his chair. Dressed immaculately he was escorted to the main Vienna railway station. On a hastily erected platform he was asked to take the prominent position beside the American Commandant General.

Soon he heard rousing martial music. Looking down the street was a continuous line of marching troops. As the troops came closer the colonel watched a hundred German officers leading over 3000 weary prisoners of war. As the tired and weary prisoners passed the reviewing stand they straightened up, marched western style and looked directly in front.

The first companies came abreast and Col. Halford Williams suddenly heard the crisp command in German. "Ryes right!" All the former enemy troops turned their faces toward the bespectacled young American officer until they heard the command, "Eyes front!"

The commandant turned to Williams and said proudly, "That salute was for you Colonel." Col. Williams was standing at full salute.

The commandant later advised Williams, "General Carl Ritter has assembled rail coaches at the station for their ride as POW's to France and Western Germany occupied by the allies."

As the remainder of his team boarded a plane for London, goodbyes were echoed and Williams took a jeep hack to the military hospital where he picked up the unknown boy. They went by rail to Berne, Switzerland where Williams had asked a banker friend, Mr. Walter Schusnick to meet him.

On seeing the manacled boy the Swiss banker phoned a displaced French banker who, because he was a Jew, had become a Swiss refugee.

The boy was placed in a hospital again and this time Mr. Schusnick brought in a locksmith. The neck and ankle manacles, with attached chains, were removed. As the terrible hardware was taken off the boy, he was seen holding his hands as if in prayer. Then he uttered his first word since redeemed from death over three weeks before.

The French banker standing beside explained. The boy simply said, "Hurrah." "The tears are of Joy, and I presume the hands say thank you, God."

The boy sobbed. "My name is Piere. Am I safe?"

The young boy's grateful father, Count Julian Rothschild, was later reunited with his kidnapped son at a Paris railway station. The ordeal was to cause the breakdown and death of young Piere's mother.

(A Williams team had rescued Mr. Schusnick's younger son who was also kidnapped for ransom the year before. When found in solitary, he was emaciated and chained by the neck. Col. Williams had brought him home safely to his parents after the team killed over thirty Nazi jailers to effect their withdrawal. That mission also began with a nighttime parachute drop adjacent to the prison where the boy was being held.)

A United States counter-intelligence team in Vienna picked up Fritz, the so-called guard at Prison "X" who was actually the head warden. His admission of identity, and his authentic information divulged about the prison atrocities and the kidnap scheme in particular, would be used at the forthcoming Nuremberg trial for Nazi warmongers.

Granted clemency for becoming a prosecution witness, his testimony would result in the conviction of Herman Goring and his ten collaborators who had planned the hideous kidnap scheme. Identifiable hostages who had been cast to the crocodiles were named. It was this criminal act for which Goring's accomplices were condemned and hung. Goring escaped the hangman's noose by taking a cyanide capsule smuggled into his cell.

The twelve escapee guards from the prison literally were trying to escape, according to their confessions that were considered valid by allied intelligence questioners. They had attached themselves to Col. Williams' commando team as being the most direct route to allied lines. In return for freedom they compiled dossiers on activities in Prison "X" which also were used to convict Goring and his defendants.

The allies bombed Prison "X" and its crocodile moat after the notorious jail had been cleaned out of remaining prisoners. Later, the Soviets demolished the structure, and the new Communist government of Poland declared the place a perpetual memorial park.

After delivering Piere Rothschild to the Berne Hospital, Col. Halford Williams managed to get a telegram off to his London girlfriend. It said he would be back on the morrow, and she probably hoped it would be his last mysterious disappearance of their romance.

On hearing that Williams had survived his sixty-second mission, the losing bettors in London left allied headquarters to drown the memory of their losses in the nearest pub. The others who had hoped the amazing young Colonel Williams would return safely perhaps went out to the black market to buy silk stockings for their wives or girlfriends. That evening they probably celebrated the hoped-for ending of the war in Europe when the lights would be lit again in London's blackout area, and a nightingale no doubt would sing in Berkley Square.

Meanwhile, Prime Minister Churchill exchanged congratulations with the Soviet and American leaders that their nationals had been saved. They themselves had been granted amnesty from immediate death by a higher power, for reasons unknown.

Chapter 13

DISMISSED

This young American war hero, code named Halford Williams, survived World War II. He completed unscathed 62 missions and cheated death hundreds, perhaps thousands of times. Hitler's $300,000 in gold for his capture went uncollected.

On May 22, 1945, Halford Williams celebrated his 26th birthday with the family of his fiancé in England and made plans to obtain a doctorate in literature at Oxford University. Life looked promising and the future bright.

As he left allied headquarters in London in June of 1945, he walked to Buckingham Palace to watch the Changing of the Guard. Standing alone in civies he felt comfortable but enjoyed the exhilaration of a new peacetime freedom and a relationship with a civilian world he was about to rediscover. He was thrilled by the splendor of the bright uniforms and drill precision, and felt like a young boy who had bypassed his childhood and was eager to flirt with the lost years.

As Williams strolled about for viewing advantage he was confronted suddenly by an old wartime acquaintance that he knew well. He heard his former buddy call out, "Colonel Williams! Hello."

The warrior with a thousand lives looked studiously at the man he knew by first name and returned the salutation almost rudely. "You have the wrong person, Sir. My name is not Williams," and he walked deliberately away. He hated the denial of his identity. He was infuriated by the edict laid down on his departure from Trafalgar Square by which he must deny his war-time role if recognized.

He smarted at the ultimatum they used in bidding farewell. "You are no longer Halford Williams. Should you be addressed as such, you will not respond under penalty of severe action. You will be under surveillance in the transitional months, perhaps years." The de-mob security officers forbade him to rehash his experiences with his top Sergeant Ian McCloskey, but he rationalized the inquisitive brass would never prevent him from confiding in Father John or General Charles Wilson, should they ever meet again.

Following hostilities Williams chose to remain in England. During this period, a major happening of heraldic importance occurred to him. While attending Oxford he accepted knighthood. It was not the ceremony itself as much as the comments made to him during the investiture and luncheon that followed.

King George VI was not in sympathy with keeping the exploits of young American Colonel Halford Williams hidden under security wraps. And he was to tell his attitude to those whom he met. Thus, on an October morning in 1946, Halford Williams found himself fully attired in officer's dress at Buckingham Palace. From his waist hung his illustrious golden sword.

In another line of celebrities stood Dwight D. Eisenhower, Omar Bradley, George S. Patton, and Bernard Montgomery. In an adjoining line were brave, but less distinguished men of battle, among them the officer lately called Lieutenant Colonel Halford Williams. And also present for the King's honors was Sergeant Ian McCloskey.

On spying Williams, General Patton suddenly broke ranks. Crossing over to the less prestigious line he stopped before Col. Williams. The general came to attention, looked the lower ranking officer in the eye and saluted. Then he burst out in praise.

"Colonel, I owe a long overdue apology, dammit. I'm ashamed I said the things I did about you. I personally acknowledge your triumphs as a soldier. Furthermore I admit it was you who saved our skins in the Battle of the Bulge and made it possible for us to knock out the enemy. If that story is ever told, you'll come out smelling like a rose and be hailed as the real hero of World War II--in fact, any war." Williams, overcome with gratitude, spluttered embarrassed thanks.

Williams was not knighted at Buckingham Palace that day. The ceremony took place at St. George's Chapel, Windsor Castle. There, King George VI knighted a kneeling Halford Williams. Later, the gracious king asked whom Col. Williams had brought with him on the special occasion. The young hero had brought his American mother and his English fiancé. All were invited for lunch, and Williams' mother remained a royal guest for three days. During the luncheon His Majesty addressed Williams' mother somewhat as follows:

"This nation is proud of your son's valor in war and I selfishly wish he had been English-born as were his father's people generations ago. I would indeed like to claim the honor of young Col. Williams belonging to us. It should not go unsaid that we allies owe him a priceless debt of gratitude. More than any other, he offered his life as a sacrifice to shorten this terrible war...except for your son's bravery, countless soldiers would have died."

But the exasperating problem of keeping his wartime activities quiet continued to plague Williams. The subject of what one did in the war was the prime conversation of the late forties, and no less at Oxford University where Williams mingled with many veterans. Hence in 1946, Williams was soon to realize what it meant to be sworn to secrecy. Rumors persisted that the greatest hero of World War II was alive and had survived combat. Called back to Washington to refute the growing stories, Williams was ushered into OSS headquarters ostensibly to be reunited with his old Chief of Operations, William Donovan. Unexpectedly he found himself seated before two grim-faced OSS officers where his entry to peace from war was re-read to him. Curtly and without acclaim they interrogated Williams and reminded him of his oath of silence. The hero status was dead they said. In its place they managed to provoke the image of a non-person sitting in judgment. By the time they had finished their coercion, they had inflicted psychological dishonor on a sensitive Williams for breaking silence about his wartime role. The grievance would not be forgotten.

In brief, Williams was reminded that he had failed to repudiate his wartime record. He was told that his reluctant career in arms would be sealed till the year 1990 or until his death. Mangling his self-image further they read the rules that his real name must remain anonymous in future years apart from his illustrious war accomplishments. They reminded him that agents would continue to report his civilian conversations in the forthcoming years. They inferred that his role in defeating the enemy was so critical on several missions that his identity forever must remain classified.

At the time of the appearance Williams did not realize the significance of this bureaucratic intimidation, but he inwardly speculated that the underlying motive of the investigation was rooted in concerns more puzzling than security demands. Charles Wilson, Deputy head of the CIA in post-war years stated that Williams' actions in certain major missions had reversed blunders committed by the upper brass, but Wilson would not name names or occasions. The general speculated that Williams' record in battle was the envy of the allied chiefs, and that this displeasure among them did more to bury the wartime record of Col. Williams than the security angle.

Pondering the achievements of Williams during his two short years of service, Gen. Wilson himself, one of America's greatest World War II spies, reviewed the format of this book. He stated that the "greatest good which should have been derived from Williams' military successes would have been allowing fellow Americans to share the glories. Such a patriotic acclaim would have been more noble than the perpetual attempt to deny the existence of Williams as the nation's greatest hero."

During the 1946 "investigation of Williams, he realized he had reached a watershed in his life and he was numbed by the edict to impose a post-war silence on him. Williams remembers asking if he must muzzle all mention of active duty in the war, and was stunned by the reply. "Say you were a desk man in London or Panama."

They informed Williams that the clothes he wore during his service, as Halford Williams, including his uniforms, boots and eyeglasses, et cetera, were already the property of the U.S. Government. He was told he must return them to be kept as exhibits for future generations--after his death. The German officers' car he had driven from the western front to London and given as a gift to General Eisenhower was already on its way to the Smithsonian Institute.

And lastly, they calmly advised Williams that G2 personnel in the near future would pick up the golden sword and all the medals then in his possession. They had been classified as property of the state. Thus, they stripped him of all his wartime honors.

Williams' face flushed. He retorted. "You would take the honors for which I was willing to yield my life so often? If I deserve one paramount consideration for my service to the cause, it is my custodianship of those medals. They belong to my children and me. You pip squeaks that go by the book have killed me twice. One, I'm not a person at all, and two, I never existed.

The reply stunned Williams again. "Remember Sir! You no longer exist. You agreed under oath that you would become a character with a code name that would be annulled when the war was over. We have your signature on file. There are many others in the same category of enforced silence.

Furthermore, your file and all records concerning your marvelous exploits which are not denied will shortly be moved to a classified section of the National Archives."

Then the dismissing officer stung the young man again with the disclosure that his secret service to the nation as Halford Williams was finished--to be forgotten--the missions sealed for posterity. Someday they consoled him, your valor in the war may become legendary and songs sung about you for generations. But not in your lifetime unless in the future the rules are changed."

As the meeting adjourned they stated he was subject to recall at the government's pleasure if his great ability in military matters was required again.

The debriefing officer in charge made the final comment. "Since this file doesn't reveal your real name, I'll simply say goodbye Mr. X."

The late Halford Williams, a name made famous by an unknown young American hero, shuffled out of the Washington building onto the street. He had been ordered to obliterate his illustrious past. His pride at being an American and his vicarious offer to sacrifice himself for others on hundreds or perhaps a thousand occasions was to be remembered no more. Halford Williams felt he had been drummed out of the service, not as a hero, but as a nameless, discredited conscript.

Little did Mr. Halford Williams realize, that in the next forty years he would become as one abandoned while struggling through the desert of his life.

The powers from beyond that had saved him from death when a young man, would not again intervene to give him succor. And as the sun set in his life he found himself alone and unrecognized. Old and unsteady, he slowly walked the streets of his native city, St. Petersburg, Florida. Occasionally, he opened the faded front page of the local 1946 newspaper devoted entirely to his homecoming when the entire city turned out to greet him -- their greatest hero.

And while those he served in World War II lived out their days in man-made glory, Halford Williams could only reminisce remorsefully, sworn to silence till his death.

It was over forty years since Halford Williams had come home a hero, his wartime pension only a pittance for his deeds of valor. No man among those he knew was grateful enough to come to his aid -- the greatest hero since recorded time.

APPENDIX A

The Origin of the Relics

How authentic are the so-called relics of Jesus the Christ as related to his crucifixion? The author sought to discover if there was irrefutable evidence of their existence and if so, what became of them when they were brought from the Holy Land to Europe. Also of interest is where did the custodianship of the relics lay throughout the centuries?

In searching contemporary literature no decisive body of information could be found that lent credence to the true origin of the relics that the team of Halford Williams found in the French cave. No attempts were made to refute the conclusions of any existing information regarding the powers supposedly emanating from other related Christian relics. Nor were efforts taken to investigate neo-pagan assumptions or beginnings said to be associated with any of the subject body of artifacts, particularly the shield and the sword of Longinus.

For those interested in deeper research, there already exists a quantity of both pseudo-historical and subjective material, for instance on the Teutonic Knights and the Cathors. These societies relate to ancient artifacts and their symbolic meanings to early Christian beginnings. But inasmuch as the theme of this book is the singular adventures surrounding one of America's World War II heroes, deeper eastern or spiritual meanings have not been pursued.

Therefore, the object of this appendix is to trace as far back as possible, the beginnings of the relics, presuming of course that they were once connected with the Christ and/or His family or friends.

High Vatican sources shared the view that the relics do exist but that the Church proper did not possess them today. A Vatican telex stated also that it was doubtful that the so-called "Holy Grail" discovered in the French underground chamber was the actual cup of the Last Supper. Furthermore, information from English sources familiar with Glastonbury, destroyed by Henry VIII, (that held early Christian relics) suggests the present whereabouts of those relics is unknown. But the English advice also suggested that the cup found by Colonel Williams' team was unlikely to be the Holy Grail or cup of the Last Supper from which Jesus the Lord drank according to the New Testament. Two diverse-interest groups supposed the cup found by Williams' team was not the "Holy Grail", but they did not, however, attempt to deny the existence of the relics that form part of this book. The Catholic and Church-of-England sources seemed to know the proper description of the "true grail" but were unable or unwilling to divulge its precise description or its present resting place. Hence, the mystery deepened concerning the origin of the cup found by Father John of the Williams' team. The question then asked was from where and from whom did the cup receive its esoteric powers? And more important to the author, what was its point of origin and to whom did it once belong?

The Vatican inquiry suggested a further investigation be made with the deposed Hapsburg dynasty of Austro Hungary. Otto von Hapsburg, son of the late Emperor Karl, agreed to help several months later. After visiting the Hofburg museum in Vienna and closely examining the sword of Longinus, Otto von Hapsburg suggested the next stop should be in a monastery in Czechoslovakia, noted as one of the world's most complete collections of pre-medieval manuscripts and books. The present monastery dated from 760 A.D., but a German prince named Otto is said to have started the original monastery on that site. Otto was reported to be present at the crucifixion of Christ and was believed to be the one who presided at the crucifixion with Gaius Cassius (Longinus). While the monastery, at the time of this research was in a Communist controlled country, during the old Austro-Hungarian Empire it was ruled by the Hapsburgs.

In 1984 the request to visit the monastery was granted by Soviet authorities. A researcher of Austrian ancestry, on behalf of the author, accompanied Otto von Hapsburg by train to the site named St. James Monastery. The head abbot, The Reverend Carl Hapsburg, met them. His name was spelled Karl before he entered the Order. Two days spent at the monastery provided unexpected clues as to the origin of the relics plus a wealth of historical information.

Discovered was a well-reserved leather-bound book, measuring about 12 by 18 inches and six inches thick, of the Hapsburg dynasty dating back to the year 996 and ending with the last entry made July 16, 1919. The book was hand written by several generations of monks during that millennium. The languages were modern German, old Germanic, and an older and cruder form of interwoven Germanic and French penmanship. The contents of the book outlined the various Hapsburg kings and family trees and apparently was compiled from papers and documents made available to the scribes over the centuries, which papers (if they still existed) were not seen by the researcher or Otto von Hapsburg at the time of the visit.

Inasmuch as the Hapsburg dynasty entries were so conclusive, the information contained therein is considered to be of a primary nature and is the main source used to reveal the beginnings of the Christ relics discovered by Catholic theologian Father John who was with Williams at the time of discovery. Where and if other source material is stated, it will be mentioned in the following narrative.

The narrative that begins was copied in brief from the Hapsburg Royal dynasty book with the blessings of the present Pope John Paul II and the Secretary of the Vatican father Brian.

The first entry of the book was started at the time of one called Otto the Bold and was written by a "Brother Rudolph", a Capuchin Friar who belonged to an offshoot order of the Franciscans. He accompanied Otto on his crusades to the Holy Land and also in the Slave Trade of that period of brutal history.

The principal character in the early history of the Hapsburgs was a crown prince named Otto. His early life, interwoven with warfare, is most memorable for his retrieving the holy relics of Christ and transporting them to Europe.

In reading the activity of Otto it is problematic in deciding whether what unfolds is a mystery of Godliness or a mystery of Iniquity. Nevertheless, though not verified, Otto was apparently born in the autumn of 970. He was the oldest of twelve children whose home was a castle near the present town of Metz, France, but in 970 it was the capital of the Grand Duchy of Lorraine, Otto's father being the reigning Grand Duke.

His mother was the daughter of the Grand Duke of Burgundy. Otto's early ambition was to become Emperor of the Holy Roman Empire and he dared anyone to stand in his way. He was knighted before his twentieth birthday. With his younger brother (by two years) named Ludwig, they later raised a troop of noble knights who in turn joined a group of French knights for a pilgrimage to the Holy Lands about 1016, the book states.

Grown into manhood, Otto stood six feet, six inches and measured thirty inches across his shoulders, probably weighing over three hundred pounds. Otto's suit of armor today stands in the Hofburg Museum in Vienna. It is made of hammered bronze and was used on his first trip to the Holy Land. After his death the armor remained in Hawk's castle for three hundred years, and it is still sworn to be inhabited by the ghost of Otto.

Because of deeds of daring and valor during the first crusade his nickname became Otto "the Brave" and finally Otto "the Bold". The knights who Otto chose to join him in the first crusade were mainly from Germanic tribes including those of Saxony, Baden, Bor and Denmark; others from Lorraine and Flanders also gathered. According to the account in the old book, much of the first crusade is filled with disagreements between the French knights led by Francis, Duke of Bourbon, and his numerous attached troops and aides.

Otto's well-aired beliefs were that killing infidels and taking their plunder was no sin, but instead would accrue favor in Heaven.

The French knights with copious baggage filled eleven boats for the first crusade and Otto and his Spartan group occupied but two boats, the narrative not mentioning the size of the vessels, other than, for maneuverability in navigation, Otto traveled with few comforts. On the way to the Holy Land they were attacked by three boatloads of pirates that Otto's knights captured. They diverted their course to Cairo where they sold the pirates as slaves and continued on.

Their ships arrived in mid-summer near a Christian port named Appollonis and stayed intact for three months because of sand storms. After venturing forth they fought their first battles with Saracens and finally reached Jerusalem. There combined Pilgrim knights breached a hole with a battering ram in the third North Wall (extant during the life of Jesus) at least half a mile away from the next wall, the book explains. Breaching the wall is described in detail after which Otto's men (no number revealed) rushed through and finding a Christian slave, they were escorted to the Old Mosque and Herod's Palace.

Advised before departing France that legend said a gold hoard was buried under the Royal treasury of Herod's former palace, (possibly the el-Asqua Mosque built in 710 CE), the gold was located after careful search in which certain of Otto's knights doubled as guards and probers. A similar find was made at the Great Mosque, (likely the Dome of the Rock completed in 691 on the Temple Mount). In total they took eighteen donkey loads from one site and thirty-six from another. Hurriedly withdrawing from the city, they left countless enemy dead (not mentioning their own losses). Otto's group then deserted their French knights and eleven days after sailing with their booty, they arrived at Marseilles. Returning over land to Lorraine, the stolen gold was secreted in the basement of an old castle and the entrance bricked over.

By year's end, Otto had arrived in the presence of the Pope and, presenting him bags of gold coinage and gold bars, the giant of a man realized his life-long ambition. He was crowned The Holy Roman Emperor.

While a youth, Otto had married the daughter of the Duke of Burgundy at Geneva, Switzerland and the offspring eventually became known as the Hapsburgs (various spellings). The first royal residence was the newly built Hawks Castle on the border of Burgundy at the confluence of the Aur and Reiss Rivers. Natives first named the place Habichtsburg because of the ever-present hawks which Otto kept for hunting, hence the name Hapsburg was coined as the family's identification. But it was Otto's grandson, Guntram "the Rich" who first took the name Hapsburg.

The gold obtained from the first crusade led by Otto, made him a wealthy potentate and placed him firmly on the road to political destiny for him and his descendants. As a result of his newly found power derived from the Jerusalem gold, Otto was able to enlist mercenary troops to dominate the neighboring dukedoms and kingdoms.

As told in the old book, the Hapsburgs were Emperors of Germany prior to extending their land acquisition to include Austria. They had begun in Lorraine, moved with authority over adjacent Swiss tribes, annexed more German territory and finally absorbed, by further conquest, all of Austria.

Therefore, Otto was the real founder of Switzerland and it was under his rule that the Cantonments gradually united into the nation known today as Switzerland. Thus, overlooking his carnal nature, Otto was a fearless man, a brave fighter, and founder of the aggregate Germanic tribal nations of this century.

The old book on the Hapsburg dynasty also deals with the capture of the English King Richard the Lion Hearted, but admits a discrepancy as to whether it was Otto or his grandson who captured Richard, demanding so great a ransom.

In spite of his newfound monies, Otto continued to acquire his wealth from the capture and sale of human beings--known as the Slave Trade. He bought all the convicted criminals from the dukedoms, kingdoms, counties, and independent cities of Europe. Then as purchaser he transported them to North Africa and sold them in the flourishing slave markets.

From the monies he made from creating human misery, Otto financed three expeditions to the Holy Land to free slaves from the infidels. Later as respect increased somewhat toward more destitute human slaves they became serfs attached to the land for work and defense. When a Noble sold such land, those serfs (formerly slaves) on the feudal land went with the sale of the property.

Otto the Bold did not forget his promise made to the Pope that one day he would lead another crusade to the Holy City of Jerusalem. Thus at about 25 years of age or later, he again visited Rome to work out the next crusade. On this occasion the Pope produced an old map showing holy relics hidden in secret chambers below the Mosque in Jerusalem and beneath Herod's Palace. The Pope, who would later commit suicide, told Otto, according to the narrative, "You are not a man of honor, neither am I. We are both cut from the same mold. Get the relics at any cost and I will make your descendants the wealthiest of men." Otto thanked the Pope, took the map, hid it in his clothing and departed.

The Pope had suggested that Otto finance his next expedition to the Holy Land out of current, profit-making ventures. As soon as possible, Otto filled three ships with convicted criminals and church felons, men and women. After selling his cargo in Morocco, Otto sailed on to Jerusalem to search for further treasures. He particularly sought hidden relics of the early Christian era, concerning which relics the Pope had provided Otto the map of their hiding places.

This time, arriving again at Appollonis, they made their way to the Holy City by joining another group of European knights. Finding less opposition than on the first crusade, Otto and his knights reached Herod's Palace site for his second looting. Led by the fierce Otto, they overcame a rather weak resistance not having to kill or take prisoner any Saracen guards. Using the map they breached the same basement as in their first attempt. Again, following the map, Otto placed guards while the other devotees went into the basement as before. Through hidden staircases and secret openings (the book describes the entry in detail) leading to three lower levels, they learned the Pope's map showed accurately the final resting place of the supposed relics.

Breaking through one remaining stonewall, they entered an underground cubicle and came upon the first object of their search. It was a copper-covered box containing the following items: One pair of well-preserved leather sandals; one leather belt, well preserved; a one-piece robe, well preserved; a gold Roman coin on a chain; a round glass dish with bottom broken off; one used metal cup on chain; one knife in well-preserved leather sheath; two scrolls wrapped in sheepskins, also well-preserved; a small metal box containing jewels and a ring said (later) to have been presented to Jesus at the time of his birth.

Breaking open the large box, Otto the Bold who slew opponents at will, who sold impoverished human cargo for gain, whose God had become greed, power and riches--found himself unable to handle the relics, all of which burned his hands on touch. Another knight evidently free of Otto's cardinal sins was able to examine the objects. From that point on the presence of the relics disturbed Otto quite noticeably, but nevertheless, he had them taken outside where his crusading band fought their way to their camp outside the wall. They placed a strong guard on the box while Otto and a remnant returned to the city. There they met stiff resistance but this time again they reached the Mosque. Using the papal map, they descended to another room filled with gold and with it another box of relics were found hidden at one end. The contents of this second box were revealed to be: the sword of Longinus; the spear said to have pierced Christ's side; the shield placed on Christ after his removal from the cross; the headless nails; the Holy Grail, regarded as the cup of the Last Supper; five bowls of hammered copper (nested bowls 10" to 16" in diameter) also said to have been used in the Last Supper; cruets (residues of Christ's sweat and blood); four scrolls; a burial shroud, including the bindings of the dead person; sword of King Solomon (which legend says became the sword of English King Arthur); and hand-hewn pieces of timber.

Although Otto had made the second crusade accompanied by another Duke of Bourbon in charge of the French and English knights, plus a few Saxons. Otto deserted them again. He then headed quickly for Appollonis, taking only what was essential to transport the relics and the gold cache. The old book says he arrived in Rome ten or twelve days later and presented, intact, the holy relics to the Pope. For his part in the agreement the Pope divided with Otto a large part of the stolen gold.

In addition, the Pope and Otto made a new agreement. Otto was authorized by Rome to receive all dissidents and felons from the Catholic churches in Europe for which permission was granted Otto's brother Ludwig to transport the tragic humans to North Africa as slaves.

Otto the Bold took his newly acquired booty of gold home to his castle.

Like Otto, the Pope found the relics too hot to handle and quickly became ill, blaming his condition on the accursed relics. The Pope therefore devised a plan to dispose of the relics to churches throughout Europe, the disbursement of which produced the legends that abound to this day.

The above information is a history of the relics (some of which were discovered in the French man-made cavern by Col. Williams and his team). But where did the custodianship of the relics lay in the years after they were brought back from Jerusalem? For that unknown knowledge, the Vatican was again asked to help.

There has never been a response.

APPENDIX B

The Nun's Story

Mother Superior Mary Teresa was about 50 years old on October 22, 1943 when members of the Death Squad overran her orphanage. Now at 93 she sat in the retirement home in St. Etienne the last week of November 1984 and told her story--the nun's story. A young novice priest from the North American College in Rome, with written permission from the Secretariat of the Vatican, had come to France to talk with Mother Mary Teresa on behalf of the author. Condensed as follows are the comments of the Mother Superior that occupied twenty-six typed pages:

"Our order, The Sisters of Mercy, was originally English in origin, and I had been in St. Etienne for over twenty years before that terrible day. The orphanage was my life's devotion--working with destitute and homeless children.

"On the day in question there should have been about 150 orphans crammed into the old converted chateau, but the number of children had swelled to two hundred because during the last three months prior to the day of the brutes, we had become a refuge for another forty-six Jewish children whose parents had been killed on sight or taken away to the gas furnaces. There were twenty-eight nuns and novices to look after our big family. We never considered the Nazi Death Squad would be informed that we harbored Jewish children, and even so, we never anticipated they would seek them out for death as their parents were.

"Yet that chilly, wet day 42 years ago will be forever burnt into my earthly memory. It was a day in which I questioned all my beliefs and I felt my faith in God had shriveled up inside my breaking heart. In anguish, I thought God would never hear my cries. But later in the day he not only answered but also dispensed justice--a justice that was overdue to those brutes who violated our institution.

"Before telling my story let me remind you I don't hate nor do I blame Germans as such for what happened. But, I can't forget that those brutes came in the name of Germany of which they boasted. I suppose ours was just one of the Death Squad's countless visits made that year as they roamed the countryside kidnapping, murdering, and raping at will. I think if the German people had known the evil committed by such brigands on that particular day in St. Etienne, Germany would have risen in revolt. Later, good Germans did find out and responded as best they could.

"Anyway, getting back to the harsh reality of that 22nd of October, forty years ago, the events are quite clear. A dozen or more of the brutes stormed up to our doors and overran the orphanage. They ordered us outside immediately for inspection and when we did not respond they took delight in dragging us out into the cold, wet air. 'Comprenez vous Monsieur le novice? Ils nous dragged cote de maison pour l'inspection!'

(The young novice, John Holmes, who spoke both French and English looked away embarrassed and Mother Teresa, observing his forced detachment, continued.)

"Those brutes lined us up outside in the raw wind. They had pulled us from dormitories, offices, and even the chapel where some had fled to pray for protection. The chief brute was Otto. He ordered us to strip off our clothes including our undergarments. We refused. I protested. He laughed. It was a vulgar laugh and he said that God might soon get the chance to see us appear before him naked, if we didn't obey him (Otto), who was the god we should fear. How right he was! His men then ripped off our clothes and mauled us amid tears and pleas for mercy. They threw our clothes in a heap. One of them poured gasoline over them and Otto threw on a match. They all laughed and guffawed at us, as we stood forlornly naked.

"Then the vicious dogs of men examined the nuns grotesquely. They dragged off the younger ones and those that appealed to their particular lusts. They took turns in brutal assaults and ravished the girls at will using whips to subdue their victims. After they finished their sexual brutalities, three of the girls were dead.

"A sneaky brute that stayed inside the building came upon a girl peeling potatoes in the kitchen early in the raid. He tried to violate her and she repelled him, stabbing him three times superficially. He chased her into the backyard, grabbing a butcher knife as he ran. Catching up with her he held and sliced open her throat. As she fell, terror stricken and speechless, he kicked her and taunted her for turning down his advances. As she succumbed, he dragged her to the cow manure pile and threw manure over her still warm face and body. That act was typical of the abominations they committed on the helpless nuns.

"Later, an officer came over and yelled. 'Fun's over.' I understand some German and I remember him saying, 'Get those Jewish kids loaded into the trucks. We have a lot more Jews to pick up before nightfall.'

"Then the officer saw us huddled and shivering. We had been left standing out in the cold while they went inside and violated the younger ones. The officer told us to get inside and that's when I came upon our girls who had been strangled, stabbed and otherwise tortured or mutilated. The children were terror stricken and those who weren't hiding were wandering around in confusion and shock. In spite of the inhuman adversities committed upon so many innocent people, we tried to develop some order out of the chaos created by beasts without conscience. However, you can understand that some of the nuns were still in hysterics and would be terribly troubled the rest of their lives.

"The experience we all witnessed that day was beyond anything we could ever believe."

The author learned that "subsequently a German detail of regular troops came in to clean up the mess in the town. One of the officers was a Captain Hans Stocheimer who came by to offer his apologies to Mother Superior Mary Teresa. He experienced surprise and genuine concern for the atrocities. Then he had his Catholic church in Munich send to the orphanage a box of new religious clothes and a sum of money collected from the Munich parish. The captain apologized on behalf of the German people who had heard of the depravity of those who called themselves Germans. He told the Mother Superior and local priest that all of Germany was under the heel of a madman and to pray for Hitler's downfall. After the war, further sums of money were sent to the orphanage from unknown German sympathizers."

Mother Mary Teresa continued, "I don't know why we were allowed to be overcome by evil men and four of our numbers hideously killed, but my Catholic point of view is that God did intervene moments later when he commissioned six men to destroy over 140 brutes. You see God could not stand by that day without intervening.

"Almost forgotten was another blessing that occurred at the same time because of intervention by those whom I like to call God's warriors. The adult Jews on their way to the gas chambers via St. Etienne also were liberated, receiving a blessing of added years to their lives.

"After that terrible day in 1943 we were given permission (the first such condolence granted in one hundred years) to say a special mass to speed on to Hell the souls of the lustful creatures who never knew the meaning of virtue or compassion. Of course we also said masses immediately for the souls of the murdered nuns and on every anniversary since that day we give thanks to God for saving the orphans and adults from the devils.

"It was not till weeks after the ordeal that I heard it was British and Americans dressed as German soldiers who freed the orphans and adults. But even when I learned the rescuers were allied soldiers, I thought for years they had been sent purposely to save us. I was unaware till today that a human government was not responsible for planning the operation. The savior was God.

"I never had the pleasure of meeting the American officer who engineered the chain explosion that killed all the evil men and I never met the Britisher whom they say detonated the chain bomb--but they have been in my prayers for over forty years--and will be till God takes me home."

APPENDIX 3

FOR THE RECORD

Actual interviews concerning the missions of OSS agent Halford Williams were obtained from him personally over seven years and verified from government sources. The spiritual involvements as recounted by him were written and approved in their meaning and context.

There was found no references, read or implied, however, in the official OSS records regarding the Christ relics discovered by his team in the French cave. But actual existence of the relics, though not their whereabouts, was later confirmed by three unbiased sources, one English, one Vatican, and one monastic. Williams' story in which he recovered the spear and sword said to relate to the crucifixion were substantiated in U.S. government files and other sources.

But the perplexing question remains. Was there a supernaturally endowed screen of protection provided Williams during his war-time episodes, assuring his being drafted by higher powers for some exalted appointment later in his life? That is, was his life tenure predestined regardless of danger?

Without a satisfactory answer there remains unsolved the spirituality of the enigma. Simply stated is the paradox that Halford Williams, who did not hate the enemy but enlisted in a war he despised, is the only person known that death in battle tried to overtake but failed to touch. Such a recompense for volunteering to serve humanity goes unchallenged.

The Man with the Golden Sword

Epilogue

by Donald M. Ware

I sense great truth in this long-hidden "documentary - drama," and I am not concerned about exactly what percentage is drama. Though I have chosen to not read fiction, except when it was required in high school, I imagine a fiction reader would find this book a good read. I do have considerable experience in observing controlled leaks from classified government sources that were not allowed to escape into the public domain without some disinformation inserted, or being released as partly drama or fiction. Our world leaders want to keep the general public from getting too excited about the new world that is emerging both below and above the surface of this planet.

I think that our human leaders may be influenced by non-human advisors who encourage compliance with galactic law. As we jointly transform Earth for the Golden Age, not everyone has evolved his or her consciousness sufficiently to graduate. If the less-evolved people knew too much they might become jealous of those who have made better choices over many lifetimes and earned their graduation. The quarantine of our world, imposed since the Lucifer rebellion, is being lifted. More people are choosing love -- becoming ready for peace on Earth.

I am a retired USAF pilot, staff scientist, teacher, and program manager with an advanced degree in Nuclear Engineering. I had a paranormal experience in 1954 when I was an 18-year-old sophomore at Duke University. That led to my retirement at age 47, no longer needing to work for a living. I volunteered to work for the Mutual UFO Network for 10 years and served as Director of the International UFO Congress for 18 years. I chose to study not only the physical evidence of a much larger reality, but the non-physical evidence too. Since 1983 I read about 1,000 books and attended six conferences each year where truthseekers share their experiences and research. I studied all of the persistent mysteries of mankind. I am now an Advisor to the Exopolitics Institute (www.exopoliticsinstitute.org) with past or current contacts by several beings of higher intelligence: a Zeta, a descendant of Atlanteans, a member of the Council of "20 and 4" mentioned in The Bible and in The Urantia Book (1955), and a high-IQ employee of the National Reconnaissance Organization. The Council of 20 and 4 seems to manage, from the Star-System level, our transformation to the Golden Age."

I recognize a subtle connection between John B. Leith's personal story and The Urantia Book, an important recent revelation. Leith apparently had a photographic mind. He said he went to the capitol of Tibet to seek spiritual growth at age 17, as did others choosing a spiritual path. The head of the monastery in Lhasa suggested a 9-month study, starting with three months meditating in a cave, subsiding on water and a daily bowl of rice. When Leith completed the nine months, he was told that the cave he used was the same cave that Jesus had used to meditate during his early years. I think that was a misperception by the spiritual teachers in Tibet, the young student being Ganid rather than Jesus..

In my copy of The Urantia Book, Part IV has 684 pages on "The Life and Teachings of Jesus." It describes the first disciple of Jesus, one not mentioned in the Bible. His name was Ganid, the son of a wealthy businessman from India seeking business contacts around the Mediterranean during a two-year trip. Jesus was hired to be the interpreter in three languages for Ganid's father and as a tutor for the son. This intelligent boy turned 18 about the time Jesus was crucified, and that is when Ganid started teaching the message of Jesus in India. Ganid was a faster learner than the later disciples. He taught the message of Jesus so well that people later thought he must have been Jesus who somehow escaped death. Books and a movie were made about "Jesus" teaching in India. I presume it was Ganid, before age 18, not Jesus that meditated nearly 2000 years earlier in the same cave in Tibet that John Leith more recently used on his spiritual path.

Leith studied law in St. Petersburg at age 19 before he entered military service.

I read Ike's Spies: Eisenhower and the Espionage Establishment by Stephen Ambrose. On page 71 it says, "They arrived at Capri, where a MacGregor team was plotting a new daredevil operation to rescue an Italian scientist from German-occupied Italy." Not only are the individual code names for the special-forces team members highly classified but the type of team is coded, such as a "MacGregor" team.

Leith was not allowed to mention his OSS-assigned code name, Col. Halford Williams, so in his book written in 1980, Genesis of the New Space Age, Leith used the code name that the Germans had assigned to him, The American Fox. Leith apparently described his most exciting wartime missions using a manual typewriter, possibly while still using the GI Bill to study for a doctorate in Literature at Oxford. Later, after writing the New Space Age book with research partner Frank Hudson, Leith did further research on his personal war-time story as late as 1985.

As the MUFON State Director for Florida and Eastern Region Director, 1984 -1993, I was highly impressed by the work that Robin Andrews did using hypnotic regression and in writing about important sensitive issues like prodigies born to ET experiencers (1992). At that time Robyn was a board member of Para-psychological Services, Inc. organized at the Psychology Dept. of Georgia State

College and directed by William Roll.

I met Robyn at several conferences, and Leith met her at a workshop she was presenting in Clearwater, FL. Leith had apparently not even told his son that he had fought in the war, following the orders from "Wild Bill" Donovan, head of the Office of Strategic Services, predecessor for the CIA. Leith wanted his two books published after his death, and he was impressed with Robyn's interests, so he gave Robyn both original manuscripts and asked her to publish them after his death. Better late than never.

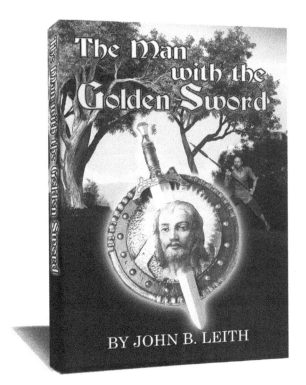